My Soul to Keep

by

V.J. Prucha

Printed in the United States of America

First Printing: September 2013
VJPPublishing, LLC

ISBN: 978-0-9850941-0-2
Ebook ISBN: 978-0-9850941-1-9
LCN: 2013914951

Thank you, Frank, for being my best friend and the support I needed; Tom, for giving me the method to release my imagination; Susan, for helping me release the book to the world. To my friends, Joleen and Caitlin for teaching me to live and ride for today and dream about tomorrow, and Beth, for making sure I never stopped writing. To my sisters, Jeanne and Madeleine, who keep me laughing. To RamaJon for helping me wrangle through the publishing process.

Prologue

Alisha came home spiritually bankrupt and bone weary. Her keys slipped through her fingers as she tried to put them on the key rack. Cursing, she picked them up and placed them securely back on one of the brass hooks. She crooked her head as the echo of clanking keys broke the silence. Something wasn't right as she tried to squash the spider of misgivings she had in her stomach. Something touched her shoulder and she quickly turned but only ghostly stillness blanketed her. Every muscle contracted turning Alisha into stone as she stood in her apartment looking, waiting for the intruder to appear. Finally, after a few intense moments, she thought nothing but a really good vodka martini would cure her ills. Whatever she was feeling was miniscule compared to the bank acquisitions, clients who needed hand holding, loans, and all the other tedious things that needed her attention at the bank. Her reservations slowly dissipated into the ether and she breathed a sigh of relief past her lips. She flipped on the tube for noise and a talking head related the latest murder in Albuquerque, another woman found naked and mutilated. She immediately flipped the TV back off. Slowly, she went into her bedroom and cast her ridiculously high heels off across the room where they landed in a beleaguered pile. She smirked; she would allow one mess. Her black pencil skirt slithered over her hips, cascaded down her legs, and pooled to the ground. She peeled her pantyhose from her long, sleek legs. "Sadistic bastard," she muttered at the inventor of hose, but smiled because she couldn't deny her legs looked damn good with them on. Silence made the air heavy as she tried to knead the tension from her shoulders away. But the annoying pit in her stomach was growing legs and crawling up her spine. She could feel each hairy leg of suspicion and paranoia stick into each nerve cell.

She sat stiff and straight as a board on the edge of her bed. Her eyes darted everywhere in her bedroom, looking for the source of her discomfort, but only silence answered her paranoid questions. "Right, no more late night news," spilled across her lips. Alisha shook her head, then deftly unbuttoned each button to her white satin blouse and tossed the delicate shirt in the basket on the way to the bathroom. In nothing but a bra and panties, she brushed her long hair and let each strand fall across her flawless skin. She watched herself smile at the memory of her boyfriend whispering in her ear about how he could lose himself in her whiskey-colored eyes. An electrical impulse of tonight's possibilities squashed the hairy little bastard feeling in her stomach. She looked in the mirror and pointed her finger, "You are getting so lucky tonight," and giggled at her audacity.

A soft scent of vanilla wafted around her and tickled her nose. It was such a delicious smell, a small growl rose from her stomach and suddenly she craved cookies and milk. She wondered where the aroma was coming from. She didn't remember lighting a candle or having a plug-in scent in the room. She stopped brushing her hair and looked at the reflections in the mirror. Every muscle tightened in place. The bathtub was full of steaming water. She commanded her muscles to move and backed out of the bathroom so quickly she slammed her shoulder into the doorframe. The pain was jarring and forced her to stand still. Each beat of her heart pounded in her ears. Dizzy from the rush of blood to her head, she put a hand to a wall. The cold, hard surface beneath her fingers became a wet blanket that embalmed her nerves.

This is ridiculous, she thought, *I never panic*, and she took a deep breath. "All right, there is a logical explanation," she commented. "Maybe a pipe broke," she knotted her eyebrows together, "maybe I forgot to pull the stopper in the tub." Her heartbeat slowed after each reasonable explanation until a million little other questions beat her reasonable explanations to a pulp. She couldn't escape the feeling that a pair of wolf eyes, slaking in the woods, was boring through her skin. "Right, time to get out," but she looked down at herself in her purple silk bra and panties. "Must get dressed first," and she scrambled to her closet. A meticulous list of things she needed formed in her scattered brain—a brush, toothbrush, clothes, deodorant, perfume, and of course, underwear. "There is a logical explanation," her voice cracked from her parched throat as she dragged clothes off their hangers.

Alisha grabbed a running outfit and quickly tried to put one foot in a pant leg, but missed and she ended up bouncing around on one leg. She caught herself against the wall, "Damn it." The smell of vanilla was overwhelming and she scrunched her nose, "Maybe the neighbors had some stupid candle lighted." A cold draft blew across the back of her neck. She stopped moving, and let her pants puddle around her ankles. Slowly, she turned clockwise, fear making her body turn to stone. A scream caught in her throat as her body was hurled across the room. Her head hit the wall with a loud crack and she slumped down the cold surface in a heap. Barely moving, she opened her eyes to a blurry figure before her. Her fingers reached out to the ethereal object for help. He caught her wrist in a vise-like grip, sending searing sharp needles down her arms.

She tried to scream, but gloved fingers lifted her chin so her eyes were looking into a deep blue abyss, "You are getting so lucky tonight." His voice, every word, sent a wave of fear inside her and she fought to stay awake to keep the demon away. Blackness encroached as thick as tar and she melted into the dark.

Alisha's eyes fluttered open, only to find she couldn't focus on anything. Only haziness surrounded her. Piercing light penetrated her eyes, exacerbating her excruciating headache. Every time she opened her eyes, a new lightning bolt of pain struck her and she wanted to wretch from the agony. Her arms were stretched taut and she tried yanking at the red ties, but with each new movement, a new wave of nausea would envelop her. Panic began to crawl from her toes to her very heart. "Help…" but the words were lost in her dry, cracked throat. She licked her swollen lips. She tasted something coppery/metallic on her tongue. A white shadow crossed her eyes and then a sudden sharp pain struck across her arm. She screamed and tried to move, but blackness stole her from consciousness. Her eyes popped open, but she couldn't figure out how long she had been out. She looked in horror as the deep color of red began to well. Rivulets of blood slowly dripped down her arm, where she could feel it pool around her neck. The scent of iron mixed with vanilla hung heavy in the air. Disoriented, she tried to figure out what was happening, but couldn't comprehend, until pain in both arms brought her to her bleak reality. A cold sensation went across her body and she knew, without looking, she was totally naked, vulnerable.

She jerked her body hard to escape her bonds, but with every jerk, there were a thousand stinging pains in her back. Hanging in front of her was her wooden rosary with the body of a man splayed out on the cross in agony, blood dripping from nail wounds in his hands and feet. Her grandma prayed with that rosary every Sunday before she gave it to Alisha for her first communion. A teardrop escaped and ran down her cheek. Behind the swaying crucifix stood a demon in a white chemical suit with piercing blue eyes.

"Hello, Alisha, awake at last!" his voice dripped liquid fire down her spine. Her body tremored from the waves of chills coursing through her body. Her eyes darted around the room, looking for something, anything that would save her. "Alisha, Alisha" he patted her face, "look at me." He forced her to look at him. "Alisha, look at me," and the killer's deep blue eyes penetrated her own. Desperately, she peered into his eyes searching for a small sign of humanity, but only found arctic ice. "If you move, dear, the glass on the bed will only cut deeper." He leaned closer and whispered in her ear, "Please, move some more." He laughed while she trembled. He raised a large butcher knife above her body. Her eyes focused on a drop of blood that slowly snaked its way from the tip, down the blade, and then splashed onto her body. She tried to scream, but his hand covered her mouth. "Shhh...." He began to sing, "Hush little baby don't you cry." He kissed her cheek. "Alisha, you and I are going to have so much fun," and she watched cold steel slash her skin wide open....

Chapter 1

"NOOOOOO!!! Miss, please don't!" he screamed.

My head rang from his screaming. Why wouldn't he stop screaming? The sound of his screams—of all of their screams—was making me crazy. I wanted to put my hands to my ears and muffle out their sounds, but I held the gun straight and steady. God, why do they have to scream? Can't they whisper? The gun was cold and heavy. Electrical shockwaves ran through my veins at the power I had in my hands. My tongue tingled with the taste of fear from the man shaking before me. Waves of panic from the bank employees huddled on the ground collided around me and I reveled in the rush of adrenaline. Behind me, my boyfriend was egging me to pull the trigger.

"Go ahead, baby, pull the trigger."

My eyes pinpointed on the bank guard's deep, rich brown eyes. His pupils were wide and black as he knelt before me. Beads of sweat rolled down his temples and dripped down his sweaty, black neck as his hands were outstretched in a sign of complete surrender.

"Please, Ma'am, just calm down. No need for this to happen."

I laughed at his sweet gentle, talk. He was following his training perfectly—stay calm, and talk softly to the assailant. All I heard was the scared rabbit sound in his cracked throat.

But, I so wanted this to happen. My finger slowly pulled the trigger to the gun that was aimed directly for his forehead. He was in my sights. I couldn't wait for the blast of light and the sensation of the bullet racing out of the gun. My head was spinning at the revelation that I was in control over everyone. Power was such an elixir and it had a taste like no other. My heartbeat drummed faster at the images of my finger pulling the trigger. My senses heightened to any movement, anyone making even the slightest sound. Tiny water droplets of perspiration budded on the back of my neck. The cries and whimpers of people cowered on the stone-cold floor were like loud screeches and made my ears hurt. They prayed and searched from a sign from God that an angel or someone would help them. But no one was going to help them. I was their savior and their punisher. They didn't do anything to deserve this, but I was the one who decided if their last breath was laid among the ashes of their dreams. My boyfriend was buzzing in my ear, "Come on, baby, shoot the fucker!"

He rocked his hips behind me and something very hard pushed into me. He was excited at the thought of death. His arm was around my neck, and the other hand was helping to hold the gun steady in my hands that were slick with sweat. He whispered in my ear, "Just shoot it."

His hot breath tickled my neck, sending a chill down my spine, and I jerked for only a moment. It was enough to break my trance and I was slammed back into my body. What am I doing here? I started to shake. The gun slipped but only a little. The guard saw the opportunity and began to soothingly talk to me in hushed monotones, "It's okay, honey, you don't have to do this."

The guard's silky voice wove a web around my erratic beating heart and slowed my pulse to a palpable rhythm. Desperation was starting to set in, the sense of power was fading, and my drug of choice was abandoning me for my sense of humanity. But the hand holding mine pressed the trigger and the blast went out, blinding my eyes. A screamed pierced the air....

I shot up board straight in bed and attempted to reorient myself to my surroundings. "Nightmare!" I whispered, "It's only..." and I tried to swallow, but my words were caught on sandpaper. "A nightmare," and willed my deafening heartbeat to a small roar. A soft sunrise illuminated the room and spilled onto the floor. Shadows dissipated slowly under the intensity of daylight, while dingy lace curtains blew back and forth in silence. A soft breeze escaped the beat of the curtains and cooled my sweaty skin. Breathing in deep, the last of the nightmare's tentacles blew past my lips as the echoes of my screams diluted into the cool air. Trails of familiar tears burned down my skin and dripped onto the white sheets, turning them gray.

This was the monotony of beginning each day in the death grip of nightmares. Swinging my legs over the bed, I gingerly touched the wooden planks of the floor. Still weak from my fractured sleep, I stumbled into the water closet, the bathroom so named because there is no other word that can describe its size any better. Passing the old pink tub with chipped porcelain and a showerhead with a never-ceasing leak, I tried to open the small window for a little air. But it wouldn't budge even with verbal threats of mutilation and deconstruction. Then, after one big slam from my hand, the window opened with an eardrum-shattering screech.

A trickle of water flowed from the lime-encrusted faucet, down the sides of the pink clamshell sink, pooled, and then circled the drain. My eyes, in a hypnotic state, stared as the clean water washed away every cell of my being into a slow lazy river. The stream of cells cascaded down the pipes, until it reached its final destination, the sewer. My hands formed the shape of a cup, and a pool of water emerged until it leaked through my fingers. Splashing my face with baptismal water, I watched the trails of pain wash away. The image in the mirror tried to match the words coming out of my mouth, "I'm Danielle Clearwater, I'm Danielle Clearwater," but the reflection just didn't feel like lying today. My brain chimed in and rang out, No! You're Carolina Stronghill! I relented and softly spoke, "I'm Carolina Stronghill." *Always one Hail Mary from hell.* My likeness shook her head and I threw a cup of water at it. My image melted down the mirror and into the sinkhole.

After wiping down the ménage of smears and water droplets, I let out a big sigh. This growing old may bring wisdom, which seems lost unto me, but it sure does bring the unavoidable signs of aging. Every morning was the inevitable inventory of age spots, wrinkles, and…as I looked closer, *damn it to hell,* new wrinkles. Some crow left his feet in the corner of my eyes and my smile lines were growing deeper around my mouth. Lord knows how I got those, I don't recall smiling all that much.

Needing to whip myself just one more time, I backed away to get a full body view. Circus mirrors would be a good idea right now. My self-deprecating survey in the morning was getting depressing, so I put my hair in a ponytail and found some clothes on the floor. My toes grabbed a white t-shirt, threw it up in the air, and it rained down like a soft cotton ball. Then I snugged into some denim shorts and headed towards the kitchen to make coffee. Not a big stretch from the bathroom to the kitchen, really; it was just a doorway. The pads of my fingertips ran along the cool adobe wall and stirred up the still water of memories of when I purchased this house.

The true essence of any neighborhood is not what is in the rays of the sun, but what creepy crawly things hide in the dark. Car lights off, my car crept down this quiet neighborhood, with only the light of the moon to guide my way. Under the silvery waves stood a vacant sunbaked house with a FOR SALE sign that hung off one hinge swaying in the breeze. I parked across the street and gazed at the forgotten adobe. The yellow lights of the houses next to it illuminated the casita, and cast an eerie glow upon the decay. Underneath the façade of chipped and cracked skin were the bones of the house grinning like an old forgotten skeleton in the desert. It was dying a slow death, and as I lay my head on my arms in the car window, I knew it was mine.

The next day, the real estate agent slammed the door open with her shoulder, and we marched into the house. Immediately, we scampered right back out until the air cleared of the foul odor. "Old houses always have a distinct odor about them, but they are certainly the most well-built," she coughed and wiped her hands on her skirt. I remained silent and lifted one eyebrow at the certainty of odoriferous old houses. A few minutes later and a cautious sniff test, we were at the threshold looking around, "Really, just a few touch-ups are all that it needs," her voice squeaked as she looked pensively around the room with her briefcase in hand. She made her way around, avoiding the streaks of light from the windows that revealed all the particles in the air. She contorted her body in various positions to keep from getting dust on her designer outfit.

Yes, I agree, the touch of a backhoe is exactly what this house needed hoping my thoughts didn't resonate around the room. With confidence, she flipped the light switch with a loud click, but only darkness answered the call. "I'll just look for the electrical panel," and she scurried off, picking her way through the trash and other debris that was on the floor. *Man, is she going to be pissed when she sees what stained her Manolo Blahnik shoes.*

Sudden luminosity hit all the crevices and chased the shadows away. She quickly came back and began proselytizing the amenities, and in hushed tones, the pitfalls of the house, her eyes darting my direction after each revealed problem.

"A new coat of plaster should take care of those rather large cracks," her face made a frown, "and then just some paint...." Her voice died into the ether as I touched the adobe walls. A quiet rhythm pulsed through my fingertips. Waves of strength and endurance embraced me, and I knew I was nothing to this house, a piece of mortal ash easily swept away by a straw broom.

"I'll take it." Her jaw dropped, ceasing the ramble of a woman's touch, paint, and something about blood, sweat, and tears, "And I'm paying cash for it."

"I'll draw up the paperwork," and she paused for a moment and looked straight at me, "today."

The aroma of rich and pungent coffee percolating tickled my noise and brought me back to the present. Unfortunately, my little casita had its quirks, and well…eccentricities. The electrical system was wired for only one appliance to work at a time. Plug in a coffeemaker and a curling iron and all of life ceased to exist. It wasn't unusual to come home, flip the switch, and remain in total darkness. That is why there is a magna light handy by the door; it's bright, and has the added convenience of braining anyone I deemed dangerous.

Waiting for the last drop of coffee, I stared at my backyard full of sand and holes, and quickly pulled the curtains together. Why take of care of something when you can hide it from view? A shadow crossed the curtains and darkened the kitchen for a split second and an eerie feeling of someone walking across my grave came over me. Shaking it off, I came face to face with two little beady eyes staring at me from the cabinet. My pig cup was a garage sale find that I couldn't pass up. Between the boxes of dusty furniture and a seventies lava lamp, sat a pink ceramic teacup in a shape of a pig, with a snout and curly tail that poked out of the cup. Pig cup sat alone and forlorn on top an old creaky table with a soiled red and checkered cloth. Its sad and lonely eyes mirrored my own, and I immediately took it home to become part of the family entourage of farm animals in the form of teacups.

The coffeemaker sighed as I poured a ton of sugar and milk in my coffee. Coffee in hand, I walked to the front porch and sat in the dawning light, letting the heat of the Southwest sun resonate around me, and chased the shadows away. Today was going to be a scorcher, and I quickly learned another quirk of the house—no air conditioning. I'm sure that was innocently forgotten by the real estate agent.

The view from the porch is less than stellar. Siberian Elms, a menace to society here in the great Southwest, line the perimeter of my house. They are a weed tree with scraggly-looking branches, scrawny bark, their seedpods forever infusing the ground with roots that reach into middle earth. They are almost next to impossible to get rid of, so I decided to be Zen and live with them—except when their leaves drop, by which time I have major issues with the trees. My revenge is watching their branches burn to ash in my small kiva fireplace. Through my sunglasses, I scanned the many holes in the yard underneath the shade of the Siberian Elms and decided some form of plant life should fill them. That was a tempting thought, but I'm never around long enough to see a full bloom. I slurped some coffee and wiggled my nose at the acrid taste, definitely more cream and sugar. Digging holes saved me a butt load of money in therapy. The intense work forcing a shovel into caliche siphoned all the frustration and anger that welled inside of me till the next round of pesky feelings came around, and since I was in self-imposed witness protection program, it would be the only therapy I would ever get.

Surrounding my front yard, I have a dilapidated three-foot high wooden fence with out-of-control ivy growing all over it. Visually, I'm sure the neighbors have issues with the front yard eyesore, but since I don't particularly mind it, I ignore it, and leave to its own devices. My side gate is clinging onto life by one rusty hinge. There is a trick to opening it: you have to lift and then move the gate at the same time to get in. A rusty cowbell decorates the aging gate and acts a doorbell for anyone attempting to come in. I thought about all of the things I needed to do and sighed. No use in fixing a house that I might have to leave under the cover of darkness.

My neighbor waved to me and I mirrored the friendly neighborhood signal of friendliness. Keeping up appearances was vital; my modus operandi is to be friendly, but keep my distance because if the neighborhood ever found out who I was, I believe pitchforks might be involved. Not to mention, my ex is a psychopath trying to find me. I smiled at my neighbor hesitantly. I didn't really want to form a bond of friendship so easily shattered. Drinking some bitter coffee, I wiped away something wet that ran down my cheek and found distraction in the scenery. The views of the Sandia Mountains were spectacular this morning. They were dressed in brilliant purples and dark blues. The sun highlighted all the cracks and crevices, revealing even more of the mountain. The Sandias, made of sand and stone, was an uncompromising mother who spread her arms out and gathered the city of Albuquerque to her breast.

A loud rumble broke me out of my tranquil morning and as I jumped out of my chair, coffee spilled across my legs. "Son of a bitch!" I yelled as loudly as I could. Luckily, the coffee was only lukewarm. My gorgeous, which I hardly noticed his looks, but rather rude neighbor—rammed the throttle on his motorcycle and spun the wheel so that greasy black smoke billowed in the air. His motorcycle reverberated as he backed out of his driveway. A slight wind picked up the burnt tire smell and came into my yard, "Freaking damn neighbor!" I hacked as I tried to get oxygen into my lungs. I'm …I'm…so not sure what I am going to do about him, but it will be something. Then I gave his lovely behind the evil stare as he rode away. "Damn neighbor," I muttered in between spasms of coughing from the black smoke. In the middle of a really nice rant I had going, the paperboy came racing by and threw the newspaper. The paper plopped right on the edge of a hole and the wind gently pushed it in. Fucking A! I belted out between cough spasms. *Stupid, gorgeous neighbor with his incredibly tight jeans. Bad neighbor, bad neighbor*, I thought as I watched him roar away in a t-shirt that stretched over his back muscles. A warming sensation in a most interesting and unused place became apparent. Then a breeze cooled down the area and I looked down at a big, brown stain on the front of my shorts. I took a long, slow deep breath out of sheer depression.

After changing clothes, I went back out and gingerly picked up the rolled up newspaper out of its cavernous hole and unrolled the *Albuquerque Journal*. Splashed across the headline, in bold, black letters were the words SERIAL KILLER STRIKES AGAIN!

> *Alisha Myers, thirty-eight, was found murdered in her Albuquerque, NE Heights home today. Her boyfriend, Carlos Martinez, who found the body, is currently being questioned. Police would not speculate any further details, pending a thorough investigation. When asked if this case looked like the other murder cases, Captain Stafford of the Albuquerque Police said, 'No comment,' as he plowed through the throng of reporters.*

A black and white photo on the front page bared the raw pain on the faces of Alisha's parents as they watched a body rolled out of the house. On the gurney was a simple human form covered by a white sheet that hid the horrors beneath it. The journal went on to describe previous victims tortured and murdered, all found in their homes. They were always women, various shades of blonde, single, and living alone in the city. A blonde strand of hair landed on the article and my muscles trembled at a sudden chill I had. Brushing the stray strand off, I continued scanning, looking for any other clues to my newest obsession.

I knew what the killer was doing. He was looking into the soul of the city and bringing Albuquerque to its knees. The killer was intoxicated with the feeling of power, attention, and control. I knew the feeling well. My fingers twitched and my palm dropped from the weight of a remembered gun. The murders occurred about once every three months. When the city would finally start to calm down, he would strike again. But if you looked at other newspapers around the state, there would be a similar murder in another city or town. He was consistently torturing his victims and then killing them. There was only one clue that the police slipped out: The victims lay in a position of prayer, with their eyes forced open to the coming sunlight. He, the killer of petitions, must feel invincible, and I licked my lips. He was a junkie. A binge of murder and then Albuquerque breathed sigh of relief when there was a respite. The victims were older women looking for love, only to find pain in their last moments. It didn't seem to matter what their socioeconomic status was, and there was no indication that women even knew each other. The police were truly baffled by this mystery, which left only more questions, and answers that seemed to be chased by the wind.

Albuquerque was awash with grieving families pouring their souls into mikes of the reporters, begging for information to capture the murderer. The vibration of sadness blasted out on the airwaves over the ten o'clock news and surrounded me in my nightmares. The police chief would take questions and as each murder happened, I saw the yoke of his burden bend him further and further. His voice was the sound of a tree bending against the prevailing winds when he explained yet another victim, no new evidence, and no captured monster.

Reporters were relentless in the pursuit of the story, always asking for more gruesome details about the deaths. They were just as insatiable as the killer. People wanted more than just generic answers as though specifics would balm their nerves and ease their fears. The story was gripping the city, the only subject people talked about as I passed them by like a ghost. I would hear bits of conversations as I shopped for groceries and heads were buried in newspapers at the coffee shop. Fear and paranoia was rampant, spreading infection to everyone. Gun and ammunition sales shot up. Brilliant stars reflected off the alarm company vans from the sun, my hand diverting the sparks as I drove around the neighborhood. The killer was a soul-stealing addict and his adrenaline rush was the last breath of life from his lambs.

Staring out into the Sandias, I thought of him, Albuquerque's serial killer, and his need to slaughter, his need for power, and the monster inside grabbed my spine and shook it to let me know it is alive and well. My heart began to race at the thought of him in the city and my spine rattled me out of my thoughts. I slammed the monster back in her locked box and disguised her as forty-year-old runaway. Unfortunately, the key to open the box was always readily available.

Chapter 2

Pig cup's eyes lasered through my caustic mental haze and not to be judged, I lifted one eyebrow right back at the painted pink image. The squealing tires of a car burning rubber broke my stare down with the cup. I curled up my lip and quelled the nasty thoughts running through my head of where the driver could go. Through the greasy haze came the irascible sounds of uncontrollable barking dogs from the yard across the street.

My neighborhood, once serene, is now filled with screeching, speeding cars, and the roar of the obnoxious neighbor's motorcycle. My usual routine was to wake sweaty and miserable from a nightmare, shut my eyes from the assault from the sun's dawning light, and put a pillow over my head. Lately, the rumble of a Harley at full throttle would bring me out of my just new state of REM sleep. One morning after a vicious throwing of my pillow against the wall, I ran out the door and tried to wave him down, to have a frank discussion about his need for a properly functioning muffler. I'm not sure if he pretended not to see me or he didn't see me through the acrid smoke. One fist shake later, I assumed he was pretending.

Across the street were the Garcia's, a young Hispanic couple with three precocious children. The timbers of my porch framed the family's house in perfect harmony in the morning rays of sun. The father always had a blue, long sleeve shirt, tan pants, and rugged boots and the mother always wore a hotel maid's uniform. They huddled their kids together and one by one kissed each of their foreheads as the kids squirmed beneath the tender ministrations. If it weren't for the color of their skin, they would be Norman Rockwell's next painting. The father grabbed the first child he could capture and hugged him close.

A tainted memory clouded my eyes and I was home getting dressed for the first day of second grade. A cold wind blew against the window and made the panes shake.

"There, you're dressed," my father announced flatly and spun me around to stand in front of the mirror. I was dressed in jeans with a strawberry patch on the knee and my father's extra-large shirt hanging down like an ill-fitting dress. Suspiciously, I eyed the jeans with a look of familiarity; they had to be from the girl down the street.

My dad, tall as a sequoia and just as round, towered over me. The mirror reflected a disheveled child with uncontrollable blonde curls with a disgusted look on her face and his face with a nervous twitch. His police uniform was sharp and ironed compared to my crumpled clothes.

"Um, it's not that bad." His eyes were searching anywhere but my face. His head dipped, "Sorry, Carolina" and shrugged his shoulder, "maybe a belt will help." He went through my closet but gave up the attempt in the mess of Barbie dolls and last year's clothes on the floor.

"Dad...I don't want to go to school." I put my hands in a fist and then crossed them above my chest. I was standing my ground; no one was taking me to school looking like this.

My dad closed his eyes and then harrumphed. He scratched his bristly chin and then rolled his bloodshot eyes. "You'll go to school, if I say you'll go to school."

I threw my hip. "I will not!" then I tightened my lips. "You can't make me!" My high-pitched voice rang off the walls.

"Carolina Ann, you will go to school!" He put his arms on his hips and straightened himself, and the sequoia grew taller. He towered over me and a dark shadow crossed over my face as I began to shrink underneath the stare. I always knew I was in trouble when both of my names were flung past his lips. His face was ironwood and in the battle of being stubborn, he won.

Chin to my chest in a sad little whisper, I said, "Where's Mom?"

The tree bent and knelt before me, "Ahh, don't cry, Carolina," and brushed my tears away with this thumb.

"When is Mom coming back?" It had been weeks since she had left to see her family. I searched his eyes for a sign of anything that would tell me a different answer, but he only looked out the window. "Dad...." My little heart was broken and the tears were dropping on the pieces. "When is she coming back?" I knew the answer long ago but I was desperate to hear something different.

He sighed. The wind blew the snow outside in circles. His strong branches swayed and gathered me up into his arms. I buried my nose in his uniform. Old

Spice mixed with sweat and sadness lingered on his shirt. He put his chin on top of my head. Normally, his voice was baritone, sweet and low; however, he choked out, "Carolina…," he swallowed, "Carolina…she's not coming back." Something landed on my leg, a drop that soaked into my jeans, and then another drop and another. Teardrops rained down around me and I was underneath the canopy, waiting for the storm to cease. After a few minutes, the rain stopped. My ear to his chest, I heard the slow thumping sound of his heart. He wiped his eyes. "Now, after school, we'll go get ice cream," and he scrunched up his face to the reflection in the mirror, "and then we'll go shopping, eh."

Barking dogs broke the silent inner storm and I was sitting on the porch basking in warm sunlight. I slurped some coffee to clear my clogged throat and cringed…*god I hate coffee*. Next to the Garcia's was Carson's home. My first day here, I walked out onto the porch, tea in hand, and watched as a nice, quiet, mild-mannered, grandmotherly-looking woman, hose in hand, flooded the dirt in front of her house. Her front yard was a catastrophe of brightly colored wind spinners, faded pink flamingos barely standing on one leg, and an old cracked plastic statue of Jesus lying on some old cement bricks. Plastic balls with puncture holes and dog toys lay scattered throughout her yard. Leaning against the post, I wondered if I had landed in some weird version of the Wizard of Oz.

My days in this neighborhood were going to be short because no matter how much I disguised myself, she would see through me. Then a car sped by and, without hesitation, the calm and serene sage screamed at the top of her lungs, "Slow the fuck down!" The car immediately braked and cruised on in an acceptable neighborhood street speed. Perhaps, I was mistaken; maybe this is exactly where I needed to be. Then, two whirling dervishes barreled out of the shadows and I understood why she was watering the dirt. If she didn't, dust devils would claim her yard.

Smiling at the memory, I chucked my nasty coffee and crossed the street to chat with the neighborhood informant—must keep up my appearances of a normal person. "Hey, what's up, Carson?" Two dogs slammed into the fence and began a cacophony of happy state of yapping. After I petted them, my shirt became a mixture of doggy saliva and mud. I tried in vain to wipe it all off, but it just smeared some more and I implored silently for help with dog slobber on my hands.

Carson, oblivious to the mess standing before her, said, "Nothing much…would you like a pair of obnoxious dogs?"

My consternations ignored, I picked up a mud-caked dog toy and threw it. Kelsey, a Red Heeler with gangly legs and long tail, tried to beat her brother to the toy and ran like the wind past Dolin. Not to be outdone, Dolin, a Blue Heeler with black polka dots scattered across his body, kick-started and bounced on Kelsey for the toy. The neighborhood entertainment rolled around in the dirt until they became one ball of fur. I couldn't stop laughing and realized I hadn't laughed in quite a while.

"Not today," and shrugged my shoulders. Carson's bright blue eyes opened wide in fake surprise and her mouth crinkled up in a smile as she picked up a dog toy and threw it. She would always joke about giving her dogs away but she loved them like her own children. I continued wiping my hands on my shorts after each dog throw pass and groaned, *I was due for a shower anyways.*

A bright red steel ghost sped past us and Carson yelled, "Slow the fuck down!" but to no avail. The red mustang turned the corner and disappeared. "Damn speeding cars, they're going to kill someone!" She immediately got on the phone and called the cops. Carson was the all-seeing eye of our neighborhood, and under her ever present watchful eye, the neighborhood was kept safe from people…well…people like me.

About that time, my next-door neighbor, Riley, came over with her five-year-old daughter, Angelica. "Hey there! What are y'all up to?" Riley's voice, with its high-pitched Southern accent and oozing of Southern charm, could be heard down the block in a rainstorm. The child within her arms stretched out to touch the dogs. Riley sighed. Angelica was wearing small white pinafore with white roses on her bodice, a magnet for dirt and doggy saliva.

"You want to play with the doggies, Angelica?" Carson asked.

Angelica buried her face in her mother's arms. She never spoke, just made motions with her hands and moved her body around to indicate what she wanted at that particular moment. Most days, I always had a small fire of turmoil in my being, but around Angelica, a sense of cool peace banked the fires within. Riley, eyeing the dogs and then Angelica's dress, took a deep breath and was about to put her down, when Angelica spied me over her mother's shoulder. Strawberry blonde locks surrounded her chubby little face and her cornflower blue eyes suddenly had a heavenly cloudy look.

"I don't know what it is about you, Danni, but she just loves to hug you." I smiled shyly, I couldn't imagine why, either, as I wrapped Angelica in my arms. "You're the only one she lets herself get close to," Riley whispered.

Angelica hugged my neck and an overwhelming sense of peace chased the shadows of my heart, then suddenly like nothing happened, she squirmed and practically jumped out of my arms. Her feet hit the ground running and the moment of tranquility was lost. She was a vision: a small white angel with dogs running around her in circles, and then a small puff of wind lifted her hair and revealed an old jagged scar across the side of her neck. Angelica giggled and, for a dazzling moment, the sunlight reflected a halo around her small head.

Carson picked up a soggy toy and threw it, "Where did Angelica get that scar on her neck?" My mouth dropped open in shock. My grandmotherly neighbor was a wee bit nosey as far as I was concerned. Riley's face turned ashen and so many painful emotions crossed her face.

Riley closed her eyes for a few moments and choked out, "An accident," and her eyes began to tear. There was so much more to this story, but Carson didn't press any further, to my relief. An awkward silence stifled the oxygen we were all breathing and then, true to form, Riley wiped a tear from her eye, "So how is the neighborhood watch going?"

Carson said, "Fine, nothing unusual so far."

"I've been looking for anything out of the ordinary but haven't seen anything suspicious," I chimed in. *Man, I'm such a good neighbor with my valuable insight.*

Riley smirked and in her Southern speech, "You mean you have been watching the activities of your next-door neighbor." She had a distinct look of a cat that just caught the rat. My cheeks burned bright red and Carson had the same look when a vulture horns in on dead prey. The neighbor wasn't there at the moment, thank god for little favors, but a nice little memory of him seemed to have sprung up unexpectedly, though. The memory coursed through me: I was surveying my last therapy session hole when a flash of bright light caught my eye. I peeked over the bushes and saw him. His backside was in my view as he was diligently working on his motorcycle, the sun shooting sparks off the tank, and I, a motorcycle enthusiast, just happened to notice the way his biceps flexed underneath his tanned skinned as he was polishing the tank.

Other details I hadn't noticed were the perfect curve of his ears, the stubble on his face that outlined his stern jaw, and his long eyelashes that defined his eyes. Carson and Riley both eyed me as I was daydreaming. It's definitely been a long time since I had any romance, except for Danielle Steel books, and the occasional bubble bath with toys. Brought back to my senses by hmmmm sound, I checked my mouth for drool and had a sudden need to check for nonexistent birds in the sky. "I hadn't really noticed."

Riley turned slightly and her hair like her daughter's hid her giggle. At thirty-five, she could pass for the everlasting age of twenty-nine and gentle beyond compare. Short and stumpy standing next to her, I looked like an ogre. I just needed the green makeup for effect. There was no man to call her wife and only a light skin band around her wedding finger to indicate there was ever a husband.

Gaining some composure but only slightly, "He's a biker, probably with a motorcycle gang," and just for good measure, I threw in, "he's just fucking rude!"

"Carolina!" Riley's stern eyes pointed to Angelica.

My neck lost a vertebrae at the admonishment; right time for a different tactic, "Doesn't the noise bother you?"

"You get used it," Carson shrugged as she watched Dolin, Kelsey, and Angelica playing with a toy. Angelica's high-pitched giggle rang through the air as the two furry creatures licked her face like she was a big dogsicle.

"Well, I live right next door to him, haven't gotten used to it yet." I made a frowny face to show my annoyance; however, I don't think they were buying my acting skills.

"Maybe you should go talk to him, Danni." Riley said as she was trying to keep dirt and doggy drool off Angelica's pinafore. She gave up and threw her hands in the air.

Inwardly, I smiled; she had no idea that dirt is a permanent way of life in the high desert. "How would he ever hear me over his Harley?"

"He seems nice enough," Carson mentioned. "He checks up on me from time to time to see if I need anything."

Riley spoke up. "He helped me move a piece of furniture the other day. He was a perfect gentleman." My brain yelled, *He never introduced himself to me!* Luckily, no one noticed my brain shout. She went on, "He just a little too …well…he just seems like he's just too much salt of the earth."

I was about to disagree about his level of nice behavior, when my neighbor came rumbling in on his Harley and we tilted our heads for a better view. He stood for a moment, then he turned around suddenly, scrunched his eyes against the assault of the sun, waved, and then he disappeared into his house. Riley put her hand underneath my chin and lifted up my jaw. I blinked my eyes and tried to clear away the last image I had of him walking in the house and the way his faded jeans hugged the lower portions of his exquisite body. Taking a breath, I turned to the trio of dogs and child to cool down the temperature in my face. The three of them at play made me laugh, until I noticed there was only the din of barking dogs but no child's words ringing in the air. *Oh, Angelica, what could be so bad that would take your voice away?* Out of the Garcia's house a boy yelled, "Dad, Dad!"

The screaming hurt my ears, "Dad! Dad!" My dad lay on the ground his lips were blue and his face starch white. "Dad," the words caught in my throat. The next sordid image was of my fingers feeling the smooth wood of the oak casket before me. The smell of sandalwood perforated the atmosphere, cutting off the air I breathed. His uniform, a dark blue, so perfectly ironed contrasted with his ashen face surrounded by white silk.

"Your father was a good man. One of the best." With teary eyes, I lifted my head to the tall man beside me. A man I didn't know but had seen when I visited Dad at the precinct. He put a hand on my shoulder, the weight crushing my body, "If you need anything…." He turned his head away and wiped a tear. His uniform was perfect and I could only read three letters from his name tag, STA.

As a teenager, I could talk it up with the best of them, today I couldn't speak, "I…I…." The pain in my throat blocked the words. His eyes were overwhelmingly sad. He patted my shoulder and walked away.

This nightmare was never going to end; so many people and yet I was the loneliest person in the world. Another stranger walked up to me and his lips moved, but the voice was so familiar. "Did you read in the paper today about the latest murder?"

"What?"

"Did you read in the paper today about the latest murder?" I was transported back to the present and gazing at Carson's face.

I shook my head. "I…the murder…um…ahh." Mr. Garcia came out and hugged his laughing son and they began to play basketball.

Riley eyebrows knitted together as I looked for an anchor in the present. I couldn't seem to orient myself to where I was. "Albuquerque is becoming such a dangerous place to live," she spoke, her voice ringing with her Southern accent.

My throat felt like it was going to collapse, but I managed to choke something out to keep any concerned looks coming my way, "This is the fifteenth one."

"Always single women." Riley continued to look at me until she heard a thump. Angelica had fallen on the ground, but she sat stunned and then got up again. "We should all be nervous."

My bearings came back and I was finally able to think. I wasn't nervous, even though I shook my head with the group. *Who would come after me?*

"Kelsey, stop growling at your brother!" Kelsey, with her tongue hanging out on the side, took a stance against her brother over a torn up bear with the stuffing coming out of its head. Angelica fidgeted with her hands and kept looking at the dogs. Noticing Angelica's apprehension, Carson shushed them and told them quit it.

"I wonder how those women didn't see him coming?" Riley posed. "He's gotta give you the creeps when he's around. Mercy, Angelica you're just as dirty as those dogs." She tried to wipe a smudge off Angelica's fat little cheek.

Carson threw another toy to the dogs to wrestle over. "Problem is you have no idea who he is. He could be anybody around here," and Carson eyed each house slowly and methodically till she rested her eyes upon my house.

I kept my silent speculation because whoever this creature of the night was, he was a killer chameleon, easily blending into society. What is the one thing that makes a human soul trust another and open their doors to the face of evil? The newspaper was not giving a profile on the man, but then again, the police hadn't released a lot of details. Maybe I would hear more in the whispers and innuendos among the patrons at work.

A police car cruised down the street looking for the speeding car. Carson and Riley waved their thanks as Angelica caught my attention and away from the policeman's prying eyes. The dogs had pinned Angelica beneath them and were bathing her in dog slobber. She giggled only slightly, her white pinafore stained with dog drool and mud.

Chapter 3

After our armchair detective speculations of Albuquerque's serial killer ran its course, I sauntered back to my house. Instrumental music, a very soulful song with wind instruments, resonated through the air, breaking my obsession of who the killer could be. Putting my head down and peering through the holes in the hedge, I took in the view of my neighbor spit shining his Harley. It was beautiful sight to behold man and his machine. The sun reflected in dazzling diamonds off his gas tank and blinded me for a second. When I tried to get a way, I tripped over my spade and landed flat on my face. "Son of a bitch!" I touched my lip, "God, that smarts."

"Yeah, that wouldn't happen if you'd put up your tools."

Fucking A, my hands clenched in disbelief at my stupidity and then cursed him. Slowly, I got up on all fours and remembered the view he had. I turned my head back. "Thanks for the concern," I said rather sarcastically.

He replied, "No problem," then walked away.

Shaking my head in disbelief, *what an asshole*, I went into the house and decided to call Harvey, my parole officer, because today's humiliation wasn't enough. Released from prison with a probation agreement signed as my short leash, I was assigned to Harvey, a bleeding heart workaholic with an ulcer and an attitude. He was in his forties like me, but the stress of his job had withered his face until he was reminiscent of an old man. My last memory of Harvey was shaded in shadows. He was standing on the opposite side of my car door.

"You'll be okay, Carolina. Call me every day, promise?" He was concerned for my life. Escaping my ex became his priority.

A soft wind picked up a soft piece of red hair and blew it away from his balding head. Tears were forming and I couldn't think of a single thing to say except, "When are you going to shave that cheesy red mustache of yours?" I hated the thing and tried with all my might for him to do something about it and eventually it became a running joke.

He smiled, rubbed his hand over it, and said, "Get in the car and go!" I hugged him quickly and dove into the car before he saw the tears flow. Backing out of the driveway, his look of concern and blowing red hair was the last image I had of him.

Dialing his number on the rotary phone, I thought about how after twenty years in the "business," he had retained his big heart and was eager to see any of his parolees making something of themselves. Needless to say, disappointment was a major factor in his life. I called him every day, as ordered, and at first, our conversations were very benign. Where are you living, are you finding work—stuff like that. Eventually, he became my lifeline and unlikely ally. In a sea of unfamiliar faces and towns, new names, he was the only one who really knew me, who called me by my real name. He was the lighthouse I drew myself to in the storm.

The click of the phone and din of the background rang through the line, "Hey, Harvey," my bored voice covered up my insecure heart.

"Hey, Carolina, how's it going in the desert?" His voice was loud over the din of cussing, phones, and fax machines.

"Dry. And you, how's the windy city?"

"Blowing as usual. You doing okay, kid?"

"Same as always."

"Still have the nightmares?"

Silence was my answer. Nightmares were my guilty conscience's form of harassment.

"It'll get better, kid."

"You always say that."

"I know because I believe it will."

"Always mister positive, aren't you?"

"Stupid, stupid kid!" *What the hell.* Harvey's voice became muffled as I heard some inaudible conversation going on about one of Harvey's parolees. Jaw intact as I realized he wasn't talking about me, I held tight to the telephone line, hoping he wouldn't decide to hang up.

"Gotta go, kid, someone has ta take care of the rat house. I'll talk to ya tomorrow, Carolina." The dial tone broke the silence as my lifeline was cut.

Gently, I cradled the phone and glanced at the clock on the wall. *Fuck! Oh, shit, work.* Work was a local pizza place named Marco's Pizzeria, a combination of tomato sauce, cheese, police officers, and parolees. It was kind of an odd place to work, a ying yang effect in the form of a pizza joint and a pseudo halfway house. Police loved to keep an eye on the parolees as the parolees kept an eye on the police. Somehow, the owner, Marco, made it work to his advantage: Criminal or not, everyone loves pizza.

When I arrived in Albuquerque, Harvey had already made arrangements for me to meet an ex parolee of his by the spectacular name of Marco Protettore. He had a soft spot for criminals largely because he was one himself and he believed in the golden rule of "Pay it forward." He hired young men who always seemed to be in and out of the penal system. He did his best to straighten them out. However, the benefits of drug dealing were enormous but the fall from grace was hard.

The day I met Marco, I walked into the sweltering pizza place and ran straight into him, literally. Dressed in the epitome of Southwestern style, I had a red broom skirt, cute cowboy boots, and a white peasant blouse. Later, I came to find out my fashion sense was all but screaming tourist. Standing in the middle of the restaurant, I closed my eyes and breathed in an intoxicating mixture of basil, oregano, and garlic. My stomach growled at the prospect of having a slice. Hoping no one noticed my gastronomical dilemma, I opened an eye and noticed little details like leftover coffee cups with cigarette butts in them. The sun beaming through the doors highlighted a greasy sheen across the tables. The floor was littered with crumbs and napkins. The ceiling had water stains and the paint on the walls was dingy urine yellow. *Right time to skedaddle* and *possibly go yell at Harvey.* Turning to hightail it out of there, I slipped on some coffee and fell on Marco. His gold medallion around his thick neck hit my eye. The coffee cup he held smooshed into his chest and coffee spilled down his t-shirt. Two feet taller than me, I bent my neck to see his protruding chin with a five o'clock shadow and a nasty-smelling cigar with an inch of ash dangling from his lips.

"Fuck!" and I sucked in my lips and scrunched my eyes. "Sorry about that."

He grunted and I swiped a towel that hung from his belt and tried in vain to wipe the remnants of coffee off his already stained t-shirt. He grabbed the towel from my hands and blotted at the stain without much success.

Reluctantly, I coughed, backed up, and tried to run but my feet stayed rooted in the ground. With a really deep sigh, I said, "You must be Marco?"

After some more useless blotting of the stain, he eyed me and then grumbled what I assumed to be was a yes. "I'm Dannielle, or Danni for short. Clearwater," and I put out my hand and gave him the best smile I could muster under the circumstances.

Turning his back on me, he waddled behind the counter. *Well, hey, this going well.* "You know a friend of mine, Harvey…I believe." My words pelting his hunched over back. Hmmm, that's interesting the back side of his t-shirt is positively white.

He turned his short, stocky frame and faced me. Yeah, I know Harvey, and you're the broad I'm supposed to hire with no references, no I.D., no nothing. I have more information on the jackoffs in the back," he replied, his head nodding at the back of the restaurant. Loud protests about name-calling could be heard from the dark caverns of the back.

"Ahh, shut up! Quit your bitching, girls, and get back to work!" After yelling whoever was in the back there, he turned to me.

A nervous grin crossed my lips and I tried to erase it, but that stupid grin stayed stubbornly on my face. He stared at me and I moved my feet apart, preparing for battle and mostly to keep my knees from sagging, "Yeah, well, deal with it, asshole, because this is my new job and when do I start?" *Hmm, that was interesting, I just grew a new spine. Hope it stays around.*

He raised one eyebrow and scanned me from head to toe, stopping, of course, and resting his brown eyes on my chest. "Fuck, just what I need, a broad in the joint. Have you washed dishes?"

"No."

"Have you waited on tables before?'

"Oh, God, no!"

By now, we were gathering an audience. The three "jackoffs" were behind him, making rude gestures.

He rolled his eyes at me, "What am I supposed to do with you then?"

"I have no idea," I replied, putting my chin down and shaking my head at his dilemma about what we are going to do with a girl like Maria, and shrugged my shoulders.

"Fuck," he breathed a heavy sigh, "you start tomorrow." He grunted and then sauntered into the abyss. I did a little victory dance and the jackoffs behind the counter made catcalls while they high-fived each other. *Oh*, I stopped in mid dance; realization dawned on me we were all going to keep each other very entertained.

Eventually, I enjoyed working with the "jackoffs"— Juan, Julio, and Diego. All of them were on parole for various felony charges. Naturally, some adjustments had to be made and a forced newfound respect for women, particularly this woman. The best teacher I had on the human soul was prison and I had my compadres figured out within minutes. I, on the other hand, was a complete anomaly in their world: white, old (to them, of course), and far as they knew, no record. Respect was quickly gained when Juan tried to grab my breast while my hands were occupied with sticky pizza dough. Behind me were the rude calls and sexual innuendos bouncing off the tiled walls. Red from embarrassment and a deep seeded anger, I quickly turned and kneed Juan straight in the balls. Standing there watching Juan, I made note of these reactions: there was the initial shock, then the bent over position, and then the inevitable grabbing of the newly inflamed area, which was then preceded by falling on the floor. His amigos became suddenly silent, their faces turned to chalk dust as they witnessed their overly affectionate friend's face turn different shades of red and white. I stared at the others with a "Want a piece of this? Because Momma's got more to give!" stare and they turned away and left their comrade on the floor crying in a high-pitched tone in agony. A smirk firmly plastered on my face, I went back to kneading the dough.

Marco walked by and stared down at the folded human on the floor. "Dumbass, get back to work!" and kicked him slightly.

"But Boss…" was a painful whine from the puddle before him.

"Get back to work, you pansy." Marco wiped his hands in a filthy towel and mumbled, "you got your ass kicked by a girl." Reluctantly, Juan got off the floor, balls in hand, and walked away completely hunched over. No one touched me again.

Juan was shy of twenty, lanky with tawny brown skin stretched across his muscular frame. He had a pencil-thin mustache above his lip and underneath his hairnet was slicked jet-black hair. He usually had five girlfriends he bragged about, but no one quite believed. Either that or girls were pretty stupid these days. I was quickly indoctrinated into the world of sexting when, one day, I came around the corner and caught an eyeful, "Holy Mother of God, what the hell is that woman doing?" When I went to prison, cell phones were big, ugly clunky things; now, they were pocket size with enlarged pictures.

Juan snickered. "That's my woman showing me her best position, amiga." I stood in horror and thought, *God, please help me erase that awful image that has just been burned into my brain.*

Oddly enough, kneeing Juan in the jewels was a bonding experience. No budding romance, I refused to be a cougar to a confused, oversexed felon. I have my standards. Behind the machismo and bravado was a lonely lost boy and lonely I understood well. Every day,

I slipped on a coat of armor to mask the frightened child inside. Juan was also the one who teased me the most and could get away with it.

"Hey, Danni, you like that sausage? I'll show you mine, amiga," and Juan pointed to his crotch and made the international male sign for penis.

"This is what I think of your sausage," and I put the fresh meat mixture through the grinder.

"Ah, Danni, why do you have be that way." Juan pretended to be hurt by such a rejection of his affection.

"Man, you're an idiot if you think she's gonna like a jerk-off like you," Julio said. "She only likes the big ones." He put his arm around me. Everyone snickered as I happily punched in the stomach. Julio, who was also in his twenties, was similar to Juan in demeanor but a little more reserved. He had honey brown eyes that spoke in volumes of a deep sadness. His stomach showed the dedication of a man who worked out and his arms were sculpted to smooth perfection. Long and rail thin, he hunched his shoulders whenever he was around the others.

The third person in this *All My Sons* episode was Diego, who didn't talk or joke. He was a stone statue. There was something about him that I couldn't put my finger on, an eerie darkness always seemed to surround him. Julio and Juan just seemed like lost puppies to me, but Diego was definitely different. He was short and stocky, with russet skin that was unevenly tanned; he kept his hair greased back in a net to "tame" it. No older than Juan and Julio, he acted like a man who had seen too much of the bad side of life. His dark, intelligent eyes processed everything around him. He kept to himself and the details about his life to a bare minimum. One day, Diego was changing his shirt after work. I squeaked at the sight of his tattoo inked into his bare skin. He put his arms down against his sides, barreled out his chest, and stood tall. He dared me with his eyes and slowly walked forward to where my hand met his warm skin. My fingertips ran along a brilliantly colored rattlesnake as it slithered around Diego's body. Finally, the serpent ended with its triangular head around his neck, mouth open waiting to strike. The snake's eyes were emeralds that shined brightly against his darkened skin and stared into mine.

Clocking in, I looked at the beehive of felons and the owner on the menagerie of orders. Without hellos, or chitchat, I began my main job of making dough, an entrancing process of mixing yeast with water, watching it rise, punching it, and then rolling it into a smooth, doughy circle. I have yet to master the art of throwing dough up in the air, most of the time, it always landed on the floor, on my head, or on the head of someone who was reflex challenged. Of all of us, Marco was the only one who was deft enough to wheel a pile of dough into a circus act and create the perfect pie.

After a couple of hours, I took a break and looked out over the faded turquoise countertop into a sea of civilians and cops, their eyes darting around as they drank their coffee. At times, I couldn't tell who were cops, informants, or criminals. The lines between good and bad seem to blur all in the name of justice. The

Albuquerque murders had made the police very apprehensive, making them very twitchy. A killer was taunting them and with all the detective work, forensics, they could do nothing but sit and wait for the next lamb. In the middle of the restaurant some uniforms ruminated over cold coffee. It just so happened that surrounding my new uniformed friends, some empty tables were in need of my meticulous attention for detail.

Grabbing a rag, I began wiping away the crumbs as I leaned closer to their table. A rotund cop with sweat rolling down his face leaned across the table, "How is it he never leaves a print or nothing?" His question was tapped out by the rhythm of his finger on the table.

"I don't know," said an older cop, who was gaunt with yellow graying hair. He was about to take a swig of coffee when he said, "Like he has these women figured out, somehow," his graying eyebrows knitted together. Then he gulped some coffee down and his face soured.

"He studies them," said the fat one, who wiped the sweat off his forehead but missed the sweat on his upper lip. The buttons on his uniform stretched beyond their limits and looked like they were ready to pop any moment. "Shit, this could be anybody."

A younger officer in an ironed uniform leaned back in his chair and said, "He drains them, like he was some kind of fucking vampire. He drains them...," and his speech dropped off into thought, "....not a drop of blood left." The cop put a hand on his belly and his face turned a soft white, but he continued talking, "Lays them on their side with their knees bent up. Their hands," he lifted his hand and rubbed a knuckle, "like they were praying." He grabbed his coffee cup. "A rosary is always entwined in their fingers." He stared down into his coffee cup, "That last girl had her grandmother's rosary in her hands." He put the cup to his lips and looked at the older cop. He shook his head and the younger one put the coffee down and pushed it away. This new information pulled me into the vortex of their conversation.

Absentmindedly, I had wiped the same spot, when a fourth cop with a moustache spoke up, "That rose he leaves on top of them girls, what the hell does that mean?" My leg hit a chair and, suddenly, four pairs of eyes were staring at me. Time for a new rag and I ran behind the counter. When I came back to my already clean table, they were in midconversation.

"...he combs their hair," the large cop remarked, "...and spreads their hair down the pillow." He tipped his coffee cup back and forth. "He even puts make up on 'em afterward, the sick bastard."

"Yeah, bathtub was cleaned with bleach, the floors vacuumed, but no vacuum anywhere, nothing. Like he's a ghost or something." The older one with years of his job etched upon his face sat back in his chair. He sipped some coffee and began to choke. Finally recovered, he looked up to find every patron staring at him. Then, they huddled closer and whispered. *Damn, why did they have to clam up now?* As I continued wiping the table, hoping for more escaped words, I came to a couple of conclusions—that either the press sucked at getting those details, or the police finally put a clamp on the leak.

"Hey, Marco, you ever going to put fresh coffee in the pot?" the mustached cop waved his cup at Marco.

"Yeah, yeah, keep your panties on," he mumbled.

Marco motioned for me and I hunched my shoulders and reluctantly grabbed the coffee pot. "How's it going?" I smiled innocently. Every member of the circle silently stared at me as I poured each of them a cup of coffee. *Assholes.* "All right then, I guess I will just move on to a different table." Refreshing some college student's cup with some ridiculously awful coffee, I thought if the police had no clue who the hell this guy was, then exactly what were the rest of us supposed to do?

Walking back to the counter, a dark shadow in the corner caught my attention. His head bent so the bill of his hat cast an eeriness over his eyes, but the fluorescent lights illuminated a creepy smirk across his face. A chill came across my back as I went behind the counter to get him a menu. When I came back out, the shadow was gone and the door was slowly closing. Right before the door closed, a crow flew in and started pecking at the crumbs on the floor. He stopped and turned his head toward me, his beady little eyes staring straight at me. Ceramic plates shattered into pieces behind me and I jumped out of my skin. My nervous energy released in his direction, "Julio!"

"Damn, Danni! Why are you so jumpy?" he scowled at me. I sneered back, *Idiot*. As I turned back around, only a black feather lay on the floor.

After an eight-hour shift, home was my only destination, and it was a relief to finally pull into the driveway. Keys in hand, I got out of my car into the inky black night and cursed myself for not having a porch light. Each hair on the back of my neck began to rise and fear slowly crept into my bones. Prison taught me some painful lessons, one very hard lesson; trust my instincts. Suspiciously, my eyes scanned in all directions, desperately searching for anything in the well of darkness. All I found was shadows and the outlines of elms and lilac bushes. The wind rushed through the trees, causing the branches to creak as they swayed back and forth. I couldn't stop the creepiness factor that made every footstep I took painstaking. My shaky fingers fumbled around in my purse for a small flashlight, and my heart skipped a beat when I finally found it. "Eureka!" My lungs burned from the breath that I was holding. Suddenly, a car came screeching by and everything I had worked for was lost in the abyss of my purse. "Son of a bitch!" Anger ran roughshod over my nerves and oddly calmed me down. Reaching down into my purse, I began the search again, when something like fingers brushed the back of my neck. I quickly turned around with my hand still stuck in the vortex and looked for the arm attached to those creepy fingers. There was nothing, except the wind and the night.

Checking every few feet, my eyes darted around, looking for any signs of a malicious boogeyman. If I didn't know any better, I would swear on a dusty Bible that leering eyes followed my every move. After scrabbling through old house keys that I have kept for souvenirs, I screamed, "Aha!" I figured that sound effect might scare off anyone lurking behind the trees. *Oh, thank god.* The house key procured, I forced it into the door. Checking one more time behind me, I saw nothing but wicked trees swaying in the wind and hightailed myself into the house.

Flinging my shoes off, I put on the old bunnies and headed straight for the kitchen to see if there was anything remotely in the great crevasse that would calm my nerves. I never kept company with men like Jack Daniels, Johnny Walker or any other of their friends; it didn't do much for me. My two farm animal cups, pig and cow, welcomed me home with soft eyes. After greetings and salutations to my ceramic friends, I peered into my International Harvester refrigerator and considered my options before me: moldy cheese, Marco's leftover cheese pizza, and Riley's homemade Southern okra casserole (I still wasn't brave enough to try it.), and a wimpy bag of salad. Nothing sounded very appealing, so I shut the refrigerator door and retreated to the living room. I bounced on the couch, settled down, and let the silence surround me. Like Kudzu, loneliness and tendrils of fear crept in and buried their roots deeply. So I drowned out the silence by turning the TV to earth shattering decibels.

The TV news babbled on endlessly over stuff I didn't care about and only minutes on the latest murder, essentially no clues left behind. One click button later, the TV was dead which threw the room in total darkness, except for light escaping from the bedroom. Shuffling off to bed, I heard the cowbell clank softly

41

and something flashed in the window. Frozen in place, I held my breath. In the windowpane was a woman stiff with fright, hair askew. She wore a white t-shirt full of holes, shorts, and fuzzy pink bunny slippers. One of the ears on the slippers was hopelessly cockeyed. Embarrassment flooded and turned my face beet red. My own fucking reflection had just scared the bejeezus out of me. My over active imagination was going to get me killed and, with that, I jumped into bed.

Chapter 4

Naturally, the night was restless from my near-death experience. I couldn't sleep, and watched the dawn break through the glass, illuminating my room with rainbow crystals, turning the dark to a soft gray. Slowly, I drifted back to sleep and then the roar of a Harley jolted me out of the one minute of sleep I got. "God damn it!"

Jerking the covers off, I jumped out of bed, threw some clothes I found on the floor, and glided into my slippers. I jerked the door open and yelled at the top of my lungs, "Hey, you on the fucking motorcycle!" Then my jaw dropped: A pair of delicate bare arms slaked around his body and closed around his stomach. Those creamy white arms were attached to a thin body with nice curves and really long legs, her red hair in a ponytail swung back and forth as she laughed. She looked at me, wickedly smiled, and whispered in his ear. He scanned me from head to toe, smirked, and backed out of his driveway. My anger abated when I checked myself at what he was looking at. I cringed. *Oh, God, I'm an idiot.* I had thrown on a holy t-shirt that revealed the racier bits and parts of me, baggy sweats with paint all over them, and to complete my ensemble, bunny slippers. My right rabbit slipper had one ear laid on the ground in defeat.

I stomped into the bathroom and looked at my face. My hair looked like I had been part of an electrocution and I had black pits underneath my eyes. Lovely. I was this year's version of the walking dead. The reflection in the mirror showed bright crimson cheeks. I had walked out into the world to fight off my ill-mannered neighbor and my suit of armor was a pornographic clown costume. All I could do was go back to bed and hide underneath the covers.

As I attempted to sleep, I thought of the rude awakening by the gorgeous neighbor with long dark hair, chiseled biceps, and the harlot with bright red hair on the back of his motorcycle snaking her arms around him, and punched the pillow till it surrendered by lying flat. Taking a deep breath, I tried to analyze exactly what I was mad about—the fact he woke me up out of a dead sleep, the latest in sleepwear fashion show, or the hot chick that was on the back of his motorcycle? Humiliation burned on my face, jealousy was on my mind, lust in my heart, and guilt in my soul. What was I thinking? I didn't have a right to any of those emotions. They belonged to normal people certainly, not somebody like me. Eyes wide open, the morning stilled in peaceful silence, and my thoughts were a ball of twisted yarn, hopelessly tied in knots. I contemplated what I had done and wondered if I would ever be forgiven and who would do the forgiving.

No sleep, I managed to put something on that resembled work clothes (no holes) and dragged myself to work. Pounding dough with every bit of strength I could muster, I watched convicts trying to function in a normal work environment. Juan was fighting with his girlfriends, Julio was making a deal somewhere in the back, Diego, dark and brooding, was chopping meat into little pieces and the cops in the front kept a watchful eye on all the rats in the cage. Then there was a shout from the boss across the diner, "Jackoffs, get your asses into my office now!" Growling, I shuffled past Marco.

"What the hell is wrong with you?" He had a disgusted look on his face.

"Nothing. Why?" I had sudden need to check myself in the mirror.

Juan piped in with the flair of turning anything into a sexual innuendo, "Long night for you, Danni, eh!" and he grinned a nasty smile.

"Oh, shut the fuckup!" and I threw a towel at him. Juan flexed to the right and the towel missed him by a hair.

"All right everybody, I have some news. A newspaper reporter is coming here to talk about my place." Everyone either chewed gum, rolled their eyes, or in my case, just stared into the distance. "Everyone is getting their picture taken." With that, a cacophony of miscreants jumped and yelled at Marco. No one wanted the publicity. After a few minutes of concentrated screaming, Marco yelled back, "Shut the fuck up and sit down!" and we all stopped talking, his booming voice still echoing off the walls. "You girls, and I mean all of ya's, is getting their picture taken. This will be a picture of a fine establishment employing Albuquerque's rejects. End of story." He was about to walk away, when he looked and said, "Anyone you jackasses thinking of leaving will be fired." He eyed us all, threw a towel over his shoulder, and walked out the door.

All of us already had our pictures taken—it was called a mug shot. I marched behind him and fell into step. "I really can't be in this picture, Marco."

He looked at me with a cigar in his mouth, ashes dropping everywhere, and a puff of cigar smoke puffed in my face. The smell was hideous. "Why not?"

After choking and coughing, "I don't know what Harvey told you about me, but I can't have my picture taken. Please, Marco?" I was desperate. If he wanted me to kiss his toes, I would do it, mind you. I would need a barf bag and some gum, but I would do it. "Please, Marco," I was on my tippy toes, moving anxiously and my hands were wringing a towel to death. I couldn't let my ex find me.

His eyes softened. "Oh, for the love of God, keep yourself hidden when the reporter comes."

"I could kiss you right now. Thank you, thank you so much!" I danced around like a little girl getting a new doll.

"Yeah, yeah, now get back to work."

Later in the afternoon, relaxed and happy, catastrophe averted, I was punching some dough at the front counter. A shadow crossed my work area, but I didn't pay much attention. I thought it was a patron just checking out the fine art of dough making.

"So how do you like working here?"

"Fine, I guess." I wonder where Marco is, he should be schmoozing the paying guests right about now.

"So what's it like to work with all these ex-cons?"

I looked up into the face of middle age white guy with graying sideburns and a cigarette dangling out of his mouth. Across his chest was a strap that held a rather large looking digital camera. *Shit, shit!* "Marco!"

He took the cigarette out of his mouth and then held it in his fingers while he wrote on his little steno pad. The acrid smoke rose from his cigarette as ashes drifted to the floor. The reporter looked at my disgusted grimace, looked at the ashes floating on the counter, and just shrugged. I shook my head at his idiocy and coughed from the ashtray smell. "Oh, it's just great." Bending my neck in an impossible position, "Marco!" What was he writing down? How many sentences could you get out of great? Something just nagged at me that this wasn't right; there was something off about this reporter. Then Marco nonchalantly walked in and began making conversation about this Shangri-la in the desert for criminals. It was a back and forth conversation about Marco's willingness to hire convicts and I just nodded my head like this was the most interesting conversation I had ever heard.

Inch by inch, I started to back up and I eyed the back door; just a few steps and I was home free when Marco grabbed me and held me next to him. We stood side by side with his hand in my back like I was his Marionette puppet. Mother of God, how do I get into these things? The reporter eyed me and then scribbled more on his notepad.

"You don't look like a convict," he said, squinting his eyes.

"Huh, um, well," for an ex-prisoner, you would think lying would come easily. "I'm just regular gal trying to work. Marco felt sorry for me. He knew my ex was a con and well, he took pity on me." I implored Marco to help me with a desperate eye stare. He grinned. He was getting free advertising and then he walked off to look for the missing jackoffs. Sniffing the reporter that waltzed through the door, the cowards had fled like cockroaches when the lights come on. Apparently, my rat sense of smell failed me.

"Yeah, I thought Marco only hired convicts."

"I'm the ex of a convict. You know, I really gotta get back to work now." A high-pitched whine came out of my throat. "Dough waits for no man." I laughed nervously, then muttered some obscenities underneath my breath such as "fucking ass reporter."

"What did you just say?"

"What? Oh, nothing, I'm looking for a new camcorder," and started wrestling the dough once more. I was trying to imagine Marco's face as I beat the holy hell out of the dough.

He stared up me dubiously, "One more question."

"Of course, you do," I said rather sarcastically, and as I looked up, a flash of light blinded me. My eyes blinked as I tried to clear out the black dots floating in the air.

"Hey, hey, you're not gonna give all your attention to just the pretty lady." Marco finally came to the rescue, towing the deserters behind him. Damsels would be shriveled up prunes by the time this white knight came to rescue them. The reporter just stood there in front of me, staring, but Marco started talking about the other delinquents and the reporter finally started to ask some questions, always looking in my direction. I couldn't shake the feeling there was something fishy about this whole thing. Backing my way behind the captured jackoff, I heard, "Group picture." *Son of bitch.* I took a gigantic step backward so I could disappear, tripped over the mop bucket, and landed on the floor with a big resounding thump. The bucket landed on its side and swoosh, all the dirty water cascaded out in waves.

"Danni! Get over here!" He looked for my five foot three-inch tall figure across the air. An exuberant Marco yelled, "Come get into the picture." Then he looked at me on the floor and shrugged his shoulders. He was not missing his chance at free publicity. *Asshole!*

My escape plan had melted into the water as I heaved myself up. Wiping myself down as best I could, I kept my face down, but my cap fell backwards as I was squished in between Marco and Juan. The smell of sweat and cheap cologne nearly made me gag. Their noses were wrinkling at the smell of Pine Sol and dirt soaked into my clothes. *Good, hope you choke on it.* The camera flashed and captured five tortured souls and one overly exuberant grin in one photo. When the agony was finally over, we all turned and ran for the back door, except for Marco, of course.

The New Mexico sun beat down upon my soaked backside as I walked out and tried to meld with the wall. Juan lit a cigarette and parked himself on the second step, head down, staring at the long line of ants heading towards the backdoor. Julio was immediately on the phone and started arguing with someone, and

Diego stood there quietly letting the sun burn his face. We had all just been used and not a word of thank you to complete the assault. My thoughts ran deeper. *God help me if those pictures get into the paper.* Even though I was cooked from the sun, my jeans remained hot and wet. "Bastard!" We all looked at each other and they nodded their head in agreement and we went back in. Fretting all day, I worked till the second hand crossed the number for quitting time and ran home.

Tossing and turning all night, I finally succumbed to exhaustion. A peaceful thought drifted into my delirium. Marco said those pictures of me wouldn't get in the paper and I trusted him. Startled out of a deep sleep by the backfire of the neighbor's exhaust, I grabbed the windowsill, hoisted myself up, and looked out at the window. Bleary eyed and squinting, I watched my neighbor back out his driveway. I had to do a double take when a white skull with wings was levitating between his legs. Shutting my eyes to refocus, I realized that floating skull was the emblem embossed on his deep electric purple gas tank. Then he and his god damn noisy steed disappeared into the greasy smoke. Skipping the bunnies, I schlepped into the kitchen, punched the start the button on the coffeemaker, and opened and slammed the refrigerator door. It wasn't the refrigerator's fault for waking me up but what the hell; it was my version of kicking the dog.

Pig cup in hand, I walked out to my porch and sloshed hot coffee on me. Cursing loudly several expletives that only sailors would be proud of, I wrung out my shorts, sat down, and surveyed my therapy holes. Some of them were mysteriously filled in. Maybe one of my happy-go-lucky neighbors from Georgia just didn't like my form of therapy.

The paperboy on his bicycle came speeding past and hurled the newspaper. It hit the window with a thud and rolled down in defeat. I gave him my best I'm-pissed-at-you stare but it bounced off his smirky little face as he squeaked on down the road. Resigned to my lack of an intimidating stare, I eased into the porch chair and unrolled the abused paper. The headline jumped out: DESERT KILLER MURDERS AGAIN. I skimmed the article looking for any details like the ones I overhead from the cops the other day. Only one clue stood out among the jumble of black words. The victim was found the same way like the others, lying on her side in a prayer position, but this time they mentioned the rosary in her hands. For her sake, I hoped her prayers were answered quickly.

Then I scanned the rest of the paper, looking for any more information, until a proverbial ton of bricks hit me. Abruptly, I jumped and pushed the paper off me like an unwanted bug and then I stomped on it, repeatedly. My picture was on the front page. There in bright colors—well…newspaper bright colors—was me standing with my mouth gaping open, my hair swirling around me like springs in a box with black shadows underneath my eyes as the camera flash hit. *Motherfucker!*

Chapter 5

After my continued annihilation of the newspaper, I crumpled it up into a little ball and threw into one of the holes. Then I stomped over to the hole, picked it back out, and unraveled it. Why? Because I love to torture myself. Desperate for a miracle, I looked at the picture again and hoped that I magically disappeared. No such luck. In Kodachrome, I resembled a clown from an insane asylum, squashed between the keepers of the crazy house. Thoughts buzzed in my over fired synapses about where on earth I was going to begin a new hole to bury this newspaper. The Zen masters in my head whispered, *Let this go*, and the monster in my Pandora's Box rattled the cage and demanded we go find the dead man walking reporter.

Marco was supposed to make sure those pictures never made it into the paper. I distinctly remember having a conversation with him about that. "Don't worry, Danni, I will make sure those photos don't get in the paper."

"Are you sure, Marco?"

"Of course, trust me," said the snake to the mouse.

Panicked, I called Harvey that morning to let him know what happened. "I've been forced to take a photograph and now that very photograph is in the paper!" I exaggerated those last few words quite a bit, merely to make my point come across.

"Huh."

That was the response, *oh bloody hell*, so I spoke slowly and distinctly, "Essentially, they announced to the world exactly where I am." Harvey didn't say a word—a very odd reaction, indeed. He was never calm about anything. He seemed to be always in the midst of disaster with one of his clients. He was doing his level best to keep society's wasted juveniles out of jail and trying to save them from themselves. Meanwhile, all that forced saving was boomeranging and killing him slowly. He had a heart attack two years ago and his ulcer never ceased to cause him pain.

"You seem awfully calm. Do you not get I was in the paper?" A car passed by and I hid behind the wall. "What if he finds me again? You know he'll find me." My voice came out a bit well..paranoid. I swallowed and breathed through my nose and then exhaled aloud. This is so not working, meditation sucks, what would really help is hitting someone over the head, preferably with a baseball bat. *Breathe, Carolina, breathe.*

"Don't worry, Carolina, you'll be fine. I have friends in high places." He had a nice chuckle, then a knocking sound, "God dammit! I knocked my coffee cup over." Good, maybe there was an angel intervening for me. He dropped the phone and then I heard the inescapable noise of an angry Harvey stomping around. In distant muffled tones, he said, "Can't I get a fucking rag around here? Fucking got it all over me!" I held the receiver away from my ears—virgin ears and all.

"Look, Carolina, you haven't heard from him in two years. Maybe he's stopped looking for you." I could hear ominous sounds in the background of objects being moved and some dripping sounds. "You never get any letters from him anymore. Son of a bitch…no, no, no, not that report! Oh, hell!"

"Just because I haven't received letters doesn't mean he has stopped looking for me. I move around a lot, remember."

I never knew how Snake found me, but he managed to fork his tongue and find my scent. Letters from Snake always magically appeared wherever I was, and not necessarily through the mail. Sometimes they magically appeared on my screen door or casually left for me at work. Their content filled with either his undying love or the nasty little things he would do to me for betraying his love. Somehow, I had managed to find a psychopath as a boyfriend.

Looking between the shutters, a crow hopped around the yard looking for any kind of crumb to snatch, and then he turned his blue-black head towards me. The shutters snapped shut as a faint memory made its way into the present. For two years, I had one solace in prison that kept me from constantly screaming. The sun warmed my shoulders as I threw stale breadcrumbs at some brave pigeons who managed to fly into the fenced courtyard. For a fraction of moment, I felt some peace as the birds pecked for the food. Suddenly all the birds took flight, their wings touching my face as a dark cloud engulfed me. Frozen in place by the sudden chill, his fingers picked up my hair and pushed on my new tattoo, making me wince in pain. Continuing to hold my hair, he moved his other hand down my neck and slipped his fingers underneath my collar. Silently, I sat and didn't move a muscle. Prisoners who made a move against this particularly malicious guard usually ended up in a most uncompromising position. All around me the other inmates went on talking, playing games, and ignoring what was in front of them. Quick glances told me they knew what was happening, but couldn't help. His fingers reached my bra line and stopped. "Your man, what's his name?" His fingers played between the edges of the bra and my skin. "Isn't it, Snake? Snake...that's it." The man I loved had been on the run since the night of the bank robbery and the event that forever chained us. "He just got arrested last night." My spine straightened, but I dared not look at the guard. *They caught him?* My heart beat faster. The guard removed his hand from underneath my shirt and my body eased somewhat. He tugged on my hair and pulled me back into him. Something hard pressed into my neck. "That hot little thing on his bike was surprised when she was thrown in jail, too. Some sixteen year old little bitch." He laughed, "she kind of looks like you." He walked away and in the heat of the day, I felt chilled to the bone.

The next day, a prosecutor by name of Argus Dunkirk came to visit me. He sat down and adjusted his eyes to the dim lights of the conversation room. He had a middle-aged face with dark bags bulging underneath his eyelids. Scruffy auburn hair with wisps of white infused themselves in the strands of his hair. He must have looked handsome at one time, but I could only guess that stress must have done a real number on him.

With my twenty years of wisdom, I smirked at him. He was losing his youth and vitality trying to prosecute innocent people like Snake. Humped over a thick manila file, he barely noticed me as I sat across from him. A corner of the file touched the roll of fat around his waist. As an adult in numbers only, I copped a teenage attitude and rolled my eyes at him.

"I need you to testify against him."

"Go fuck yourself." Snake was my hero, my rescuer from pain and anguish. He was no knight in shining armor—he was better. He terrorized people when he walked through any door. They seemed to shrink in their chairs underneath his stare. Sometimes, just for kicks, he would come up on some innocent person and yell at them for no reason and they would pee in their pants. I laughed at the stooge's suffering as I hid behind Snake's rage and insanity. Arms crossed over my chest, I gave Argus a look of defiance and popped my bubblegum. Yes, at twenty, I still blew bubbles like I was sixteen.

He made a disgusted sound. "You know that he's committed you to this life." He looked around with his eyes as if I didn't figure out what kind of small hell I was living in. "Carolina, he deserves to go to prison," he sighed, "just as much as you do." I turned away and stared at the green yellow paint with leaky brown stains on the walls. The conversation room reeked of cigarette smoke and sadness. The silence was becoming unbearable and I couldn't stand it anymore.

"Do you have a point?" I was a pool of malice, and spite cascading out of every pore of my being. Guilty as sin, but that didn't stop me from being angry at the world. I hated everyone, especially me.

He got up out of chair, sat on the table, and got within inch of my face. "Witnesses tell me that he is just as guilty as you are, that he helped you pull that trigger."

"How would they know? Their heads were all on the ground shaking behind their hands." My lips twisted, "They were scared little sheep," and I shot out of the chair and tried to put some distance between us. My monster was rising out of its box, the nails scratching at the lid. I faced him again and swallowed some air. "It was all me, I pulled that trigger, me, no one else! Me!" and I pounded on my chest. My eyes were cold, hard steel, and I felt the slow creep of anger crawl up my arteries and ooze into my brain. I would protect the man who loved me. At the time, I didn't remember Snake was also the man who left me lying on the floor, passed out after it happened. I had selective memory back then.

Argus' chest moved up and down as he observed me on the edge of reason. I could tell he was frustrated. He was trying to run a scare tactic of intimidation, but he saw the monster inside and lost the battle. It was an enemy he couldn't fight. He sighed in defeat. Panic welled up. He was going to leave and I almost backed down from my stance. He fished around in his briefcase and pulled out a new manila file. He displayed its contents like a perfect hand in a poker game. My eyes shot up to the ceiling to observe the round circle patterns of brown stains from numerous leaks. Some photographer should take that picture and put in a modern art museum and call it "Ode to the American Prison System."

"Look at it, goddamn you!"

Tears welled up in my eyes because I knew what it meant. If I looked at that picture, my sense of self and who I believed in would be shattered into shards of glass like a rock through a mosaic window.

He tapped the picture and said in a quiet voice, "Look at it." I wearily glanced at the picture. Glass shattered in my ears as I slowly opened my eyes to the colored slivers of the past laid before me. My breath caught in my throat and my fingernails dug into the table.

She was so young; she looked like she was twelve dressed up in my clothes. She was a younger version of me with long brunette hair showing blonde roots and angular cheeks. Her almond-shaped eyes were hazel with sparks of gold, and they looked so defiant in the police mug shot, but I knew it was an act. She was scared. One eye was almost swollen shut, black, purple, and some faded yellows surrounded her eye socket. She was a lost sheep protected by a wolf. A teardrop soaked into the skin of my hand.

"Look at her, Carolina. You can save girls just like her. She was lucky."

"How so?"

"She was a juvy and didn't have a record. She'll be released on Tuesday." He walked away from the table. "Her records are sealed. But if he gets released, they'll be more just like her, more like you rotting in here." He looked all around the room where we were speaking. The room was a wasteland of inmates whispering to their loved ones, searching for a moment of privacy, stolen touches, and broken smiles and dreams. We were lost souls in a sealed container made of bricks and steel.

My time was up and the guard led me away. I looked back at Argus sitting at the table deflated like a worn old tire. "Think about it, Carolina."

The lights clicked off, but the image of that young girl burned bright before me. That messed up picture of her stayed fresh in my mind for days. I searched in the eyes of the incarcerated in food lines with haunted faces and in the library, the lost searched for a chance of hope. I went to rehabilitation meetings and listened to their hearts resonate of regret for the crimes they committed. I heard the deep pit of venomous anger they felt at how life turned out.

There was evil here for sure and I passed by her cell every day. Her name was Cecilia Baptiste and she guarded the collected girls in her family like a rabid dog. Her girls called her "Mama." She was in jail because she butchered her boyfriend to death and laid his skull on an altar. One eye was normal and the other eye was a blue, hazy, round ball. Rumor had it that she practiced an evil form of voodoo. One day I passed a book through the bars, her scaly black hands grabbed my wrist. She had the strength of Hercules and pulled me into the bars. She stared me down, her eyes were cold and I melded into the steel. With the back of her hand, she caressed my cheek, "Such a pretty thing you are." Her Louisianan accent was deep, her belly moved as she chuckled,

"Hmm, I see your demon, child, embrace him." She let me go and I nearly fell to the ground like some force had pushed me away. Tail tucked between my legs, I ran as fast as I could. Fate would intervene and I became one of the collected with her symbol permanently tattooed on the back of my neck.

The girls who rearranged my thought processes and bent them like steel were the young, misguided street girls. Abandoned and abused, they acted like lions in cages—so tough, but hiding their tears and anger from the children they couldn't wait to see. I wondered, *If someone would have given them half a chance, would they have ended up here?*

My days were spent with constant thought vacillating between the past and present. No letters would arrive for me as I passed them out to other inmates. I rather thought I would get a note of undying love or something to that effect from him. Maybe a letter in indelible ink that he knew the sacrifices I had made for him. But certain thoughts rocked me to my core, that I had followed a horse-drawn cart with no driver into the desert.

Months had passed by; the idealistic dream of Snake evaporated into thin air. Images of the rebel coming to rescue me, police sirens screaming behind him, became replaced by how sick and pathetic he really was. Afternoon light spilled through the bars of the prison library. A cockroach scrambled across the bars of shadow and light and it was so easy for him to weave himself between those areas. Then an inmate flattened the cockroach in one step. The splat snapped me out of my haze. As a prison librarian, I shelved the well-read books that desperate inmates used for moments of hope. Putting one ratty-looking book away, I chipped off the rest of the gold letters that identified the author, Ralph Waldo Emerson. A page fell out of the book and floated to the ground. *Fuck*, snatching it off the floor, a sentence jumped at me from the torn sheet: "Be an opener of doors for such as came after thee, and do not try to make the universe a blind alley." It was the universe's answer to the question that had been racking me for weeks. I needed to testify against Snake, or maybe it was just a torn page out of broken down book. Damn, I hate existentialism. I went to the payphone and called Argus to let him know of my change of heart.

Argus came by often to coach me for the upcoming trial. I learned more of Snake's insidious manipulation. I wasn't the first girl he conned so easily with a slick smile, an overabundance of confidence, and whispers of love. He had many strays, castaways, always young, naïve, so easily convinced that crime was passionate love. Snake changed their hair to jet black, black fingernails, short skirts, and hose. He kept them close so that every thought only belonged to Snake. He created malcontent Barbie dolls for his own playhouse. Oddly enough, I turned out to be the lucky one. Many of his throwaways turned to drugs and prostitution to the ease the pain of being used like a ragdoll. I wasn't around him long enough to inhale the poison. Also, in a small twist of fate, Mother's abandonment made me distrust anyone, so I wasn't so easily bought.

The day finally came for his trial; I was more than ready to testify against him. I was called to the witness stand and my blood drained—Snake was dressed in a suit and tie and his hair was cut businessman-short. There was not a nose or ear piercing to be found. He was dressed like a puppet for the show and he looked like the all-American boy. I, on the other hand, came in shackles and prison wear. My hair returned to its natural state of blonde and electrified. Snake acted like he didn't even know me, but underneath his eyelids, power radiated from his eyes and crashed upon me. For a split second, all thoughts of betrayal had left me— then, I glanced at a teenager in the back of the courtroom making doe eyes at Snake. She had short black hair and a dark t-shirt with a dog collar around her neck. She scowled at me and raised her lip like she was growling. Determination sprang up and speared my false love for Snake through the heart. That young teenage girl was going to be saved, whether she liked it or not. The words came out tortuously slow from my mouth. Questions assailed me from both defense and prosecuting attorneys. I did what I could to bring Goliath down and then it was over. The guards led me past the defense table in chains and shackles and were completely oblivious when Snake mouthed the words, "You're dead." My legs seemed to turn into liquid and I hoped to reach the door before I was nothing more than a pool of water.

I hadn't heard from the prosecutor in a few days. When finally I got a visitation from him, he looked sad and destitute. "What, did your dog die or what?" A smirk crossed my face. I still didn't like him.

"Carolina, Snake got off on a technicality." The moon fell and landed on me. This was all for nothing.

"Guard!" My hands began to ball into fists and my body shook from anger. Something told me inside that Argus' face would make a really good punching bag. I needed to leave, now! "Guard!" I kicked and screamed at the door.

Over the din of my confusion and explosive anger, I heard, "Carolina, I'm sorry. I tried everything."

Rushing back over to him, I said, "You didn't try hard enough." My face was in his and my finger shaking before his eyes. The guards looked at me and then nervously looked at each other and grabbed me. Facing the door, I looked over my shoulder and hoped my stare would turn him to dust. The guards threw me back in my cell and I paced till exhaustion consumed me. Blood pulsated through my body and fought my own anger. There was undeniable need to hit something, anything. But, I would just be hitting solid concrete walls of my own making. Flattened, I curled up in a ball on my standard issue prison bed.

"Wake up, Carolina!" It was a guard yelling and bagging his nightstick on the steel. Through groggy, bloodshot eyes, a white envelope was pushed through the bars.

"What's this?"

"What's it look like?" Ask a stupid question and get a stupid question back. I grabbed it from him. The front simply had my name and I turned it around. "It's open." The guard shrugged.

"Looks like your lover boy wrote you a pretty note." Sneering at the guard, I tore it open. The first words were written in red ink.

Carolina,

You fucking whore! You're dead. I'll get you back and then you will know pain. You can't hide from me. When we are together, you will know how much I love you.

Snake

I balled up the letter and threw it against the wall and watched it roll down the bricks.

"God dammit! There's coffee everywhere!" I was pulled back to reality by Harvey yelling. "Carolina, you'll be fine. Don't sweat the small stuff."

"Okay, Harvey, if you say so." But I wasn't so convinced. Fear had taught me to become a dark shadow. Slipping in and out, praying that I would be undetected. Sixteen years of prison and five on parole hadn't cooled his feelings; if anything his obsession burned hotter. How hard could it be for a criminal like Snake, stupid as he was, to search for me on the Internet? I learned quickly early on an assumed name meant nothing compared to the World Wide Web.

There were faint whisperings from his end of the world. "Carolina, I gotta go. Some kid is about to commit a felony and I'm gonna see if I pull his head out of his ass."

"See ya, Harvey," I tried to say it with confidence; mostly, my voice just sounded pathetic. Images came to mind of me being alone on a life raft drifting out to the sea.

"Carolina, it will be fine," and he hung up and I strangled the phone till the damn thing beeped a nasty tone. My head bounced against the wall several times because that old familiar feeling of "Time to pack it up" came over me. God, I was so tired of running away, and exhaustion leads to unclear thinking.

Chapter 6

Contemplating the latest pothole in the road of my life, I decided it was time for tea. Bad coffee had kept me from plowing face first into the dough at work, but it was fast becoming my enemy. My stomach revolted the last couple of times and I was a mess of jitters and nerves.

I searched the barren cupboards for a calming elixir, specifically chamomile tea. "Good luck with that." First sign of crazy, talking to yourself, but I heard answering back was the real sign of total mental breakdown. We'll see. If I find myself talking to the walls, then we got serious issues. Lo and behold, a lowly box of chamomile tea was hidden behind a sneaky cat-shaped coffee cup. I gave the cup my best stink eye. It was deliberately trying to keep me from eternal bliss.

My teapot screeched because it had to conjure up boiling water after a long restful state. The teabag sat innocently in the teacup as I tortured it to death with the slow meticulous pouring of boiling water. The sun blazed down as I passed through the front door. Squinting across the street was Carson and Riley chatting it up over the fence. Behind Carson were two blurs running around Angelica as though she was the center of the universe. I waved and lifted my right foot to walk over when a guilty string of memories sliced across my consciousness and my feet became stone. Cool waves of loneliness collided with my heart and I would forever be a prisoner. My mind and body were fighting for control on whether to turn around to finish my prison sentence or go over and continue the pretension of someone with no past. Indecision buzzed into a hive of chaos and then I heard, "Fuck!" and glanced over the fence. An old yellow 1950-ish Ford truck was swallowing a man alive. Lovely—must be my neighbor.

What was left of the truck's lunch was a long-legged man clad in jeans with ragged holes showing off some rather nice skin. I particularly enjoyed a large hole on his left side that revealed slightly brown skin highlighting a soft, round butt cheek. Scanning more of the leftover carcass, my eyes beheld the undone button on his jeans. Immediately, my eyes shut themselves to all the possibilities. Temptation made me open one eye and sunlight reflected the sheen off his sweaty back. His shoulder blades were defined underneath smooth tanned skin. Both eyes were now fully wide open as I gazed at his side and saw a wicked scar that started underneath his jeans and ran up almost to nipple height.

That stopped all the porno thoughts in my head and then feelings of pity crept in. *Damn it!* I liked those porno thoughts. But my little monster inside Pandora's Box made its two cents known and told me he is a bad, bad boy. We should meet. I tossed my cup in a hole and my legs detached from my brain and carried me towards him, when I heard muffled expletives rang out of the defunct Ford. The ringing in my ears seemed to have brought me back to my senses. The angel and devil on my shoulders picked a fight with each other as I started to leave. The angel of evil won and I snuck up behind the carcass and said, "Hello!" loudly. He jumped and hit his head on the Ford's hood.

"Ow, son of a bitch!" His hand touched the sore spot and then he stared down at me, and I defiantly stared right back at him. Hopefully, he didn't notice that I nervously swallowed my tongue. Wow, he's a lot taller than I thought. *Oops, I think I just pissed off Paul Bunyon.* He was also quite... well, beautiful, actually, but he wasn't perfect. Remnants of battles before left small indents in his skin as well as other jagged scars. A bead of sweat ran down his squared chest and over every ripple of his muscular stomach. His skin was baked to a golden brown and glinted in the sunlight. Entranced by his body, I didn't notice when he yelled, "What the hell was that for, lady?"

His tone of voice broke me out of my trance, "Payback for waking up me in the mornings," there, simply stated—no need to mince words here.

He stared at me for a really long moment and then went back to banging on things in the old worn truck. "What do you want?" came a muffled voice.

"Oh, just being neighborly," sarcasm dripped down the side of my mouth.

A muffled grunt came out of the truck.

"You need to stop throttling your motorcycle so loudly in the morning!" I waited for what seemed like an eternity for a response. Then I stared at his physique with my most indignant look. "Are you even listening to me!" Anger began to swell; if he didn't look so good in his jeans and that top button wasn't undone, I might have gotten really angry. *You're an idiot, Carolina, an absolute fucking idiot.*

He pulled his head out of the old Ford, grabbed a dirty rag, and wiped his greasy hands on it. He smirked a little. "I tell ya what I'll do," and he towered over me as I bent backwards slightly. His eyes were a beautiful shade of amber brown surrounded by long black eyelashes. "You wear that t-shirt you had on the other morning" and he looked down at my breasts, "and I'll keep the noise down." Instinctively, I crossed my arms over my chest and my cheeks blazed red. He stood for a few minutes while I gaped like a fish out of water, he cranked a victory smile, and then dove back into the truck.

Lesson to self: Pick your battles. My brain desperately searched for the last word. Unfortunately, nothing brilliant came to mind, so I went for the lame, "What are ya fixing up, there?"

A muffled, "Golly, I don't know, a lawn mower."

"Really, because I was thinking it was a Ford 150 with a hemi engine from oh, I don't know, say 1955."

He just kept working on the engine, but there were no expletives coming from it. Hmm, silent treatment from gigantor. *Asshole.* I spoke underneath my breath, turned, and walked away.

"Can you hand me that wrench?"

I tramped back and looked on the ground, picked a wrench out of a sea of metallic shiny objects and handed it to an arm with a wiggling hand attached to it.

He lifted his head out of the beast's belly and examined the wrench. "You know your tools."

"Well, I definitely know a tool when I see one," and stared straight at him. A big grin came across his face and I couldn't but help smile, too. I did a half pirouette, walked away, and claimed victory. *Yeah for me.*

"Not gonna stay and talk?"

I turned back around and thought a girl could get really dizzy from all the turn arounds. His black, silk hair was streaked back in a ponytail and grease smudged his cheekbones, highlighting them into a distinctive angular shape

"You're not really talking."

"I thought women did all the talking."

"No. Some of us actually like to listen. I am Caro….Danni by the way." Mental note got to practice my fake name more.

"I know."

My mouth opened. *How did he know my name?*

"Except I thought it was Danni and not CaroDanni."

"Just Danni. How did you know my name, Gabriel?" My turn, ha ha, caught him by surprise. Hormonally, I am still a teenager at age fortyish. One eyebrow rose up on his face.

The same thought must have struck us both at the same time because we both stared at Carson and Riley across the street. They just waved and smiled at us.

"You know how you women like to gossip and talk about men?" His face was concentrating on the rag in his hand but he looked at me under hooded eyes.

"Really, that's kind of an egotistical observation, isn't it?" I couldn't tell if he was joking or not. "As though men were the center of our universe."

"Not an observation, it's the truth. Women have nothing better to do." There was poison in his tone and the conversation came to a dead stop. Obviously, he had some kind of anger issues. I was about to go into a diatribe of the finer features of women and decided his preconceived notions weren't wasting my breath over.

"Huh, well...think I'll just leave now."

"Yep," and he turned and dove back into his Ford.

He's a real conversationalist. He could kiss my ass. Actually, that thought warmed the cockles of my heart. He really could kiss my ass and I wouldn't mind that at all. As I walked back over to my house, heat rose into my cheeks that couldn't be directly attributed to the sun. Pushing the door open, I found my favorite wailing wall and banged my head against it.

Chapter 7

After some needed self-flagellation and some indecent thoughts of Gabriel at the same time, I went into the kitchen and eyed my display of animal cups. A cup was missing. *Damn*, I had forgotten about the coffee cup that the devil made me toss in the hole. So I grabbed the nearest farm animal. Moo cup had large patches of black with white spots mixed in between with Meeks Dairy Farm emblazed on front. It brought a smile to my face and a soft memory formed in the waterfall from the faucet. In my need to run as far as I could, I went to Wisconsin. I didn't think Snake would look for me in a state full of farms and cows.

The memories dripped down into the sink. The sound of water mimicked the gates opening from prison as I stepped out into a new world, new freedom, and fresh air. Nose in the air, I breathed in oxygen that didn't smell of disinfectant, smoke, or body odor. The guards outside the gate eyed me from head to toe as they shook their heads in laughter. My apparel was a black t-shirt full of rips with multiple safety pins threading the loose ends of the shreds together. A black pleated mini skirt barely covered the black tights with large runs down the legs. Thick black motorcycle lace up boots went up to my knees and a bright yellow plaid shirt tied around my waist. I was quite thankful that at least I had a shirt to cover over my ass because the skirt was a wee bit too short, now. Everything seemed tight and parts of me bulged in certain places. Definitely did not have that eighteen-year-old body anymore. I looked absolutely…ridiculous. I had on a rebellious teenager gothic clothes on a thirty-six-year-old just released from prison body. My clothes were presented to me in a dusty covered box by a guard who could barely keep the grin off his face. The guards at the gate tried to keep from laughing and ended up laughing even louder. Just great, my new life started as a comedy skit. Mercifully, a Lexus pulled up and I quickly got into the back of the car with a tall, thin, stern-looking man. His face was long and aged with stress. His eyes, small and intense, were engrossed in a newspaper but I knew he saw every detail about me. His hair was dark sky gray mottled with snow white strands.

My thirty-six-year-old body fitted into the plush seat and shrank to the size of an admonished five-year old, "Hey, Uncle Tony." Uncle Tony had been my father's friend for a lifetime and they treated each other like blood relatives. When my father passed away, Uncle Tony could not be the father I wanted but kept himself as the uncle when I needed him. My eyes were cast to the floor and I had a sinking feeling I would be sent to the corner at any moment. Maybe I could get some cookies and milk out of the deal afterwards.

"Ah, Carolina, it is good to see you," he said in perfect schoolmaster vernacular. My uncle glazed over my attire, shook his head, and pursed his lips. At front were two large bodies shaking with laughter, although they had enough grace to do it silently. They had been my uncle's bodyguards for as long as I can remember.

"Hey, Mikey," and I patted his shoulder. In the rearview mirror, he saw my uncle's stern face and replied to my hello with a grunt. For a silent killer, he was a giant of a man. His face was pockmarked from childhood disease and a disposition only a salivating pit bull could love. But I remember him as the man who walked me to school and scowled at any kid if they came near me. After school, on some occasions, he would get out of the limo in a black suit and tie, eyes darting everywhere looking for danger, and in his hand was a dripping ice cream cone. Rumors and innuendos swept in my house and left with the dust about Mikey that always left my spine in a state of disarray. No enemy crossed Mike Salvatino's path without seeing the underside of a coffin lid.

Next to Mikey to was the teddy bear with a dark soul, "Hello, Shadow."

"Carolina," and he covered his mouth for my dignity, but he couldn't stop laughing at my attire. He was my uncle's shadow and the angel of death to any man that my uncle called enemy, or so I was told. He was wicked fast with a knife and he used a gun purely for backup. He was growing older and age was leaving him with a permanent scowl. He was shorter than Mikey, and he had a meat locker for a body.

Shadow would come over to our house when I was younger with my uncle and melted into the walls. He usually sat in a corner, always keeping a constant eye on anything that was a portal for my uncle's foes. My fondest memory was of me as a heartbroken child, nose to the window, looking for the any sign of my mother's return. The thrum beat of the ceiling fan was in the background as my father and uncle were in heated whispers. I was dressed in a white brim hat, a buttery-yellow sundress, and lots of fake jewelry with lacy bobby socks, and adult red high heels that fell off my feet when I kneeled on the chair. I jumped at any sound outside that sounded like a car door closing. But no car arrived and, slowly, I sat back in my chair in front of small table with chipped blue paint. It was set for four people—me, my old teddy bear with one eye, ruffled and stained from a child's grubby hands clinging to it for comfort, an old rabbit made out of flour bags with one stuffed ear hanging down and one ear sticking straight up. The sun came streaming through the window and created highlights and shadows across the teacups decorated with tiny pink flowers. Those tiny teacups were placed delicately on top of saucers, and a white teapot with a long spout sat in the middle of the table. The lint in the sunbeam floated all around me as the scent of roses from my mother's flattened dress hung on the door wafted through the air. The sunlight floated across the table and struck an empty chair. I went back to my chair, sat down with my head in my hands, and looked upon the haphazard party waiting for their air tea to begin. I stared out the window at nothing, disappointment drowning my soul. Then, I heard the creaking of the empty chair under a heavy weight; beside me was a man holding a tea cup.

"Tea, my lady," he said in a thick Chicago smoke-infused accent. He was a huge man sitting in a child's size chair, adjusting his tie around his thick, beefy neck.

I was intimidated by one droopy eye and his sagging lips, but he held the teacup and motioned for me to pour him some tea. My eyes were big and round trying to adjust to the being in front of me. He growled, and I jumped out of my chair and pretended to pour him tea.

In a perfect English accent, I asked "how is your tea?" He sipped his tea with his little finger pointed out, and cleared his throat. I continued to pour for my other inanimate guests and went on with how the lovely the day had become. He never said much, just sipped tea, and just agreed with my entire little girl conversations. I have loved him since that tea party and have always thought of him as big teddy bear with a really big gun in his back.

Freshly released from prison, I was in a Lexus with three very dangerous males who worked for a Chicago organization with a very nasty reputation. They managed somehow to keep free and clear with the law, so I was not violating any parole terms. My uncle was the organization's lawyer and kept a very low profile. My father and uncle ran in the same circles on the streets of Chicago as children but life gave them very different paths. My father became a detective with the Chicago police force, but they remained brothers in arms, though not in ideology. However, when my dad died, I became a secret member of my uncle's family, always hidden from prying eyes.

I leaned over and gave my uncle a kiss on the cheek. "It's good to see you, too." He had a distinct aroma of expensive cologne and Cuban cigars. He only visited me in jail a couple of times. I think he would have liked to have visited more, but it just wasn't possible to blur the line of lawyer for the crime syndicate and a visiting relative in prison.

My uncle sat stoically and continued reading the paper. "So, Carolina, what are your plans now?"

"Take a hot bath. A really hot bath." My uncle crooked a smile. "Honestly, I don't know. I've been thinking about it and going over it in my mind. I just can't quite think what to do or how to do it." He put the newspaper down on his lap and stared out the window at the passing fuzziness of suburban life. I had battled my life and lost the war, and now, I couldn't find all the shrapnel to even begin to piece my life together.

He turned his head back to me and with distant eyes, said, "I think you start by going home, familiarizing yourself with your furniture, curtains, the layout of the house. You begin a new routine, wash some dishes, do the laundry, vacuum the floor, and maybe watch some TV." He returned to staring out the window. "Begin again."

"Sixteen years in jail and I'm back to doing housework. How poetic."

"Ahh, Carolina, life is in the details, not in the bigger picture. You pick up the puzzle pieces and eventually you make a beautiful picture. Along the way, you have a glass of vino and a hot bath." He smiled to himself. "But first, we need to find you some new clothes. Mikey, let's drop by the mall," and I heard the slow whistles of laughs trying to be held back.

My cheeks began to burn as I kept trying to pull my plaid shirt down over my knees. My skirt seemed impossibly short. I must have grown a couple of inches in jail. I accidentally caught a fledgling piece of material in my shirt and it pulled against the safety pin and ripped an even bigger hole. There weren't enough safety pins in the world to begin to close the shredded material. My stockings were nothing but shredded black nylon; I put them on strictly for the underwear aspect. How could I have possibly thought this was so cool?

"You might want to step on it before all my clothes disintegrate," and they all began to laugh.

Chapter 8

After getting a whole new wardrobe that didn't have safety pins in them, I began the slow process of getting used to my home. It was a small arts and crafts cottage that seemed so small back then, but was now much bigger than the cell I was used to. Familiarizing myself with old forgotten things, I pulled the dusty sheets off the furniture and they floated down to the floor like deflated ghosts. I tore the plastic away from atop of the four-poster bed in the master bedroom. A musty smell mixed with my father's cologne tickled my nose and I couldn't stop sneezing. The closet door hinges creaked when they were opened and all of my father's suits were in a perfect row. In the very back corner was his policeman's uniform with all the medals of valor on the left breast. I quickly closed the doors and left the suits entombed.

Closing the master bedroom door silently, I crept into my old bedroom. Posters of old teen heartthrobs lined the walls, a black quilt laid on my bed, and various black candles encrusted with dust were everywhere. Morose curtains hung from the window and filtered the sun in gray. Clothes in my closet were black t-shirts with various pieces of safety pins and metal. Plaid shirts were the only color that illuminated the closet. Old converse tennis shoes, black sandals, and worn out boots littered the floor. Underneath the litter of canvas and leather laid a cassette recorder. It was my dad's present to me; he had attempted to calm my childhood fears by using a tape recorder to capture all the ghosts and monsters of my nightmares. Laying the recorder on the bed, my reflection from the mirror on my dresser picked up black lipstick and twisted it, moved a bottle of black nail polish, and touched pans of dark purple eye shadow. I turned on the old Walkman that I left behind and listened to the music of The Cure. The song was "A Funeral Party" and I immediately turned it off.

A purple stuffed dragon occupied a rocking chair in the corner. Soft echoes of giggles drifted in my ears as my father read me a story and tucked me in at night. I flipped the switch off to the mausoleum of Goth and childhood memories and drifted through the house, trying to gain what I had lost. In the kitchen, I pared an apple. The scent of green apple awoke the painful memories of my mother and I left the apple on the counter. In the living room, ghosts of my disintegrated family going about their everyday business passed before me in a home that seemed so strange to me.

Weeks passed into months and I began a routine of cleaning the house, mindlessly eating, and watching TV. The seasons changed from green to gold, then eventually to winter white as I walked hopelessly all around Chicago. I had endless sessions with Harvey and his dogged determination for me to reenter society as a convict passing as a newly formed human being. There were infinite possibilities of dead-end jobs and going back to school. But everything he said just seemed to echo around and bounced off the walls of my head. I took his advice on some things, though; I visited museums, malls, and tried to catch a tidal wave of modernization in my hand that had happened in sixteen years of isolation. Cell phones were rapidly gaining popularity and computers were new and expanding at light speed when I went into prison, but it was still beyond the everyday person to have such items. Now, everyone had a cell phone, a computer in their lap, and, suddenly, you were friends with people you hadn't seen in years. I was afraid of it all and how much I missed out. I was forced kicking and screaming into a technological age I didn't understand.

I kept everyone at a distance and let loneliness surround my heart and invade my soul because I was determined to get used to the empty feelings of everyday existence. After one of my many walks, I came to find a letter taped to my door. The handwriting on the envelope immediately made my knees melt into the snow. I couldn't tell if my fingers were numb from the sheer cold of winter or the blood that had drained from my fingertips as I shakily opened the letter from Snake. Cast before me in black ink was remorse for letting me get away and the plans he had for my return, but what scared me was the line written in red: "Carolina, I can't wait to begin where we left off." I was clawing my way up a slow tunnel and had no intention of falling back to the sewer I came from. I called Harvey, told him the circumstances of my sudden departure. He and I had an understanding from the beginning of parole that if I were ever to encounter Snake again, I was to run as far as I could. He made all the arrangements and permissions ahead of time. I met him later to get all the paperwork and one last face to say goodbye. I left a message with my uncle and immediately began to pack everything I owned in one bag. Hastily, I began the process of putting the house and ghosts back into hibernation to wait for me again. I grabbed my bag, turned to look once more, and the house went back into the shadows and waited for my return.

Slamming the garage door shut, I went into the garage and eyed pensively the one thing my dad cherished most besides me—his '69 GTO Judge. He bought it before I was born and reconditioned everything in painstaking detail. His blood, sweat, and tears created the soul that returned the car back to its original condition. I uncovered the shiny black Judge and the car door creaked like an old man coming to life when I opened it. I held my breath, turned the keys, and prayed for resurrection. The engine just clicked as I turned it again; a slow rumble, a gasp, and then black smoke infiltrated the garage. Desperation set in. This car was part of my runaway plan. I needed to take the shortcuts and remote highways where the Greyhound bus failed to go. Exhaust fumes mixed with sweat, the dust particles were settling all around me, and I closed my eyes, coughed, and pleaded, "Please, Dad." I slowly opened my eyes and a hint of sunlight hit the keys, and glints of steel darted around in the car. I turned the keys and the car roared to life, "Thanks, Dad." The garage door opened and I backed out. The Judge rumbled out of the driveway as the house was blanketed with snow.

I found an out of way town that technological time outpaced and left behind in its bandwidth. My room at the Sleepy Time Inn was well someone's version of an old country themed hotel, including a sagging hole in the middle of the bed and dust on the lampshades. I put my bags on the chair, coughed, wiped my hands, and closed the door and began my walk down the only street in town, Main Street. My fingers glazed across the rough carved stone of some of the old Victorian stores. Brass door handles with a patina glaze protruded from doors with cracked and peeled lead paint. An empty rocking chair sat behind a dust-encrusted storefront window. On top of the chair lay an old oily rag. Gold Victorian lettering arched over the chair was peeling off in bits and pieces. Spots of glue with dust stuck outlined the title of the lettering, Mason's Sundries, Your Last Stop for Goods.

The wonderful aroma of bacon wafted through the air and my stomach churned in anticipation. My nose led me to Paulson's Diner. The bell on the door made tinkling sounds as I entered the diner. Mostly, old farmers were conversing with each other and a couple of older women staring off into space. I definitely was not in Chicago anymore when I noted what the patrons were wearing while they were eating: They were in grungy baseball caps, overalls with smears of grease that were worn at the edges over thick leather boots with cakes of mud on them. Every eye stared mercilessly at me as I stood in the doorway and looked for an empty seat. I was out of place in my new leather bomber jacket, blue jeans, and a white t-shirt. After close scrutiny, all the occupants looked at my shoes and sneered. I was in farm country with bright yellow Converse high-tops. Pensively, I sat down on a stool at the counter top while every eye in the diner kept staring.

"You're not from around here are you, sweetheart?" She gave me a half smile. "My name is Janine." She patted her white nametag with faded blue lettering. Janine, a tall, thin woman stood at the countertop with a coffeepot in her hand. Her pink uniform wrapped around the curves of her thin frame. Her face had wrinkles around her lips, and crow's feet surrounded her eyes. I guessed she was in her fifties, but I would never say it out loud.

"I'm Jenna," I mentioned as she put a cup of coffee in front of me. I sighed, "What gave me away," as I looked at her underneath my eyelids. I poured copious amounts of sugar and cream into my coffee and stirred until the black became liquid brown.

"Woman like you, out here in the middle of the sticks," and she looked around, "and no man, I see." She raised one eyebrow at me. I stirred my coffee faster and bounced my knee uncontrollably. My back felt as if a thousand tiny holes were being drilled into it.

"It's okay, honey, we mind our own business in this town. Don't we, boys?" Grunts and reluctant acknowledgments could be heard behind my back and I slowly stirred even more sugar into the coffee. She put the coffeepot down on the counter and tilted her head. "I think you been through a lot." Her eyes were a soft gray and she had a mother's look of concern. She was like looking into the sun and she had lit up the dark shadows of my heart. I wasn't sure if my eyes would get burned if I looked back in her face and went back to concentrating on my coffee. A warm heat enveloped my hand and her delicate fingers surrounded mine.

"You'll never be able to run far enough, I know," and she pointed to a scar on the top of her right eye. "But you can certainly take a break for a while." She pulled her hand away and a chill crossed my fingers. I didn't realize how much I ached for the simple touch of another. "Now, you are way too skinny looking. How about some bacon and eggs?" Skinny looking, me…I love her. A delicious plate of bacon, ham, and eggs, with toast piled high was set before me, and I ate like I hadn't had real food in years.

"You might want to slow there down, hon, there's plenty." She laughed and poured another cup of coffee. Damn, more coffee, but I didn't want to seem ungrateful by asking for tea. Distorted jaws dropped wide open as I looked in the reflection of a steel shelf above the serving window. Hadn't anyone see a hungry person eat before?

A little wisp of paper flapping to the ceiling fan caught my eye and I went over and unpinned it from the corkboard. It was a note from some farmers looking for a farm hand.

"Who are the Meeks?" I asked Janine. I figured she was the conductor of grand central information here.

"Oh, the Meeks family. Sweetest family you'll ever find." She picked up my empty plate and wiped away the crumbs. I licked away the jam on my lips and eyed the pies behind her—no, must stop eating. "They tend to keep to themselves, though. They run a small family farm." She poured some more coffee into the cup of the gentlemen next to me. "Just a farm house with a few animals and a small corn field." Sounds like my kind of people as I plunked some cash on the counter and smiled at Janine.

I wondered if I could blend in with a few sheep and some cows as I knocked on their door. The rusted hinges creaked open and an old man opened the door. "Yes?" he looked at me like I was an odd alien who just flew in and landed on their doorstep.

"I'm answering your help wanted ad from the diner." I handed him the paper, which was a mess of bacon grease and hand sweat. He looked at my yellow Converse shoes and instantly, my right foot crossed my left foot. Maybe the dirt would drown out the color. My reflection in the door glass made me cringe; my hair was a wild mess of curls and as I looked closer, I saw egg drippings on my shirt. He looked behind me and I closed my eyes when he peered at my GTO.

"Mother!" he yelled back into the house.

We all sat around a kitchen table laid fresh with a red and white checkered tablecloth and dried flowers in a vase in the center. Coffee in cow-like cups was set before all of us. The clinking of time on an old German Cuckoo Clock and the ceiling fan's trhrwp-trhrwp rhythm was the only sounds in the room.

The Meeks were coming into the twilight of their life. Arthritis was eating Mr. Meek's hands till they were knobby branches, his hands shook when he tried to put sugar in his coffee. The light of the afternoon sun highlighted Mrs. Meek's round face. Her features were soft with only a few wrinkles around the eye to show her age, her lips small and pink. She kept her eyes down on the ball of yarn and needles clanking together. Her deft little fingers were knitting some baby booties and I had the warm, fuzzy feeling I was sitting across from America's grandma. An awkward conversation revealed that they were slowing down considerably, but they were not quite ready to give up on their farm. Their children were scattered like seeds in the wind, and they had been looking for a strong back. No one had applied for the job because I was just guessing here, but no man in his right mind wanted to work that hard for little pay and be out in the middle of nowhere with only sheep to call for friends. For me, the job description fit the bill perfectly.

"So, you're looking to move from the city," he said as his spoon went for the sugar bowl and missed. Mrs. Meeks pursed her lips and clicked her tongue as his spoon scooped some sugar, on the second attempt. Mr. Meeks begrudgingly put the spoon down and white crystals danced over the tablecloth.

"Yeah, just need a change of pace. City was getting to be too much." I lowered my eyes. Lie, lie, and lie, and I mixed more sugar in my coffee and eyed Mrs. Meeks. She squinted her eyes and I put the spoon down.

"This is hard work, ya know. You'll come home tired and exhausted. You wake up every day at five am and you don't quit till eight pm. Every day, you will have a set routine—milk the cows, take them to the pasture, then come back here and start processing the cheese. Then, you go to the fields, put the cows up in the barn, and feed them. And you'll have to feed the pigs as well." He emphasized the word "every day"; I think he was trying to discourage me.

The routine sounded like prison, except I would have fresh air, no people, and elderly couple for guards. "Sounds like heaven." I knew I couldn't possibly lift bales of hay, but I'd give it my best shot. Mr. Meeks implored Mrs. Meeks with her eyes and she just shrugged her shoulders and went back to knitting. Apparently, I just got hired.

The learning curve was pretty horrendous. I learned to milk cows the old-fashioned way, and had wasted a lot of milk and changed my clothes often. Ever graceful, I would trip and fall into cow poop, dumped over pails of milk, and had a horrible time pouring the whey into cheese molds. Mr. Meeks kept his silence and mostly just shook his head. He was disappointed but I was the best he got. As predicted, I came home exhausted and sore, but a slow burn of happiness was beginning to form within me.

Eventually, I became stronger, faster. The bionic man would have been proud; in actuality, I was the same. I still tripped and copious amount of hard wrung milk doused the floor, eggs were broken, and cows mooed at me and turned away. It did get easier, though. Bales of hay became easier to lift, I didn't curse the sun as it came into my window and blasted a ray of light in my eyes, and I loved to hear the rain on the barn. I traded yellow Converse hardtops for leather boots and won approval at the diner by a nod.

I was a tenant in their household. From my bedroom window, I would gasp as a ball of fire woke up the fields in salute to another day and said goodnight as the darkness doused the sun. My window had the perfect view to a night full of cascading, twinkling stars. On rest breaks, I walked into the fields of corn and let my fingers hop across the tasseled tops. Other times, I sat on sweet smelling hay and told the gated cows my life's story. They were attentive listeners as long as there was grain in my hand. Their noses were so soft in mornings as I petted them before I began my familiar routine of milking them. Dinnertime would be a discussion about what animal was in need of what and the ever-present chores to be done. I kept to myself with a book to keep me company at night when the house was settled and put to bed. I steered the conversations to general things such as where I was from, what had I been doing before I moved here. I managed to skirt their questions for a while, but I could see that curiosity was starting to get the best of them.

One evening, Mr. Meeks sipped his potato soup as I was buttering my bread with fresh cream butter. "So what are you running away from, Jenna?"

I tried to put my bread and butter down gracefully, but my hands just shook as the butter knife slipped from my hands.

I swallowed hard and my throat became suddenly dry. "Nothing really." It was my best nonchalant voice, but I think there was a turn tail squeak in there.

Nervousness built up in my stomach and then spewed forth nonsense. Hard to say what the next string of words that came out, something about an ex and midlife crisis, blood rushed to my ears and drowned all the words that passed my lips, till the string of lies broke. Mrs. Meeks just stared at me. I knew that she saw through all the scaffolding of lies I had built, but she pursed her lips and didn't say anything, just slurped her soup.

Mr. Meeks took another swallow of soup and his cataract eyes pierced my own. He wiped his mouth with the checkered print cloth and put his spoon down. He interlaced his knotted fingers; his skin was paper-thin and deep purple blue veins roped across the back of his hands. He had age spots like the spotted brown eggs that I stole from the chickens in the morning. I noticed every detail and burned it into memory. My heart sank into my stomach because I just knew they saw through the paper-thin shell I created and I would have skulk back into the night. I shakily picked up my butter knife and let the silence engulf us all.

"Well, then, Jenna," he shook his head and licked his lips, "that is quiet a tale you have there. Tomorrow.."

"Yes."

"Mrs. Meeks and I are going into town for the day." He dunked some bread in his soup, "make sure you close the gate to the barn before you go to bed." I let out the breath I was holding, let out like a balloon that had a sudden opening. Life went back to normal the next day and I settled into my routine. Mrs. Meeks kept her silence as usual, but I would catch her stealing looks at me when she thought I wasn't looking. Looks aside and questions abetted, I began to feel part of this familial circle. Until one day, I walked out of the barn after milking the cows and heard the roar of a motorcycle down the farm road. The rider had a black leather jacket and black boots like the ones I was so familiar with. A red bandana crossed the rider's head and goggles covered his eyes. Milk slopped over the pale as I stood straight still, shaking, blood drained from my face and my feet sank into the ground. The rumble of the motorcycle faded quickly into the fields until I heard only the sound of the wind whipping across the tassels of corn.

"Did ya see something, Jenna? You're as pale as a ghost." Mr. Meeks must have seen me standing there like an idiot.

I turned to face him, mouthing gaping, and he was there in his blue jean overalls holding slops for the pigs. "There was something in my shoe," and I picked my left foot and tried to pretend something was in there.

He looked out on to the road and stood for a moment, clicked his tongue, and said, "Hmmm, well, Jenna, let's get back to work," and we continued with our day, not saying another word about it.

The whistle blew on the teapot and I snapped back to my present Albuquerque surroundings. I poured the boiling water into my cup and unconsciously steeped a teabag. I couldn't help but smile at the recollections of the farm and a teardrop fell into my tea. My last memory was their small kitchen lit only by the moon and a note I had left on the checkerboard cloth. I scribbled something about my sudden departure, but I always felt like a thief in the night that stole their hearts and kept them for myself. I drenched the teabag one last time and raised the cup to my lips; steam rose and tickled my nose. I wondered if they missed me.

Chapter 9

Sentimental cup in hand, I padded my way out to the porch and reveled in the clouds peaking over the Sandias. Monsoon season was here, an atmospheric event in the desert on a daily basis. The morning would start with bright yellow ball of heat beating upon the parched land, baking the sand and clay into hard earth. Then little wisps of clouds like cotton balls began to rise one by one over the mountains. As they floated across the sky, they morphed from soft cotton balls into massive clouds of deep blue, purples, and grays. When the time was right, the pregnant clouds began their labor drop by drop, pelting the earth with earth-quenching water, each drop coming faster and faster, till a shower of rain poured down upon the city. This was an experience that no one would miss. The denizens of Albuquerque would stand in their doorways and bear witness to their gift. By afternoon, a sheet of rain whisked away the dust and dirt, leaving only rainbows crisscrossing the sky and cactus as the pot of gold. The air would be fragrant with fresh rain and dirt.

The sun beat down upon my arms as I watched the clouds transform from cotton puffs to angry thunderheads. In the distance above me was an unusual black cloud that, upon close observation, was a flock of crows. They were flying in a circular pattern, diving, and then rising up again to meet their clan. I wondered what they were searching for. Their caws pierced the air as they answered each other's calls. Their bodies were large, with midnight black and blue feathers. All of them formed a heart-shaped fan guiding them across the thermals. They were fascinating and I lost all notions of time and space, engrossed in their flight.

"Hello!" That greeting from nowhere startled me, and I jumped out of my chair as hot tea splashed down my shirt.

"Son of bitch!" My eyes were blinded from looking into the sky, so I couldn't see clearly who was at the gate. Squinting, all I could see was a tall blur. A warm wet sensation touched my stomach. "Ow! Fuck!" A big brown circular stain formed on my white t-shirt. Lifting my shirt off, I exposed my pasty white stomach with a big red tea burn. "Damn, that hurts," and looked around for something to staunch the pain.

"Sorry, I didn't mean to startle you," the distortion chuckled.

My eyes finally adjusted to the blur standing on the other side of the gate and, lo and behold, there was a tall, handsome man standing there. His hair was ice blonde and his skin was white that was reddening in the sun. His eyes had the look of age with some crinkles and lines, but they enhanced his face. He looked wise with an air of kindness. I couldn't tell the color of his eyes this far away, but it made me wonder with blonde hair like that if his eyes were blue. He had high, sharp cheekbones and his chin was freshly shaven. He radiated a gorgeous smile with perfect white teeth. His neck was red and was decorated with a white collar and embarrassment flooded up my face at my earlier remarks. I was a semi sort of good Catholic girl. "Father, you scared me."

"I can see that," and he tried to hide a smirk. He put out his hand over the fence. "I'm Reverend Seth Whitehouse."

Quickly, I pulled the hem of my shirt down and wiped my hands on the back of my shorts. Reaching out to shake his hand, he slid his cool hand into my overheated palm. There was a slight electrical charge to his touch that shocked me. Did we just connect in some way? Questioning my insanity, I said, "Umm, I'm Danni Clearwater, Father."

"Actually, just Seth would be nice. Priests can't marry." An awkward silence impregnated the air as he continued to hold my hand. "I'm new in town and thought I would meet my flock."

I cringed and pulled my hand away. Churches and I were like oil and water. I didn't think God would appreciate a stained soul like mine mixed in with all the other purer souls. "Don't go to church, Father...ah....I mean Seth." I hesitated calling him by his first name, I got the message loud and clear as a kid: Clergy were better than everyone.

"That's too bad, I would have liked to have seen you in the front pew." Under hooded eyes, he started looking at my feet and continued to follow up the path of my body. It was quite unnerving. He finally met my eyes, quietly he said, "It would make my day if you came...," and his eyes captured mine and I was mesmerized, "...to church." His eyes were the color of a deep blue ocean with irises that were surrounded by an intense black band. Inside the black band was a halo of gold encasing the ocean. Shivers ran up and down my body. Maybe I should reconsider going to church if I didn't think I would catch on fire as soon as I walked the door. "Besides," he said, "with language like that, going to church wouldn't be such a bad thing," he grinned slightly.

Fresh embarrassment rose to my cheeks. "You never know," and I broke away from the close proximity of his body. "Would you like to come in?" That question slipped out of my mouth before I had a chance to think about it. What the hell was I going to do with a man of God around here? "Maybe some tea or perhaps some lemonade?" Oh, I did it again, fuck, fuck. I racked my brain thinking what I could use for lemonade. I mentally did an inventory of my refrigerator; I think there was some old shriveled up lemons in there. He turned away and glanced up and down the neighborhood. That gave me the perfect opportunity to scrutinize the man before me. He had on a purple button up shirt that hugged tight and flat against his chest. Underneath his khaki shorts were long, tanned legs with defined muscular thighs. I was so going to burn in hell twice because I was having indecent thoughts about a man of God.

He flashed his beautiful smile and I had a sudden outbreak of shyness. "I would like that," and a crow squawked above us as we turned towards the door. Just then, Carson came out of her front door and started beating a rug, and dog hair flew all around in the breeze. Seth's face became stone cold and he stopped in midstep. "Unfortunately, I cannot right now, I am on a mission to try and get to know everyone, see if I can get more souls to church." His voice seemed to have a sense of regret to them. Well, at least, that is what I would like to think. "But, I will take you up on the offer to come over for lemonade sometime soon." He put his hand out again.

I found myself leaning forward slightly as I slid my hand into his. A breeze came by and a sweet scent of soap and vanilla drifted around me. Looking into his eyes of blue, I replied, "Anytime, Seth," and I gave him a shy, sweet smile. We lingered for a moment and then he walked away. There was something so familiar about him and I tried to figure out what was I connecting to. A shadow crossed over me and as I looked up, a group of crows passed over and disappeared from the sky. *I guess they found what they were looking for.*

Chapter 10

With the exception of few noisy mornings that made me jump out of bed and fall on the floor, I had finally gotten some sleep—with the plague of my nightmares as my alarm. Continuing with my routine, I let the door hit the frame hard and plopped myself in a chair on the porch. The sun struck upon my face and chased the shadows of my nightmares away. The photographs in the newspaper was cause for concern over the past few days, but I finally relaxed into Harry's idea that Snake had finally let me go.

"Fuck! Gawd dammit!" Then there was the clink-clink sound of tools hitting the concrete. Oh, good, the truck was eating Gabriel again. That poor Ford truck, it was going to have major indigestion. Inwardly, I couldn't help a moment of glee. A mechanical woman was putting him in his place.

"Are you going to come over and help or are you going to sit and there sulk in the sun!" he yelled from inside the truck. I assumed he was shouting, but the truck muffled out the yell to a tinny voice.

"Was I supposed to help you?" I yelled back. I figured he had a hearing problem from the loud exhaust of his motorcycle.

He pulled his head out of the truck, "You can help me fix this truck, or I can go back to the motorcycle—your choice."

Good point. I meandered over and the scent of lilacs perfumed the air as I brushed by. On my way, walking oh so very slowly, in front of me, a roadrunner snatched a worm from the ground and ran across the street to chomp on his newly acquired prize. Finally, I had arrived and peered into the old, greasy engine block.

"Are you going to stand there or you going to hand me that tool?" A greasy finger pointed to a pile of flashy metal objects splayed across the concrete. I picked up a random shiny silver wrench that was sulking away from the hornet's nest of tools.

He glanced over. "No, not that one. The screwdriver over there. You know a screwdriver. Has a flat head, turns things," and he cranked his wrist in a turning motion. That was a whole mess of words with random bits of sarcasm that I didn't quite appreciate.

I grabbed the screwdriver. "Well, be a little more specific, you jackass!" I yelled back in his ear just in case his ego was blocking his hearing. "Here, take it," and I shoved the tool in his hand. I stomped off, mumbling about jackasses and all egotistical men should be hung by their entrails.

"Wait! Danni…please, wait," and I stopped for a moment and faced straight out, arms crossed. I was not going to turn around, not for all the tea in China.

"Would you face me?" and I turned around, cocked my hip, and stared at him with the coldest eyes I could muster.

"Huh, that's interesting, your eyes get a really deep green when you're mad." That was an odd observation at the moment that broke me out of pissed-off-ville. "I'm sorry. That truck," and he looked back and sneered at the old Ford, "just drives me a little nuts, okay. I didn't mean to take it out on you."

From inside his house, I could hear a police scanner squawking about a car getting a ticket on Central, a nostalgic street from the days of route 66. "What are you doing with a police scanner?" His head popped up and he hit the rusted hood.

"Fuck!" and he grabbed his head.

"You should probably wear a helmet when you work on her."

"Only around you."

I smirked. "Whatever. So what do you need a scanner for?" I am nothing but persistent.

"I like to keep myself out of trouble, listen in, make sure my name isn't on any arrest warrants." He did look guilty of some crime and my prison spidey sensed there was more than what he was telling. "It's a form of entertainment, okay."

Couldn't argue there. I always thought listening to people get arrested made for good entertainment. Gabriel dove back into the belly of the beast and soon expletives rang off the steal of the truck. *Good truck! You go, girl, give 'em hell!* More assaults of the English language in the form of damn, fucks, and hells in a string that made one long sentence and I couldn't help but laugh.

"Sailors would be proud."

He wiped his hand on his right butt cheek and left a smear of grease. An overwhelming need to wipe clean off that grease stain with my hand came over me, but I opted to occupy my hand with some shiny metallic tool. He looked behind him and noticed what I was staring at.

"Like what you see?" He reached over and slid the tool out of my hand.

Yes, as matter of fact I do, but hid that thought behind some other indecent ones. I wouldn't want to inflate his ego any further. I wasn't blushing, although my cheeks were beginning to warm up—must be getting hotter out here. Gabriel threw down the used cloth on top of a heap of dirty cloths. He leaned his whole body against the truck and faced me. Beads of sweat slowly dripped down the side of his face and his t-shirt was fast becoming wet with perspiration. The shirt stuck to his skin and followed the curves of his pectoral muscles. His chest began to move up and down, displaying his finer qualities. Quickly, I rummaged in the tool pile for anything that would quell my laughter. When I came back up, the arm he was leaning on began flexing. I began to cough to stop the smirk I was hiding, "So, am I done here?"

"It's pretty hot!" he raised his eyes to the sky at the bright sun's pelting rays, "and she's not cooperating." His eyes came back to me and blinked several times; he must be trying to rid himself of all the black shadows of me. He leaned against the truck that was befuddling him so much and shook his head. "Typical woman— you try and do something for them and they never like what's good for them."

"Hmmpf! Typical man, always deciding what the best thing is for a woman."

A broad smile went across his face and it was like rain in a desert. Suddenly, I didn't feel like laughing anymore. An eternity passed between us in an awkward silence.

"Come with me." His eyes were the color of hazel brown with gold flecks randomly placed throughout his irises.

Marry me. At least that is what I think he said. "What?"

"Something to drink." He gestured holding a cup and pouring it into his mouth.

"Oh, of course." Yes, alcohol might actually help quell the anxiousness I felt.

We drove down Central and stopped. *Damn*, not the place I was hoping to calm my nerves but a coffeehouse across from UNM, where the homeless and college students imbibe in caffeinated drinks. This quaint little place was a beehive of activity with students nose deep in their books and vagrants dodging the cars as they crossed the street to beg. Gabriel and I sat underneath an elm tree that only made the pervasive temperatures slightly cooler. A disheveled *Albuquerque Journal* crinkled up with coffee stains laid across the table while the wind whipped up the corners, I swear to god it was calling my name. The coffee he had ordered for me swirled around and around as I tried to lose myself in the waves of brown liquid. A thick layer of sugar remained congealed at the bottom.

"Something wrong with your coffee?"

"No, not really." Nervous and excitement broiled a storm in my stomach mixed with caffeine and I was becoming a tornado of jitters. He, on the other hand, was seated comfortably in his chair, legs crossed, taking in the view of his surroundings. *Damn him, Why can't he be nervous like me?* His black hair cascaded in waves down his shoulders and reflected sparks from the sun. He had a choker of turquoise around his neck and one single silver feather leaf hanging from the center. "So," and I waited a lifetime for a response to that. Sighing, "Do you read any books?" He whipped his head my way and raised an eyebrow at me.

"Of course, I read. I'm not an idiot, Danni." He chugged some coffee and crushed the cup underneath his hand.

"Well, beside motorcycle magazines and girlie pictures, what exactly do you read?" I was being sarcastically pleasant.

"Actually, I just got done reading *Metamorphosis* by Franz Kafka."

"Oh, uhm, well," that was unexpected.

"Well, what do you read, then?"

"Definitely not that," then I looked for a different topic. The wind knocked over the newspaper. Picking up the paper, a section slipped out and the headline caught my attention.

"No really, what do you read?"

"*The Cat in the Hat* by Dr. Seuss," but I was no longer concerned with our conversation anymore.

He blew out his coffee and coffee droplets stained the crinkled paper. I checked to see if he was breathing, after a second consideration I went back to the headline. THE DESERT KILLER STUMPS ALB POLICE. In between the circular coffee stains, the journal reported "police still investigating…coffee stain…blood drained…. hands… coffee stain…hands tied together….coffee stain, coffee stain…police did not reveal any other clues at the scene of the crime. *Well, at least they got a name for him.*

"*Cat in the Hat*, huh?"

I turned beet red; oh, still on that conversation. Okay, it was childish to read children's stories but I liked *Cat in the Hat* and *Green Eggs and Ham*, gawd dammit.

"Now, why would a woman in her forties read children's tales?"

That tore me away from my obsession. "Who said I was in my forties? Exactly." One eyebrow went up at me; well, that sucked, I don't seem to be able to pull off that twenty-nine age anymore. Taken aback by his question, I felt ridiculous that I was bothered so much by my age.

He grabbed my hand, his eyes were so engaging, "No, seriously, why do you like Dr. Seuss books?"

Nervousness coiled into my stomach, "They remind me of innocence and of simpler things. A life lived in harmony before the monsters come." My heart dropped a beat and my throat became choked as I watched coffee swirl in my cup. Silence came between us again and I hadn't a clue what to say and desperate to hear his voice again.

"This is ridiculous." He grabbed my coffee and poured it out in the bushes. "Let's go," and I stared at his open hand. He shook his hand again. "Come on, let's go."

"Where?"

But I didn't really get an answer. We got on his motorcycle, rode out to the Bosque trail, and walked along arroyo. Geese flew above our heads in a perfect V and roadrunners scampered past us. We watched the river go lazily by as we walked into a grove of trees. I marveled as the Titans rose above us and their branches grasped pieces of heaven. Their green leaves so vivid against the azure sky. The fragrance of detritus and earth mixed and awakened all my senses and a calming sense of peace blanketed over me.

"You don't talk much, do you?' His voice deep and thoughtful broke the silence of the wooded church.

"Neither do you."

"I'm the quiet strong type," and he flexed his bicep.

"Yeah, I see that," and I couldn't help but laugh a little.

"Most women can't wait to tell me all about themselves or ask me a million questions about me, but you, I don't know...."

"I'm trying to be mysterious." I did a little coy smile and bashed my eyelashes. "I heard it's supposed to keep a man interested in you."

I shied away and tried to keep two steps in front of him, but his presence sent electrical sparks through my body. The wind gently picked up a few fallen leaves on the ground and they swirled in a tornado, circled, and then they landed gently back on the ground. Deep purple and blue clouds formed menacing thunderheads as the geese called to each other above us. As I started to look down again and blinked to accustom my eyes back to normal, Gabriel was standing in front of me. He stood a breath away.

"I'm definitely interested in you." His finger followed the curve of my cheekbone. My knees trembled at his touch and then a feeling that this is probably a big mistake crashed my newly built house of dreams. He looked concerned but didn't pursue my sudden change in mood, thankfully. I walked to the edge of the bank and listened to the water rush by.

Searching for a way to keep connected, I asked, "So what do you do?" He looked away sharply. "You don't have to tell me if you don't want to." I kicked a rock in the stream.

"Ah, well, it's hard to explain and I'll just leave at that." Great, he's a drug runner.

"Okay, well…." Think, Carolina, think, but I couldn't get past his job, curiosity was going to skewer the cat here. We continued to walk. The sound of dead leaves beneath our feet was the only conversation. I thought when you met your heart's desire you had those late midnight conversations and endless phone calls. "You're a hard man to have a conversation with, you know that?" I was trying to make a joke but it came out with an edge of anger.

"I usually don't have conversations with woman beyond "What time do you get off work? Where is your place?" and "No, I'm not staying for breakfast."

Well, that was some information I didn't need to hear. Let's review: I'm walking with a nonconversing male who likes to flex his muscles, and one-night stands are considered a relationship. He was one of the grouchiest people I ever met. Wow, I really know how to pick 'em. But I couldn't deny that I was attracted to him. *Oh, Carolina, do you really have to be such an idiot. Yes, yes, I do, and I'm a raving idiot most of the time.* My useless conversation continued in my head until I smacked myself straight into him.

"Oompf, hey!" My head hit the back of his shoulder blades and the scent of Tide, musky cologne, and sweat infiltrated my bent nose. *When did he get ahead of me?*

"Shhh, look over there," and he pointed to the river's edge. It was a coyote padding in the tall grass on the bank of the river. The coyote silently searched among the grass and leaves for his next meal, always keeping a watchful eye on his surroundings. He had a beautiful red coat and bushy long tail. Behind another bush, another smaller coyote shyly looked out from underneath the leaves. She looked directly at me for a moment and went back into hiding. Trying to get closer, a branch snapped underneath the weight of my foot. The precocious coyote quickly looked our way, stared directly at both of us, swished his tail, and then continued behind the bush to join his mate.

Gabriel turned around and whispered in my ear, "I'm a more of show you kind of man." The wind blew slightly and a stray hair crossed my face. He gently pulled the hair behind my ear and rested his palm on my cheek. I couldn't help it and let my face rest in his hand.

"Let me see what else I can show you," and we continued down the path.

We walked slowly, always near each other as I waited for the touch of his hand that never came. Our conversations were short, with dashes of small talk, never asking those questions that new lovers ask— "Where are you from?" "Where have you been?" "Who are you?" It seemed we both had something to hide and it was easier confining our conversations to weather and traffic. At the end of the day, I got off his motorcycle stiff and sore from bracing myself against the wind and holding him tight. He remained seated. Our faces met and our eyes locked and so many emotions swirled around. I couldn't tell if it was the start of something or the ending of something.

Unable to handle the silence any longer, I finally said, "Well, thanks for the coffee," I said jokingly.

"Yeah, no problem. See ya later," and he turned on his motorcycle. Exhaust billowed around me and the sound of his motorcycle exploded in my ears. He backed out of his driveway, leaving me in a pillow of blue-gray greasy smoke. I was so stunned that I just stood there like an idiot as I heard the last echoes of his motorcycle rumble down the street. *I just got blown off.* I rolled my eyes and walked back home with the cacophony of anger, disconcertment, and what-the-hell-did-I-do-to-deserve-this-all feeling, banging around in my head.

The sounds of dogs yapping grabbed my attention. Carson seated on the porch threw dog toys to the two whirls of fur in the front yard. That is exactly what I needed right now, two furry circus clowns that I knew would cheer me up. They ran up to the fence, wagged their tails, and yapped incessantly, Carson shushed them, instantly. They were a sight with their grass-laden tongues hanging out of the sides of the mouth. Dolin offered his doggy drenched ball to me. Well, at least there was one male in my life that was happy to see me.

"Hey, Carson," I said as I scruffed up the top of the Dolin's head. Both of them were caked with grass and drool, and they started to argue in doggy speak over who got the ball. They lightened up my mood considerably.

"What's going on, Danni? I see you had a good day," and she looked over at Gabriel's house.

"You could say that." I really didn't want to discuss it. About then, Riley came over, Angelica's little hand in hers. The small angel was in a white pinafore with little pink flowers all over it. Angelica tightened her grip around her mother as they got closer to the excited dogs. A grim look crossed Riley's face.

Riley tried to distract herself. "What is this about having a good day, hmmm?" She had one eyebrow raised up and a little smirk on her face. God, what was it with this neighborhood that my love life seemed to be an interest.

"Yeah, it was a great day," I said rather sarcastically.

Both women looked at me and said, "Oh!" in perfect harmony. Man, women are the worst when it comes to gossip! I looked at their faces and they were salivating at the prospect of more information. But, honestly, I just didn't have much to tell them. Actually, it would have been nice to talk about it, but I needed to keep my distance. "So, you guys heard any more on Albuquerque's killer?" Both of them had sour expressions on their faces, like they had just been in the desert with no food and I had just eaten a steak in front of them.

"No, not much. The news said there were no other leads," Riley said distractedly as she watched Angelica cling to her.

"What's wrong with Angelica today?"

"She gets like this from time to time. She'll be a happy child with smiles and light in her eyes. Then, the next day, she will be scared and shy." Riley's eyes were glistening and she turned away. "I am just not sure what to do for her." Carson and I shrugged our shoulders. We were helpless against a little girl's sadness.

I took a big risk here, not to mention it was a bit hypocritical of me to delve into someone's past and not reveal my own. "Does she miss her father?" I asked very gingerly. Sudden hands covered Angelica's ears and a liquid sheen formed in Riley's eyes.

"I can't really talk about it—not just yet." Angelica reached up to her mother and Riley scooped her up and held her for dear life. Clinging to her mother, Angelica raised her head and, with bright beautiful angelic eyes, stared at me. She unglued one arm and stuck her chubby little hands towards me. Her eyes became lighter, almost ghostly, and I had an overwhelming need to hold her. She placed her hand upon my cheek and soft beautiful warm light filled the dark caverns of my being. They both walked away and, in the middle of summer, I felt the snow of winter.

Dolin and Kelsey came over to the fence and watched Angelica and her mother walk away. Both of their heads just cocked to one side, watching the other puppy walk away. Their eyes jumped to mine and they began to wag their tales. Nothing fazes those dogs. I picked up a gnarly, drooled on, mud cake toy by the tips of my fingers and threw it. The next moment, I saw a pile of red, white, and black fur swirling around in the mud.

Both of us ignored the fact that I had asked a personal question that crossed the neighbor conversation lines. "So—have you met that Reverend yet?" I asked.

Carson just gave me a quizzical look. "What reverend?"

"Ah, Reverend Seth somebody," and it took me a while to remember his name. "Whitehouse, Seth Whitehouse. He came by the other day to introduce himself to the neighborhood."

Carson, not afraid of drool, picked up the dirt-encrusted ball and threw it.

"Ewww, that's disgusting!"

She shrugged her shoulder and threw the ball to the whirling dervishes. "No, no one has come by as of late."

"Hmm, that's interesting. He said he was out meeting the neighbors. I think he was trying to recruit people to come to church."

"Well, good luck for him trying to get me to church."

"I know what you mean." I figured I was going to burn in hell eventually, why start early. Although he was a rather handsome-looking man and, suddenly, I envisioned him in front of his enraptured congregation preaching the good word with those striking blue eyes and god-like blonde hair. There was a fire in his voice and a slight reddening to his cheeks from the proselytizing. "But then again, a little church never hurt anyone." Carson shrugged and threw the toy. I must be lonely. After a few more words on the latest in the neighborhood, I went back home and opened my creaking gate, hanging on for dear life. The cowbell just clanked tiredly as the gate relented with a cringe when I opened it. The hinge encrusted with rust hung by a thread and next to it was an empty black screw hole. *Right*, good thing there is no homeowner's association and, if there is, they are ignoring my house. Glancing over to Gabriel's house, his adobe home was quiet and sullen, with a big, droopy elm tree and tire marks on the driveway. Lamenting, he was one confusing man.

Chapter 11

The heat of Gabriel's hand on my cheek lingered, even though it had been hours since we had been at the Bosque and the anger of his sudden departure burned all my organs into cinder. Who does that? Obviously, he does. The door opened to my hideaway and I stepped into the cool adobe casita and, immediately, the hairs on the back of my neck rose. Nothing was amiss, but all my muscles were in flight position, ready to jump at any moment.

I looked everywhere for what caused the sudden need to flee, but there was nothing except well…except the picture frames were perfect. They seemed suddenly straighter than when I hung them. When I first moved in, I hung "art" from garage sale finds and Goodwill just to make the place homier, more so to hide all the cracks that tore through the walls. I could never quite get them level. As soon as my muscles released from the flight response, I slowly searched the rest of the house with my handy Magna light. Nothing but those frames was amiss, but still I had the feeling someone walked across my grave and I was writhing beneath their feet. I pushed the frames until they were slightly off kilter.

The next day, Gabriel's motorcycle backfired. Excited to see him, through the window, Gabriel was firing his obnoxious cycle and the redhead was at the back, holding him tight. *Oh, I am so gonna kill him.* Not really kill him, but yeah, I really wanted to kill him.

I schlepped into the kitchen and slammed things around for a while. Furiously, I looked for coffee, tea—anything to calm me down—but I all found was hard and cold frustration. Moo cup and pig cup looked at me innocently and I just growled at them. Damn it, I would have to make a coffee/tea run. Feeling absolutely bitter, today, I figured coffee would be the best thing—dark roast to top it all off. I got dressed in a simple pair of jean shorts, a peasant blouse, and ropers, just to make the whole ensemble. I tried in vain to tame my hair, but the curls were temperamental and could not be rationalized with.

I stomped out, slid into my GTO, and roared down the street to the coffee shop. The universe in its infinite wisdom opened up the only table at the coffee shop, the same one that I sat at with Gabriel for our date. Was it a date, a meeting, a get together? What exactly was all that? Frustrated, I opened the newspaper and skimmed through the pages, trying to keep my mind off things like red hair, red lips, and hands holding Gabriel's body, but somehow, New Mexico's gubernatorial election couldn't compete with my acidic memories. I attempted to read about two New Mexico women running for election. It would be a tight race and each took the latest headlines and ran with how they would be tough on crime. Blah, blah, blah, it was time to go.

Out of the coffee shop and down Central, the goat rumbled past the homeless, the shops, and the university. Today was a beautiful day just to drive. The leather seats cupped me and soothed my nerves. The dashboard indications of gas and speed let me know I could run away all day. A phantom scent of my father's cologne mixed with leather tickled my nose. The wind whipped my hair and straightened out the curl that I had tried in vain to tame.

The car seemed to drive me and we came across the church that Reverend Whitehouse—I mean Seth—was currently residing as a pastor. On the radio, the song by the Fray belted out, "I found God at the corner of Fifth and Armistad," and in my case, I found God on the corner of First and Sanistevan at St. Stephen's Episcopal Church. I stilled the beast in front of the church and gazed at the stark white cross on top of on old adobe. It was an old church with one big, round stain glass window at the entrance. A short adobe wall surrounded the church in a protective circle. Beautiful sand plaster tinted the church blending God's fortress into the desert, with only a cross to lead the parishioner's home. The doors were heavy oak stained brown and worn with time, but they withstood against the elements. A testament to the church's congregation, that they were safe from the outside world and people like me. I felt compelled to go in and seek the peace I remembered as a child. Childhood memories came flooding back; I couldn't stand church because it was boring—no one talked, people stood there staring at the front of the church mesmerized by an old man in front on a pedestal. I can still feel my father's heavy hand of on my shoulder to keep me from fidgeting. But now, there was something about the quiet of the church that I longed for. I cautiously put a hand on the door and waited for a bolt of lightning to strike me down.

The heavy wooden doors groaned as I walked in. I stood at the apse and felt the peaceful silence drown out the din of my head. A tall marble stoup graced my right side and out of old habits, I made the sign of the cross. I stopped in midcross when I realized what I was doing. Then, I moused my way to the last pew and settled in. The scent of burning candles and incense made me dizzy.

All around the church were intricately hand-carved Santos made out driftwood keeping vigil. In between the forlorn saints that gazed to the heavens were stained glass windows. Beams of radiant sun poured through the glass and cast jewels of gold, green, and red upon the church floor. As the sun progressed, the jewels danced up my legs and rested at my waist. Slowly my hands became encased with shards of colored light.

Raising my eyes, I caught the sparkle of light from this one particular stained glass window. Swathed in glass, St. Michael stood tall with an angry warrior's face. Thick, powerful muscles controlled luminescent wings that expanded across the windowpane. Each feather looked like it was ready to take flight. Robes of white flowed all around him. In Michael's hand was a huge sword above his head and he was waiting to strike down the very object of his fierce eyes. I followed the Saint's blade to a hideous creature below it. The red-skinned monster was writhing around a rock, gnashing his teeth and clawing at the ground. He had black tipped horns on his head and yellow piercing eyes that seemed to show anger and pain at the same time. The creature on the ground had muscles protruding ready to fight, and his forked tail swishing above his body. His feet were pointed hooves and I had a sudden need to shove my feet underneath the pew. The devil's red arm was stretching out to the pitchfork that was so close but still unreachable as St. Michael looked on. After looking at the minute details, the glass window expanded to the whole scene that good conquers evil. I imagined the hand of St. Michael was going to slash his blade upon my soul and I would be no longer. I couldn't look at that image anymore and wanted so badly to flee. But another part of me remained rooted to the oak pew.

Memories of all the masses I was forced as a child to go to rolled back from the forgotten closets, and I remembered the old crusty priest with flowing robes raising the gold chalice above his head and wine was miraculously turned into the Blood of Christ. I never bought that story, but at thirteen, I thought it was so cool we could finally drink wine. Before me, the ghosts of families, friends, and strangers reached across the aisle to say, "Peace be with you." The sound of my voice echoed in the church.

"And also with you," was whispered in my ear. Stunned out of solitude, I turned around and found Seth sitting behind me.

He grinned and said, "I didn't mean to startle you. I seem to have a habit doing that, don't I?"

"I didn't expect you...." I was looking for Seth when I came in but had forgotten him when I stood waiting to be burned in the fires of hell. He moved around the pew and sat right next to me, the heat of his body warming me from the cold of the church. Incense and vanilla scent mixed all around us and tickled my nose. I had a sudden need to scoot away, but I willed myself to remain there. Maybe my monster couldn't take anything good surrounding it. We sat and stared straight at the altar in complete silence. My knees jumped up and down, incessantly.

"Why are you so nervous?"

"Do you think evil can walk in a church and survive?" So far, I hadn't caught on fire as of yet, but I didn't want take any chances.

His pupils turned from wide black deep circles to pin points and then he laughed. His easygoing laughter eased my consternations. He leaned his head close to mine. The soft scents of soap and vanilla from his clothes mixed together and formed an intoxicating aroma. His chin had soft bristles that made his jaw quite masculine. In a low growling voice, he said, "I believe evil can walk in here unhindered and face God down himself." His hands grabbed mine and they were ice cold. Splinters of ice rose through my veins and I froze in place.

He looked at the altar with a smirk. A cold, hard mask encased his face and his eyes were a defiant, brilliant blue. He stared so hard at the crucifix upon the mantle that I thought the church would explode in flames. Never have I seen anyone with a look of disdain like he had when looking up to God.

He felt me shiver and then he stared right through me as though I were made of glass. Then I saw a flash in his eyes and his cold mask vanished instantly. A kind, gentle face replaced the icy veneer. He smiled.

"But, I believe God stares right back and sends evil back to hell. No evil can survive heaven, as far as churches…well…. Churches are nothing but brick and stone unless you truly believe God resides here."

His face lightened and he said in a lighthearted manner, "But truly, God resides in your heart." Something a well-rehearsed revered would say and my frozen body eased only slightly.

In front of the church, a man came in with the same type of religious garb Seth wore, a purple button down shirt and a collar around his neck. Seth's hand was sweaty when it had been so cold and dry before. The reverend at the altar was beginning preparations for mass. I turned to Seth. I was going to ask about the other reverend, when he squeezed my hand a little. "How about some peppermint tea? I believe it's your favorite."

How did he know that? His frame stretched tall above me and his shadow engulfed me as he stood. His eyes were no longer a brutal ice storm but lakes of serene blue. He held out his hand and I placed mine in his, but deep in my being, bells were ringing in warning, but I blew them off as an overactive imagination. We met at the coffee shop on Central. All misgivings went away as the breeze moved the trees in a soothing rhythm and cooled my neck.

"How did you decide to become a man of God?" I ceremoniously opened sugar packets, poured milk into my tea, and slowly drank. Each sip I took made my taste buds burst with the cool sensation of mint and the heat of hot water. Drinking tea was an experience for

119

me. Seth watched my every move, entranced by my fingers tearing open a small pink package. His smile was warm and easy and I found myself captured by the web of his good looks.

"The usual."

"The usual what?"

"The usual story: God calls you and you are inclined...no... required to follow the calling." He drank his coffee and a breeze picked up the aroma of coffee and infused the air.

"'Required...,' hmm, that's interesting, I never heard it as a requirement. No, angels descended upon you or echoes in your mind from God's word," I said jokingly.

"Yeah, all that." He spoke so nonchalantly like this was a boring subject. A police car passed by and his eyes darted everywhere and he suddenly seemed very uncomfortable. He must have seen the question on my face and sighed. "I was in college doing drugs, the whole nine yards, drinking stuff like that when...." His voice drolled on and I became lulled by the rhythm and my attention sailed to comparisons. Like the way his eyes were so expressive when he talked or thought about something. They crinkled when he smiled and were so blue and I couldn't help but to compare them Gabriel's warm brown eyes. Seth's cheekbones were soft underneath his skin and Gabriel's was angular and cut lines.

His muscles were developed but they weren't defined like Gabriel's. They seemed like a soft layer of skin wrapped around hard sinew. Seth was charming and polished, while Gabriel was rough like fine grit sandpaper. When I imagined touching Gabriel, my fingers tingled as they felt the rough texture of his skin. Seth's hands were moving like a symphony conductor. Then, I noticed a deep gash on top of his wrist. I was surprised that I hadn't noticed it before.

"Chopping vegetables."

"What?"

"Chopping vegetables. You were looking at my wrist and I assumed you were wondering what made that gash." He seemed annoyed with me. I would be, too. I hadn't been listening to a word he was saying.

"You haven't been listening to me at all, have you?"

A really great lie would be great here, but nothing came to mind. How did others lie so well? I need a whole lot of practice. "I'm sorry, Seth, I haven't been sleeping well lately. I guess I've been working too many hours at the pizza place." I swished cold tea in my cup. That and too many nightmares. His face softened and he put his hand on mine.

"Why don't you go back and get some sleep?"

I did suddenly feel very sleepy and the thought of soft pillow underneath my head gazing at Gabriel's eyes was very appealing. I shook my head to liven myself up.

He looked at his watch, "I have to get back to my flock, as they say."

We both got up at the same time and he gave me a hug and a peck on the cheek. "I will drop by again sometime."

"I look forward to that," and I actually meant that. Seth was…nice, although I still couldn't put my finger on what was bothering me about him, probably the whole man of God, thing. Who could think erotic thoughts about a reverend? Me.

I lay down and looked at the pillow next to me and a sense of loneliness draped over me. I'm not sure how a simple walk in nature, meaningless conversations, and a few glances made me think of Gabriel so often. It must be some kind of weird chemical running through my synopsis that women my age get.

Chapter 12

Summer was coming full force and it was time to plant the lavender I bought at the nursery. A sorry ass attempt at distracting myself from thoughts of who shall not be named. Little wisps of clouds formed over the Sandias and they would be full-grown monsters in a few hours. Yep, today was planting day. There was a plant of some kind at all the places I have been, at least there was something living to remember me. A whooshing sound came by my ear, a flying missile came over the fence, and I managed to duck my head just in time. That paperboy is going to be a world-class baseball player if he didn't get killed for breaking someone's window. Unraveling the projectile, the headline splashed across the paper: POLICE GETTING CLOSER TO CATCHING THE DESERT KILLER!

Quite excited, I dove in searching for more details. Some undisclosed source close to the police thought they found more clues. My head played armchair sleuth thinking about what they had found, like a broken rosary bead, one blood spatter, and all the other clues found on the latest praying body. Eh-aw! Sound made me jump out of my skin. The wind caught the paper and blew it on the porch, where it rested haphazardly. A big black crow sat on the fence and continued to curse at me. His head was shiny—or was it her head? How could you tell? I picked up my spade, waiting for more expletives in crow language. His beady eyes were staring me down. He opened his beak and I yelled, "Don't you dare!" and he shut his beak and flew away.

My knuckles turned white as they held the spade. Shaken, I went back to digging and talked to the lavender I bought at the nursery. I was trying to cheer it up and talk to it in soothing kiddie language. It really missed its nursery and was not particularly happy about being moved. Its leaves were drooping into endless tears, evidence of its depression laid all around me. I sympathized with it, moving did that to me, too.

The monotony of digging, the beat of the shovel in the ground, and the smell of fresh dug earth made me forget that crow. Each mound of earth I moved, the thoughts of Gabriel drifted in and out of my consciousness. Deeper in the ground I dug and let the images of his body moving in synchronicity with mine entranced all my thoughts.

The clang of the cowbell broke my daydreaming and there he stood before me, but not the one I really wanted. Seth stood devilishly handsome in an oxford t-shirt, not a wrinkle in sight, and perfectly ironed shorts. My attire left little to be desired. Dirt handprints smeared my shirt, dried mud was caked on my legs, and sweat stains were underneath my armpits. This was really not the time for casual lemonade.

He flashed his smile. "Digging?"

Embarrassed of my previous images, I cleared my throat. "It's good therapy."

"What could you possibly need therapy from?" *Oh many, many things,* I thought. "Perhaps unrequited love."

That made me shirk back a little and I hurried back to my digging. I implored the lavender psychically not to give out any secrets. "Something like that."

"Now, who would walk away from someone as beautiful as you?"

"A fool."

He cracked a perfect white smile. "Do you need some help there?"

"Love some."

We wrestled with the lavender. Its roots were holding onto the pot for dear life. When it was finally extracted, we both lifted the plant and put it in its new roomy earth station with solar power and all the water it could want. I sent it mental images, *it'll be just like at the nursery, honest, just more room, no encroaching neighbors to worry about.* I couldn't tell who I was trying to convince—me or the plant.

I filled in the hole and then clawed at the ground to cover up the roots. "Ow!" I pulled my glove off and looked at my index finger; one drop of blood was beginning to form.

"What is it?"

"Oh, I was digging around in the ground and a thorn, or maybe a piece of glass, or something sharp bit me," and I put my finger in my mouth.

"Let me see," he said, and I pulled my finger out my mouth and bright red drops dripped onto the lavender bush.

He put his lips on my finger and sweetly kissed the wound. My insides did a little flip, until he started to gently suck on my finger. Hazy clouds formed in his eyes and he drifted away.

"Seth!" I freaked out and pulled my hand away. "I think I need a band aid," and he seemed to come back to his senses and rubbed his hands on his shorts. A dark, red smear left a stain on his khaki shorts.

"Your pants," and I pointed to the stain that had smeared the perfect crease.

He peered down at the stain, then he looked at me and his eyes became dark blue. Nervous, I stepped back. Then they returned to normal in a flash, "Not to worry, they will wash out."

Hmm, I guess overreacted and I shivered in the heat of the sun. "Want something to drink?" I asked.

"That would be great. I would love a cold glass of water right about now. Digging always makes me thirsty."

I went into the house and remembered to ask if he needed a cloth for his shorts. Through the gray screen, a distorted image of a happy-go-lucky Seth picked up the newspaper and smoothed it out until there was hardly a wrinkle. He read the title of the latest murder. He sat back like he was a king, his shoulders dropped, and his lips twisted sardonically. If I didn't know any better, I thought I saw the remnants of a rat's tail in the corner of his mouth. He stared straight out but he glanced at me out of the corner of his eye. His shoulders became square as he flipped the page and casually read on. A disconcerting feeling crept back into my stomach.

After gauzing and tying my wound up with string (I had no Band-Aids to speak of), I gathered up drinking items and placed them out on a tray. Wound care had taken my mind off my unsettled feelings and concluded I was just being paranoid. Too much TV, I would have to starve my curiosity in order to have sanity. Tray first, I headed out and watched a brilliant sunset splash red, golds, and purples across the sky. I was amazed as the last ray of the sun went down underneath its cloudy covers.

"Where do you think the neighbors are out on a night like this?" Seth said and broke the stillness.

"I don't know really." I put the tray down beside him, "Carson may have left for dog training classes. Riley and Angelica went to dance class, I think." There was no sign of life at Gabriel's, but I think I will keep that little fact to myself.

Seth cleared his throat, "Do you mind if I use your bathroom?"

"No, knock yourself out." He got up with cat like reflexes and went into the house. "I'm sure you won't miss it, it's by the kitchen through the guest room."

He just flashed a smile and slowly closed the door. A loud growl in my stomach replaced my misgivings and, well, it was time for dinner. Enchiladas tonight with green or red chile would be the best course of action to calm an angry stomach. Chile roasting season would soon be here, perfuming the air. My stomach was protesting to my musings on the flavors of chile, and I muttered something to the effect of "All right already," and went into the house.

There was only the small tell-tale signs of the sun's last lingering light when I saw a tall dark shadow move quickly. Nerves quickly took over my growling stomach, and my heart skipped five beats. I groped for the light switch. "Seth!" With a flip of a switch, the low yellow light of my living room bathed Seth in an eerie glow. He stood before the paintings like a stone statue. "Seth," but he didn't respond.

Hand over heart to stop the irascible beating, I walked over to him, "Seth, you're scaring me." Then I bent over to stop the sudden dizziness in my head and caught my breath. When all the bees in my brain stopped buzzing, I straightened up to see Seth staring at me.

He looked at me underneath his dark eyelids for a few moments and then, like a chameleon, his appearance changed. "Sorry," he whispered and put his hands around my head and lifted my face to his. Gone were the dark shadows from earlier and his eyes were a pale soft blue. "I didn't mean to scare you."

A sudden growling noise from my stomach broke the silence and my face turned red.

"Hungry?"

"How could you tell?"

He brushed my cheek with the back of his hand. "I will help you with dinner," and he walked into the kitchen and left me standing there.

Apparently, the handsome reverend was staying for dinner. I needed to quickly pick up the living room. How embarrassed would I be for Seth to see my living room in chaos. I had thrown the blanket on the floor, some magazines were haphazardly thrown around, and the paintings—okay, garage sale finds—all hung askew. Organizational queen I'm not. However, when I looked at the room and expected my cheeks to turn bright red, I noticed that Seth had straightened each painting with level precision. The blanket was folded on the couch and the magazines were stacked in order.

I slowly walked into the kitchen, brushed past him, and felt a sinking feeling. He was at the counter with a blade in his hand that was nothing but a blur as he diced a whole onion into slivers. I shook my head to release the cobwebs of doubt that had crawled around and looked into the refrigerator. "Red or green?" and when I didn't hear a reply, I reached out to grab the red enchilada sauce. The lid of the jar fell off.

"Either," his breath tickled my ear. I jumped and spilt red enchilada sauce all over his ironed shorts. He hopped back and his ice mask encased his face. His calm sea eyes turned violent and dark and his pupils became wide. The moment was instantaneous. This time, I wasn't scared, I was attracted to the darkness, all the doubts I had before disappeared. I was enthralled by the pale color of his skin and his blue eyes. Playing with fire, I licked the flames. I moved within inches of his body and felt the waves of heat all around him. I reached around the stone creature and grabbed a towel that was behind him.

"I'm so sorry about that." Every muscle in his neck and jaw were tight metal cords protruding from his neck. He grabbed the towel from me and started to wipe away the thick enchilada sauce, but the towel had merely smeared the stains. Now, he had large dark red blotch on his shirt and red on his hands. His eyes were crystal blue and under their weight, I acquiesced, humbled by the power he radiated, and looked down at the sauce spreading across the floor like blood from a wound.

My shoulders slumped because the spell was broken. "Damn, this is going to take forever to clean up!"

"No harm done." Mask torn away, Seth smiled and handed the sopping wet towel back to me. "Gee, thanks" and both of our hands were red with sauce. "I guess you'll be going home now," disappointment crept in.

"Nonsense. I just need to wash these out right away. I will just go use your bathroom."

Really, a naked man in my bathroom—haven't had that in a while. "Let me get you some towels."

"No, you have got a mess to clean up here."

No offer on helping, typical man, the red sea of sauce was getting wider. My eyes and nose began to burn from the chile "Fuck" and thought about all the crap I need to get to clean this mess up, when powerful hands began to ease my shoulder muscles. It wasn't until all the knots started to ease did I realize how tense I had been.

"Where are all the towels?" he whispered.

Momentary good feelings blocked my mouth-brain connection so I pointed to the closet door. I had one closet in my house right next to the back door. There was no way to have both doors open at the same time. Seth walked into the closet and I went back to mopping up the mess. The more I cleaned, the more I smeared red chile sauce everywhere and the tiles became stained with red. After a few moments, it was time for fresh rags. The used towels had to be thrown away. Otherwise, red chile smell would forever permeate the house.

On my way out, I pushed the closet door and walked outside to deposit the chile-soaked rags. The air was quiet and still, until ferocious eh-aw sounds from a few crows above broke the silence. Maybe the acidic red chile smell would burn their beady little eyes and they would think my house was from hell. I mused on what burned feathers would look like, when I heard the most gawd-awful muffled scream coming from the kitchen. I ran back in and looked everywhere for Seth, but couldn't find him. He screamed again and, finally, I followed the terror from his voice to the closet. I threw the closet door open and the light from the kitchen cut his face in a diagonal across his nose and left one tear-soaked eye open. He was hugging himself like a parentless child in the street, alone and afraid.

"Seth!" I shouted, "It's me, it's me, Danni!" But he couldn't hear me over his own shrieking. "Seth, it's okay." I touched him and he jerked back. "Seth, it's me." A spark of recognition flooded his eyes and the screams became whimpers. He was so childlike, so afraid. My heart saw the fear in his eyes of things that go bump in the night.

"Seth, it's me."

He looked straight through me. I gently touched him but there was no reaction, so I pulled him into the open. He was a mess of sweat and tears. My nose crinkled at the pungent smell of chile and urine. The enchilada sauce covered his shorts and saved him from anymore humiliation. He regained composure and his crimson cheeks returned to a soft pink.

This was definitely an awkward moment, "Umm, well..huh…dark spaces." I scratched my head, trying to get a clue on exactly how to help him. His eyes darted around and his shoulders began to unhinge from his neck.

"Let me get you a towel." I went back into the closet/pantry to look for monsters, but it was only me in here. But I knew of monsters that stalked in the dark crevices of the mind.

His hands were still shaking when I handed him the towel. He was still distant and child-like. He took a moment to look at me, then he shuffled off to the shower. The shower turned on as I continued the business of cleaning up. The enchilada sauce stained the old tile floor. I stood and contemplated the pros and cons of letting enchilada sauce become the new décor. Strong hands began to massage my shoulders, again, and wet heat seeped into my back. He whispered, "Thank you." My spine tingled from the touch of his fingers. I turned around and stepped back. He was dripping wet with a very holey towel wrapped around his waist. Droplets of water ran down his chest, glided over his chiseled stomach, and became absorbed by the soft cotton. He stood like a Greek statue, except for the deep penetrating look that shook me to my very core.

Seth's eyes had been tumultuous seas and now they were a calm ocean in the moonlight. Sparks of light from the kitchen light made his eyes become alive. He gently pushed me against the adobe wall and I was pinned between a rock and a hard place. His hand glided up the inside of my shirt, underneath by bra, and found the bounty he was looking for. Softly, he kneaded my breast and every cell in my body turned to water. All the blood drained from my head and pooled below. I licked my lips as his thumb flicked the captured nipple between his fingertips, sending charges of electricity throughout my body. My will became enslaved to his command, and I was lost in the momentum of the moment.

My fingers ached to touch the white stone god, to feel his porcelain skin against my own. He left a wake of goose bump down my arms by his fingertips. My fingers slipped between the towel and his warm wet skin. It dropped to the ground and pooled around his ankles. He jerked my head back and my neck stretched causing my mouth to open for a deep kiss. His knee pushed between my legs and I was ensnared.

His teeth caught my earlobe and I felt little soft bites. "You are mine," he whispered in my ear. "I am going to enjoy every minute of you," he growled. I stopped still, but then small sweet kisses ran up the side of my neck and my apprehensions ceased to exist. Towering over me, he stole the air I breathed and I grabbed his muscular shoulder, but I wasn't sure if it was to come up for air or to hold on to him as I died. With closed eyes and lost in lust, I thought Gabriel was touching me.

Something buzzed in my ear and the deep kiss stopped, "Danni! Danni! Are you here?"

That voice was so familiar and my senses reached out to the one I really wanted. Suddenly, I found myself between Seth and the wall, and I didn't like it and I tried to move. Seth pushed me harder against the wall. A wave of anger crashed into me and I pushed back.

"Be quiet!" His hand covered my mouth.

That really pissed me off and I kneed him. Unfortunately, I missed and hit the side of his leg. He stared at me and stepped back only slightly. His body keeping me caged.

"Danni, are you here?" Gabriel was in the living room and by his footsteps, I could hear him getting closer.

"Move, gawd dammit," I growled and pushed against his rock hard chest. He relented with stone cold blue eyes and backed off. I walked through the kitchen door and straight into Gabriel. "Hmmpf."

"Danni?"

"Gabriel, what are you doing here?" said the cat with bird feathers hanging out of her mouth.

"I was worried, the door was open," he was looking around me, "and I tried knocking but you weren't answering" and I moved into his line of sight at every bend as he tried to look around me.

"Oh, I'm just fine, just fine," I grabbed his arm and tried to steer the mountain towards the front door. "Stupid me left the front door open," and I hit my head like I was hitting wood.

He suddenly stopped. "You look flushed and your shirt is all wet."

"I do," and I crossed my arms. Well, I was stumped. Almost having sex in the kitchen didn't seem like the appropriate thing to say right at the moment. I stood up and turned my head towards the kitchen floor and spoke really loudly, hoping upon hope Seth got the hint and put his clothes on. "Umm, I...umm, spilled enchilada sauce on the floor. I was just cleaning it up now." Hey, there really are happy accidents. Feelings of guilt crisscrossed all over me and hoped he bought my story. His hands were holding a thin blue book. "What's in your hands?"

His face had a question mark and then he looked at what he was holding. His face softened, "I got you this." He handed me the book, *Cat in the Hat* by Dr. Seuss.

"For me?"

"Yeah, of course, it's for you."

My heart did tiny leaps of faith. I opened up the cover and a big Dr. Suess signature covered the page. Taken aback by his gesture, I held the book to my heart. When, Crash! Something in the kitchen had dropped and I wondered if not on purpose.

"You're not alone, are you?"

Right about then, Seth came out of the door with a towel, drying his naked body. "I didn't know you had company, Danni." Seth put his hands on his hips and stood there like a nonmoving Greek statue. Where is a fig leaf when you need one?

Gabriel looked at me with hurt in his eyes and stomped out the door. Any chance I had left was walking out the gate and I started to run, when I was jerked back by hand grabbing my arm.

"Let him go, Danni, let's go back into the kitchen and finish what we started."

I pushed his hand away. "No, I—Seth," damn, I was flustered. There was a naked man in front of me that I didn't want and the one I wanted naked was walking out.

He gave me a look of disgust. "You would choose that ape over me." He straightened his back and reigned over me. "I am perfect for you." He had an insidious grin and moved towards me. Nervous, I jumped back like a rat on hot butter.

His face turned cold. "I see where I stand."

Oh, hell, it wasn't supposed to be like this. "Seth, you're a nice guy, but…."

"But, what?"

I was at a loss for words.

His whole demeanor changed before. A chameleon would not have been able to change any faster, and then he said loudly, "I am a man of God!" He pounded on his chest. "God sent you to tempt me into wicked ways!"

My mouth dropped open. "What?" Well, that came out of nowhere. "Wait, Seth, I'm sorry. I just…."

"You led me on."

"I did what?"

"You led me on. You are nothing but a whore."

"A what?" I stammered out. I felt like cold water had been splashed upon my face.

"You heard me!" He bore down upon me, his eyes changed to crystal blue, and he looked like a predator in a snowstorm. "You were sent here to tempt me!" He quickly turned away.

No one calls me a whore. "Fuck you! Don't you dare turn away!" and I grabbed his shoulder.

With lightning speed, he turned and slapped me across my face. A sharp stinging pain burned across my cheek and I fumbled backwards. His face was a cold hard mask and unrecognizable. He stared at me for a few microscopic seconds, his mouth twitched, and his face eased into the charming Seth. "No, this not how I wanted it," he mumbled. His eyes quickly returned to calm seas.

"I am sorry," he said as a matter of fact. "I will go and get dressed."

Seth walked into kitchen and I stumbled out to the porch to see if I could catch Gabriel, but only the faint scent of Gabriel lingered in the air. My legs were shaking to the point I wasn't sure if they would hold me up. I plopped down on to the porch chair and placed my cold sweaty palm to my burning cheek, and tried to figure out what just happened.

A less than perfect, fully dressed Seth walked out a few minutes later. He looked straight through me and a spark of fear punctured my stomach. Some crows cawed as they landed on the gate. Ignoring them, Seth had a kind look on his face and stood before me in a crinkled shirt and wet, stained shorts. He looked a little pathetic. "Danni, this didn't go as I planned. I had something different in mind for you and me." His voice was so soft and apologetic. I melted a little. I guess this is what I do to people. I make them crazy and then destroy their clothes.

"Seth, I…don't know what to say."

"You don't have to say anything. Let us just forget this day."

"I just don't feel that way…." He put his finger on my lips.

"Shhhhh, I will change your mind. Trust me, I will be all you think about," and he walked away into the midst of flying crows. They flew up chaotically and brushed their wings around Seth's head. He batted at them and then disappeared into the cool, inky night. The clank of the cowbell and the beat of wings was the last thing that echoed in the air.

Chapter 13

I was fraught with indecisiveness. Should I go plead for mercy and make him understand this was all a big ugly fucking mistake or should I stay? The sun went down minute by minute as I watched the ball of fire escape into the darkness. Exhausted, I burrowed underneath the covers and hoped I would succumb to the night's passing, but a motorcycle loud exhaust broke the silence. The engine stopped and laughter pierced the air and shattered my eardrums. Red hair flowed across my imagination, along with big red lips kissing his neck. The door of his house slammed shut and I punched my pillow. My fluffy down pillow had nothing on the sounds of that woman's voice. I had really screwed up this time, but how? We weren't exclusive or anything. He barely even noticed me. He saw me when he wanted. But my heart softened at his smile and the image of his fingers gently putting a strand of hair behind my ear. The Dr. Seuss book lay across the nightstand. *Damn it! I have a right to have some man, even a naked man, in my house at any time. Preferably, that man should be Gabriel, but I have rights, you know.*

All night I tossed and turned, nightmares plaguing my short catnaps. Guilt ravished me, then anger over my guilt, mad that I was angry. In between the moments of madness, I thought of Seth, but I couldn't tell if I was the cause for his schizophrenic reactions or was he just completely off his rocker. Until the morning spilled across the empty pillow next to me, I threw the covers off and made my way to the bathroom. I wasn't even going to look at the mirror today. What was it going to do, lie, tell me I looked fabulous, you belong on the cover of *Vogue*? That would be a great circus mirror. Women would be lined up with cold, hard cash at that opportunity.

Slipping into my bunny slippers, I schlepped out to the kitchen. My nerves frazzled beyond exhaustion, I by passed pig cup, found an old coffee cup, and poured day-old coffee in it. The refrigerator door squeaked open; I fumbled for the milk, and then nearly dropped it. Poured it into my coffee, said a sarcastic hello to the morning, took a big swig, and blew coffee chunks back out. The milk had soured.

Right about that time, a dull thud hit the window and a crack formed a spider's leg crawling across the pane. *The newspaper boy must die.* I'm headed straight for hell anyways. The battered and abused paper was a little hard to unroll, when Eureka! The pages fanned out. The headlines screamed out: ANOTHER MURDER VICTIM IN ALBUQUERQUE. Scanning the article, this murder seemed different, but still with all the same characteristics; the same middle age, blonde hair, and single. However, the victim, Dahlia Tatum, 35, was found strangled to death amid a torrent of tossed clothes and upended furniture. The body crumpled on the bed, beaten and broken, no time to for her to pray. Rosary beads scattered across her body and on the floor. The police speculated that murder was unrelated to the other victims of the Desert Killer because of the circumstances of her death. They were looking into old boyfriends, known associates, and relatives. Dahlia looked more like a victim of domestic violence, an all too common occurrence in New Mexico. My gut feeling told me that this was the same killer but something royally pissed him off. This was personal, the slayer of souls was enraged.

A reverberating motorcycle broke my obsession. My imagination kicked in, and thoughts of a redheaded hussy with a hot young nubile body, perky breasts, and no stretch marks to found anywhere seared through my brain. I could hear her laughing as she hung on to Gabriel as they rode away. Hate poured out of me in rivulets and I crumpled up the newspaper and tossed in the can. Time for work.

The back door smacked against the brick wall, announcing my arrival. I stomped in and crossed the kitchen. Juan, Julio, and Marco just stared at me with wide eyes like they were viewing a tornado headed straight their way and I stared right back, daring anyone to speak to me. Marco's lips began to move. "Don't you dare say a word to me today." He clamped his lips tight. I threw my purse down and started in on the pizza dough, pounding and beating it within an inch of its floury life. I must have radiated "Stay away from me" because nobody said a peep to me all day. At that moment, I decided there must be a mandar. They sent signals to each other: When one man messed up, they knew they all did. My coworkers were drug dealers and felons, and they skirted around me like mice around a hungry cat. They had no idea what to do with a female who was in a state of frenzy.

After the beating and pounding, I was physically tired but mentally wired. Going for ride in my dad's goat seemed like the perfect balm to my shattered nerves, but white puffs of smoke that I had seen in the morning had turned into raging purple clouds. Their wrath would turn into a downpour. I could empathize. It was late anyways; the light was succumbing to the dark as the clouds melted into the ground. Driving for long periods in the dark on wet slick roads seemed like an accident waiting to happen. See, I can be reasonable at times.

The GTO turned slowly into the driveway. Emotionally and physically exhausted, I got out of Dad's car, when I had a sudden sense that someone was watching me. All the hairs on the back of my neck stood tall. Panic arose in my throat, my hands started to shake, and then invariably, I dropped my keys. "Damn it to hell!" I still hadn't installed a night light in front of the house so it was pitch dark. Knees to the ground, I searched the cold, hard concrete for those damn elusive keys. A twinkle from underneath the car gave me a clue that they might be there but I had to get flat on my stomach and reach underneath. My life really sucked. My fingers reached out and finally touched a pile of metal. *Yes! Thank God!* Then I got up too suddenly and hit my head. "OW! Fucking, son of a bitch!" Dragging myself from underneath the car, one cold drop hit my head, and then another. *Thank you, Dear Lord, for reminding that I am not allowed any breaks.* I yelled some other choice expletives and out of the blue, the wind whipped my hair around my face. A faint caw sound echoed across the storm-heavy air and rattled my bones.

The keys were a jumble in my hand as I tried in vain to the find the right one. With metal clanking sounds, "Aha, found it!" I pushed the key in the lock and the door moved in without effort. Frozen in place, my thoughts rang. *I swore I locked the door this afternoon.* I flipped the switch and no lights came on, just the click clack sound of the switch going back and forth. Pushing the door further, it creaked open wide, like it does in all the horror movies. I hadn't realized I was in the flight or fight position till my back began to hurt. "Oh, for god's sake, this is ridiculous!" and marched in my house and ran smack into a chair, "Son of a bitch! Where in the hell did that come from?"

Talking to myself, I hoped the wave of panic enveloping my body would abate. *The stupid refrigerator probably tripped the breakers, how very Friday the thirteenth.* My stomach flipped. *Damn, no more thinking about horror movies.* Lightning flashed, then thunder clamped, ringing madness in the air. *Just thunder* and tried to still my beating heart with a deep breath, *just thunder.* My jaw popped to release the tension. The air became still again. There was a light scent in the air. *Vanilla?* My frazzled nerves were affecting my sense of smell. Then the sound of a kitchen cabinet door slammed shut and I froze. My stomach suddenly did loopty loops. The room was murky black, with only flashes of lightning to illuminate my way. I should run out the door, but the monster inside said, *Let's go find Jason. Besides, the lights go out all the time and you probably forgot to lock the door, you stupid idiot,* all very reasonable explanations. That little conversation in my head was a nice stall tactic on my part. I yelled, "Jason, come out, come out wherever you are! It's late and all Caspers should leave, it's past midnight!"

Something dropped on the floor. All right, this was royally pissing me off, and well anger quelled the frightened little girl feeling. Stupidly, I fumbled my way to the kitchen. *Probably some stupid teenager lurking around.* "Bastard!" But silence was my only reply. A bolt of lightning struck and flashed the room, turning the living room into a disco nightmare. Then a sharp crack of thunder made me jump and hurt my eardrums. Then absolute quiet—good, I scared them off. I didn't hear anything else so whoever it was must have slipped out or maybe it was all my imagination and I'm actually in bed dreaming.

Continuing my darkened journey to find the elusive control panel, I ran my hand along the textured adobe walls, their solidity and coldness balming my nerves. Bang! "Ow! Fuck!" My foot was in excruciating pain and I began to hop around on the one not in pain. After the pain resided, I grasped the concept of soft flesh hitting hard wood is never a good thing. Growling and spitting mad, I made my way to the kitchen. My foot was throbbing as I gingerly felt my way looking for the closet door. So far, there was nothing in the kitchen to indicate an intruder. Maybe it was one big one rat, although I don't know how a rat managed to open a drawer.

Another flash and then loud thunder struck, ozone perfumed the air. Vivid flashes in rapid succession and a shadowed man appeared with a glint of steel and in another flash, the man was gone. A shriek was about to come out of my throat, when a powerful hand covered my mouth. Panic flooded all of my senses as I was struggling with the vise grip around my body. My hands struggled to release me from the boa-like grip of muscular hairy arms. I squirmed and kicked my foot back, hoping I could damage something really delicate and soft, but my foot kept hitting air. I struggled to breathe.

"Shhhh," the human vise grip whispered, but when I didn't comply, it growled, "Would you shut up, I think someone is in your house."

Hey now, I mumbled through covered lips. His grip got tighter as I struggled some more.

"Calm down, Danni." He knows my name, now I'm terrified and squirmed in his arms but I couldn't fight him, he was too strong. "Danni, it's me," he whispered. "Shhh, it's me, Gabriel," and my body went slack from shock. *What the hell was Gabriel doing in my house, in the dark?* A stark realization hit me: He was trying to attack me. This really was a horror story, the man I really liked was a murderer, or worse, a rapist. *Damn.* He let me go and my feet hit the floor with a thud. He left and with a few clicks on the panel, all the lights chased all the shadows away in blinding light.

"What the fuck are you doing in my house?" This is after I tried to get my eyes adjusted to the light and convinced my heart the race was over. Feeling dizzy from all the blood rush, I uttered, "I really…need to sit down." I pushed past Gabriel and made my way into the living room. Nothing but dead silence ensued. Hmmm, I guessed he left and closed my eyes.

"Here, drink, and put this on your forehead."

Eyes snapped open, there was Gabriel standing with a glass of water and a dripping washcloth. I saluted him and did as I was ordered because frankly, I was thirsty. He left and my eyes tracked a tall Gabriel walking through the house, eyeing everything in sight.

"So what are you doing in my house, exactly?" I yelled loudly.

"I noticed the lights weren't on so I came over to check on you, and the door was open," he yelled from the bathroom. I heard the squeak and then a slam, *Good luck on closing that window.* Gabriel's voice echoed in the bathroom, "I flipped the light switch but nothing came on." Back from his excursion, he leaned against the living room wall and crossed his arms, "then," he scrunched up his eyebrows. "I thought I heard running water." He stood lost in thought, "also I thought I smelled something like vanilla."

"Vanilla?"

"So I made my way to the kitchen to check it out when you came in."

"Why didn't you say anything when I yelled out?"

"I wanted to make sure there were no other naked strangers in the house," he said rather sarcastically.

"Jackass."

"Is that the only name you have for me?"

"Well, it's the only name that seems appropriate at the moment." I bounced up, stood, and watched the living room spin. My knees buckled underneath and I was back on the couch, hoping the world would stop going around.

"Are you all right?" The concern in his voice sounded like silk.

"Yeah, just no sleep, no food, and a whole lot of adrenaline." I closed my eyes with the cloth in my hands. I expected him to leave, but the couch seat sank next to me and the scent of cedar, musk, and rain drifted around me.

"Here, give me that." He took the cloth out of my hand and put it over my eyes. The room was spinning into one big whirlwind.

"Why are you here?"

He grumbled, "I told you why, I was checking your house for you."

"No, I get that, but why are you here?"

He sighed, just then a flash of lightning followed by a clap of thunder rang through the air. The lights flashed off and on and then, finally, we were in pitch black again.

"Damn, I never catch a break!" I got up to go fix the lights. He grabbed my shirt and pulled me back down.

"Just leave it, okay, the lights will come back on eventually."

Well, this was turning out to be an interesting situation. Two people in the dark having no idea what to say to each other with only flashes of light to prove we existed in the shadows.

"Is he your boyfriend?"

"Who? Oh, Seth. Oh, god no. I dropped red enchilada sauce on the floor and…on him." I pulled the cloth off my face. "He took that opportunity to show how he felt about me and well…I kicked him out after you left." A sense of guilt washed over me and I laid the cloth back over my face, more so to hide my embarrassment than anything. "I'm sorry." My voice sounded desperate, needy. He slipped the cloth off my face, the lights flashed on for only a moment, and he was a breath away from me.

Then the house plunged into darkness. He whispered in my ear, "Shh." His lips gently touched mine and thousand butterflies launched flight in my stomach.

The lights miraculously came back on. *Thank you very much.* I catapulted off the couch to quell the thousands of wings fluttering around, no peep from the monster within, damn her, where is she when I needed her. "I don't think I should be involved with anyone right now." Pacing back and forth, I added, "I mean, my life is so complicated" *to say the least,* "and well…" and then suddenly soft lips stopped all the useless chatter. A slow heat replaced the shockwaves that rolled through my body. A cold hard thump hit my head, then another drop, all in midkiss and then the cold seeped into my scalp and the hot moment was doused by the rain.

He backed off. "What's wrong?"

"Leak," and what were just drops became a stream. *This sucks eggs*, I moved and he pulled me out the deluge and into his arms. The heat of his body blanketed me. Lulled into a haze, I mumbled, "I can't get involved."

"Danni, I know you're afraid." *You don't know the half of it there, buddy.* "It scares me, too."

"You're scared of what?" I searched for something to say and bunch of thoughts jammed into my brain, I started mumbling incoherently, "My life is so crazy and…." His finger covered my lips.

"You're loud, obnoxious, you swear like a sailor, but I find myself looking out the window wondering when you're getting home." He shifted slightly and, somehow, I was deeper into his embrace. "He was standing naked in your living room and I wanted to rip his fucking heart out." He embraced within the strength of his arms, "You drive me absolutely fucking crazy, but I can't seem to stay away." He cupped my face, "You're so beautiful," his eyes were an intense hazel surrounded by a brilliant gold. "I don't know what you're running away from, but it doesn't matter." The house plunged into darkness but I wasn't afraid anymore.

"I…." He lips touched mine and I was lost in a deep kiss, then he walked out the door. Stunned into silence, the lights broke the darkness and flooded the living room. The last sound of thunder rolled away and my only thought was, *Fuck, I'm in really big trouble*!

Chapter 14

My eyes fluttered open to my room bathed in sunlight. Beams of light washed the red and black colors of my blanket into pinks and grays. My fingers captured a ray of light and for just a moment, I thought I had touched the hand of God. Then, a cloud blanketed the beams and my room returned to a dull gray.

God's hand disappeared, so I got out of bed, wiggled into some cutoff jeans, and slipped a t-shirt on. Found my loafers, no bunny slippers today, and walked out the porch to check on my weeping lavender. It was much perkier, dare I say enjoying its new digs. Grabbing the hose, I wrestled with it and then gave the lavender a lifesaving drink. Water swirled around in the hole, creating a white froth mixed with chocolaty earth. *Hmmm, my lavender was having a spa day.*

The sun was hanging low in the sky and the air was crisp and cool. The long summer nights had faded into darkness and the days turned into fall. Fall fairs, crisp apples, and of course, the aroma of fresh roasted chili had perfumed the air. Halloween would be soon be here. Christmas was no longer a joy for me, but Halloween was my night. A night made for monsters.

Gabriel had disappeared into the ethers that night and while I missed him, his kiss lingering on my lips, I was a bit relieved. All notions of Seth had slipped my mind. I was finally able to breathe. Both of them really complicated the hell out of things. Tea would help unravel my life so I headed out to the coffee shop. The college kids next to me were studying and drinking copious amounts of coffee. *Must be midterms.* I would never know what college would be like. I never thought of myself as an academic, book bags, learning, being part of a crowd. Actually, I always thought of myself as a prisoner. I just exchanged a prison cell for lockup within my mind. A dark shadow crossed over me and I shivered.

"I thought I would find you here."

Startled out of my thoughts, Seth was hovering over me blocking out the sun. He was dressed in a purple button up shirt with a white collar and black pants. Everything he wore was ironed to perfection. Peals of laughter from behind him broke my stunned silence. We both looked down at the crow pecking at discarded bits of muffin.

"Seth, I haven't seen…" a vision of his nude body popped in my head. I cleared my throat. "I haven't seen you in a while."

"Church business," a horrible screeching sound rang through the air as he pulled out a chair. "I have been thinking about you, Dannielle Clearwater," and he flashed a smile that made his eyes crinkle like Santa Claus as he sat down.

"Oh," that sounded ominous, he never used my full name before.

"That last encounter I had with you did not go as I planned."

"Things did go a little awry, didn't they?" I smiled. "Sounds like a funny story you tell someone over drinks," and I chuckled. His smile faded in a callous frown and his eyes turned dark gray. Evidently, it wasn't all that funny to him.

"Yes, well, I know the next time we meet will be under better circumstances."

Oh, hell, "Seth," this could get out of hand if I didn't do something quick, "I think of you as a friend."

"Good, then you and I will go on a friendly date."

"Seth…."

"Say dinner tomorrow night around 8:00 pm." He got out of his chair.

"8:00 pm," *What?* "Seth, I…."

"Good, 8:00 pm, I will pick you up." He leered at me from the top of my head to my loafers. He pursed his lips from the invisible lemon he just ate. "Danielle, do wear something nice." Then he walked off.

Hey, what just happened here? The crow picked up a morsel on the ground, eyed me with one beady little black eye, and flew off.

The next morning, I woke up out of solid state of sleep from the persistent banging on my door. Through hazed covered eyes, the clock read a blurry four am. The knocking was relentless and I shoved the covers off in a fit of madness. *Who in the hell would be knocking in the morning like this, fucking A!* I grabbed my clothes and almost fell because I was disoriented and slipped on the bunnies to go meet the new corpse at my door. Stumbling, I wrenched the door open to find Gabriel all dressed up warmly in a blanketed leather jacket. The cold air dissipating any warm fuzzy feelings, I tried to leer through my hazy eyeballs.

"Wow, you're not a morning person, are you?"

"You think? What the hell do you want at four am in the fucking morning?"

He smiled like a very proud Cheshire cat. He stood there while my head pounded from the sudden rush of blood from being woken up from a dead sleep.

"Get dressed, we're leaving."

"What," I was yawning, "what are you talking about?"

Gabriel pushed past me and found his way to the bedroom. I followed dopily, wondering how he got in the room so quickly and what were the possibilities of keeping him there. He started looking around and picked up my bra from off the floor. "Here," he said, with a smile, "you can put this on, preferably in front of me." I grimaced, grabbed my bra, and hugged it to my chest. Then he scrounged more through the pile of clothes and found my panties with some interesting holes in them. He held them up, "Don't you think it's time for some new underwear and threw them at me."

"Hey, now!" The cobwebs in my brain dissipated and now I was getting pissed. "Get dressed for what, it's freezing out."

"Yes, I know, and it'll be even colder on a motorcycle, you'll need to dress warmly."

What kind of fucked up way is this to ask me on a date? He started digging through my drawers. "Looking for something?"

He kept prowling through my underwear and sock drawer, "Forms of entertainment, what do you think I'm looking for?" He pulled out a thong, eyed it, and then gave me a raised eyebrow. I grabbed that as well.

"Get out of my drawers! Asshole. I'll get dressed, all right." I pointed a finger towards the door, "now leave." He lingered for a moment. "What?!"

"I thought I could watch."

As I pushed him out the bedroom door, he stopped and grabbed the hammer that was on top of the dresser. "What's this for?"

I snatched the tool from him and put it back on the dresser. "Protection from intruders at four am." Then I booted him out the door, he turned around as I slammed the door in his face. I collected my scattered thoughts and jumped in my clothes. What the hell I am doing? God, how did he do that? I was sleeping, now I am dressing for who knows what? Did a quick breath check and ran for the bathroom for a teeth cleaning. Five minutes later, I walked out to the living room where Gabriel was looking at this watch.

"Bout time."

"Shut up."

"Here, put this on.

I questioned his soberness when I inspected the helmet, "Why am I getting a helmet with masking tape on it? I won't be able to see."

He looked at me like I was two years old, "That's the point. I've got a surprise for you."

That brought a five-year-old giggle and smile to my face. "A surprise?"

"Yeah, now get your jacket on and hurry up. We're leaving."

We rushed out the door and this time I double-checked the locks. I got on his motorcycle, put on my heavy-duty blindfold, and was encased in the dark. The vibration of his motorcycle rumbled through my body as we left. Movement without my eyesight left me befuddled as I floated above the ground. This is definitely where trust and faith comes in and I hugged him harder. Since I had no idea where I was going, I had no idea how long it took to get there till we came to a dead stop. I was about to take off my helmet when a warm hand held mine.

"Wait. Keep your eyes closed." As ordered, I kept my eyes closed as he gently took off my helmet. *Oh, god, I hope I don't have helmet hair.* Still dizzy from my early morning flight, a wave of early morning chilled air hit my face. The roaring sounds of fire surrounded me.

"Where are we?"

"You'll see in just minute." I forced myself to keep my eyes closed. My face was so cold and then soft, warm lips were on mine that turned to a deep kiss. The sweet taste of his lips lingered as he spoke. "Okay, open your eyes."

Impatient, my eyes sprang open. I tried to catch my breath as colossal, multicolored hot air balloons slowly rose from the ground like dead spirits coming to life. Giants before me wobbled back and forth, bouncing off each other. All around in different rhythms of fire rushed to propel the sleeping giants into the sky. Awestruck, I was stilled into silence at the sight of hot air balloons illuminating the dark morning sky, casting shadows all around. Gabriel just grinned at me.

"This must be what is like to watch a child open a Christmas present," he said. "Your eyes are so big."

"I'm trying to take it all in." I tried to see everything and watch each individual balloon, but there were too many of them bouncing in the sky. Some balloons were still on the ground waiting for the breath of life. They would fill with cold air and heat with each succession of propulsion. They would flatten and arise like a primordial heartbeat. My soul rose with every balloon and my breath released when the tethers broke away.

The flames that rushed to invigorate the heart of the balloon heated the outside and kissed my skin. His presence and his gift of love warmed me like a pool of molten metal from the inside. Then, I heard a cracking sound like ice underneath the sun and realized it was my heart beginning to thaw. A beautiful silent thought crept in. He was becoming home to me, and I shivered in his arms.

The sky was a kaleidoscope of balloons, colors of the rainbow with different sizes and shapes were everywhere. Each giant rising slowly until they became nothing but colored balls that could fit in my hand. More balloons replaced the ones that had ascended and it started the heartbeat process again. Floating candles lit the sky like fireflies. Mother Sandia was letting her kids play while she slept and I tried to memorize the colored light bulbs against an azure sky. Twinkled stars receded into the sky and blinked before they said goodnight.

A giant polar bear in a sitting position like a small child surged above the others and slowly faded away.

Gabriel gazed at me and then suddenly his warm hands were underneath my chin, lifting my lips to meet his. He backed away and left me shivering as the rays of the sun cascaded down on us. I put my arms inside his jacket and the warmth of his body replaced the chill. The flood of chemicals in my brain crashed the tide of cells and each nerve tingled with waves of sensations. He let go and the chill came back over me as we both watched the mass ascension.

The show was over, the balloons had risen, and the landscape was a dull brown with floating toys above us. The surprise was gone, the package opened, but it was a beautiful sight forever burned into memory. We walked back to his motorcycle and I picked up the helmet with duct tape crisscrossed against the visor.

"You'll have to take it off if you want to see." He got on his motorcycle and revved it up. *Guess the romantic moment just ended.* With all this newfound trust and faith, I decided to put my life in his hands and hooked the helmet on the back of his Harley. Then I heard the best words ever. "Let's ride."

We thundered out of the parking lot and on to the highway headed north. The New Mexico landscape rushed around us in waves of sand-colored houses and blue green sage. I was a child again, letting the neighborhood boy push the merry-go-round as I lay on the surface and watched the clouds spin into circles. Purplish-blue mountains passed by and all the trees were an artist's palette of color. The world zoomed past in a flash as I was holding on for dear life.

"You need to let go. I can't breathe."

"Oh, is breathing important?" My hands released each finger one by one, as I tried to convince my brain that this was the right thing to do. His chest heaved up and down as he laughed.

We glided past Santa Fe and made our way to Taos. We glided along a U-shaped turn in the highway and then parked at a rest stop, looking down into a massive panoramic view. Below us, the Rio Grande snaked its way into a sleepy little town protected by massive blue gray mountains. Above it all were pregnant clouds heavy in labor. We continued on till drops of rain pelted our bodies. Forced into hiding, we pulled into a gas station and awaited our baptismal turn.

Sheets of rain poured from the merciless sky, and I shivered from the cold even though I was holding on to a flame. "Cold," he whispered.

"Not anymore," and hugged him more. The rain finally stopped and the sun peeked above the mountain. Taos Mountain had a rough craggy texture, with rocks jutting out between dark angry clouds. But around the peak was a halo illuminated by the sun and I thought this was what God's face must look like. We left our gas station shelter and the sound of his exhaust reverberated through the twists and turns of Taos canyon. We finally came to a small cabin and the noisy beast ceased its chatter.

Moving my body and awakening stiff muscles, I scanned the horizon and breathed in the cool, crisp air. The landscape was picturesque of distant mountain scenes, tall green grass, and towering yellow aspens, quaking in the breeze.

"Where are we?"

"A friend's cabin. Unfortunately, it looks like he's gone." He was clamoring around the log cabin and peering into the windows.

"I think he's been gone a while." Tufts of weeds were bending in the wind and there were spider webs with dust encasing the thin strands.

"Yeah, I guess I should have called first. I was hoping we could crash here," and his hazel eyes were a mixture of mischief and lust.

Ignoring him, I peered in the window and willed the butterflies in my stomach to desist in their incessant wing flapping. The cabin was a small idyllic place with the mountains as the backdrop. This was a Lincoln Log cabin like I played with as a child, except in major proportion and I chuckled at the thought. The logs retained their skin and the bark was rough against my palm as I lifted myself up to look inside. The kitchen was simple, a couple of open pine cabinets with a few dishes, a wood-burning stove, and a small propane refrigerator. The living room had an old fireplace with burnt logs tucked safely inside it. A stone mantle with old wooden snowshoes crisscrossed above for decoration. On the floor were large planks showing every knot the trees had and in front of the fireplace, a bear skin rug was spread out, his teeth gnashing at the ash covered stones. Two leather rocking chairs with animal skins lay over their tops quietly, waiting for someone to begin rocking them.

"Come over here." I was so preoccupied with the cabin's décor, I didn't notice he had left and was

159

walking through the wet grass on a deer trail. I hiked along the rocky little path that led to a grove of trees. Putting my hand in his, we continued walking further into the quaking aspens and the air became still and quiet. It was a natural church made of wood as the aspens with starch white and black knots arched above us in brilliant gold. A river swirled around a bend and bubbled around boulders and stones. The sounds of rushing water soothed the riptide of nervousness I felt.

"It wasn't really the cabin I needed you to see." He licked his parched lips; his pupils became wider, and my heart quickened in a response to his eyes. He bent his head towards my ear and spoke in husky tones, "It was the bedroom I wanted to show you."

"Oh," was the only thing I could manage to say. The grove opened further down. He grabbed my hand and we walked past deer grazing in a field. Above us, pregnant, dark skies were waiting for the moment of birth as I followed him past a grove. A weathered old chair almost falling over marked a turning point in the trail. He led me to the bank of the river and laid an old Mexican blanket down.

The river sang a sweet lullaby and my heart slowed down to its pulse. He lifted my hair and moved my shirt off my shoulder to reveal a small patch of skin in the sunlight. My skin blossomed underneath the soft touch of his lips.

"What are you thinking?" he whispered.

Soft kisses followed the curve of my neck into a sweet surrender, but the shadows remained in front of me. I thought I had locked them a way, but they escaped their keyhole as an ever-present reminder to who I was. "Nothing, just listening to the river," and my voice drifted away because I had melted into his touch. He lifted my hair up more and then all his gentle ministrations ceased. It took me a moment and then I straightened up in tension. *Damn.*

"Danni, why is there an evil eye symbol tattooed on the back of your neck?"

I closed my eyes and racked my brain, searching for any word. How do I explain this? How do I explain the voodoo woman in prison branding me with her protection sign for helping one of her own? It was my saving grace from other tormentors in prison. But I wasn't completely sure if I had sold a large chunk of my soul to the devil in the exchange for peace.

"Stupid teenager and a dare." I turned my head to meet his eyes and kept my silence. He shrugged and bundled me up in his arms. It started so simply, a few stolen kisses as I touched his arm and entangled his fingers in mine. His hungry fingers lowered more of my shirt and exposing more of my skin to his warm fingertips, sending chills all through my body. I unbuttoned his shirt and put my ear to his chest so I could listen to the beating of his pulse. Gently, he brought my head up to meet his lips. The deeper the kisses, the more our hands looked for more skin to touch, each piece of clothing cast away. The universe pulsated around us as I laid the angel down beneath me. I straddled him and guided his way in.

With the strength of his arms, he held me up as he thrusted into me. "Don't turn away." He brought my face close to his and his hazel eyes burned into mine. "You're beautiful." My internal muscles reeled from the constant rhythm. The pulse of our bodies became faster and harder, until the final climax melted us into one. We collapsed as two souls blew apart and released the energy between the flesh. I fell hard from the sky and landed on earth. Our breathing was heavy till we finally heard the lingering adulations of nature in the echoes of the canyon. Around us, we lay in a bed of sweet smelling grass, earth, and the crackling leaves of fall.

We lay quietly in each other's arms and then reality literally bit me and my hand instinctively slapped a mosquito. Shaking, Gabriel pulled me closer and wrapped the blanket around me. Even as his body warmed mine, the woods become a cold and uncomfortable, beautiful place, and I began to fidget.

"Problem?"

Something hard and pointy was poking into my back. Somehow, I didn't think it was Gabriel. "Yeah, there is a rock underneath me."

Exasperated, he said, "You're not much of an outdoors girl, are you?" as he pulled me up. Naked in the woods, I suddenly felt very vulnerable and began looking around for any garment I could find. They seemed to have been flung here and there.

"How did ya guess." I swore we gently laid our clothes aside. Something white caught my attention. He saw them first, grabbed them, and swung them in front of me. With one raised eyebrow he said, "Silk underwear." I grabbed them back. It was my new choice to replace the holey underwear. I maybe guilty as sin, but it doesn't mean I have to wear cotton underwear in hell.

Gabriel was half-clothed, leaving only his bare chest exposed. Underwear in place and pants on, I was still searching for my elusive bra. How far could one bra go? I was definitely starting to feel some gentler parts of my body react to the cold.

"You must be cold," his voice muffled as he poked his head through the t-shirt.

"Really, what was your first clue?"

He had a huge grin. "Hurry up and get dressed."

He laughed at me, and at first, I felt indignant. Then I started to smile at the absurdity of being naked in the woods. He came closer and uncrossed my arms. Each of his ridiculously warm hands held each breast and his thumbs encircled my erect nipples.

"Stop," I choked out, although I really wasn't sure that was the word I wanted to use.

"Are you sure? They seem cold to me."

He pulled me closer to him as the sun peeked through the clouds and disappeared, leaving only rays of light to guide our way back. Looking up at him, the light from the escaping sun reflected from his hair and created a halo effect. I quickly turned away and looked for other far-flung garments. Finally clothed, we stood there amidst the cooling air and listened to the wind enrapture the trees, bringing a slow, soft rhythm to our ears. "Are you ready to go?" His head was on top of mine, his arms around my waist.

"No," I whispered. I didn't want any of it to end.

"Neither do I." We scampered up the trail and looked behind us. Our nest disappeared into the church of the aspens and behind the veil of sunset. I wondered if we would ever see it again. A sudden wet blanket covered my heart and smothered it under the weight of the wool.

We made our way back in the cool water of the night and the sound of the motorcycle broke the song of the crickets in the woods. Headlights whizzed past us like the fireflies I tried to catch as a child. My eyelids grew heavy as the cool wind whipped by and I laid my head on his back. The lights of the circus were below me and the stars above merged into one. I felt so small, like a little lost girl, and I kept calling for my daddy, but I couldn't get off the Ferris Wheel. The wheel kept spinning and I would come close to the tents on the ground and my little hand reached out. But the wheel kept scooping me away, suddenly I was atop, and then I would swoop down again, reaching out for anyone to help me. Then the Ferris wheel came to a sudden stop. Warm fingers were wiping my tears away as I came back to reality.

"We're here." The sound of Gabriel's soft voice cleared the dark fears away. We had arrived back at his house. My heart was starting to calm down from the free fall. "Was it that bad of a ride?" He inquired with a grin, although his eyes remained heavy with concern.

Stiffly, I got off the bike and looked at his watch. It was two am. "Shit, I have to be at work in the morning."

"Go to sleep, I'll be here when you get back." He nibbled on my ear, "Come straight home after work."

I brushed his cheek and his lips explored my own. Walking away from love, I felt the last tips of his fingertips fade away. In a dreamy haze, I began my journey home, when I was grabbed from behind and tipped over.

"That is to me remember me by." He gave me a deep, lingering kiss.

Spinning me back up, how could I forget him? He got on his motorcycle and backed out. I started singing, "I can see the red tail lights heading for Spain, oh, and Daniel…."

Until questions broke the song, *Where was he going this late?* But warm feelings and sleepiness fuzzed over the puzzle pieces and they vanished into thin air. Dreamily, I floated above the sidewalk, thinking about the man on the motorcycle. But in the hollows of the streetlight, a face from the past floated around me, his face turning ashen as he faded into death. A sickening feeling came over me and my feet landed hard on the sidewalk. My foot stuck on a crack and I put my arms out to catch myself but managed to find my balance. *Fucking A!* My feet dragged as I came closer to my house and shadows of fear crawled up my body.

My house had no lights on and I racked my brain for a logical explanation. Of course, I was rudely awakened, which made me grin from ear to ear. But as I got closer to the house, uneasiness had settled in, and I chanted, "There's no place like home, there's no place like home."

The gate creaked open but nothing else, and I thought something was missing. Fatigue settled into my shoulders and I shrugged, trying to release the tension. The door was steps away and lovely illusions of grandeur crossed my heavy eyes as I wished for a tall, dark, handsome Gabriel to be in my bed. Thoughts about downy feathers floated around me as I fumbled around looking for my keys.

"Damn it, where are you?"

A flicking sound broke the silence, as a flame illuminated his ghostly face with two soulless eyes staring at me. The small flame lit the cigarette and then with a click it was doused leaving us in heavy shadows.

"You're late." His words were ice-cold as he stepped out of the shadows.

Petrified, all my muscles froze; the apparition stepped into the light of the streetlamp. "Seth." My body eased and quickly, I went back to digging in my purse. "You scared me. I didn't see you...I didn't see you standing there." *Damn, damn,* where are those keys? I shook my purse, hoping that a forced earthquake inside my purse would shake them up. "What are you doing here?" I remembered the answer before the question was finished. Oh, yeah, fuck, I had completely forgotten about the dinner I never really had agreed to. "Seth, I'm so sorry." I really wasn't, but it seemed like a good thing to say.

He took a seat on the porch, with only a small burning light illuminating his mouth. The acrid cigarette smoke scented the air and burned my eyes. "Do you know how long I have been waiting?" His voice made my skin crawl, and my spine cracked as my back muscles pulled on each vertebra.

The chair screeched and suddenly, he was before me. A weak streetlight illuminated half his face in eerie gold and the other side remained in dark black. A cigarette light tip came to his lips and highlighted a hideous grin. He put his hand on my shoulder and the weight of his hand bent my shoulder down, "You do not ever keep me waiting." Icicles came out of his mouth, and I shivered. The light of his cigarette fell to the ground and I was frozen to that ash. "It's all right, though, I forgive you." His voice suddenly changed into the Seth I knew. He kissed me on the forehead. "You and I will make another dinner date." Then he walked by me and left me standing with the sounds of my bones rattling.

Chapter 15

The next morning, I bolted up and then held my head. I felt hung-over without the fun effect of alcohol from the night before. Dawn's early light came roaring past my curtains and pierced my eyeballs like bolts of lightning. My body ached from the long ride and quite possibly the misuse of other muscles. Sleep deprived, I tried to remember the paranoid dreams of black and white feathers drifting down from some enormous battle from above. But I could never see what was happening, only wisps of smoke that always seem to cloud the battle up above.

What woke me up abruptly was the incessant phone ringing. Through hazy squinty eyes, I checked the clock's bright shiny numbers, indicating it was only ten in the morning. I threw the pillow against the clock and knocked it over, *who the fuck calls me at ten in the morning?* I slammed the bunny slippers on and picked up the phone.

"What!"

"Rise and shine! It's going to be a beautiful day."

"Harvey, shut the fuck up."

"Bad night," I heard him snicker.

I just growled. There was nothing like a happy Harvey when I was feeling particularly grouchy. I heard the loud exhaust of tailpipe blasting in. I looked between the shutters and it was Gabriel in the same outfit he wore yesterday. My fist slammed the shutters closed.

"Carolina, still there?"

"Yes, what the hell do you want?'

"Well, aren't you a ray of sunshine."

"You know, Harvey, this not a particularly good day for chit chat." I looked down and my bunny slipper ears were all asunder. I kicked them off and flung them against the couch.

"It's probation call time. I'm checking on my little angel to see how she's doing."

I peered between two shutters and couldn't miss the pile of used cigarettes. A small, very hairy chill slowly crawled up my body. Each leg of panic stuck its leg in every nerve.

"I heard there was another murder last night."

That shocked my fuzzy brain cells back into existence. "What?"

"Yeah, some girl a few streets down from you." I had a sudden craving for a morning newspaper. My stomach turned to knots, but I didn't know what it was, could be early morning interruptus.

"Carolina, are you there?"

"I'm here, Harvey," but just barely.

"Carolina, are you being careful? Maybe, it's time for you to leave."

"Define 'careful.'"

"Carolina! I'm serious."

"Yes, of course, I am." But I had no inclination to run at the previous moment. I was so tired of running and well, it had been a while since the photograph. Maybe this time, Snake would leave me alone.

"That girl was murdered only a few blocks from you."

"It was probably a house invasion."

"No, Carolina, um…it's like all the other murders."

With that announcement, my blood began to drain. I peered out at the window again and watched Gabriel clean his bike. "How would you know, you live in Chicago."

"I have my ways of keeping up."

Harvey's voice faded out, as I looked closer at Gabriel's gas tank. Soft, white feathers reflected Gabriel's every move. I blinked and they were gone. Great, now I need glasses.

"Carolina! Are you listening to me?"

That snapped me out my haze. "What!" I heard a deep sigh in his voice.

"Carolina, I'm just concerned."

"I know, Harvey. How's the wife and kids?" I needed to change the subject big time. We talked of other things and for one small second, the warmth of someone else's family calmed my nerves.

After our conversation, I went outside and pushed the pile of cigarette butts off into the dirt and tried to cover them up with my foot. Then, I picked through the defenseless lilac for the newspaper and whispered underneath my breath, *Damn paperboy*. I had anticipated big headlines, but there was nothing about a new murder. Maybe Harvey was thinking of a different murder; however, he knew one small detail. His voice was in my head. *She was only a few blocks from you* and I rubbed my arms to calm the hairs that were rising. Heavy metal music broke my fear momentarily. I would have to ask Harvey about that little tidbit of information later and that train of thought left the station and never came back.

I glided over to Gabriel's house and watched his body move as he cleaned his bike. Each bicep moved in rhythm to the music of the rag going in endless circles, he stopped, glanced over his shoulder and caught me staring. He kept cleaning, but with much more vigor and many more muscles being exposed.

"Just gonna stand there and watch me?"

"Why not, it's good entertainment."

He turned around, threw the rag down, and held out his hand.

My fingers entwined with his. "I missed you, where did you go last night?"

His face turned dark and he popped his jaw. "Work."

"Oooh, touchy, so, what's the issue with that?" His muscles tensed up and his biceps became hard rocks. The lines of his cheeks became harder and his eyes were intense shade of golden brown.

"I was hoping we could avoid this."

"How do you avoid where someone works?"

He unlocked himself from my hand, picked the rag up, and started cleaning again.

"Gabriel, tell me, I've pretty much heard it all before." I touched his arm and he jerked his arm away. "Fine, asshole," and took a step to leave. *No one needs this kind of shit in their life.*

"I work for Michael's, does that satisfy you?" He kept wiping his motorcycle, making the skull in the tank shine with an eerie grin.

I finally tore my eyes away. "Michael's?"

He turned back around. "You've never heard of Michael's?"

"Nope."

He breathed a resigned sigh, "How can you be the only girl in town who doesn't know what Michael's is?" I shrugged my shoulders.

He licked his lips. "I work for a gang, all right? I'm their bouncer for that bar."

"Oh," still no light flashing on what the problem was.

"Don't you get it, I work with criminals. Probably am one, except I manage to keep my head above water." I couldn't stop it. It began in my belly with a chuch and then out my mouth, a deep laugh that bent me over.

"Are you psycho? What are you laughing at?"

Between bits of laughter and trying to catch my breath, I said, "You're worried about what I think of where you work and of you?"

"You're laughing at me?" His face was turning red and his eyes were becoming enraged.

Stifling the laughter, I was finally able to gather my composure. "You're a fucking idiot."

"How so?" His arms were crossed.

"Do you not know where I work? I work for Marco's." Now, his face drew a blank and then finally the moment of *Oh* crossed his face. "There are convicts on parole who are my best friends, not to mention Marco has a bit of a crime reputation himself." There were rumors that he had some ties to a crime family in Chicago, but I don't go chasing rumors. His face eased and his eyes calmed down from enraged to hazel. My laughing hysteria eased but I couldn't stop smiling.

"Just shut the fuck up and come help me." He put his hand out and I grabbed it, but I couldn't help but break up in fits of laughter all day.

Gabriel and I spent some days together in the Indian summer, riding in the Sandias, following the roads like meandering snakes. We hiked different trails in the mountains and looked for forgotten coves of trees. We would take day trips to small sleepy villages like Madrid and talked of nothing in particular while we looked in the shops. Nights were spent in passionate embraces as we tried to tear at each other to get our souls. Sometimes, we just sat in my kitchen and drank tea or coffee, depending on the mood.

Afternoon light spilled in from the window and the scent of fall permeated the air as I was paring an apple. I peeled away the skin in one long green and white spiral until it fell into the sink.

"I never saw anyone peel an apple like that before."

My heart sank as I stared out the pane of glass. Memories of my mother bubbled and ran over and I tried in vain to stop the flow. The material from the back of her coat, the heavy suitcase pulling her shoulder down, and her walking out the door into the bright sun came pouring in. A peeled apple she handed me in fall. "This is how my mother peeled apples."

"I've never heard you talk about your mother."

My throat tightened and I could hardly speak, even though it had been thousands of years, I was pushed back into pain of the moment. "She left when I was very young." The silence blanketed us both.

After a while, he looked at his watch. "I think it's time for you to go to work." He pointed at his watch like he was an old school marm and I had just showed up late for school.

"So," I walked over and put my breasts directly in his face and stood over him. "Maybe I'll call in sick," I bent my head down and placed soft kisses on his neck.

"No," he pushed me away from him, "you need to go."

My voice had a distinct sound of huffiness and hurt, "Sounds like you're pushing me to go."

"No," he pulled me back and whispered in my ear, "I've got some stuff to do and if you're here, I will never get it done." He wiggled his eyebrows at the hint as he stood and towered above me.

"Just stuff?" He shrugged his shoulders, gave me a kiss on the forehead, and left. Well, huh…I just got blown off. Work was the subject he avoided as much as possible. But since I was avoiding things about my life, it was only fair he got to be vague as well.

Later in the afternoon, the phone rang and I was expecting to hear Harvey's gravelly voice. Instead, just some stupid asswipe was breathing into the receiver. "Hello, hello!" More sounds of deep breathing. "Whoever you are, I advise you seek help," and I hung up the phone. I went to go take a drip shower to erase the creepy feeling I had.

It was late in the evening when I got home from work and my back and feet were killing me. Gabriel was waiting for me on the porch, kicking the rest of the cigarette butts off that I had missed. He had a worried look on his face but when he saw me, he lighted up and immediately my body responded to his smile. Cigarette butts be damned.

"Let's go to bed." Walking right past him, I went to the bedroom, slithered out of my clothes, and stood naked before him. A moment later, the heat of his skin touched mine. He kissed my neck and began a symphony of soft touches across my body and suddenly, I didn't feel so tired anymore. Melting into his warm embrace, my fingers caressed his back and shivered at my touch. Laying him down, I engulfed his body with my legs and drew him into me, letting pulsating senses dictate the rhythm of the music we made. He brought me to a crescendo with each push and pull and the sounds of our lovemaking ended the symphony. Afterwards, I started to drift off into never never land when I remembered something and jumped out of bed.

"Hey, what are you doing?" His arm that had been holding a warm body a second ago plopped on the empty side of the bed.

I picked up a white cloud on the floor and put my arms through his t-shirt. Soft cotton drifted down my body in a large formless dress. The rush of air cooled my skin and I crawled back into bed and knelt before him. My hair fell past his face and his nose crinkled in reaction. My fingers unknotted the leather tie that bound his hair and waves of black cascaded down his back. His muscles twitched underneath as I ran my fingers across his bronze skin.

I pulled back the curtains and opened the window. The fragrant scent of autumn drifted in as he put a finger down my arm and he left a trail of goose bumps behind. He nuzzled my neck, "You're cold, come lay down." He tried to pull me back down into the mattress.

"Give me a minute," I whispered softly. His hand went under the t-shirt and felt up my back and bolts of electricity jolted through me. The reaction was immediate and I arched my back and my breasts were in his face. Warm liquid enveloped my nipple and I looked down to find his lips sucking through the t-shirt. My mission was starting to fade away and all I wanted to do was go back to the warm body next to me. "Stop, just …uh…um… just one more minute…oh, gawd, and you can do whatever you want."

"Oh," his hand seemed to be in all the right places at once. Reluctantly, I pulled away and felt one hand remain curved nicely around my butt cheek.

"You're full of goose bumps," he chuckled softly. I gave him little wet kisses on his forehead as I fumbled for my battery-operated candle on the windowsill.

My face and other hand were occupied as tried to feel for the switch. I'm way too safety conscious to have a real candle. Finally, goal found, I switched it on and a pretend flame fired up and a soft glow was cast across the room. Dark shadows and soft light accentuated all his muscles and made the scars shine even brighter. I couldn't but help touch them. But I didn't ask about the reminders of the pain he endured. I wasn't sure I could handle it.

"What's the candle for?" He nuzzled my neck.

"Safe harbor."

I nestled back into his perfect spoon shape. He was so warm against the cool night air as I started to drift away. In the haze between awake and sleep, Gabriel's placed feather kisses on the back of my neck while the slightest scent of fall leaves and musty earth wafted all around us. Outside my other window dry leaves crackled. Something was outside as I looked at the window, a faint shadow passed by. All my muscles tensed as my skin crawled. Then the wind whistled around the house and I eased back into his body. *It was only the wind.*

Gabriel apparently had heard nothing as he whispered in my ear, "safe harbor," as he was making lazy circles in my back and caressing my skin, easing the goose bumps back down.

Sleepily, I said, "My father told me about these lighthouses. In the midst of a storm, the lighthouse keeper would light a flame from the shore and sailors could find their home while they battled the torrent seas." I yawned and drowsiness was starting to take over my senses. "I figure my house is my safe harbor." Lazy circles on the small of my back got lighter and then his arm came under mine. He hugged my stomach and drew me closer to him. Delicious heat from his muscled body poured in waves across my back and I was completely encapsulated by warmth and love.

In my sleepy haze, a memory drifted in through the window of playing with sand castles on the shore with my dad. I mumbled, "My dad loved the sea so much that he named me after one of his favorite places."

The pillow moved under his sudden weight and his mouth came closer to my ear and nibbled, "There's a place named Danielle?"

My eyes snapped open. "Huh, hmm," and I pretended to go back to sleep.

He lay his head back down and started to breathe heavier. "Dannielle by the sea, maybe we can go there," and he drifted off to sleep.

I was wide awake.

Chapter 16

In predawn's light, I started to finally fall asleep, when I heard screaming from the man next to me. "No, don't! Leave him alone!"

"What! Gabriel, what's wrong?" Gabriel was thrashing around in his bed, tearing the covers off him. He was still not waking up to the tone of my voice.

"Gabriel?" I tried to touch him, but that made him jerk harder.

"Leave him alone! Leave him alone!" Then he grabbed his side with the long-jagged scar and the nightmare receded into the shadows.

He jumped out of bed and the sheets floated around me. His secrets were begging to come to the surface and they found a way through the crack of nightmares. Gabriel searched around and picked up his pants. "Gabriel, talk to me, tell me what's going on?"

"You got a lot of nerve. Talk to you," he said sarcastically, "I have my secrets, too."

That stung and then his pained expression clouded my hurt. His cheeks were still flush and tears were beginning to well into his eyes. "There's nothing to be embarrassed about. It was just a dream." He gave me a cold, hard stare and continued to clothe himself. "Gabriel," I whispered ever so slightly.

"Don't!" His voice was cold and sharp. I pulled my knees up to my chest and remained still and silent. He was fully dressed now and walked out the bedroom. He hit the bedroom door as hard as he could and stopped. He bent his head down and his hair cascaded around his shoulders.

He choked out, "I'll call you tomorrow."

"Sure." Then he left.

All day I waited for his call. I cleaned around the phone, jumped at every sound, but the phone never rang. My life continued but I replayed exactly what happened that night like a constant spinning wheel, but I could never figure out what the problem was until a revelation scorched through me. The secrets we held between us made the wall of concrete that couldn't be torn down. Maybe this was the sign, time for me to go. But it didn't feel right. It didn't seem the right time to leave. Fall was the worst time to leave, I determined, that's my story and I am sticking to it. The war between, who would control the weather, summer or fall, resulted embattled thunderstorms.

A few days have passed and no word from Gabriel, *what did I do?* Seth, neither called or dropped by, and I hoped he never did. My emotions over Gabriel twisted like a tornado through me and ran ram shod over the landscape of my soul. However, those deep breathing phone calls continued to haunt me. Maybe I should pay a little extra for call id, but I figured it was stupid neighbor kids with nothing better to do.

The phone rang. I ran towards it, hoping I would hear that familiar voice on the other side. But it was just heavy breathing. I slammed the phone down and went to the bathroom to wash the disgust off my face. *Damn kids.* Raising my head from the sink, I had sudden sense that eyes were boring into my back and I turned to see a dark shadow quickly pass by. I ran outside to my bathroom window, but there was nothing but a tall weed moving back and forth in the wind and a faint scent of vanilla that disappeared with the breeze.

The *Albuquerque Journal* was stained, beat up, and flaccid looking as it laid across the counter. The latest murder splashed across the front, DESERT KILLER STRIKES AGAIN. Harvey was right. But how did he know before the paper did? The question rolled around in my mind as I wiped tables down. The cops surrounding the one table were in a buzz. Lucky for me, there were some tables that needed to be cleaned right in the same proximity. After the routine items of no blood, rosary, and all the other unhelpful information I wanted about the latest murder, the name Dahlia was whispered across the lips of cop I had not seen before. That definitely piqued my curiosity. That cop sat back with one arm over the chair and a toothpick in his mouth. The nametag on his uniform was Chavez.

"Hey, Sarge, do you know any more on the Dahlia Tatum case?" He was one of the cops I had seen earlier.

The sergeant grabbed his cup, swirled the coffee around, then he put it back down, his eyes looking pensive. He pursed his lips. "They found a clue. One hair was found on the body."

"Well, hopefully they catch the bastard, probably an old boyfriend of hers."

The new cop sat there. "Yeah, I guess, but something didn't seem right about that scene. I think there is more to it." The transmitter on his uniform squawked and both cops paid their tip and ran out the door. Putting the change in my pocket, *cheapskates*, that latest clue burrowed itself into my conscious like a thorn and I could never pick it out all day.

Driving from work early, I noticed my neighbors in a deep conversation. Angelica was playing with Kelsey and Dolin. Since Gabriel had not been around, I was feeling a bit lost and decided neighborhood gossip was just the key to lift my spirits.

"Hey, guys, what's up?"

"Nothing much, just talking," Riley said in her Georgian accent, but her eyes had darted over to Carson. They were up to something. Angelica ran over and put her arms out. I scooped her up and gave her a tight hug, filling an empty space in my heart. Riley beamed; Angelica seemed to be breaking out of her shell.

"So, tell us about Gabriel?" Riley chimed in. "We're dying to know."

The heat rose to my cheeks. Not knowing who the neighbors were was definitely an advantage.

"He's a great guy," I blurted out through a pink mottled face and put Angelica down to run with her pack.

"Oh, come on, I think you can give a little more that!" Riley said with exasperation. She acted like I was denying her the greatest gossip in the world.

"Well," my eyebrows raised and the heat from my cheeks could cook an egg. I squeaked out, "I don't know, I'm still getting to know him."

"From the looks of things, looks like you already know him well," Carson mentioned as she was watching her dogs play with Angelica. I don't think Christmas tree lights could be redder than me.

"Ahh, you're blushing. Oh, well, another one bites the dust," Carson teased. "No woman can stand a chance against those eyes." Very true, I never did stand a chance.

"He is one good-looking man." Riley said in a lustful Southern voice. Carson just cracked a smile and I blew bangs out of my eyes. Right about then, the devil so to speak came home; he looked over and went immediately into his house.

Riley tilted her head and then spoke, "I wonder when he stopped dating that redhead he brought home the other night."

"What!"

Riley looked at me, "Uh, oh." She turned her head quickly away.

"What redhead?" I just gawked at Carson.

Carson just shrugged. "I've been noticing a redhead go in and out of his house for a couple of months. But I'm sure it doesn't mean much." She quickly looked away. It was starting to mean something to me. A need to go kill something came over me. Without saying another word, I marched over to my house and began slamming and kicking anything not nailed to the ground. I was being played for a fool. In a frenzied moment, I picked up pig cup and flung it across the room. The cup hit the wall and the sound of breaking porcelain rang in my ears.

Looking for anything else to take my aggression out on, I found the refrigerator. I did a swift kick to the door and hit it hard. "Ow, son of a bitch! Mother fuck a duck, ow! My foot! My foot!" I grabbed my foot and hopped on one leg like a lunatic. Then I limped into the bedroom and hid underneath the pillows.

"What the hell is wrong with you? I heard you yelling from next door."

Startled, I cracked my skull from hitting the windowsill. "Son of a bitch!" I yelled and grabbed my head from the sharp, piercing pain.

"I was worried about you. Are you all right?"

Now he is all kisses and kindness. I threw the feather pillow at him and he caught it right before it hit his face. *Damn it.*

"Would you like to tell me what the fuck is going on?"

"Who's the redhead, Gabriel?"

"Redhead?" Sudden dawning came across his face, "Oh, you mean Charlie?"

"Is that her name, Charlie? Where have you been? You haven't called or anything?" The whine in my voice pierced my ears. This wasn't supposed to happen; I wasn't supposed to like him this much, love him. *Oh god help me.*

He put his hand in his hair and slicked it back. "Sorry, I had to take care of some stuff and I really couldn't talk about it."

"What stuff?"

"I can't talk about it."

"So who's the redhead?"

"I can't really talk about that either." I got off the bed and grabbed the pillow from his hands and hit him with it. This time, I heard a rip and an innocent looking feather came out of its protective home.

"Well, you better start talking."

184

"Look, Danni, I can't discuss anything with you."

I started to cry. "Is she your girlfriend?" I picked up the pillow and threw it at him. This time, he just let the pillow hit him. More feathers came out of the pillow and gently drifted around us. It was beginning to look like winter and it matched my heart.

"Danni, you're starting to lose it. Did you really think you would be the one I would date exclusively? I mean, look, we just started and well…I'm not quite sure I was ready for a relationship anyways."

"So I'm a series of one-night stands?" I could feel the tears well up in my eyes. *I'm not gonna cry, I'm not gonna cry, damn it, I'm gonna cry.* I thought we had something more. How come I am never clued into these things?

"Danni, we'll talk about this when you are more rational."

"Rational!" I gave him a cold hard stare. "Oh, I am very rational," and I crossed my arms. "So what, am I a midnight booty call?" My voice was quivering and my foot began to ache. He stood there like a deer caught in the headlights, "Get out! Get out!" I screamed at the top of my lungs.

He put his hands in a fist. "I'm not leaving, so just fucking calm down."

"What did you just say?"

"No, of course not!"

"Of course not, what?" Blood was roaring in my ears.

"You're not just, just a one-night stand. I can't tell you what's going on." He started to pace back and forth. "You don't understand, I wasn't supposed to get this close to you, this was not how this was supposed to be." He was talking to himself and then he reared up and slammed his fist into the wall. Dust fell from the vigas on top of his head and shoulders. When he turned back around, both of his hands were in fists.

"So gonna hit me now," I sneered.

He looked at his hands, "Fine," and he stormed out and slammed the door. *Why was he storming out?* And I threw another pillow at the door as it vibrated from all the assaults. I marched around in circles and then I paced back and forth, but nothing would abet my anger.

"Holes, I need to dig some holes." Flinging the backdoor open, I stomped out to my backyard and began digging one monster hole to China underneath the Siberian Elm. Dirt flew everywhere and once in a while, a feather from my head would gently drift down into the hole. I loved good old-fashioned anger; unfortunately, it was also the key to unleashing my insane side. Anger was an adrenaline rush and I was this close to opening Pandora's Box and releasing myself upon the world. The monster within me was rising and crawling up my insides. My friends from work could provide me with the very weapon that would do the most damage. I envisioned the frightened look on Gabriel's face as a bullet pierced his skull. I wanted to watch the blood pool around his head. My monster was sending images as I braced the handle of the shovel.

After hours of nonstop digging, my energy finally gave out and I plopped onto the ground. Hurt, sore, and tired, I just lay there and encircled the rim with my body. I wretched into the hole and then cried some more. The monster encased in a tired body receded into the black depths. I think sanity was starting to come back to me. I hated sanity; it made sense of things.

Pushing myself up, I limped back into the house and followed the feather trail to the bedroom. The bed was a mess of feathers and dishevelment. I plopped into the middle and all the feathers flew into the air. Little feathers puffed up around me and gently fell across my body. Exhaustion overwhelmed me. I could no longer move and cried myself to sleep as the rays of the afternoon sun washed over my back.

After my tantrum, well, my major blowout and then rest period, I went to the kitchen to look for pig cup and then the sound of porcelain hitting the wall made me cringe. The wall had splattered black and brown drips down to the floor. Pink porcelain with black spots littered the ground and a piece with a sad little eye stared straight at me in dismay. This was what my heart must look like, shattered pieces and none so easily glued back together. Amongst the chips and broken pieces was one whole piece, a swirly tail. As I walked out of kitchen, moo cup followed my movement with a look of shame and fear etched across his face.

Sunset was fast approaching. I peeked out the front door at the house next to mine. There were no lights on, no movement, just a dead stillness at Gabriel's house. Resigned to my fate, I went back inside and decided now was the time to begin packing and steal away in the night. Then I stopped in midtracks and surveyed the landscape of my home.

My house looked like an explosion from the feather factory hit it and not to mention various other things that got thrown in a rage of passion. *Oh, hell!* I went to go look for a broom, mop, rags, my brain, my sanity and searched the closet for rational behavior. I dug every cleaning tool out and began the process of putting pieces of my life back together. I spent what seemed like hours limping and cleaning up feathers, broken glass, torn up papers, and anything else that got in the way of my rampage until I was utterly spent.

Hot and sweaty, I limped out unto the front porch into the cool night to check out the neighborhood, well really to check on Gabriel's house. Disappointed that I still didn't see any telltale signs of life, I parked myself into a chair and surveyed the homes down the street. The neighborhood seemed eerily quiet, and wondered where everyone was tonight? Our street looked black as coal, with only the mismatched patterns of porch lights and streetlights casting surreal ghostly patterns.

Humidity was rising and the sweet scent of rain was christening the air. The moonlight illuminated heavy, dark ominous clouds. A soft breeze picked my hair up and cooled my sweaty skin. Dad's goat was parked, waiting for action. The windows were down, huffing, *Can't I ever catch a break*, and limped out to the car and rolled them up in record time. Disaster averted, let's be real, no one likes wet leather in a car and hauled myself back to the house. Seven crows flew in and lined themselves on the fence. Each black bird screeched at me one right after the other. Incensed, I hobbled over and waved my arms, "Damn birds, get out!" Their wings flapped and circled around me as they took flight from their indignation of leaving their resting place. Pushing the gate open, the slow creak of rusted hinges grinding against each other rang through the air, but no clank from the cowbell. It must have dropped on the ground, *huh, I wonder when that happened,* and tried to recall the last time it rang. Something else to put on my to-do list for tomorrow.

A low growl emanated from my stomach, breaking the still of the night. Right, food, and I hobbled into the house, flipped the switch, and nothing happened. Son of a bitch! The lights were out again. A flash of brilliant blue light streaked down and broke the darkness of the kitchen. Crack! The sound of thunder reverberated through the air, making me jump and I clenched my toes, causing the abused foot more radiating pain. "Ow!" *Lord, help me, this was going to be a long night.* More streaks of lightning flashed across the backyard and, for a moment, everything in the backyard was cast in a beautiful radiating blue light. Searching the cabinets for anything that would dull the pain, I found some aspirin and felt my way looking for a glass. By touch and feel, I found the cold, hard steel of the faucet and got a glass of water. Another lightning strike and a dark shadow of a man was in my backyard. The glass slipped through my frightened hands and shattered into a thousand pieces. The lights turned back on and there was nothing in my backyard but the elm tree swaying in the wind. There was a monster in the backyard and I realized it was just a projection of me. The glass sparkled in the sink but I was too tired to care about cleaning it up.

Feeling restless, I hopped to the door and leaned against the frame. I wondered what he was doing tonight and hoped he was just as miserable as I was. I really wanted to talk to someone, but my recent scan of the neighborhood indicated that no one was home. Disappointed with no one to rant to, I decided to go stand underneath the showerhead and have slow, big drop of water pour on my head.

After my "shower," I toweled off the remains of the day. There was an old, white t-shirt of Gabriel's hanging flat on the hook. The scent of his cologne had saturated his shirt and I buried my nose in his scent and floated the shirt down my body. Tea would help soothe my ramshackled nerves and headed towards the kitchen. A soft vanilla scent permeated the air and wrapped itself around my senses. I pushed the door to the living room open. SLAM! My body was thrown like a rag doll against the wall. My head cracked loudly as it bounced against the adobe. I tried to get up, but my head felt like a knife went through it. My eyes were completely crossed as I tried to concentrate on the blurry figure before me. My chin was forced slowly up.

"I'm going to enjoy this," was the last thing I heard from the familiar voice. I tried to form the word "Help", but I took a breath and felt fire run through my lungs. Dots formed and bounced in front of my eyes, blackness encroached upon my vision. Then the last remaining light faded into black.

When I came to, I lifted my arm to touch my head, but my arm was stretched and I couldn't move it. I tested the other arm, but it also was too stuck. *What the hell! I must have really slipped on something.* My eyes opened slowly to piercing light, which brought a bolt of pain. "Ow!" A wave of nausea followed the dagger of light that sliced its way through my eyes. I slammed my eyes shut to stop the blinding pain. But I had no choice, I needed to move. Reluctantly, I lifted my eyelids cautiously so only bits of light could get in, which was better. It wasn't blinding anymore, only searing. Finally, both eyes wide open, I twisted my neck both ways and was shocked to find that both of my arms were tied with a red chord cutting into my wrists. There were a thousand stings all across my back and legs. When I wiggled, I heard a crunching sound that coincided with a thousand more stings. Looking down, I was tied spread eagle, a red spotted sheet laid across my body. Blood had formed in spots, marking my pain in psychedelic dots. My heart sank and panic enveloped me, I had been laying on a bed of glass that cut me every time I moved.

"You're finally awake. Oh, good, I thought it might be getting too late in the evening for you and me." He clasped his hands together. "Such a naughty girl being with that other man. I thought you only had eyes for me."

I swallowed hard, his eyes were flaming blue. "Seth!"

Chapter 17

He was in a chemical suit from head to toe and his hands were gloved in blue latex. "I am going to enjoy you so much, Carolina." He lowered his body close to my own and inhaled and slowly breathed out. "I do love the smell of that soap." Quivering from shock, I looked into his lifeless eyes. "Surprised, are you?" He put a blue latex finger to his lip, "I researched everything about you. You are a very bad girl, Carolina." His eyes became gentle and soft. "I can release you, Carolina. I can ease your pain."

Fear curled from my toes to the very tips of every single strand of hair. I started pulling on the red chords willing myself to break ties that bound me to him. A thousand sharp cut stung my back and I screamed with every inch of my being, "Fuck you!"

His pupils were wide, black, soulless disks. Shaking from pain and fear, he whispered right in my ear, "You are going to be so delicious," and he took the knife and slowly sliced a cut across my upper right arm. A blood-curdling scream reverberated off the walls, the sound of my pain pierced the air. He dipped his gloved fingers in the knife wound and dabbed it on his lips. His tongue came out his mouth like a snake and he licked his bottom lip. His eyes got dreamy, "Yes, you are very delicious, maybe a little bit too salty," he cocked his head to the side like he was tasting batter, "but definitely worth waiting for."

The tang of fear on my tongue, my throat parched from all the screaming. Every little twitch I made cut me further. I was completely vulnerable, spread eagle, a sacrifice on an altar. Nausea was gripping my stomach as I was going in and out of consciousness. He was stroking my hair, the latex pulling on my scalp. Pain pulsated as blood dripped down my arm. "Oh, Carolina, let us take a long look at you and then pray." He slipped the sheet off. Gabriel's t-shirt was in bloody shreds across my body. Seth knelt beside me, knife in hand. "Relax, Carolina," he said, and patted my stomach, "this is going to take all night. So do enjoy it, won't you?" His eyes were large black holes, with only a small ring of blue that surrounded them. A rubber-gloved hand lifted one breast. He made concentric circles on my nipples and they responded hard to his touch, humiliation burning through my body. "Isn't this like how Gabriel does it? I have been watching for pointers." Tears welled and dripped down the sides of my eyes.

I was going to be sick and yelled, "You fucking bastard!" to the stop the bile. *Please, stop.*

His hand released my breast and then they crawled down my stomach, inch by inch. A stream of tears wet the pillow as his finger circled my belly button. Then, slowly, he worked his way even lower. He toyed with the most sensitive part of me and I willed myself to remain like a stone to avoid the glass shards invading my skin. He fingers encircling and moving in a rhythmic motion sent electrical impulses up my body.

Ashamed, at my body responding to his unwanted touch, my mind screamed no.

"Ah, yes, I think you like this, Carolina." His voice faded in and out.

"No," was all I could whisper.

"Oh, but yes." His hand became harder and deeper.

My tongue tasted like steel where I had bit it when I landed against the wall. My body was shaking uncontrollably, but I didn't know if it was from blood loss or sheer panic. Then all sensations stopped. Too afraid to look, a drop fell upon my cheek. My eyes fluttered open for a second and caught a shiny bright star. A blurry image of me reflected in the knife before me.

"This is my favorite blade. It is quite dull, you see." The latex glove shredded when he touched the blade. "Carolina, Oh, Carolina." He closed his eyes. "You don't how much peace I get from cutting your skin in two." Then he opened them again and stared into space. "Watching the skin split apart. Blood released from its vessel." He stood up and there was strange calm about him. "Let me show you," and slashed my thigh. I screamed out, but it didn't sound like me, it sounded like a wounded animal. After the initial shock of excruciating pain, black dots floated in my vision. I was fading fast. He lifted my head so I could see the rush of fresh blood pool spill over the side of the bed. Tink, tink was the sound each drop of blood made as it hit something metal. Blackness crept in and I dove deeper into my darkest dream. Something shocked me back to the present. I couldn't tell if a few minutes had passed or hours. My cheeks burned white hot. His hand stopped slapping me when my eyes opened.

"Don't think, Carolina, you can fade away. We have so much time together. Here, drink this, my dear, it will perk you up a bit," and he gave me a small sip of something sweet. His hand was on my stomach, making small lazy circles that grew ever larger further and further down. I was bracing myself for more degradation when he stopped abruptly. "Hmmmm, it's time." The blade dragged across the path of a rib bone leaving only a superficial well of red. My voice wailed, so alone and pathetic, like a distant coyote call.

He slithered back up to my head, "Carolina," his face was so close and the vanilla scent turned my stomach, "You are going to be my best ever." His nose was in my hair and he took a deep whiff, "I will savor our time." Blood was on his lips as he kissed me. I tried with all my might to turn away, but he held my head in his hands like a vise grip. "God, you taste delicious!" and smacked his lips. My body was trying to save me from any more torment by shutting down. My arms and legs were becoming numb. The more I reacted, the more his face seemed to glow with pride. The more I tried to slide away from him, the more the glass effused into my skin, becoming one with all my cells. Pressurized sand mingled with my life force, and I was becoming see-through, a pane of glass for the madman.

I managed to choke out, "Why?"

"Why?" Seth clicked his head to the side, "Why, to save their souls of course." He sat on the bed and the color of his eyes returned to serene blue as he was contemplating something. "Except I love…. I love watching them die, laying my hand on their chest and feel their last breath's vibration through my fingers." My eyelids were becoming heavier and heavier. The thunder outside was getting closer. Death would ride upon the clouds and save me.

"Awwwww!"I shrieked as took the tip of the blade raked down my arm.

"Shhh, I need to just…." His hands were inside his suit. His face turned soft and dreamy. "I just need time." Essence of me was pooling on the floor in rivulets of red, tink, tink, as blood hit the pan. I had to think of something that would make him mad, something other than me to focus on. I tried to speak, but the words were sand in my throat.

"Oh, your poor throat is so dry, drink some more." He put the cup to my lips and I turned my head.

"Now come on, dear, we must keep up your strength." He tried to pour it in my mouth but I rebelled and paid for it dearly as the glass moved deeper into the already forged cuts. "You are not playing nice, Carolina, but I do love when you act like that." His eyes sparkled like diamonds every time he cut me. I searched deeply into his eyes for a spark of humanity, but all I saw was the deprivation of broken soul in a cracked mirror. He was simply a cold-blooded killer playing with his food.

Something clicked in my haze, whispered conversations from men in blue. "You really messed up on Dahlia, didn't you?" He straightened up, his shadow from the bedroom light loomed across me. The thunder was booming in rhythm to its own symphony and my eyelids were so heavy.

"No, no, no Carolina, you are not going to fade away on me!" His voice lilted up an octave as he was trying to bring me back with little slaps, "We have so much to talk about. Revived once more, he asked, "What did you mean I messed up with Dahlia?"

His face was chiseled into angles, his skin stretching tight across his cheekbones. I had struck a nerve. "They found a hair of yours." Enlivened by this game of cat and mouse, I continued, "Did she pull your hair?" I said mockingly. I laughed at him like children who tease each other, nah, nah boo, boo. He stared at me and then his face turned from cold hard stare to soft glow.

"No matter, they'll never catch me." He paced up and down at end of the bed, his back muscles flaring. "Stupid bitch, when I slammed her against the wall, it didn't seem to faze her. She was a karate champ who tried to do those karate chops on me." He mocked her karate chops as he paced. "She was a cunt," he stopped in mid pace, "which made her blood all that more pleasurable," his eyes drifted out the window, "to watch her die." He sighed, "The harder she fought, the more she bled out. Her death was quicker but she screamed just the same. Actually," he put a finger on his chin and tapped it in deep contemplation, leaving a bloody fingerprint, "she thought she would always be safe. Yes, I must admit I was a bit careless on that one."

Mistakes, mistakes, I had to think of more. But my mind was so cloudy and there were little tiny dots again bouncing around my eyes. For some reason, I started to hum the national anthem. "For the rockets' red glare…" my parched throat faded my voice into thin wisps.

"Here, drink this," roughly, he picked up my head and exposed my neck so that my jaw was slack. The fluid came faster than I could swallow and I was going to drown in sweet liquid.

Gasping for breath, he stopped pouring. "There you go, my dear," and then he patted me on the shoulder like I was a little blonde child in pinafore and a red ribbon bow tied in her hair.

Choking from the assault, I said, "Rockets' red glare gave truth to the night that our flag was still there." Growing weaker, a thought passed, *Please let this end.* Thoughts of Gabriel drifted in and out of my consciousness and a deep, encompassing warmth filled my empty heart. I loved him and he would never know how much. My angel who saved my soul from the darkness of loneliness and I had slammed the door in his face. Tink, tink, tink the drops were slowing. Ethereal visions of him came to life. "I'm coming, Danni, stay alive!" *I'm fighting, I…will stay alive for as long as I can, please hurry.* "Awwwwww!" another cut, another slice, and the visions disappeared. All the pain was blending into one and sparked one last taunt. Lifting my head to face him, I said, "They have your hair now. It'll be no time at all. I heard they have more hair on file," then I slowly lay back down. That was the last grain of sand I had in the time glass.

He ceased all movement and stood as cold as stone, "Impossible, I am meticulous." But I thought I heard a slight crack of uncertainty in his voice.

Things were getting blurrier and it was impossible to think, "Rockets' red glare" and my body shook. It was very cold and I wished for the heat of Gabriel's body next to mine.

He got close to my ear and whispered sweetly, "This is what Gabriel does to you. I've seen you and him, your nights together." His fingers were inside me, pushing in and out, "Oh, yes, I've watched you very closely." He stroked harder and I shook in revolt to stop the violation.

"There it is, the shake, your body trying so hard to keep warm. Whew, I am so very hot in here, I think I will open a window." My battery-operated candle, my safe harbor in the storm, was knocked off the sill and bounced into the weeds.

"Tsk, tsk, Carolina, you should have replaced that screen." Normally, the cool would have been of relief but now it seemed as cold as winter. The scent of the impending storm was wafting through the air. I breathed in the aroma of earth and rain mixed together, my last breath would be of something beautiful.

"Rockets' red glare… bursting in air, you're going to jail and they will fry you…flag was still there." Still humming into the fading darkness, a memory invaded my dreams. "Small cell, dark and closed."

"Shut up, you stupid whore!" He yelled at the top of his lungs.

Oh, *did I just hit a nerve*. "Do you know what they do with evil like you? They put you in small, dark places."

"Shut up, shut up!"

"And then they shut the door!" My eyelids grew heavy, his voice ranting in my ear about death, blood, his mother as I hummed about small, dark, and lonely places. I opened my eyes just to see the cold steel above me ready to slice. Looking straight into those ice-cold eyes, I muttered, "Small space, four by six jail cell, small, ever so small." Beads of sweat formed on his temple. A singular memory of him pushing me up against the wall waded through the clouds, "No wonder you had to restrain them. You can't get it up unless they're tied down and screaming." A small giggle was coming out of me; like a cascade, the laughing became uncontrollable. He was nothing to be feared. Something clicked, a childhood memory flashed back of monsters in the closet and a tape recorder, *Oh, dad, where are you*?

Seth was all over the place. He looked lost and confused, and definitely angry. He wasn't deriving pleasure from me anymore. Little shivers were starting to spasm through my body. I found a purpose for my life—if not for me, then for the others who needed to be saved.

My throat was closing, "Seth" but he couldn't hear me. He was too busy ranting and knocking things over. I mustered all my strength and yelled, "Seth!"

He quickly came over to me. His eyes were pools of ice blue madness. The knife was above his head, poised to slice. A thin red line streamed down the blade and one fat drop plopped between my eyes.

"Seth," the knife drew closer. Slowly, I spoke concisely, "The cell was so small. I couldn't breathe when I was in there, so small, so constricted." He ceased his taunting and stood, his eyes turning from cold seas to frightened blue. "The lights…," and I swallowed hard, "…goes dark at night, pitch black." The blade started to shake in his hand. "You don't know what you're doing, you really messed up on that last one." His face turned white, a blue vein formed in the corner of his eye. "Dahlia must have been your first. You're a fake, a copycat, you're not the real killer." With that, he screamed and tripped over a pan. My ears detected a faint splashing sound as blood rushed over the bowl in a tidal wave. My blood spilled on the floor, seeping into the corners and crevices where it would congeal and crust.

He came close to my face, spittle on the side of his mouth. "I'm the only one!" and he beat his chest with the bloody knife, "I'm the only one, no one else," the knife in his hand slashed across his arm. Blood dripped down his arm onto my body. He got quiet calm after his release, "Look at what you made me do. Well, I'm just going just have to wash you even harder, aren't I?"

"You lie. You know nothing about the real serial killer."

"You think those idiot cops at that pizza place know something. They know nothing!" He growled. "Those rosaries on the girls and the way I positioned them in prayer, I did that for show, Carolina, just for show. I was bored and wanted to watch them speculate on the symbolism of it all. Being a reverend was a way into their door. Who would you trust more, a reverend or some guy off the street?"

Good point. "If you know so much, tell me more about what you do with those girls." My body did an uncontrollable shake that stiffened my neck. My head was spinning.

He laughed. "Trying so hard to stop the inevitable." He sat on the bed next to me. "I have time, Carolina." He licked his lips and wiped his face of splattered blood. "Just before they die, when their breathing grows shallower, I cradle them in my arms and gently place them in warm water. Gently, I bathe them and wash all the filth away." His eyes were dreamy, "Shampoo their hair, put conditioner in it. They become so beautiful, so innocent, so clean." His mouth slacked, his eyelids were drooping. He became deathly quiet as he drifted into a murderous heaven.

I had to keep him talking, "You only killed what, a couple of girls? I think that other serial killer killed more."

He bounced off the bed and yelled, "There is no other serial killer! It was all me!"

A cold chill seeped into my body like a mist coming ashore. In the distance, I heard a faint rumble. Bursts of lightning flashed quicker, the thunder exploding in quicker intervals. *Just a little more time till the rain comes.* "Prove it." He stood over me, the seas of his eyes were raging. "Prove it, prove it, prove it!" I was yelling to keep myself from washing away.

"I killed in almost every state," he sneered, "but nothing gave me a sense of peace, until I came here." He drifted off as though musing on something. "Maybe three, in Utah. Hmmm, I forgot about Utah. I like Albuquerque. Its women so easily culled with a cute smile and a dashing man with a collar. All those idiot religious people telling them to trust in a man of god, their faith in me was laughable," he said like it was sad comment on life in Albuquerque. "Besides, I like the weather, adobe walls, nobody hears the screaming."

Sharp pain ran through me like sharp bolts of lightning striking all over. Close to my ear, I heard "It's okay, Carolina, you're going to be fine."

"Gabriel?"

"No, no, it's me, Seth," and he had that beautiful evil grin that used to melt my heart.

"Ahh, you are shivering." He pursed his lips, "Poor thing."

Brain fuzzy, I tried to think. He pulled on the shredded and bloodied sheet to cover me. As he was tucking me in, he hummed the national anthem. I licked my lips, my last ditch effort for more information. Shivering, so cold, "I bet they laughed at you," and he turned on me.

"I know what you are trying to do, trying to hold on. You keep hoping for miracles, Carolina." Outside the sounds of thunder mixed with the roar of his motorcycle. "You think if I talk more, I won't kill you. I have been dreaming of this night. I am going to put my head, right here," and he dipped a finger in the knife wound and drew a heart on my chest, "and listen to that last thump, that last slow beat of your heart." He whispered in my ear, "But, since you are so interested in my past, I will tell you everything you want to know. Keep in mind it will makes things that much slower." He pounced on the bed, straddled me, and showed me the bloody knife, a glint of steel against the drying crust of my blood. "Yes," and his eyes turned away from me. "Yes," he laughed, "I do want to tell you everything, I want you to know all about me," he sounded so surprised. My eyes grew heavy as he began his story.

A loud thunderclap drove me out my haze, "Small cell!" I heard him laugh very hard.

"You fell asleep on me, no matter! I'm getting tired. See this rosary?" My eyes went down the wooden beads to the body of Christ stretched out in agony. "Time to put your rosary on and then I will make sure you have it between your hands. It really does throw the police off." He lifted up my head gently, placed it over my head, and put the cross between my breasts. The time was coming.

Seth whispered, "Let us say a prayer together: Now, I lay me down to sleep."

I closed my eyes and echoed his words, "I pray my soul to keep." There was a cooling sensation from where a tear dropped out of the corner of my eye into my hair.

"Good night, Carolina." He grinned and the knife rose above me. A clap of thunder rang in the air and vibrated through the walls. A flash of light blinded me as something heavy fell across my body. Water droplets glistened on my face. The rain smelled so sweet. *I made it*, and darkness encroached on my vision and I rescinded into the blackness.

Chapter 18

"Danni!" The voice seemed so familiar. My body felt released and became lighter than air. "Danni! Wake up, please!" Gabriel's voice was only a whisper as the pulse of my heartbeat rushed in my ears. "Danni, come back to me." His breath brushed across my cheek like soft feathers. "Carolina, don't go."

My eyes fluttered and looked into the eyes of love in shades of gold and deep brown. Behind his shoulder were beautiful white wings engulfing me in a protective bubble of light. My hand reached out to touch the rounded edge of his soft wing. My fingers deftly played with the feathers. They were so soft and a brilliant pearlescent white that I had never seen before. They were unearthly. Every feather was layered perfectly on top of each other and my hand slipped and left a smear of blood. Guilt and shame encompassed me because I had left a poisonous stain on something so beautiful. "You're so beautiful, Gabriel." My breath was becoming slower and the fear of my death was dissipating into the air. I wasn't afraid to die anymore.

"You must be in bad shape," he smiled. The room and Gabriel became wrapped in a veil of haze. His lips were moving. "Just stay alive for me. Please, Danni, if you can hear me. You're gonna be okay." The haze blanketed his words and then I felt a vibration beneath me. Every cut was becoming electrified with pain. I was being cut again, "No! Please, stop!"

"Carolina, just hold on a little longer. We're taking you to the hospital. I'm so sorry I left you."

With what strength I had left, I choked out, "Don't let me go! Don't let me go!"

"Carolina."

"Dad?"

He was hazy and I was trying to reach out for him. "Don't worry. You're safe."

Peace came over me in waves as I told him the three words I never got to tell him before he died, "I love you, Dad."

"Shhh, Carolina, I love you, too. Now, go on and play, you'll be fine." I turned around and went back to the swings on the playground. I kept swinging until I was above the treetops, waiting for the moment I could fly away.

Something painful poked my arm, the room was white and hazy. Where was I, heaven can't be this painful. Oh, god, I was back in the room, screaming, "Seth, please, don't. Stop!"

"Shh, Danni, it's okay, you're with me. The nurse is just giving you something for the pain. I won't let anybody hurt you again."

"Seth?" I said weakly.

"I shot him." The pain stopped as I drifted into slumber.

My eyes popped open as I looked for Seth and his knife. But I didn't see any threats. The ceiling was gray and white. I rolled my eyes around and saw green-shaded walls. Panic struck through me. Oh god, I'm back in prison. I tried hard to remember what happened, but my thoughts were like thick tar. Did I do something bad? Faint, constant beeps invaded my ears like mosquitoes in a swamp. Plastic tubing filled with swift cold oxygen coursed through the cannula and into my nose. Warmth seeped into my cold hand and distant voice said, "It's okay." But it wasn't okay. I wasn't okay.

"Dannielle, it's me Gabriel." My arms moved freely—weren't they tied? With one hand, so tired and weak, I grazed my throat.

He brought a small plastic glass to my parched lips. The water ran down my throat and cooled my thirst. The nurse came in all chipper with a happy smile and I wanted Gabriel's gun. Couldn't she see I was trying to die? "Hello, Miss Clearwater, you're up when you should be sleeping."

She was puffing up my pillow. My voice cracked, "So sue me," and I tried to sit up but a thousand little Seth knives just skewered me and I lay back down.

The chipper ass nurse stood there for a moment, wrinkled her nose, and then she turned around and hustled out of the room. A second later, she came back with a little white paper cup, "Here, take this," she commanded. All her chipperness had disappeared. Slowly, the milky liquid oozed down my throat as the bitterness made my face scrunch up. In lightning speed, my body turned to mush and there was no more pain.

"This is good shit, more please," and everything turned to black.

I wondered in a haze of soft gray walls that disappeared underneath my fingertips. Soft, billowy sheets surrounded my every move and I was trapped by endless material walls. A long, white cotton hospital gown covered my body, except for the bandages that were wrapped over every cut, every slice that Seth had made, they oozed blood and pus. Struggling to breathe, I ran around in circles looking for the exit, but I found nothing but the soft feel of silk running through my fingertips.

My heart beat erratically and loud drums banged to the rhythm of my heart. Bandages around my legs and arms unraveled into bands of dark crimson. Red strings cut into my wrists and ankles and pulled me like a marionette. A large white door appeared before me and I knew that door would lead to my salvation. Desperate, my hands reached for the golden knob, but my fingers touched only the still air, it was moving away inch by inch. Anger and frustration filled my lifeless body as I tried to grasp that handle, but my feet were stuck in red-caked mud. Red chords lifted my arms and legs and hoisted my lifeless body above the mire. Now, I was dancing to something or someone else's rhythm, my body controlled by an evil force as the white door disappeared. The air rushing through burned my lungs and throat.

A familiar voice whispered in the nightmare. "Shh, shh, Danni, it's okay, shhh, go back to sleep." That voice so rich and deep, so loving, cooled my fever and the gray receded to dark.

The blackness and gray shadows returned to my dreams. Hellfire burned through my body, but I did not see any flames, just gray and peeling ash. My monster rose and tried to protect poor Carolina. A tall mirror edged in red stained glass crept up from the shadows. In the mirror was an insidious being who was twisted and torn, a deep gravelly voice spoke, "I must take care of you!" Bile rose, burning its way up my esophagus; weakened, I fell on fours, heaving. "No! I refuse to let you be!" I screamed at the reflection and heaved some more, twisting and willing my body to keep the monster captured. Death and destruction would scourge the earth if it was free. Howling like a dog, I tore off the bandages that held my skin. Globs of skin oozing like melted plastic came off my hands and puddled on the floor.

The monster tried to break free by scratching from the inside out and in the process killed the last shredded remains of my being. The last remnants were in a pile slowly dissolving, melting into the shadowed gray floor. Something crawled out of the remains and began to grow, but I was fucking helpless. I was nothing more than a puddle of skin and bones as I reached out for the monster.

I tried crawling across the haze and screaming, "No! I won't let you!" Nothing but goo and bile slipped through my fingers. The pain was excruciating as flames burned through my bones and licked my skin. I was in hell but I could not, would not, let the other escape. It must be consumed by hellfire as well. I must bind it and swallow it whole.

A cackle ricocheted all around me, "Oh Carolina, I have something of yours. Come find me." Seth's voice rained down in echoes, "Oh, Carolina, come play with me, you are so delicious. I want you." A crow's voice called my name, "Carolina, oh, Carolina." The sound of his voice made me retch. Death and disease permeated the air and suffocated me. The floor melted as I slipped through the threshold. Screams of all the women murdered shattered my eardrums.

Landing hard, I pulled myself up and I was standing in a circus funhouse surrounded by multiple deformed me's. Seth stood there with a huge bloody knife scraping his cheeks with it, a crow on his shoulder cawing with teardrops of blood coming from its eyes. Ash and cinder floated all around me. In one mirror, my skin was black, tarred, and oozed fire like an exploded volcano. Seth was behind me in all the mirrors and I turned to reach for him, but he stepped back and revealed the being on the floor.

She was the most beautiful and ethereal creature splayed across the floor. Her face was soft and pale like a lily, with pale green eyes, and luminescent skin. "Carolina, it's me," she echoed my voice. "I have always been here but you must fight for me," and then Seth brought the blade across her throat and a bloody line formed above the blade. My hand turned to ash when I reached for her. Something strangled me as I tried to scream. He taunted me, singing, "I'm going to kill her, I'm going to kill her!" My feet were frozen.

But Seth was slowly morphing, his features changing before my eyes. As I reached for him, his cheekbones and eyes changed to something eerily familiar. His face dissolved and reappeared as mine. Pale green eyes and cheekbones like mine reflected back at me. His lips became my soft red lips and Seth's hair had become long and curly. His body took on my curves. Seth's transformation was completed and I faced myself. The only difference was now, I had the eyes of a predator. An evil grin smacked across my lips and brought the knife across the beautiful light and killed my soul.

A deafening scream echoed in my skull and I awoke thrashing in white sheets. My wrists were still bound. I thought I had been saved by an angel but it was only a dream. I was still tied to a bed of glass. Seth was restraining me, holding me down. "Get away from me," my voice was nothing but parched earth. Panicked blurred my vision and all I could see was a tall, shadowy man. "Get away from me!" The dim vision yelled as he held me down, "Nurse! Nurse! It's okay, Danni, shhh," I kept thrashing but Seth kept holding me down.

I fought the shackles and the lights came on and blinded me. "Danni, this will help," and it was a woman's soothing voice. I didn't remember Seth ever having a high-pitched voice. This was a new game he was playing, but I opened a teary eye and took a breath. It was a woman in a teddy bear scrubs injecting something into the I.V. Sunset crept across the landscape and I had no more strength left to fight.

"Go back to sleep, Danni," and I looked over at a hazy figure. My vision cleared momentarily. He had dark circles underneath his eyes and his long black hair was escaping from his ponytail.

My eyelids grew heavier and heavier. "You look horrible, Gabriel, you should get some sleep."

"Thanks a lot."

"Hmmmmm," and I became lost in the darkness.

211

My eyes would open to sunlight and other times a black and gray room. Fatigued and soulless, I chose to remain under the darkness of my eyelids. When I could no longer avoid asleep, I saw Gabriel slumped over across my legs. His magnificent hair splayed out and his chest ebbed and flowed with each sleeping breath. My eyelids closed like a coffin lid, and I had a most subtle dream that I had crashed upon the barren landscape filled with dark grays and shadows. The sun was distinguished, leaving a permanent sunset, and I wondered if I would ever see the dawn of that luminescent light again.

Hushed male voices awoke me out of light sleep. I opened my eyes slowly, to see two fuzzy shapes by the door. I concentrated on the whispered voices and one hazy figure spoke. "You need to leave, Gabriel, you can't be here." His voice was gravelly and had seen too many days of smoke passing through his lips.

"I can't leave her. Not like this," Gabriel said in hushed voice. The heart monitor beeped in rhythm as the two men seemed to be at a pissing contest of major proportions.

"Fine, Gabriel, but bring her home and that's it." The man shifted his feet, "You leave her till after the trial. You're a liability." Under hooded eyes, I could see the other man tapping Gabriel's chest hard with finger. Slowly, my lips said the word "asshole". Both of them stopped talking. I slammed my eyes shut, then the testosterone babbling began again. I lifted one eye to see Gabriel glaring at the figure before him. The other man was decked out in policeman's uniform and a hat underneath his arm. *Was this Halloween? Did I miss the policeman's ball? Dad didn't mention it.* "I'm serious, Gabriel."

"Whatever." *Nice comeback,* I thought sarcastically. In a drug-induced haze, I was worn out trying to identify that strange man in the costume and deduce any information from that conversation. Last sound I heard was the creaking of the seat next to me. A warm hand covered my own and it was slice of heaven. "Go back to sleep, Carolina," Gabriel's voice whispered in my ear.

He called me Carolina, and my frozen heart locked behind a safety barrier called out for him, but the sound never passed my lips. As I fell asleep into a nice, warm, fuzzy feeling, a twinge of fear crept in, but I couldn't put my finger on what.

Chapter 19

As the haze of dreams and nightmares were receding back into the closet, I became more aware of my surroundings. Every cut from the glass burned and I swear I could feel every stitch holding my skin together. It was much easier being in a drug fog, where reality did not cut so deep. Finally awake, my mind became sharper as I waited for the pain to numb. I took in my new prison cell. I noticed an old, cracked TV with a fuzzy picture fading from life. Its tube was growing tired with electrical impulses.

My room was institution green. The floor was white tile and the fluorescent lights illuminated every boring detail, no paintings, no color, only a box. Rays of the sun streaked around the cracks of the blinds, struggling to chase the darkness away. A tear formed, and then spilled down my cheek. I was a manifestation of a human being neither living nor dead. A spark of light tried to reach me and I put the pillow over my head to escape.

"Hey, Danni, are you awake?" he whispered the question.

I moved the pillow slightly and saw a floating bouquet of flowers of gold, reds, and greens bounce up and down. In the bouquet was happy daisies and bright yellow roses bounded by green leaves.

"You're finally awake," the flowers spoke. I was on a hell of lot of drugs. Gabriel put the flowers down beside me on the hospital table. Each daisy seemed to eye me with big eyes, judging my happiness. I quickly looked away. They could shrivel up and die as far as I was concerned.

"I take it I have been out for a while," I croaked, my new talent would be frog impressions. He poured some water in a glass and brought it to my lips. I wondered if my lavender plant needed a cool drink.

"It's been about five days," Gabriel said, just looking at me perceptively. What could I say? His put his hand on my leg and I jumped. His touch seemed like a pulse of blazing energy that I wasn't used to and he quickly pulled his hand away.

"Sorry," he cowered. I wondered if he thought he had touched a cut on my leg.

It wasn't pain but I couldn't describe to him that love was burning a feeling I just couldn't take at the moment.

"How are you doing?" he asked sheepishly.

"Good, I think." I wasn't ready for the pity party quite yet. I don't know what I needed at the moment— an axe, a gun, something very pointy with Seth in front of the target, but pity wasn't it.

"Good...that's real good, good, umm, more water," and he jumped, poured air into the glass. He looked down the pitcher and pointed towards the door. He seemed rather excited to get some more water.

My throat felt scratched from the tube that was in it or I was just really irritable, who's to say? This is going to be a long day at any rate. Tension was thick in the air between us, and I found it hard to breathe. I didn't have the energy to ease whatever thoughts he was having about me.

"You know..." he kept clearing his throat, "if you need to talk...," he shuffled his feet and looked away. "I'm..." he swallowed, "I'm here for you," He was looking for a place to put his hand, gave up, finally rested his hand on his knee. It was painful watching him trying to acknowledge the pink elephant in the room. I, on the other hand, am a master at avoiding all pink elephants.

"Noooooo, all good here." I heard sound come out of his chest in sigh of relief. "I don't think I will ever want to talk about it," and I meant it. I'm sure that pink elephant can be locked in a small ring box.

"Damn...." He began to breathe heavily and paced around the room, "I won't pretend to know what you went through. But I think ...you need to tell someone, a therapist, maybe?"

I shook my head.

"Danni, please," he looked at me with his achingly beautiful brown eyes.

"I said no, Gabriel." The words came out much harsher than I anticipated.

"Danni...."

"Can we talk about something else for just a little while, please?"

"Okay, yeah, whatever you want. Let's watch some TV." I breathed a sigh of relief, conflict avoided for now, but it probably would rear its ugly pink trunk again. *Punk ass elephant, stay in your fucking box.*

During my recovery, fall had collided into winter in a storm's heartbeat. A growing silence crept between us and coldness seeped from my skin. I couldn't keep warm and kept Gabriel at a close distance. He seemed so hot to the touch and I was afraid I would wash away in the tide of sadness and depression. I was trying to hold onto something, something that I was losing on a daily basis. So many things were lost in the storm, pieces of me were scattered all over, and I had no energy to look for them. Finally, the day came; I was released with drugs in hand and dressed in really loose clothes. My destination was back to the house of pain and torture. An evil ship had crashed upon the shore and destroyed my safe harbor.

Gabriel drove me home in his beat up pickup truck and the trees whirred by into one blur. The cracked window framed a picturesque scene of snow falling gently to the ground. The clouds were heavy in various shades of ash and mimicked the weight I felt. All the colors of the world had drained into one, an endless gray. We drove up in front of my home and without my permission, my body shook uncontrollably.

"Are you all right?" His voice was soft and full of worry.

"Yeah, just cold," I was an existing human being with no soul and the fury of the wind and snow was blowing straight through me.

"I thought maybe you would want to stay at my house for a while. I could make a fire for you." His voice was becoming distant as I fixated on the front door. My house looked like a picture perfect postcard with snow on the flat roof and, in front, piles of puffy white snow lay on the ground. Brown vigas poked through the winter puff and guided my way towards the house.

The windows were black as coal, creating a ball of fear in the pit of my stomach. My house had lost its soul, too. Outside the house, the Siberian Elms were naked and hung low with the weight of the snow. At one time, winter had been the most magical time for me. The peaceful solitude of soft, velvet snowflakes drifting all around me, catching snowflakes in my hand and watching them melt.

"Did you want to go in?" His question broke the stillness and a moment of peace.

Am I wanting to go in? No, not really. Under soft eyelids, I glanced at Gabriel. He was hunched up with his jacket collar over his ears, concern riddling his face. "No, of course not, but it's something I gotta do." My feet crunched in the snow as I got out of the truck. The sound broke the eerie silence of winter and all before me the landscape was a frozen hell. Standing at the gate, the fence was empty of cawing crows that had taunted me earlier. *Fucking birds.* We went up to the door and stood silently. He reached for the doorknob and I stilled his hand, "Alone," and he stopped in surprise. His face became awash with questions that I couldn't answer. His eyes were such a beautiful brown, full of light, and warmth against a painful cold background. He nodded his head and stepped back. He understood all demons were faced alone, but it was nice to have backup.

His fingers touched my frozen hands, "I'll be right here if you need me." Flakes of snow blew all around and landed on his outstretched ethereal wings. Last time, they had surrounded me in feathery warmth; now they were ready for battle. Remembering the bloody spot I had left on his wings, I slipped into the house like a thief.

Gloom and depression reached out like fingers against my skin and down my neck as I started to choke. Immediately, I wanted to run back out. But by steel determination, I stayed my ground and let the house get familiar with me again. Step by hesitant step, I walked further and what seemed like miles was only a few steps into the doorway. The walls seemed like they were closing in on me as I continued my battle into the house.

The adobe walls were smooth and cold as I ran my hand along them. With the flip of a switch, my house was illuminated. I stood in shock. I had imagined my house in disarray with yellow tape crisscrossing everywhere, furniture tumbled, blood spilled and splattered across the walls. But it was pristine. Gabriel must have come and cleaned everything for my eventual arrival. I couldn't decide if that was a good thing or bad thing. The house creaked as though it was settling to my presence. My fingers came to the indent in the wall, the roundness of where my skull matched perfectly the mar left behind. Crack! The sound reverberated all through my bones. I covered my ears to muffle out that sickening sound. Finally, the sound faded away and I rubbed the phantom pain. A painful spot I couldn't rub because of the ties around my wrists. My body trembled and I couldn't stop the bile that was coming up. *I can't do this. I had to. I can't. You have to*. I was having an endless soldier's conversation before battle.

Wiping the tears from my eyes, I willed my foot to take a leap of faith and came to a dead stop. Vanilla scent wafted through my nostrils and sparkling lights from the shards of glass danced upon my bed. A nude woman was tied to the bed spread eagle, her body deathly white as she writhed from the cords. She screamed for help in endless waves. Blood dripped down the side of the plastic and onto the floor. The screaming was becoming louder and I couldn't catch my breath. I was amalgamated to the door, my wrists tied with blood red cords. My knees shook and I could no longer hold myself up, and I puddled to the floor.

A warm embrace surrounded me, but my fear and panic guarded me against the warmth. It was Seth! Oh, god, it was Seth! He has me again! I was only dreaming I was free.

"Danni, Danni, it's Gabriel! Stop fighting me. It's me, Gabriel."

His familiar voice cracked through the screeching and the bedroom became pristine. The bed was made with white linen. He picked me up and cradled me like a baby. Then, he carried me, mass of sobs and tears, to the living room and held me there till the thunder of screams and the river of tears ceased. Shivering uncontrollably, he put his heavy canvas jacket on top of me and the scent of Gabriel's cologne mixed with body heat tickled my nose. *Home.* My last thought before I closed my eyes and drifted away.

Chapter 20

The aroma of bacon and eggs wrinkled my nose, and I popped an eye open to that delicious scent. My body stiff and sore, I achingly sat up in bed and began the process of where the hell was I exactly. I was blanketed by an ocean of soft greens and blues. The edges were worn with a few strings coming out of the hem. My body was engulfed by a large king bed with no headboard, just an adobe wall. An old thrift store dresser with paint peeling off sat against the far wall, and on top gold chains and jewelry were scattered about. The curtains on the window were faded yellow, thick with dust on them, and on the right side of the bed stood an oak stand with a bed lamp. His room brought a smile to my face. No woman in his life would ever leave the decorations to this standard.

"Hey, you're awake." Gabriel was standing dressed only in a tight pair of jeans, the button open at the top. Sunlight reflected off the waves of chestnut hair mixed with gray streaks, that I had never noticed before, cascaded down his shoulders. My eyes began the slow process of familiarizing myself to his body. Each pectoral muscle so perfectly shaped in squares that were above his flat stomach. His skin stretched taut over his muscles, my fingers aching for the touch of his skin. My memory drifted back to the day of being in the woods, when all I wanted was to fuse with the essence of his being. My skin felt the heat of those hands from that moment, and my wounds began to blaze. They caught fire and burned away the feeling of Gabriel's touch. Gabriel's eyes became wider and his face became filled with concern. I gathered my knees to my chest. I was dirty, unclean. Bandages spiraled around my arms mixing pink skin against the white gauze. They were keeping my skin tied to my body. Gabriel put the eggs down and started messing with one of the bandages. I flinched and hit my head against the wall.

"Ow!" and rubbed my hand over the new area of pain.

"Are you okay?" He quickly pulled back from the wound and looked at the bedspread, "Danni...I...."

I was still rubbing my head trying to figure out where that wall came from. "How long have I been sleeping?"

"At least twelve hours." He sighed and got off the bed. He looked at me pensively and got the tray full of food. The smell of bacon and eggs came wafting up to my nose, and pangs of hunger came over me and then a sudden state of nausea came right after it.

"Danni, what's wrong, you're turning fifteen shades of white."

"I don't know...just" and I swallowed back some bile, "the food," and I gave it back to him.

I took a deep breath and the feeling passed.

He sat on the bed very carefully. I think he was afraid he was going to break me but it was too late, I was already broken.

"I'm here if you know, umm...if you need to talk or something like that...."

Oh, god, what's worse, the pain or pity? "Nope, I'm good. I don't want to talk about it," I picked up the plate again and stabbed some eggs.

"You're gonna have to some time. You're the one who told me that."

"Like, you tell me everything," I sneered. "What are those nightmares about," I said rather sarcastically.

His eyes became cold, "Oh, keeping you awake, was I?"

Good, he was getting angry—better than those pitying looks I was getting. "Every night you scream like a little girl. What aren't you telling me?" I stabbed at the helpless eggs.

"Like a little girl, huh?"

He paced back and forth. I may have gone a little far. He made a sudden jump on to the bed. By sheer panic, I jumped out and I found myself shaking in the corner. Seth was in the man before me and I tried to melt myself further into the wall. I couldn't breathe and every muscle seemed to betray me.

"Danni... Danni.... I am going to just sit on the edge of the bed and ..." the voice was changing from Seth's back to Gabriel. I concentrated on his voice and it brought me back to his room. Every muscle in my body eased for the moment. Embarrassed, I found myself staring at his carpet and thinking it needed a really good vacuuming. Shaking in the corner naked and vulnerable, I felt the pull of marionette strings.

"Danni." He slowly got off the bed and he came closer to me the cold adobe wall pressed into my back. "Danni...shh, you're safe with me." His gently lay his head on top of mine, a heavy weight bearing down on my own. His arms wrapped around me and I was in his sweet embrace, my cheeks wet with tears next to his warm, dry skin. I willed every muscle group to release until they were no longer on defense.

"I didn't mean to scare you." He was holding me softly and rocking me. "I'm so sorry."

"No, it's my fault." I smiled weakly. Why was he apologizing, it's not his fault that I'm a freak. "Just need" and I didn't know what to say, "just need some time, that's all." I wasn't so convinced that time heals all wounds, but I hoped to God it softened the edges.

"I'm so incredibly tired." Where does Frankenstein's monster begin to return to a normal human being.

"Do you want to go back to bed?'

"Yeah." He lifted the covers and I slid in.

"Do you want me to hold you?" I closed my eyes and backed into him. His arms came around me and I had to tamper down the feeling of panic. His body used to fit my own so perfectly and now I felt like I was forcing a puzzle piece into the wrong shape.

Weeks passed by and I attempted many times to go over my house and sometimes I won and was able to stay for periods of time. Other times, I couldn't step inside. The dark pit I was in seemed to grow bigger as each day passed. I couldn't sleep at night and when I did, nightmares would displace any dreams I had. Eating was a chore and my body rejected any source of life. I was becoming a zombie, a walking dead, and losing any connection I had to life.

We quickly set up a routine: He would come and go and I didn't ask any questions. I sat on the couch or went to work and watched the world go by. He walked on eggshells around me and I stomped around. It was increasingly harder to be around him. I was becoming a cave dweller and he was light that was too bright for my eyes. In the dead of winter amongst the snow and ice, I walked for hours until numbness was the only feeling I had. At the Bosque, where I once had a romantic walk with Gabriel, now black barked barren trees against the pale of winter surrounded me. Snowflakes fell around and froze against my skin. I was filling the empty spaces with hate and my monster hidden behind tears and self-pity was emerging, transforming on a daily basis.

Sitting on the couch at Gabriel's house, I rubbed my hands incessantly. I wanted to kill Seth and feel the last pulse of his life leave his body. I understood what Seth meant of finding peace in their last breath. It was where I would find my peace. My hands could feel each heartbeat in Seth's neck, his breath strangled as it passed blue slips. So consumed by that very thought that my name seemed like incessant buzzing in my ears, "Danni, Danni…." I raised my head slowly up to find Gabriel staring at me, "Uh, your eyes are dark green."

Without a word, I plowed through the snow to my house. My fear had dissipated into the ether of winter. Standing in my house, I no longer heard the screams or witnessed the visions of pain and torture. Turning slowly around, my fists clenched, I faced Gabriel standing in the doorway.

Light escaped around Gabriel and cast him a dark shadow and blinded my eyesight. For a brief millisecond, the curve of his wing floated above his shoulder and then the image dissipated into the shadows as the sun went down. An insatiable need to be held, to feel the warmth of his body against my own drowned me. I imagined his hand leaving my skin in radiating light and then I saw my wounds bleed with black ooze.

"Danni, talk to me." He came closer and I stepped back. I had stained him once, I would allow myself to do that again.

"Danni, please tell me how do I help you?" He was pleading, his voice cracked and dry. I turned away and blinded myself from the look of love. His warmth engulfed me as he put his arms around me. For a minute, his warm embrace felt like a soothing balm, until the panic arose.

I turned out of his embrace, "You can't," and one tear burned its way down my cheek.

His arms dropped. He put his hands through his hair, "You're driving me crazy. You're tearing my heart out," his hands became fists. "I would climb mountains for you if you told me that would help you." His voice got deep and low, "I would kill for you." Bile was beginning to rise and I ran towards the bathroom, purging any remains of the old me out of my system. At the sink, I looked up to find through my scraggly hair a person I didn't recognize. Sharp green eyes, a gaunt, pale face was staring straight back at me. My clavicle bones were protruding through my shirt, the edge of my ribs defined. I was returning dust, but my funeral was taking too damn long. I needed to be buried, alive. His cell phone rang and Gabriel's muffled voice broke me out of my vision as I cracked the door of the bathroom.

"I'm not leaving her." His voice seemed so determined. There was a pause for the other caller. "I don't care about the investigation. I can't leave her." A deep male voice was all I could discern from the other side of the conversation.

"I said no…. Fire me all you want, I don't care!" The other voice chimed in with its opinion. "Sir, you don't understand." *Who would he be calling 'Sir'?* "No…I know. But… Sir! Bullshit…. That doesn't matter…I can't leave…I will not run…I can't, yes Sir!" He threw his phone against the wall.

I opened the door more and saw him kick the hard, adobe walls. Dirt was falling from the vigas like rain and dust drifted down in soft, billowy sheet. "I'm impressed. I wish I could do that without breaking any toes." He looked at me but all I saw was rage in his eyes. "Gabriel," I spoke his name gently.

"What!"

Startled, I backed up a step. He seemed to come back to himself and his eyes were bloodshot, but the irises were still beautiful shades of amber liquid. "Are you okay?"

"You're asking me if I am all right?"

"Well, yeah."

He stood and looked up at the ceiling, then back to me. "You're as pale as ghost, and becoming nothing but a skeleton. You won't," he kicked the wall again, "you won't," and he closed his eyes, "you won't sleep and you scream when you do sleep. I try to touch you and you act like I'm burning you. You won't talk to me."

That was a fairly good assessment and I shrugged my shoulders. "I don't know what to say."

He made a fist and hit the wall. Weeks of pent up frustration were lashed upon the walls by fists of pain and fury. He stood there so defeated and lost. "Danni, you got to let me in."

"No, I ...can't... I can't."

"What are you afraid of? How do I fight for you? Please tell me."

I don't think the warrior could slay this dragon. He walked over and put his arms around me. Embraced by love, I felt for the wings and found just a man underneath my fingertips. Shutting my eyes tight, I said, "You don't know how much it means to me for you to love me." Truth is, he saved me before Seth, but he couldn't save me now. "But this is a battle you can't fight."

His shoulders slumped and his head fell forward. I stepped closer to him and put my arms underneath his. He was giving up on me. He bent down, put his head on my shoulder, and crushed me until the weight of us brought us to our knees.

Chapter 21

My life had become twisted steel that I was desperately trying to mold back into normal. Gabriel and I were growing farther and farther apart. The more he tried to come closer, the more I pushed him away. He was standing on a shore and I was in the boat paddling away in the depths of mist and despair until I saw him no longer.

Gabriel received constant calls and broke more cell phones, to the point that he had backups just in case he needed them. He was staying because of me. I still had no idea what he did, there was just a wee bit more to his story of being a bouncer at a bar. Every once in a while, a fuzzy memory would come of a man in a policeman's uniform yelling at Gabriel, but I took that for a drug haze, *so many secrets between us.*

I was on the porch after one particular phone call in which another cell phone was innocently rammed into a wall. My tea had grown cold inside my plain boring white cup. I knew what was coming next; it was inevitable that he had to leave. "Danni," he licked his lips and closed his eyes.

"You need to go," he knelt before me and put his hands on mine. I held my breath and didn't pull away. Would I ever feel the touch of another without feeling invaded?

"I don't want to go…there is so much I need to tell you but I can't," he whispered. Slipping my hand from underneath his, I grabbed a lock of hair. My fingers moved through the soft strands of hair, weaving black threads around my pale fingers.

"I know." I kissed his forehead and we watched the sun drift down into a sea of darkness. We were just ether and shadows now. Maybe a little space would bring us back to center, but I had no idea how. A few days later, he walked out the door. Only silence was his goodbye. He stared long and hard at the house, his chest rose and fell in deep waves. The sun was setting, his body turning dark and melting into the air. My hands had bars of light and dark running across the back. When I looked out again, he was gone. I didn't bother to wipe my tears away as I sat down. What was the point, and let them run rampant. Finally, the stream ceased and I looked up to the phone. There was a number written on a wrinkled piece of paper, taped to the receiver. Gabriel's phone number was scribbled across the note. I kissed it gently, crumpled it up, and threw it in the trash. I could no longer cause him any more pain.

Healing knife wounds, broken heart, and soul, I tried with all my might to return to the normalcy of work. My identity was kept secret, but I had been in the newspapers as the "victim" who survived. Everyone knew of my ordeal and I walked around dead in a haze of shame. My wounds were healing quickly on the outside but on the inside, I still looked like a hospital experiment gone wrong.

Normally, I walked in, threw my purse around, and began work. This time, I stood at the door of the pizza place and surveyed my surroundings like I had just been hired. Everything seemed so unfamiliar and strange. I felt like a ghost that was just passing through. The men I had so diligently worked on a friendship with stared at me with looks of concern and pity. I so wanted to run away at that moment but I plowed forward, threw my purse down in an act of this-was–the-old-me, and didn't talk. They shrugged their shoulders and returned to work. It was like back to normal for them and stranger in a strange land for me.

After a while, I fell into a routine of working the dough, beating the holy hell out it, rolling it, and then beating it again. "Hey! Danni, you ever going to get that dough ready?" Marco croaked. But, he said in such a way that was four tones lower than his usual voice.

"Yeah, Boss." I needed a coke, I needed a new life, and I needed something to bring me back to myself. I decided to take a break and go out back. Coke in hand and jacket on, I stepped into the back alley and into the blasting cool air and sat on the back step. A big red brick wall was in my view. It could have been a beautiful scene but it didn't matter my mind couldn't seem to concentrate on anything anyway. I looked at each brick with its intricate patterns, rough texture, and like usual cried for no reason.

Juan, Julio, and Diego came outside and took various positions of sitting and leaning against the wall. They smelt like cologne, sweat, and pizza spices all mixed into one. Each of them had serious looks upon their faces and their eyes were darting around like they were looking for something or someone.

Juan spoke first, "Danni, you going to be okay?"

"Sure," I shrugged my shoulders and wiped my tears away. How could you possibly define "okay"?

Diego brought out his switchblade and began cleaning his fingernails one by one with the point of his blade. A glint of sunshine reflected off the metal and after a burst of pure sunlight bounced in my eye, panic began to swell. I had to take a deep breath and remind myself where I was. Diego saw my eyes and then he looked at his own blade. The starburst was doused by the clicking of its sheath and I let out a long held breath. "We'll cut him, Danni, we'll fucking kill 'em." I looked into his eyes so serious and so willing to shed blood in my name, for my false name.

"Yeah, how you going do that?" I replied, sipping some Coke, the bubbles soothing my throat and wishing there was something stronger in the can.

"You leave that to us." And he pulled back out that same knife that reflected the sun's image and with a flick of his wrist, the knife popped to a five-inch blade.

I sighed softly, the idea that these kids were on my side made me a little less lost and lonely, "You would go to jail for me."

"We are going there anyway, hermana, we'll do you a favor," Julio smirked and then did a high five with the others. They didn't have a clue as to what they were giving up, a gallant gesture from three young men. Trouble is they would really kill Seth and make him suffer, which gave me a small feeling of comfort. Images of Seth laying on a dirty jail cell floor, his lifeless eyes watching his very fluids go down the drain and into the sewer were pervasive in my thoughts. But, my dark soulless monster had a deep-seated need to personally kill Seth and listen to his heartbeat as he died.

Lost in thought, I saw the boy's eyes, "I appreciate it guys, I do, but…."

"But nothing," Diego spoke up. He wore a white t-shirt and long khaki shorts that went down to his calves. How was he not freezing out here? The head of the tattooed rattlesnake poked his head out his collar, the green eyes of the snake looked into mine, sharp and piercing. Diego took a cigarette out his pack and Julio lighted it with an old steel lighter. He breathed in a drag and blew out acrid smoke. He looked at me with no smile in his eyes and without a hint of jocularity, "You're our hermana. We take care of our own."

It struck me that I had a family, a really dysfunctional family at that, but a family no less. I put my hand on his arm and he pulled away. I wasn't offended. I don't think he knew the touch of friendship, especially from a woman.

"I really appreciate the offer, I do, and God knows I want to see the bastard dead…." My throat went dry and I was going to cry again, but I held back the tears. I looked at all three of them square in the eye. I was going to give them the lecture about freedom, stay out of jail, live while you can, go have a life, and don't have sin upon your soul. But they all stared back at me, their faces dripping with attitude. They had heard all that so many times.

My voice became deep and low. "I'll kill him myself" and I got the knife from Diego and snapped it shut. I made the sign of cross, made a gun out of my hand, aimed at the wall, and pulled an imaginary trigger. They grinned and nodded their heads. I had earned a slight respect by threatening to take someone's life.

Marco came out and bellowed, "You lazy asses get back to work!"

"Yeah, hefe, we're at your service," Julio commented.

"Yeah, man, you think we're your slaves?" Juan took a stance. "Why do you have to be like that, man?" Juan asked, but couldn't keep the grin off his face.

"Shut up and get back to work." Julio and Juan laughed and hi-fived each other as they went in with Marco. Before we started up the steps, Diego caught my arm and he stared at me. I nodded. We had an understanding; one of us would see Seth dead.

Chapter 22

Gabriel was gone and the tide of loneliness and despair would rush in and wash away with bitterness and anger. Seth, from my understanding, was healing nicely from his gunshot wounds and hired a well-paid lawyer. I, on the other hand, had to deal with paperwork for the alleged attempt at murdering me. The tediousness of dotting the i's and crossing the t's of being an almost murder victim. The police took my statement down at the hospital but a phone call said I had to go down to the police station and finish some paperwork. My horror would be written in duplicate on a clean sheet of white paper.

Riding in my dad's GTO gave me the feeling of power and the rumble through my body made me feel like I was hellfire bitch about to cast doom, which for a little while replaced the scared little girl with a lollipop in her hand facing the fire breathing demon feeling I had.

The goat rumbled into the police station. The creak of the car door as I opened it signaled I was here. Several police offices on the corner watched me closely and smiled. Chagrined, I gave attitude back and thought, *Isn't this what all possible murder victims wear?* A cowboy hat complete with feathers, jeans, a leather jacket and cowboy boots to match or was it the fact I just yanked myself back when I locked the door with my purse dangling out of the door. "Damn it." Thank God for long hair. It shielded me from the smirks I got from the men in blue.

Dignity all lost, I thought, *Yep, this was the time to go into the police station and face the story of my torture printed on black and white and red all over*. The police station was a mass of chaos; ants running to and fro like their house was a fire. People incarcerated yelling, prostitutes in shorts and low cut shirts picking at their nails. Pushing my way through the throngs of antlike activity, I established myself in front of very bored, fat, policeman. His head was in one hand and the other hand writing mercilessly away. He must of have been the cop they called for crimes at fast food scenes. He had graying hair that matched his big, bushy eyebrows. A bead of sweat rolled down his jowly neck and into his blue collar. It was ten am and he already had a five o'clock shadow on his face that rolled with the jowls. His blue uniform stretched tight across his chest and one button was holding on for dear life. His collar cut off his neck from his uniform, making him look like a talking pudgy head. Continuing on down this lovely sight, the lines of his uniform followed the bulges of his stomach, *Wow, anyone's grandma could outrun him*.

Ignored, I pushed on, "Hmmm," I did best clearing of my throat, "hmmmm." Then I kicked the desk. Not the most lady-like but what the hell, I wasn't here to be a lady.

"Yeah, yeah, don't get your panties in a wad, I'll be with you in a minute." Deciding on whether I should file a complaint, I stole a glance at the officer's nametag, Wiltrout.

Indignant, I looked around and behind my new sweaty, rude friend, was someone I thought I recognized. Desperate, I tried to pull something out of my garbled images. My eyes became fixated on the camera around his neck. *Why did he seem so familiar?*

"Hey, who's that man over there?" and I pointed to the man who glanced my way. The cameraman's face turned white and he quickly turned away.

Donut boy preoccupied with paperwork in front of him, finally looked at me with a toothpick in the corner of his mouth. Then he turned at the now suddenly shy cameraman, who was hastily trying to leave a most engaged conversation.

"Who that guy?" he asked with a gravelly voice, was that from too many cigarettes or donuts?

"Yeah, that man." Would I be remiss in saying yeah Sherlock that guy? *Asshole. This is a police station, Carolina, this is a police station, just keep your mouth shut.* I should probably engrave that on my hand.

"That's the forensic photographer, Ruiz." The cop took the toothpick out of his mouth and laid it on the counter, where it rolled with brown spittle on it, *ewww.* "He takes pictures of all the crime scenes." Absentmindedly, he picked up the toothpick and put it back in his mouth. "Poor guy took pictures of those murdered women that psycho killed, so glad we finally caught the bastard."

"Yeah, so glad you did, too," I said under my breath. A remembered flash of light stunned me, he was the "reporter" who came into the pizza place and took my picture. I started to disconnect from my body and my hands turned into hard balls.

My brain was beginning to paint a picture that I didn't want to see and the monster inside popped one eye open and growled. My breath became ragged and I began to tremble all over. Deep inside, a really big scream was slowly making its way up from my stomach through my lungs and up to my throat. The eyes on Wiltrout got bigger, although, I don't know if it was recognition of who I was or the sudden reaction a man has to a female scorned. I shut my eyes and prepared to scream.

"Miss Stronghill." Before me was a tall thin man, with a shiny balding head, sharp cheekbones, and deep set gray-blue eyes. He had a nervous smile, his eyes were darting around looking for something, like maybe other cops to restrain me. He peered down at me and planted himself into the ground, my view blocked of the reporter by the sudden appearance of a mountain. I could tell he was a man who did not appreciate chaos ensuing on his smooth running ship. However, I believe I was about to create some ensuing chaos. The man was desperately trying to stop my line of vision.

Calmed for the moment, I took a deep breath and then someone called for the captain. He turned only slightly left but it was enough to put Ruiz in the crosshairs of my myopic vision. All the panic, fear, and anger rushed. "You did this to me!" and I thrust out my arms out and showed my wounds in various stages of healing. "You did this to me!" my arms spasmed and the police station whirled in a tornado-like frenzy.

Tears ran down my face, but all the shame and anger whimpered out, "You did this to me." Ruiz froze in position his mouth gaped open. Everyone stopped putting handcuffs on, stopped moving prisoners, everything ceased to be in motion, time stood still. Even my jowly friend just stared at me and his toothpick fell out of his gaping mouth.

"I'm Police Captain Stafford," he blocked my view again of Ruiz who was trying desperately to get out of my line of vision. "How can I help you?' As though nothing happened, the ants returned to work. I couldn't stop shaking.

"You wanna know how you can help me?" My voice became four octaves higher, "you can arrest that man," and I pointed towards the photographer's back who was speedily rushing towards the exit.

The captain's eyes darted around. He looked desperate for someone to throw him a life raft. "Carolina, you need to calm down now," his voice was so low it was almost inaudible.

Both of my eyebrows raised, he just said calm down, my head was spinning. I'll show you calm down and then in the recess of my frantic mind, something hit me like a ton of bricks, "How did you know my name?"

He grabbed me by the arm, "Ow!" He looked down at my arm and quickly released his thumb that had dug into a wound. His face changed to crimson and god I hoped that was shame. He said gently, "I think you better go into my office."

We walked down the dark hall that was painted in institution green with layers of slime, coffee stains, and *oooh, god knows what that stain was*. We walked past hookers, drug addicts, amid stares, arrests, spit and yelling. We entered the captain's office. I know this because across the glass was CAPITAN STAFFORD in big bold gold letters. He shut the door and all the sound from the outside became a dull silence.

His office was a quiet respite from the outside awash in complete Navaho White paint. He settled behind his desk as I perused his office. His oasis was a sea of chaotic pictures, awards, and accommodations. Compared to the gritty cop shows I've seen on TV, his office was huge. I know, you would think given my history, I would have seen a lot more police stations. Prison I knew, police stations only one other time. Facing east, there was a large window that encased the city with Mother Sandias watching over the city. He had a beautiful panoramic view that I didn't think he quite appreciated, since his desk faced away from it. I sat down in one of his standard come-to-Jesus meeting chairs, cozy enough from the padding on the seat but straight enough to indicate you were not supposed to stay long.

The Captain opened his desk, pulled out a whiskey bottle, and poured some into his standard issue police coffee cup. He didn't offer any to me. He sat down, eyed me for a second, and took a big swig of "coffee". I resisted rolling my eyes and turned to something that caught my eye. In the corner of the room was a palm tree desperately stretching for the light, behind it, a glint of sunlight sparkled off the corner of a picture. Like a raccoon attracted to shiny objects, I left the captain sipping his "coffee" and looked closer at the photograph. It was an old faded picture of young police officers with pride on their faces and steely determination in their eyes at their graduation ceremony. They were all dressed in blue and I scoured each face, looking at all the different features and smiled. They had no idea what they were in for. Then I recognized the familiar features of three of them. One young man's taunt skin and gleaming bright eyes were reflected in the wrinkled skin and the blood eyes of the man before me. I peered closer, then I recognized the face of someone I thought was a friend, and I put my finger up to one I recognized the most. My heart sank.

"When did you become police chief here?"

"Uh" was the gurgle that came from his throat.

"You know who I am, don't you?"

He put his coffee cup down and swallowed hard. His Adam's apple moved with the swallow. "Of course, I know who you are." I turned away from him and stared at the picture, feelings of betrayal were spilling over, "You're a convict, the worst kind." He said it with acid in his voice with no regret whatsoever.

All the blood drained from my face. Tendrils of cold, hard comprehension ensued through my veins causing me to be dizzy. I was the sad little worm he put on the end of hook to bait the soulless killer. "You bastard, you set me up."

"Now, Carolina, let's not go jumping to conclusions about this." He said it as though I was a child looking up to him and a big lecture was coming my way.

"You set me up with that reporter…" My fists were beginning to shake…"and got my picture in the paper, knowing I was his type, his type of victim." Bile was rising and I was going to be sick. My legs were buckling underneath me and I staggered towards the confession chair.

Stafford just rolled his lip out, "I was not allowed to give any details before the trial but, yes" his eyes turned toward the picture, "yes, you were an intricate part of this investigation and Seth's capture." He lifted up his chin. "You should be happy," then he sneered, "you caught a killer."

Without even realizing it, my fists slammed into his desk and I was above him, "Do you know what I went through?" A tear formed in the corner of my eye, *I will not cry.* I was getting a headache from the adrenaline rush of bitterness and anger. My monster was climbing tooth and nails up my insides and I adjusted my spine and clicked my neck to make room for my friend. The tear dropped on my shaking hands.

The police chief got up out of his chair and stared at the picture, "You have to repay society for your crime, Carolina," he turned around and looked at me. Then he looked at my scars, "this is repayment." Guilt outweighed my anger and I slumped down in to the chair. *Damn.*

Chapter 23

I slurked out of the police station, puddled into the GTO, and drove like a bat out of hell. Hot tears ran down my cheeks as I rolled the window down to feel the cold wind blow across my face. Every emotion was welling inside me and I tried my best to stamp it down. I drove past the city streets in the midst of a cold winter's blast and watched the highway slip under me. Streets, mountains, deserts, people rolled past me in flashes of undistinguishable light and color. My thoughts were guilt, betrayal from a friend, and Gabriel's last moment of grief. I had sent away the one person who would save me. Exhausted, I drove into a parking lot and laid my head against the steering wheel. Rage spilled into my fists as I slammed the steering wheel with my hands until they were red and sore. Finally tired of beating my car into submission, I eyed my surroundings and realized where I was. Oh, hell. Sunset was shutting down the light of day fast, but one last ray shined upon the building in front of me, Michael's the roughest biker bar in Albuquerque. It had the reputation that this was the last step before you plunged into hell, and nothing, I mean nothing inside me said this was where I should hightail it and run. If there was an angel on my shoulder, she probably passed out from trying to save me from killing myself on the highway. The bar pulled a string and tugged at my monster to come in the door and my feet scraped along the parking lot after it.

The door was solid gray steel with a rusted handle that was semi held on by a rusted screw. I pushed the door wide open and heard it bang against the bricks of the building. A streetlight illuminated the entrance and everything was cast in shades of yellow and gray. The atmosphere was dark and heavy with cigarette smoke. Various neon beer signs and small lights filtered through the dark gray smoke. My nose twitched at the rancid smells of old beer, sweaty men, smoke, and activated hormones. All eyes were looking me up and down as I stared straight back at them. Every member of society's castaway of drunk, rejected, and embittered stood around in various form of leather outfits. Women of all shapes and sizes displayed their skin to their partner's hungry eyes. They turned their eyes away from me and went on with their business. For the first time in my life, I fit in. I had put the last puzzle piece and made a complete picture.

As I walked further, each foot stuck to the floor but I kept my eyes cast forward because I absolutely refuse to see what was on that floor. Loud banging music played on an old jukebox in the corner with a broken neon beer sign. An old wooden bar was only a foot away from the door and I bellied right up to a long brass bar that edged it. The bartender saw my reflection in the abused mirror, and turned around. My heart stopped beating for a second. He wore a large blue bandana across his forehead that edged his one eyebrow. A scar was over one eyebrow and continued on to where his left eye should have been. His long greasy hair splayed across his shoulders and mangled with his black and white peppered scraggly beard. He was cleaning a glass with a filthy rag and opened his mouth full of rotting teeth, in what I presumed was a smile. "Want something, chica?"

"Shot of whiskey."

"Whiskey is not for tourists." He was leering at me from head to toe, beginning with my cowboy boots, broom skirt, and finally ending at my sleeveless top that had a picture of crying angel sitting on a gravestone. He must have been enamored with the picture that stretched over my breasts, because he continued to stare. I turned away, the denizens of this establishment were dressed in jeans and leather, nothing of mine indicated that I belonged here. Nobody could see my insides, though. I looked like Pollyanna in a pretty broom skirt that had just walked into the den of iniquity.

"Just give me the goddamn whiskey." He pulled back his lips, grinned with his teeth in various stages of decay, and left. When he came back, he poured from a long, sleek bottle with amber liquid into a shot glass.

The shot of whiskey sat before me and I glared back at it, "You going to drink that or stare at it." The bartender choked and lifted his lips in a smirk. I grabbed the shot glass, swallowed the whole amount, and slammed the glass down in front of him.

"Another one!" and I looked straight into his one eye. As I waited for the next one, I turned around quickly so the bartender didn't see me turn green. The whiskey had followed the path of my bloodstream, and pooled at the base of my spine. Each molecule of alcohol burned and replaced every blood cell. It eased my pain, guilt, and anger. My eyes started to cross and I saw way more bikers than before, or at least there were suddenly a lot of identical twins. I understand now why they called it liquid courage because I could take them all and began to chuckle. All those monster scratches on the inside began to sting and my stomach flipped on itself. That powerful feeling overwhelmed me as I licked my lips to taste the last drop of courage. It felt good to be home. There was a small remnant of Carolina fighting to stay up front, but I squashed her and put her in a box.

"Here, you stupid Gringa, try this one." I turned slowly around and noticed the faces surrounding me. They were daring me to slam another shot. The grease monkey behind the bar grinned, revealing bits of dinner in his teeth. My stomach revolted, but I was determined to destroy myself one way or another. "Gonna stare at this one, too?" and he wheezed out a laugh, coughed, and spit something black on the floor.

"Fuck you," I said to the bartender and drank the shot in one swallow, again like a complete idiot. My knees began to buckle, but I held myself from crumbling to the floor. Even my monster had limits of what kind of filth it wanted to lay in. My stomach almost upheaved, and my knuckles turned white as my hands gripped the wooden bar. Deep laughter from the men at the bar reverberated through me. The drink burned everything up inside me and melted my brain into mush. The floor began to list up and down; fighting to stay above water, I held on so tight I left scratch marks on the wooden top.

Sinking slowly to the floor, a hard slap came across my ass and my hair was pulled back, exposing my neck. Too intoxicated to struggle, I just stared into the eyes of a doped up, nasty smelling biker, "Look at you, bitch, coming in here all tough." He kissed me hard and rammed his tongue down my mouth. Nearly gagging from the taste of stale cigarettes and beer, I bit his lip till my teeth touched. He slammed me against the bar. "Bitch!" He backed off and blood began to bubble up from the bite. He rolled his tongue across his lips and closed his eyes. Shivers racked through my body as I replayed a memory of Seth cutting my arm, then licking the wound. He grabbed me and twisted me around like I was ragdoll. One hand cupping my breast hard and the other arm around my waist. "You're going to make one fine piece of ass for my collection," and bit my earlobe. The more I struggled, the more he coiled around me. I struggled to breathe as all the faces around me became twisted and distorted until all that remained was laughing skulls.

My fingers searched like a slow tarantula across the bar, looking for anything that would cause damage. They found purchase with a tall bottle. I grabbed it and swung as hard as I could muster, but my arms felt like jelly from the alcohol that was coursing through them. It was definitely not like the movies, where the bottle breaks and the guy crumbles to the ground with a stupid grin on his face. But it was enough for me to twist out of his deathly coil. He stood there with blood running down his forehead. "You stupid cunt!" Finally, something we agreed on. He grabbed the dirty towel from the bar and wiped his face. He growled with blood on his teeth. "You're going to be one feisty bitch in bed." He made a move forward but I sidestepped. He slipped on something nasty on the floor, possibly his own blood, and fell to his knees. God bless him for being in a drunken stupor.

Too stunned to run, I had a chance to look at my newfound suitor. He was dressed in a Hell's Angels black vest with long stringy blonde-gray hair flowing down his shoulders. It was hard to determine if the drugs and alcohol created the lines in his face or if it was just his perverted creepy age. He had a beer belly that protruded over his jeans and leather chaps with chains wrapped around his belt. His eyes seemed like black coals, lifeless in their sockets, and I looked away. They reminded too much of what I saw in the mirror every day.

He grabbed my ankle and I kicked him in the face, "Back off, you son of a bitch! You have no idea who you're dealing with." I really didn't know who I was anymore to be dealing anything, but no one was going to touch me again. For the second time today, I showed my vulnerability in an act of defiance. I stuck out my arms to show my wounds that were red and puffy, Frankenstein's cousin. I don't know if it was from the whiskey, the adrenaline rush, or how tired I was, but I started to sway a bit. The asshole in front of me seemed to grow many heads. *Not good.* My rebellious stint was starting to look a lot like Custard's last stand and no word from the monster that led me here. He looked at my wounds and stared. For a fat guy, he got up off the floor way too quickly. A smirk came across his lips, the blood drying to his face. *Fuck, I'm in trouble*. Backing out slowly, I hoped the door would spontaneously get closer to me. I backed up into a solid human being who hadn't showered in days. As he held me close, he smelled my hair and breathed. It took everything I had not to gag.

"Oh, you're not going anywhere, bitch!" He grabbed my arm and pulled me towards him. "You're staying right here with us and keeping us entertained. What do ya say, guys, up for a little entertainment?" I heard the bar break out in various hoops and calls. "Go, Rat! Fuck her hard!" *Rat, what kind of name is that?* Maybe I could throw up on his nice leather pants. Rat put his grubby fingers around my neck and forced me to my knees to the slimy floor. My hands were held by the foul-breathing ogre behind me. Face to face with Rat's zipper, he yelled, "Swallow this bitch!" He started to unzip his jeans. Terror struck me, and all that liquid courage drained out of me. The inner monster that hungered for this squeaked and pulled the curtains. Tears rolled down my eyes as I relived my nightmares. Thumbs were crushing my windpipe, any screams that managed to come out was muffled out by the music and the din of male laughter.

"Leave her alone!"

I couldn't see who was talking. I was eye level with an opened zipper and a pair of tidy whities. I tried to get up, but there was a hand on my neck keeping me solidly in place.

"I said leave her alone!"

My heart did a small leap at the sound of Gabriel's voice. *Oh, a possible rescue from my own stupidity.* The atmosphere went completely silent and the soft flutter of wings filled the air for only a split second, then all the sounds came back to a deafening roar.

"What the fuck do you want with her, Gabe? She's just trash anyways. Tonight's entertainment." The bar patrons broke in a loud cacophony of laughter.

"She's mine!" Sudden oxygen alleviated my dizziness and I could move but I wasn't sure I really wanted to. "Get the fuck up," he put his hand underneath my armpit and lifted me up to stand on my own two legs.

Firmly on my feet, I surveyed the situation and saw blood had dribbled down Rat's face in streams. Gabriel's eyes were cold metal as he stared down Rat. A glint of light sparkled from the long bladed knife Gabriel had focused squarely on Rat's stomach. Rat looked at Gabriel and then at the knife and my fondest hope was that Rat was weighing his options.

Rat put his hands up, "Take her, I don't give a fuck, she's old," he spit on my boots and left. All the other men who gathered for tonight's entertainment melted back into the haze of cigarette smoke.

Gabriel's warm, solid body was behind me. Empowered, I opened my mouth to say, "Yeah, you fucking bastards!" but before I could get a word out, I felt a kick on the back of my leg and was hauled out. We backed outside and the gray metal door closed with a bang. The air was crystal pure with the scent of winter. Gabriel pushed me against the cold adobe wall and he kissed me hard. For a second, I panicked, then my brain acquiesced and I matched the intensity of his lips. I couldn't get enough, all the fear and adrenaline exploded between us as we were trying to tear at each other. A loud bang snapped from the door opening and we both froze. We looked around but there was no one there. The moment was gone and the cold hit us both.

"So what the fuck was that all about? You nearly ruined it all."

Apparently, the romantic damsel saved by the prince moment was over, "What are you talking about?"

"You need to leave!" He grabbed me by the arm and I yelped because he grabbed the tender part of my wound. He didn't even flinch and forced his hand tighter around my arm. He yanked me forward and I tripped on a pebble.

"Gabriel? Please, you're hurting me." I put my feet out to stop him from dragging me further. He finally came to a dead stop and stared at me. His eyes seemed so unfocused until they came back clearly.

He took a deep breath. "I'm sorry," and a small white puff of smoke came from his breath. His face softened and he was the Gabriel that I fell in love with. All the pain of the past and the loneliness of the present came rushing in. I was done resisting and melted into his arms.

"Gabriel." I didn't know how much I missed him.

Right then, a deep-throated man's laughter and high-pitched voice of a woman streamed out of the bar. He unlocked himself from our embrace and, quickly, he walked me back to my car. The door to the goat screeched open from cold metal scraping against metal, then he shoved me into the seat. His beautiful brown eyes bore all the frustration, pain, and anger I felt. He yelled, "Go home!" and slammed the car door.

"But," I was stunned. "Hey, wait a minute!"

"Go home. I'll deal with you later!" He walked away from me and slipped back into the bar. My body trembled from the adrenaline rush, sheer exhaustion, and the encroaching cold. My hands shook as I put the keys into the ignition and revved the engine.

Bruised, broken, and shattered in so many different places, I drove all night just listening to the sounds of the wind whistle through the car window. Lost in a sea of thought, I had nowhere to go and nowhere to run. Finally, I parked on the side of the highway. Walking to the edge, I stood silently. The stars above me twinkled and below me was a deep, black ravine. Drinking in the darkness, I let the inky blackness of my soul match the night. A deep-pitted anger rose and the monster crawled up. It scratched and clawed its way up and I threw up everything I had in my stomach. All my thoughts turned crystal clear as I tore off my shirt and looked at each wound. I remembered every means of how those scars were acquired. I relived the fear, my weakness, humiliation from unwanted caresses, the smell of his breath on my cheek. Staring deeper into the darkness, memories flooded me, Mother walking out the door, Father's death, and the isolation of prison. Each scar still displayed the holes from the stitches and I could no longer keep myself bound. That face in Capitan Stafford's Academy picture haunted me. I threw up more and scratched at my scars until they bled. I felt the searing knife inside cut away anything that resembled the person I was and in its place, a monster patched together by stitches. Oblivious to the effects of winter, sunrise came over the horizon and illuminated my surroundings. My insides were splattered everywhere, my arms were stained with drying blood and mud, and I had been completely transformed into the monster I had tried to keep so long locked in a box. I got into my car and drove home.

My goat slipped into the driveway like glass and across the street, rays of light broke through the clouds and highlighted my neighbors. Carson and Riley were whispering as Angelica played catch-me-if-you-can with the dogs. Through their smiles, all I saw was pity on their faces and when I didn't return their friendly waves, they put their arms down. They glanced at each other underneath their eyelids. I didn't need their sympathy. The dogs barked and jumped on the fence and the noise was incessant, they seemed liked they had turned to snarling beasts protecting their owners from me. Glancing again, they were playing happily chasing their tails. For a moment, Angelica's innocent face was bright like the sun and she held her hands out to me wanting that familiar embrace. A lonely soul feeling tugged deep inside my belly, but then I stood straight up. It was too late.

I turned my back on them and opened the gate. The gate clanked with the replacement cowbell. In mid clank, I threw out into the yard where it landed in a hole with a dead thump. As I walked into the yard, a snake crossed the path in front of me and we faced each other.

He— at least I assumed it was a he—I really wasn't in a position to test his gender—was coiled up in front of me. His body was long and thin with green shading underneath him and his forked tongue slinked out of his mouth, feeling for the vibration of fear. His eyes were elliptical shaped, and he hissed and rattled his tail. I hissed back and he put his head back in his coil. For a long moment, we had a Mexican standoff and then he stuck his tongue at me one last time and slithered off.

The rumble of Gabriel's motorcycle was down the street and my heart began to rise. Nerves formed in the pit of my stomach. He had saved me from a disastrous decision earlier. I waited anxiously for his presence when I saw his luminescent smile head straight for me. I had hoped last night was forgiven, then he turned into his driveway and there was a woman on the back of his motorcycle. They parked and she took off her helmet and all this shiny red hair cascaded down her shoulders. Her melodious laughter rang out and shattered the last pieces of my broken heart.

They hadn't noticed me and I envied their deep conversation, till a speeding car broke the spell, and the inevitable screech of "Slow the Fuck Down!" from Carson, my cue to exit the land of Norman Rockwell. The key turned in the doorknob and I pushed the door open. Immediately, my hackles rose up. Fear washed over me and I crouched in the fight or flight position. The only noise in the room was the creak of the door as it opened wide and bounced on the wall. Cautiously, I stepped into the house and looked around for anything amiss. There were no smells, sounds, or anything I could detect, but I couldn't stop the feeling that something wasn't right. But there was only dead silence. I broke out into a sweat and panicked to the point where all my muscles had turned to rocks.

The phone rang and I jumped out of my skin, dropped my purse, everything cascaded onto the floor. Fuck! I humpfed over towards the phone and picked it up; still hadn't gotten caller id. The only people who called were telemarketers, the creepy deep breathing which stopped suddenly, and Harvey, "What the hell do you want?"

"Well, hello to you, Sunshine, bad day I take it?" It was Harvey's nice happy shiny voice.

"Well, hey, if it isn't fucking Harvey. What the hell do you want?"

"What's wrong?"

"I know what you did."

"What I did? What are you talking about, Sunshine?" But his voice sounded thin and pale.

"I was in the office of that fucking asshole, Captain Stafford. He had a really interesting photo."

"Now, Carolina, don't go jumping to conclusions."

"What am I supposed to think?

There was a nervous shaking in his voice. "You weren't supposed to get hurt, okay, I made that clear to the captain."

"You set me up, you bastard!"

"Just to catch the killer, Carolina, that's all. He wasn't supposed to get close. But you were his type…and" all the blood drained to my toes, nausea replaced the empty feeling I had. I wrapped the cord of phone between my hands and stretched it out tight. I imagined Harvey's neck in the chord turning white as I squeezed the life out of him.

"Carolina, please, it wasn't supposed to get this far. He was never supposed to hurt you." I couldn't stand it anymore. Harvey's voice was yelling through the receiver as I picked up the phone and threw it against the wall. It burst into a thousand little pieces. Steel parts, wires, tiny metal objects were scattered upon the floor and I heard every echo as they landed. My one friend, the one I counted on had set me up for bait. I was nothing to anyone but a worm on a hook. My head began to explode and I felt the need to crawl out of my skin. Two visions appeared, the light and ethereal me and the dark one that ravaged me. I saw the light me, she was scarred, frightened, beat up, and dark me looked at her with disgust and threw her back where she belonged, back in the dungeon. The last image I saw was of old me curled up in the corner whimpering in the dark, and I slammed the door on her.

Stillness settled in and peaceful quiet blanketed me until the sound of boots scuffing the floor came right behind me. "Hey, little girl, I missed you." I turned around quickly and kneed him right where it mattered the most. His knees hit the floor with an unmistakable cracking sound.

Looking down, I saw what I had just emasculated—"Snake."

Chapter 24

I stared at him and crossed my arms. He was visibly in pain, curled up in a ball, and it didn't matter—not one iota. He rolled onto his elbows and grinned at me between coughs. This time, I saw him differently, without the veil of memory to cast shadows on his face. The boyish features that I had fallen in love were still there in the older man before me. His eyes were sunken and he had scars among the wrinkles and lines that made him even more dangerous. His face was gaunt and his skin stretched tight over his cheekbones. His pitch-black hair shortened for trial long ago was now long, with strands of gray and white mixed in. Snake's right shoulder had a devilish looking skull with a snake coming out of the eye socket. Across his neck was a webbed tattoo with a black widow on the Adam's apple. Curiosity got the better of me, and I hungered to see if it was still there.

It was. The tattoo of me inked when I was a wild sixteen-year-old. It had faded, of course, but the eyes were bright green still, piercing, looking straight at me. The tattoo beckoned me to remember that young girl with fierce determination and the rotten attitude towards anybody who tried to help. The one who felt so rejected by the world. Mother gone, Father lost forever. The girl in foster homes moved around like cattle. I turned around quickly and closed my eyes to squelch the tear that was going to drop. The heat of his body was on my back and his arms surrounded me. Momentarily lost in time, I leaned back into him. *Damn, I'm sixteen again.*

"It's still there. I never forgot you."

The girl in the dungeon desperately pounded on the door and I heard the faintest sound of "No, don't!" He held me in a tight embrace and rocked me back and forth. His voice flowed like Tupelo honey. "Look at you, just as fine as you were back then."

His lips were following the curve of my neck as my neck stretched to the heat of his breath. He cupped each breast, lifted them up, and they no longer burdened me. All the raging power that had coursed through me seeped out into his arms and left me weak and vulnerable. His hands kneaded the flesh, then he pinched my nipples till they became hard little knobs in his fingertips. Lightening sparks flashed from my feet to my brain igniting all the dark places that I thought were dead. A momentary thought danced across my brain that this was wrong and the girl in the dungeon screamed louder. I pushed against him, but his brute strength held me tighter, and I was rendered helpless. Blood rushed into my ears, drowning out the banging sounds in the dungeon. Turning into his embrace, I searched in his eyes for something, but I hadn't a clue what I was looking for. I didn't care anymore. My hand reached behind his head and forced his lips to mine. He had a familiar taste of strength and fear mixed in an ashtray full of beer. I was back with the leader of the pack.

I took him to my bedroom, stripped him bare, and laid him across my bed previously made of glass. I didn't have time for pleasantries—"Where have you been, what have you been doing." I frankly didn't give a shit about any of that. His past was not my concern. My eyes wandered over his body and noticed the once youthful skin was now full of tattoos, scars, and bullet hole wounds. My finger followed the edge of his thigh muscles, till I my hand caressed the soft sac and felt the weight of a man between my fingers.

"You've changed a bit." He choked that out when my hand ran along a particularly sensitive area. "I think you and I are …" he sucked in his breath and leaned his head back, "…you and I have a lot of catching up to do."

My clothes pooled around my ankles as I moved slowly like a cat stalking his prey; I slithered over the top of him as his eyes followed every movement. Straddling him, he easily slipped into me. He tried to speak, but I laid his head back and whispered, "Shut the fuck up." The rest of the night, we spent underneath the sheets in a battle of who would control the other, the snake or the monster.

Nightmares drifted across my psyche, waking me in a scream that was all too familiar. The sound of a bullet leaving the gun and the shrill of screams woke me up out of dead stillness. Sitting up in a dark room, I couldn't recall where I was, or who I was. Sweat ran down my sides and back. I rubbed my wrists to stop the stinging pain. My hand immediately went to the body next to mine but it was unfamiliar terrain. Before I could pull away, he grabbed my hand.

"You're insatiable, darling, but I need to get some shut eye." Snake flipped over, pulled the covers off me, and fell back to sleep. Alone with only the shadows of the night as my only friend, all I could think was *What the hell did I just do?*

He finally woke up and lit a cigarette. My body was paralyzed as I stared straight at the wall planning different scenarios of exactly how I was going to get out of this. This cur rearranged and changed everything that I was till I became the person I am. I tried to run as far away as I could, but he found me weak and vulnerable like last time. How easily I slipped into his trap once again. He lifted the sheet off me that I had managed to steal back. His eyes glossed over me as the cigarette dripped off his mouth. "Well, you are still a fine looking woman, a little wear and tear, but fine enough." He took a puff of smoke. He put his hand between my legs and started to play and that brought me out of my paralysis. I jumped out of bed and rushed to put my clothes on. I don't suppose he would catch the hint and hoped my recluse lover would take his nasty ass out of my life.

"Where are you going in such a rush?" The cigarette smoke was graying the early morning light. I picked up his clothes and threw them at him in a show of fake courage.

"You need to leave." I stood there with my hands on my hips. *Please, God, make him leave.*

He licked his fingertips and I glanced away towards the window hoping for a better view. *What the hell is wrong with me?* He slithered out of bed and sauntered over to me. He wrapped his naked body around me and I was trapped like a fucking proverbial rat. He pushed my hair aside and began kissing my neck. I protested his advances but he reticulated his arms around me and squeezed even harder. One hand slithered down my pants. He bit my earlobe. "I'm not going anywhere, darling," and pushed me back to bed.

Later in the day, Snake wanted something harder than tea and we drove around Albuquerque, his arm crushing my body next to his. The car sputtered as he parked. "This looks promising," he said as he lit a cigarette. *Oh fuck me*, we had stopped at Michael's, the place of my previous brilliant encounter. He pulled me out of the car and we walked past the devil's gate. He had all the confidence of the angels and I, the shame of the devils. Gabriel was nowhere to be found and was grateful for dumb luck that he wasn't there, disappointment seeping around edges of gratefulness. All the patrons, some in a drunken stupor, looked up to the newcomers and then went back to their libations. No one looked at me the way they did that night. Actually, no one even looked at me. Their fascination had been with Snake, alpha males sizing up the enemy or determining he was one of them. I couldn't tell as I was pushed towards the back of the bar. We sat down at a table and yelled our drinks over the racket of AC/DC's "Hell's Bells." This bar was a cesspool of human sadness and deprivation of soul, lingering smoke lurked all around the edges and corners. I looked into the eyes of all the human waste and saw reflections of what my life had become. It seemed fitting, but a vague notion welled up in my stomach that I missed my old life. I sipped some stale beer to chase the bitterness in my throat.

"Hey," and he caressed my arm. I withdrew from his touch. "What the hell is wrong with you," he asked as he grabbed his beer with the hand that I had refused. He scowled at me.

"Nothing, nothing at all." He looked at me strangely for a moment and then his face returned to normal.

"How did you find me?"

He laughed and took another drag. He leaned back, snuck his hand in his jean pocket, and threw a crumbled piece of paper on the table. I knew what it was immediately before I unraveled it. It was the photo of me sandwiched between Diego and Juan plastered in the journal to catch a killer. "Bait for two hooks." I put the newspaper article over a flame from a cheap red candle and, in a flash, it had turned to ash.

"What did you say?"

"Nothing."

"You are one fucked up chick, but I like it," and he reached underneath my arm and grabbed my breast and squeezed.

"Ow!" I grabbed his hand from my shirt but his strength superseded my own.

He grinned. "I'm leaving town in a few days."

Thank God, "When?" Which came out a little too abruptly and I drank some beer to cover my faux pas. My imagination began to roll with packing my car, hitting the highway, and me alone… on the road again.

"Hmm, you look sad," he smiled and he pulled my head towards him. "I won't be gone long, just need to pick up a few things, make some arrangements." Then he kissed me on the lips and left a lingering taste of ash.

"You gonna share her with us?" It was Rat from that night, although his eyes seemed too glazed over to recognize me. He just leered down my t-shirt. My hands balled into fists and stared straight into the soulless demon.

Snake sat there and took a long swig of beer. Ice was forming through my whole body, I was nothing but a toy to be shared in the sandbox. Something in Snake's eyes clicked and he changed instantly into something I immediately recognized. He took a long puff of a cigarette and then with his hand in a fist, Snake backhanded Rat right in the nuts. As the lowlife fell to his knees, Snake slammed his head into the table. I glanced down at the sight of Rat's broken and bloodied nose, his hands cupping his assaulted jewels. Laughter from my belly came roaring up and I couldn't stop cackling. The monster was laughing at that man's pain and blood. The copper scent of blood drifted to my nose and I licked my lips. I backed my chair out and slowly got up. All the anger, fear, and panic I had felt for so long began to emerge.

Energy and power coursed through my body and down my leg, the point of my boot hit him straight in his ribcage. My foot felt the soft give of the human body and then the vibration of bone. A crack rang through the air and then a pop followed by a muffled scream of pain. The crumpled human being just shoved himself into a ball and I kicked him even harder. Flashes of blonde hair and blue eyes came across my eyes, an evil grin with a knife, and the smell of vanilla in my nose. The more those images incessantly looped in my thoughts, the more I kicked, the angrier I became. I continued to kick him until he was nothing but a flesh pile in clothes.

Snake pulled me back. "You've got a lot of fire in you, don't you, darlin'?"

My eyes tried to adjust back to reality, but they were still clouded by anger and resentment. A rush of blood poured into my head and replaced any common sense I had. I turned to Snake. "Go ahead, leave, I'll be just fine." I was alive again. A smile came across my mouth, death's grin. He grabbed my arm when I was about to kick my delusional Seth some more and he dragged me out of the bar.

Chapter 25

Passion fueled by anger and then sexual release created an electric pulse across my skin that I hadn't felt since before that night with Seth. My brain was intoxicated with the rush of feelings encased in my blood cells and I couldn't have enough. All my neurons pulsed with fire. The guilt of the past that had driven me into hiding was no longer and I found myself walking in the daylight, my arm entangled with Snake's, whereas before I lurked in the shadows of the buildings. I watched the sun scan across my walls and turn to the graying shadows of moonlight. I couldn't sleep and I didn't feel like eating, I was burning inside out and I wanted to run forever.

Days of this electric energy had finally burned me out and I slept like the dead with no dreams. Finally, I woke up to the sounds of Snake coughing and belching. He got dressed and threaded the belt through the loops of his pants. In the crook of his elbow, I saw a drop of blood rise from where a needle had been. His eyes looked glazed over and he seemed to be struggling with the holes on his belt.

"Where are you going? Come back to bed." Lying on my stomach, I reached my arm out so that I could pull him back in. My fingers stretched in the air, but they suddenly ached with the need to touch Gabriel's skin. I quickly pulled back my hand and retreated underneath the covers. He pulled a cigarette out the pack and lit it. Puffed on it for a while, then lifted the sheet and looked at me with hungry eyes.

"I gonna miss this fine piece of ass," and he smacked my right butt cheek.

"Ow!" I slapped his hand away. He raised his hand above his head in a fist, pulsating above me. With the look from hell, I dared him to try and hit me. Moments passed in deep silence. I wasn't the sixteen-year-old girl who lived and breathed on his every word anymore. He slowly put his arm down and went back to dressing.

Ignoring the earlier encounter, I asked, "How long are you gone for?" I watched sunlight come through the curtains and turn my white bedspread into a moonscape.

He puffed on his cigarette. "Gonna miss me?' He smiled at me as he put the rest of his clothes on. The smell of sweat and the faint odor of Old Spice cologne encapsulated my breathing space and I tried not to gag.

"Hardly." I smiled as though I was joking, but it was the truth. Honestly, I enjoyed that drug of power I felt around him, but the after effects was a real bitch.

"A day or two" and he put his hand on my face and cupped my jaw. "I have a few things to tie up." He leaned over for a kiss and his rancid breath made me flinch. He backed off. "You and I" his face became hard stone. "Things are going to be different when I get back." Then he walked out, a lingering shadow of acrid smoke was all that was left as I lay in bed.

The sunlight hit my scars and little sparks of light danced all around them. I jumped out of bed and tried to brush off the glass that I knew was embedded in my skin. The snakes inside my body wouldn't stop writhing and terror began to flood over me. Out of the sunlight, I stopped for a minute, shaking, and reluctantly looked at my scars, but there was nothing there.

Snake was gone but there was no peace. I missed the rush of power but not the man it came from. It was spring, scents of sage intertwined with the fragrance of new flowers hung in the air. Trees were turning shades of bright green and buds on flowers were ready to burst. A sudden heat wave had scorched the earth, and the winds blew Albuquerque into a brown ball of sand and dust. Mother Sandias was blinded from her idle children. I walked past the lilac, desperate for a drink of water, its leaves drooping and buds hanging low, and continued with my mission to the mailbox. The door was rusted as I pushed the lid down with the screech of metal ringing through the air. I rifled through all the gardetto that was sent to me, credit card approvals, money for charity letters, and one letter that I ravaged through that made me break out into a cold sweat.

Behind me, the dogs barked continuously and their obnoxious yapping brought me out of my concentration. They were at the fence, wagging their tails, and I stared straight at them till they backed off and ran the opposite way. Angelica was in Riley's arms, stretching her little fingers toward me, trying to reach the divide and take my hand. Riley turned around to see what Angelica was looking at, she turned back and held her daughter even tighter. Her little head popped up over her mother's shoulder and stared at me with her deep blue eyes. They had shunned me, but I couldn't really blame them. The tides had changed upon the wind and I was not the neighbor they knew before.

I retreated back into my cave, which was still cool from the night passing into day and looked closely at the letter. It was from the prosecutor's office and I was subpoenaed to testify against Seth. The trial had been sent for July 1, and this paper with certified authority requested in lawyer speak that I make an appointment with the district attorney, at my earliest convenience. With brute strength, the letter became a crumpled up ball within my palms. My fingers released the summons and it dropped to the floor where I kicked it away. It rolled solemnly underneath the couch. A little ball of fear formed in the pit of my stomach, but I blew it off by because I would be long gone by then. No one would ever find me this time. I went into the bedroom, fell on the bed and closed my eyes. Seth's face was in red and black and my scars began to burn. On fire, I ran out the door.

I dove into my father's car and sped past all my demons. The windswept desert passed me by in blurs of brown and gold. I tried to drive the tortured images from my head away and hypnotized myself between the yellow lines of the road. I switched on the radio to drown out the screams in my head. My back itched with imagined pieces of glass melding with my skin. The car seat no longer seemed to fit me. I couldn't catch my breath as the crushing metal suffocated me. Knocking noises drowned out the loud music I was playing and then steam burst from the hood. "No, Dad, please don't," and the car began to slow on its own. I was in the middle of nowhere, "please, not here." I hit the steering wheel hard, "you can't do this to me, you can't! You can't leave me again! Please, Dad, I need you."

The tears blinded me as I looked into the rearview mirror. My reflection through the haze of mist and pain was that of a red-eyed hellion with wild blonde hair. The car forced me to pullover. The door hinge screeched in protest as I pushed it open. A dirt devil whirled around me and lashed my skin, then disappeared into the sky. My tongue tasted dirt and salt. Anger welled, and I kicked the front tire and beat on the hood with my fists until the skin was red and my bones were bruised.

Steam rose in spits and spurts. The monster in me began to tire because it was losing against a wall of sadness and despair in the mixture of metal and rubber. I plopped down on the ground and scanned the horizon for clues of exactly where in the hell was I. The wind whipped my hair around and lashed against my face. Sitting on a cliff, I looked out into the abyss of endless blue mountains fading further and further into the background, with red cliffs jutting in and out of my vision. Tears mixed with sand and burned my eyes.

I put my hand on the bumper and acquiesced to his wishes. I was no longer his little girl. The car ceased all sound and steam was no longer coming from the engine. He had made his message clear. The wind calmed down and large drops of rain plopped on my head.

Nice, I got the message, Dad, but do you really have to make it rain, too? Large drops of crystal clear water fell upon my head as the squeal of car brakes rang through the air. Still sitting in the rain, I cocked my head slightly to the sound and watched standard issue boots with black pants step out of the vehicle. There was a perfect crease from his boots to his waist, a mean looking Smith and Wesson M&P .357 in his belt. Continuing my scan with my new best friend, he had a long sleeved shirt with three stripes on the sleeve. His state patrolman's hat covered his eyes in shadow as he walked over to me. The big drops of rain stopped pelting me and the sun came out from behind the clouds. Earth mixed with rain drops perfumed the air. As I sat there looking out, his shadow loomed across me and ended at the edge of the cliff. *Fuck.*

Chapter 26

I pulled the storage door down and gazed at the last remnants of sunlight chased by the encroaching darkness. The car may not belong to me anymore, but it didn't belong to anyone else either. After the cop found me alongside the road, we started the engine and somehow it miraculously worked. I popped my eyes up to the heaven and sneered at the clouds. *Nice trick, Dad.* Then the cop part of him kicked in and he wanted all my personal information. I shook my head, he couldn't just help a stranger, he had to know my identity. "You look familiar to me." I shrugged my shoulders and looked out to the panoramic view. Technically, I haven't done anything wrong in quite a while and I did do my time but I would forever be under suspicion. I gave him my fake I.D. anyways and sweated it out a few minutes as he went back to his cruiser to look me up in cyberspace. As far as he knew, I was Danni Clearwater, who had no prior arrests and was a devil wearing an angel's suit. I did my best calm face and kept my fidgeting hands under control. In his cruiser, he stared through the windshield, his eyebrows moved up and down but the rest of his face remained stone cold. He would be ideal in a poker game. After a few intense moments, he walked back and he gave me back my I.D. "Miss Clearwater, I'll follow you back to Albuquerque."

"No need, Officer, Officer, uh…" I squinted my eyes at his badge, I hate that I need glasses, "um, Officer A.

Sanchez. I don't want to waste your time and all," and I looked behind me at the car, "I'm good to go." *We're good to go. Right, Dad?* I prayed. He lifted one eyebrow and followed me straight into a repair shop.

The cop kept staring at me as I was conversing with the mechanic the language of what needed to be repaired and how much. When recognition of my face hit Officer Sanchez, his eyes widened and his mouth opened for a few moments. Damn, he figured out who I was, Albuquerque's famous resident now, the one who got away.

The police officer sauntered over and I knew the litany of questions that was coming, especially the one where I just lied to him about my identity, "Are you going to be all right, ma'am?" His face showed no emotion but his voice was tender and sincere.

"Good question." A big question mark crossed his face. "Oh, you're talking about the car?" Insecurity enveloped me and I felt strangely out of place. "Yeah, the car will be fine. They can't seem to find anything wrong with it." I looked behind me at the old goat, and could have of sworn the tires got slightly flatter. "It seemed to have spontaneously combusted on its own and then repaired itself." My voice had a wee bit too much sarcasm in it.

"Well," he looked at me for a moment pensively as I waited for the question that will haunt me for the rest of my life, *What happened that night?* "If there is no need for further assistance, I will be on my way." That was a surprise, maybe he was the one person in Albuquerque who didn't want to know. "Call me if you need anything else, Dannielle Clearwater," he said my name like it was typed in bold letters as he handed his NM State Police standard issue business card to me. Officer A. Sanchez, the address of the state police with with a cell phone number.

He turned to go and I couldn't help myself, "Wait." He stopped. His back was straight as a board and he turned around stiffly. The gold from his badge flashed in my eyes for a second, blinded, I squinted, "What is your first name?"

He glanced away and his chiseled cheeks and closely shaven face turned red. He said his name with a Spanish accent, the g coming out like an h sound. He got into his black and white patrol car and took off. I watched him back off and silently whispered his name, Angel.

Watching the mechanic do one last check, I thought of all the times I watched my father work on this vehicle. The never-ending expletives from where I get my colorful language now, the tools thrown on the ground, and the gray cover I put over it the day I buried him. I began to itch all over and scratched in various places, trying to relieve the feeling of worms in graveyard dirt writhing underneath my skin.

The car was in perfect working condition. I paid the man while I cursed the bill underneath my breath. I drove to the nearest storage unit and paid for a year. They asked for a family reference and I didn't hesitate to put Gabriel's name and address. Walking past the frame of the door, something pulled me back. "Can I see that contract?" The bored looking clerk reluctantly handed it back to me. Searching for what had been missing, underneath Gabriel's name, I scribbled, if after a year you do not hear from me, give the car to Gabriel.

The bus maneuvered down Central, avoiding hitting hapless homeless people and absentminded university students. The bus screeched to a halt at my destination. I traipsed down Central, window shopping and silently said goodbye to my old haunts. People walked past me, staring at my scars, looks of disapproval crossed my body as they pretended to be in deep conversation. I cocked my head in defiance of their judgment and resisted the urge to cover myself up. Something caught my eye in front of this store and was horrified at the image. A woman with wild blonde curly hair, sunken eyes, and angular cheekbones looked at me with deep sadness. The reflection had an army green shirt, cut off shorts, and wrapped around my neck was a ghostly image of a rosary. A river of blood drained from my face, a ghostly white image was standing frozen in place. The heat and the sunlight surrounded me like a suffocating blanket and I looked up to see the title of store, "Reflection of Soul." My eyes adjusted back to reality and behind the store front window hung many rosaries in different shapes, sizes, and colors. Bibles displayed open to various books of Matthew, Mark, and John with white candles illuminating the pages.

My hand lingered on the window as I walked away from that reflection. Lost in thought, I had managed to find my way home. Gabriel was washing the big yellow beast and in the back window was a For Sale sign. "How's it going?" Silence was my answer to the question, so I tried another route, "Why are you selling the Ford?"

He looked at me for a moment and went back to scrubbing the truck. His long, sleek hair tied in a ponytail swayed across his bare shoulders. His body was slick from the wet of the water and his skin tanned from the sun. I had a sudden urge to reach out to touch his skin again and feel the warmth of Gabriel's body against my own. My fingers curled inward before I touched him. "I haven't seen you in a while." He kept wiping down the truck and would only look at me out of the corner of his eye from time to time. I sighed. So this is how it was going to be, "Look asshole, I want to buy it, all right."

"Where's your car?" and he looked around for the invisible GTO.

"Gone, sold it." It was just easier lying than explaining the ghost of my father didn't want me to have the car.

"800 hundred."

"What? For this piece of crap, you're kidding me, right?"

He continued washing the yellow behemoth without a word and a really big ball of anger and annoyance started to bounce against my insides and make its way up my throat. Why wouldn't he look at me? What did I do to him? I turned and walked away and wondered if he couldn't stand the sight of me. I heard footsteps and my skin crawled across my back as I felt his presence behind me. He grabbed my arm and turned me around.

"You know, Danni, you can stop beating yourself up. You can stop making this your fault. He came into your home and...."

I had to stop the words because they were like a train barreling down the tunnel, "What are you saying, I'm emotionally masochistic?" I laughed but he wasn't smiling back.

His stare was intense and I thought I would become ash under the amber brown rays. "He broke into your home and beat you, tortured you...."

The well of pain and fury rushed up. "Stop! Stop! Stop saying it!" I screamed at the top of my lungs. "Please, stop!"

Between the screams and sobs I heard in a calm low voice, the voice of reality I didn't want to face, "He invaded your home, beat you, tortured you and he rap...."

"Stop! Please stop!" I was crying uncontrollably. Why was he ripping all the scars to shreds that had healed over so well? Why was he taking this emotional knife and slashing open all the old wounds? I covered my ears to stop the sound of ripping skin and to dampen the sounds of screaming.

"Danni, let me help you." He reached out to me but I had been violated enough and backed away. My wounds seeped blood down my arms and dripped to the ground. Gabriel ran a hand through his hair in frustration, his head bent solemnly, his wings expanded into bright white translucent feathers that burned my eyes. My hands were slick with blood that reflected the sunlight and I took off running. Gabriel's call was in my ears like a raucous wind, "Danni, Danni!" Running away from the hand of God, I sprinted the short distance home and held onto my wounds tightly to stop them from bleeding. Finally, I fell onto my porch, the blood oozed between my fingers and onto the planks of wood. The tink, tink sound of blood pouring into metal echoed in my ears and drowned out the chirping of the spring birds. Reaching for the doorknob, my sunbaked skin had become white as snow. The blood had completely disappeared. Now, I'm haunted by illusions and they're not even illusions of grandeur. With all the strength I had left, I willed myself up and pushed the door in. "That fucking sucks!" and crossed the threshold into my cave, back into the dark womb. I laid my heated forehead against the cool of the adobe to ease my delusional fever.

"What sucks?" Startled out of disillusionment, Snake put his arms around me and forced me back into him. "Did you miss me, baby?"

My body stiffened in his embrace. Not really, "Sure." He shoved his hand down my shorts and cupped the curve of my butt. His touch felt like the pieces of glass were twisting deeper in my skin.

Apparently, waiting for my appearance, he had already begun to entertain himself. Lines of white powder and a razor blade decorated my table, along with a big bottle of vodka. He maneuvered me to the couch and made me sit on his lap.

"Try it," he licked his cracked lips. His eyes became glazed over and I'm not sure but I think he was going to drool. "You might like it," and he rolled a dollar bill and snuffed a line in his nose.

Was this the man I was really scared of the whole time? He was just another illusion. At the moment, all my illusions were chasing me and I needed a break in the marathon. Which is worse, a drug addict or an alcoholic? I didn't need any more marks upon my body. He began to snort each line and I picked up the bottle of vodka and drank like there was no tomorrow. Because frankly I could care less if tomorrow ever came.

Snake and I danced around the house like a fools in a drunken haze, giggled, tripped, and fell a lot. I'm not sure why I fell so much, I had always great balance. I played hide and seek with Snake and then quickly forgot what I was looking for. All my thoughts became paralyzing crystal clear as I poured more vodka. I had no belief in anyone or anything. Where was God when I was being cut into pieces at a madman's buffet? Where was He when I needed him the most? My anger was an everlasting riptide that swelled and ebbed with every passing moment. Where was God? I slurred out loud, "Where were you, you left me to die? Mother, Father, you left me. I was left like trash used and discarded. To be bled like a pig before slaughter. What was I, some sacrificial lamb for You? I was twisted and mutilated for Your amusement. What kind of God are you?" And I searched for the answers in the bottom of the vodka bottle. I swam deep in the ocean of intoxication, looking for the retribution I deserved. No father to hold my hand across the pit fires of hell. God had a lot of explaining to do. He had a lot to atone for. Eventually, I schlepped my way to bed before my stomach took off for the bathroom. Emptying all that I had across the bathroom floor, I lay in bed and watched all the vigas spin in a fast moving wheel and disappear into darkness.

Something was loud, waking up my beleaguered brain, finishing a conversation I had started earlier, believe in Him, ha, and what is that god-awful noise? Something bright was piercing my eyeballs. Slowly, my eyelids lifted to beams of sunlight. *Oh, God, please make it stop,* and placed pillows over my head and plunged myself back into darkness. *Suffocation would be the ultimate act of kindness*, I thought, rather sullenly but this irascible constant banging noise, although muffled wouldn't stop. The bottle fell to the floor as I pushed Snake's arm off me. Spilling out of bed, I staggered to the source of the noise so that I could stab it and kill it.

"For god's sake, please stop!" My head was in one hand and the other hand was in front of me stopping me from running into anything. My brain was looking for an exit. My stomach flipped on itself and the floor seemed such a long way down. I opened the door to stop the incessant banging and yelled before I saw who it was, "What the fuck do you want?" Bright light pierced my eyes and now I knew my brain was trying to escape its toxic shell.

I was about to slam the door and save myself from the intense light when a hand stopped the motion of the door, "Danni?" I opened one eye and stared up into intense piercing brown eyes with a bright halo around his head.

"Danni, what the hell is wrong with you?"

"I have no idea." The other eye was trying to open but it wasn't happening by any means. It was safely glued shut. I had a bad case of cottonmouth and I just knew I would cough up a hairball at any moment. "Did you want something, Gabriel? It's early."

"It's twelve."

"Like I said, it's early."

"You don't look so good."

"You have amazing powers of observation." I began to close the door but this time, he stuck his foot in the door and held it. I hadn't the strength left to fight and stood there, swaying like I was on a rocking boat. Bed, I need my bed back and I turned around and looked for my coffin.

"Danni, I'd like to talk to you."

"Shh, you're way too loud."

"Danni, I'm barely talking."

I turned slowly around so the waves of pain in my head didn't crash too hard in my skull. "Talk softer," now there were two of him and four sets of wings. Wow, that's really unusual. I need a drink.

"What's unusual?"

"Did I say that out loud, nothing, it's just morning, can't think?" *Oh, the pain.* "You wanted something?" Holding my head because any movement started a new wave of agony, skipped the coffin, and found the couch instead.

"I wanted to bring you the keys to the truck." Silvery reflections from the keys shot sparks of light into my eyes. My eyes slammed shut and snuffed out the light. *God help me, I'm not surviving this day.* "You ran away before I could give you these." He moved the keys and the clinking of metal hurt my ears.

"Shh, be quiet."

"Danni, it's just keys," and he threw them on the coffee table with a clank. *Oh my god, those had to be the loudest keys ever* and I put my hands over my ears. The cushions next to me sank and radiation of heat from Gabriel's body reignited the burning sensation in my scars. "Danni, if you need to talk, I…."

"Please not this again," and laid my head, which felt like molten rock, on the head of the couch. Through my teeth, I whispered, "What are you, my therapist?"

"I'm not going to stop. Danni, I lo…."

"Hey, what's going on out there?" Snake yelled from the bedroom. Gabriel's mouth tensed up. "Keep it down, I'm trying to sleep." I covered my ears from Snake's voice. It felt like fingernails across the chalkboard. *Why did he have to yell?* Gabriel's eyes radiated anger and hurt in different flashes like fifty-two card pick up. Every emotion was out for display. I was ashamed, embarrassed, and oddly, I felt vindicated all at the same time, then a big wave of nausea came over me. Vindication had a price.

"I see you've got company." I just closed my eyes and hoped all this would go away and there would be peace on earth somewhere. "The truck is out there."

"Thanks," I muttered. My stomach was sending me nasty signals. He got off the couch and stopped for a minute. In a moment of weakness, I reached my hand out to him but his back was towards me. Shards of sunlight crossed his back and his gossamer wings had disappeared. Then he walked out the door without saying another word. The last remaining piece of my heart was on the bottom of his boots crossing the threshold.

Chapter 27

I was one breadstick away from getting fired, but I managed somehow to keep my job. Marco was unimpressed when I would schlepp into work without a second to spare with barely one eye open and dark circles puffs that highlighted my bloodshot eyes. The joking stopped between the boys and me, and was replaced by looks of concern from the bruises across my arms and neck. We were on a strictly don't-ask-don't-tell policy around here. I didn't ask about their sexual encounters and mine was none of their business.

After work, the goat rumbled into the driveway and as I slithered out of the car, I glanced across the street. Angelica was in midst of tea party with two drooling dogs as her other companions. Each dog showed immense patience as they eyed the dog treats on the table. Angelica was in a beautiful yellow cream dress that highlighted her saintly smile as she poured them tea in tiny teacups. My car would wake up anybody out of deep sleep but Carson and Riley didn't even look my way as they pretended to be in deep conversation. Pushing the unlocked door in, depression hit me in waves when I walked in to find Snake and two other men around the coffee table. *Oh, good, the gang is all here.* Snake popped out of his chair, beer bottle in hand, smacked my ass, and gave me a deep kiss. His eyes turned cold when he saw me cringe at the sour taste that was left in my mouth.

"Hey, darling, I want you to meet some people. This is Luka," he pointed to a guy with incredibly long legs that stuck out from the couch. The back of his greasy hair moved as he turned his head sideways to face me. He had one long jagged scar that went from his eyebrow, across the nose, and down the side of his jaw. He lifted a lanky arm off the back of the couch in apparent acknowledgment to my presence. He had a full sleeve with artwork of various naked women in different submissive positions, chains, and skeletons. He lifted his lips and exposed brown, slimy teeth in what I think was supposed to be a smile and a queasy feeling roiled in my stomach. Hand on my ass, Snake pushed me into the living and introduced me to another member of Snake's fan club. Snake slapped him on the back, "This is Damon." Damon was wide as he was tall. He had a hairy stomach that bulged over his baggy jeans, a dirty t-shirt underneath a worn leather vest with patches slowly coming unstitched. He had only one tattoo on beefy sized arm, a skeleton riding an evil looking motorcycle. Thin wisps of dark brown hair curled haphazardly around his head and ended at his fully pierced earlobes. Round cheekbones highlighted his narrowed eyes. He sneered at me with thin little lips surrounded by a wiry looking goatee and stared back out of the window across the street. My neck cracked from the chill that just ran up my body.

Snake ushered me to the couch and put his suffocating arm around me, and smirked at Luka. Luka quickly looked away. *Fabulous*, I was the bright shiny toy in the sandbox. Snake took a slug of beer. "The boys and I are thinking about heading out west." He took his arm away and lit up a cigarette. The smell of cigarette smoke quickly suffocated the room, and my lungs burned from the evasive smoke. He couldn't leave soon enough. I seemed to be under his watchful eye as of late, quite possibly because he found my bags packed in the back of the truck the other day. I was hoping to make a run for it when Gabriel opened the door to his house and saw me. I froze and felt the hurt look in his eyes. Snake slithered out, saw Gabriel, and kissed me in front of him. "Going somewhere?" He nodded towards Gabriel and grabbed my bags, brought them into the house, and I remained always within his sights ever since.

"When?"

"Soon." He took another drag, "You'll be coming with us, darling," and he looked at me out of the corner of his eye. He wasn't asking me, he was commanding me. "We'll all have a real good time," and he patted my knee.

A deep growl entered my throat and I stuffed it down and struggled out of his embrace.

"Where are you going?"

"I have to pee." I walked into the bathroom and hit my fists on the sink. *How in the hell am I going to get out of this?* I did some necessary personal things, opened the door, and ran smack straight into Luka's chest. He didn't waver from the sudden assault.

"Scuse me," and I tried to get around him. He just moved to where I was going. "What?"

He grabbed a lock of my hair and twisted in his fingers, "You smell good."

"Fantastic, shampoo is in the bathroom, try it sometime," and I tried to walk past him. "Get the fuck out of my way!"

He leered at me. "Snake said I could have you." He sniffed around my neck, "When he's done with you." He grinned with brown stains on his teeth, and the scar on his face stretched into a silvery white, "Generally, I don't like anybody's seconds," he kept twisting my hair in his finger, "but you might be worth it." Locks of blonde curl swirled around his index finger like a snake coiling around his prey.

Medusa might have had the key there with a head full of snakes and the ability to turn men into stone. Of course, it really wasn't her choice. "Leave me the hell alone!" I stared directly up into his eyes as I pushed his hand away. "I'm not anyone's seconds!" The corner of my lip rose in half sneer as I looked him up and down and stared squarely at his crotch. "Besides, I want a man, not a little boy." I walked around him and into the living room. Damon continually stared out at the window with a glazed look in his eyes. I followed his line of vision to where Angelica was playing in the front yard. He was rubbing his hand along his thigh methodically and if I didn't know better, I thought he was about to drool.

"What are ya looking at there, Damon?" He barely noticed me and swatted his ear like there was something buzzing in that pea-size brain of his. I became more direct, "Damon, what are you looking at?"

Finally, he looked at me with his eyes glassed over, "Just looking at all the pretty things in the neighborhood."

He made my skin crawl. I whispered, "Touch one hair and it will be the last thing you ever do." His tongue with a big metal piercing licked his lips and left a sheen behind. Mind you, I hadn't a clue what I would do, but I'm sure there is an elephant gun at the zoo I could borrow. Snake came up behind me and laid a heavy hand on my shoulder.

"Come on back to the couch, darling, we got future plans to make."

I couldn't tear my head away until I heard something that made my heart sink. "What future?"

He sat down and lit a joint; my house was fast becoming a bottom of an ashtray. "We have some plans." He took a puff and blew out acrid smoke that billowed in the air before it slowly dissipated. Luka came back and sat across from us. He stared straight at me. "Isn't that right, Luka?" Snake questioned as he passed the joint to Luka. Snake began to rub around my thigh and was beginning to go between my legs. "You're part of those plans." Luka leered at me as Snake took the joint back.

"No, thanks, got plans of my own." Well, at least I was starting to form some.

Snake pushed his thumb into a just healing scar on my thigh. I gritted my teeth but didn't make a sound. "You got away from me once, it won't happen again." Snake got up from the couch, "Luka, call some people and let's get this party started."

Chapter 28

The dreams of guilt no longer plagued me. Tonight, I dreamed of death, torture, and the demise of a grinning head cutting off my soul. I sat up suddenly and tried to familiarize with my surroundings. Sweat rolled off me and I was dying for cool air. I picked up an old t-shirt on the floor, sneaked my way into it, and tiptoed past the "guests" laid across each other in various forms of drunkenness. When I walked past the thrall, I thought I felt Luka's eyes upon me but when I looked back, his head was slumped over in sleep and I continued on to the kitchen with a creepy crawly feeling.

Through my kitchen window, I spied the man in the moon, it was so full and glowed bright white against the onyx sky. It fit perfectly between my windowpanes. For a moment, I tried to touch the white silvery powder that seemed to mix with the gray seas. The moon brightened the room and everything turned silver. My fingers became like eerie bones that waved in the moonbeam's light. I flipped the handle on the sink and cupped my hands. Shimmery water danced in my palms and then dripped over the sides with diamond sparkles. A familiar scent floated all around me and I put my nose into the t-shirt and sniffed Gabriel's cologne. The scent woke up my memories of him and his face became alive in the moonlight. Cool air brushed over my sweaty skin and cooled down the aching feeling of loneliness. The girl in the dungeon missed him and the monster receded to the black shadows of the night.

Footsteps behind me broke the peaceful moment. A hand came up my shirt and cupped one of my breasts. I tried like a mother to push his hand away. He pushed me against the sink. Fully trapped by his body, his hands roamed freely, his touch felt like eels were swimming across my skin.

"Stop," I whispered. I couldn't stop the wave of panic crashing into me.

"You smell like candy." He pinched my nipple and the sudden electric sensation made my head pop back. His hand caught my jaw and I couldn't move.

"Don't." I was trying to push his hand away. "Stop," I choked. My neck stretched tight beyond the point of pain. My pleas seemed to have egged him on more. He pushed Gabriel's t-shirt up and exposed my breasts to the silvery light. Moving to get out of his embrace, he slammed me harder into the counter. My hipbone hit the edge of the steel counter.

"You're ready for me, aren't you, darling?" His fingertips were crawling in between my legs.

"Sto…!" his hand slipped down and squeezed around my throat, his thumbs digging into my airway. My head began to swim.

"Shhh, you don't want to wake the others."

Something shifted in the darkness. Someone was in the shadows. I prayed silently for help. Snake pushed me over the sink, kicked my legs apart and slammed into me. He released his grip around my neck but only slightly enough to get some air. "Help." My voice sounded gravelly and pathetic. He covered my mouth and the other hand squeezed my breast with every thrust. Moonbeams highlight the sheen of my scars and cast my arms into an ethereal light. Tears streamed down my eyes as Snake continued his hammering. With one last thrust, he was finally done in a spasm and I stood there stunned, naked, and vulnerable. Afraid to move, I stood like a stone as I heard the refrigerator door open and illuminate the kitchen in yellows and grays. A diamond star reflected off the metal knife that was beside the sink. My fingers easily curled around the shaft of the knife. The clinking of glass was unmistakable as he moved around bottles on the refrigerator shelf. He took one out, rubbed it across my butt cheek, and then popped it open. He swallowed hard, "Here's one for you, too."

I didn't want a beer, I wanted to kill him. The dark shadow on the wall moved closer. The moonlight exposed the shadow's face and my heart dropped. Luka had been standing there the whole time. Snake slapped my ass and then walked over to Luka. He patted Luka's face, handed him the beer, and walked out of the kitchen. My fingers released the hilt of the knife as my chance had slipped away. I pulled Gabriel's t-shirt down as far as I could pull it and tried to walk out. I came face to face with Luka, who was still standing there leering at me with a beer in his hand. Semen ran down my leg as I stared at Luka. Silvery shadows splayed across the landscape of Luka's face, the moonlight turned his teeth bright fluorescent as he smirked a hideous white grin. His hand curved around the shape of my breast, whether from fear or stupidity, I had nowhere to run, no one to turn to help, so I stood my ground. His fingers played with my nipple, tears burned my eyes, and I spoke in a whisper, "I will see you dead one day." He took a swig of beer, licked his acrid teeth, and left me standing there.

All hope was lost; the pit I had dug was muddy and slimy as I tried to crawl my way out of my nightmare life. Clawing and screaming to get out, I had slipped further down into the pit of venomous snakes. As I lay there, the sun crept up on my bedroom wall and turned it into brilliant white. Frozen in bed, Snake's arms had coiled around me as I tried to breathe. I was suffocating slowly. In the pit, I made a silent plea, *I know that I haven't been one of your best souls, not really sure if I was a creation gone wrong, I won't bullshit you with promises of how good I'll be or I'll go to church every Sunday. No, definitely won't do that, but maybe could you see your way in finding a way to help me?* The brilliant white wall turned to ash as clouds covered the sun. Not the sign I was looking for.

It was noon and Snake released me from his chokehold, and I made my way out to the den of inequity. Some questionable characters were making their way out the door, followed by drugged out skanks who were with them. I picked up a rug full of cigarette butts and ashes and walked out to the front porch. Across the street was a symphony of Angelica's little girl laugh and barking dogs. I shook out the rug and watched all the cockroaches scamper away. One cockroach slipped his way past me, a black cloud the size of my foot was about to snuff out its life but I watched it run in desperation and left him to his travels.

Rug, semi clean in hand, I walked back inside and saw Damon entranced as he stared out the front window. The front part of his jeans formed a tent shape. "Get the fuck away from the window!" Snake came out of the bedroom half-naked with his pants sliding off his hips.

"What are you going to do about him?"

Snake buttoned his pants and took a cigarette that was in between his greasy hair and his earlobe. "Do about what, darling?" He lit it up as Luka slimed his way into the room and leaned against the wall and leered at me. *Fantastic, hail, hail the gang is all here.*

"What the fuck are you going to do about him?" and I pointed toward Damon. "I think he's got some serious mental issues."

"Who, Damon? Nah, you got him all wrong." He looked out the window as Angelica played with the dogs. Right about then, Riley walked out to her car. "He likes women," he grinned, "some younger than others," and he laughed, which caused a hacking spasm. My stomach flipped as I watched Riley get into her car and leave.

"He's not going anywhere near her, do you hear me," and I poked my finger into his chest.

He grabbed my hand and twisted my wrist. "Look, bitch, don't you worry about anybody else." His eyes bore down on me, clouds of gray moved around in his irises and his breath smelled like jack and coke. Just from the fumes alone, I was getting slightly dizzy. His arms were full of small needle holes and smeared blood. He pushed me against the wall and began to nip at my ears. Anger swelled and I had a knee jerk reaction straight up into his balls. He went down to the ground and grabbed himself. "You leave me hell alone!" And I reared back to kick him in the face.

However, he quickly recovered, caught my leg, and slammed me back into the wall. The wind was knocked out of me and I gasped for a breath. The air suddenly swooshed into my lungs and I could breathe again. Snake punched me square in the stomach, my body doubled over in vain. I desperately tried not vomit.

"Don't you ever do that again, bitch!" He pulled on my hair and I was straight up against the wall. Snake brought out his switchblade and snapped it open right besides my right eye. There was sharp pain on my cheek, but my stomach had taken center stage. Behind Snake, Damon walked nonchalantly out of the door. I knew what he was about to do and hoped Carson was watching Angelica. Fear made me slide down the wall in defeat and I tried to find courage in my sheep's heart. Wiping a tear, my fingers were smeared with blood.

"Get up, you stupid cunt. It's time to teach you a lesson." He grabbed my hair and shoved me into the bedroom. "Luka, get in here! You wanted your chance, now you got one." He slammed me into the dresser and then kicked my legs apart. Lying on the dresser was the instrument of my rescue, it isn't that God suddenly appears and saves you, but he gives you the tools to save yourself. I grabbed the hammer that had lain forgotten so many months before, turned, and smashed Snake's face. A sickening crunch sound echoed in the room, and he crumpled down to the ground. I picked up the switchblade that had fallen beside him and ran for the door. Luka tripped me and I fell flat on my face, as the switchblade skidded across the floor. He flipped me over like a rag doll, then swiped at me with his blade. My body moved just in time for the blade to hit the floor. I must have moved too quickly because my side began to burn. For a few milliseconds, he was stunned by the fact that the knife was stuck, so I kneed him in the gut so hard he lost his breath. I struggled to release myself from under him but it was no use, he quickly regained his composure, grabbed his knife, and raised it above his head. For a split second, he stared down and his eyes were black empty coals. His hands came down, but my fingertips scrambled for the blade behind me, and I plunged the knife into his side. Shocked, his face turned white. He clutched his side and fell over. I scrambled from underneath him, pushed him off me, and ran out the door.

Searching frantically, I found who I was looking for. "Don't you touch her! Don't you dare touch her, you fucking bastard!" Damon was in the middle of the street and turned his beefy neck only slightly. My side was burning, my hands wet with blood. My legs couldn't carry me any faster, I was running in slow motion. Hideously, he smiled at me. I was so close, then my knees crumpled beneath me. "Don't you dare touch her!" I reached out for Angelica, *please God*.

A speeding car roared around the corner, hit their brakes, and slammed straight into Damon. He hit the lid of the car and smashed the windshield into a perfect spider web. His body rolled down the hood of the car and onto the street, where he lay like a carcass for the crows.

Slowly, I managed to get up and get to Angelica. Her eyes were wide open as I scooped her up in my arms.

The sound of sirens screamed as they came around the corner. Carson rushed out the door, phone beside her ear. I rocked Angelica back and forth in my arms, holding her tight. Her eyes were becoming so beautiful and ethereal, so angelic. Then everything faded into white.

Chapter 29

All around me was golden light and ether, but nothing I could touch or feel. I sensed a peace I never have felt before. I walked along into the clouds of white and wondered where in the hell I was exactly.

"Definitely not hell." Before me, out of nowhere stood Angelica, but much older. I couldn't help but stare and then she began to morph into many different faces. Faces I had all seen before, people that in some form or another helped me over the years. "No, I'm not Angelica." She had turned into the waitress at the diner that I stopped at years ago.

I take it you know everything I'm thinking.

"Yes, I do." She was beautiful, standing in an indescribably radiating light.

"Thank you. We are made from the Great Creator. He makes everything beautiful."

I hate it when somebody reads your thoughts. It's an invasion of privacy, actually. She smiled and bowed her head slightly.

"I take it I'm dead. I really don't have dreams like this."

"No, not dead," she morphed into Mr. Meeks. She smiled, or rather, he smiled, "a temporary reprieve, let's say."

Damn.

"You're forgiven, you know." She walked along, clouds moved out of her way, and bits of white light bounced all around her. I looked down and fidgeted with my feet.

"Humans really have no understanding of the concepts of forgiveness and love, do they?" She turned back into the older Angelica, so serene, a bright halo encircled her head. "You must be wondering about Angelica and why you sense something about her." Her face was so gentle, with a hit of sadness in her blue, ethereal eyes. "She is an angel in training, but she had a hard lesson too soon. We're trying to coach her out of her shell, as you say." She turned into the bank guard from that fateful night, and my heart started to bleed.

With sadness and trepidation, "When do I have to go back?"

"Now," and she faded into the ether, with only whispers of her voice all around me, "forgive yourself."

"Danni! Danni!"

I fell hard from wherever to earth and I felt like I hit a rock on the way down. I grabbed my side.

"Good, she's responding."

"I am?"

"Do you know what day it is?" He was a rather nice handsome young E.M.T. flashing a light in my eye.

I pushed his penlight away, "Get that penlight the hell of my eyes day." He seemed astonished at first, then he chuckled slightly. I grabbed my side, "My side is on fire."

"It's a pretty good slice, but it should mend pretty quickly." He was putting one last piece of tape on a large padded bandage, "We need to get you to the hospital for stitches." He motioned to the lump underneath the blanket. "So, did you have a fight with that guy?"

"Something like that." He shrugged his shoulders to the lack of information I gave. My wound was throbbing and burning from the inside out.

"Where did you get all those scars?" He kept writing on his pad and never looked at me.

I hope God gives me another step to heaven every time I hear that question. "I'm a knife juggler, had to give it up," and I shook my head at the sadness of giving up my career. "I was really bad at it." The E.M.T. smirked and continued writing. "Are you going to be much longer?" The E.M.T. looked up from his important paperwork and stared a little bit too long. Then, his face had that dawn of realization look. *Fuck.* He recognized me. He quickly went back to writing. *He should write a novel or something.*

"No, he's quite done. You may leave, Henson." The E.M.T. glanced back and forth between me and the captain and, smart person that he was, skedaddled.

"You've quite the knack for getting into trouble, don't you, Carolina?"

"I would never be in trouble if it weren't for you, Captain Stafford." Dickhead just made the handsome E.M.T. guy leave.

"Care to tell me why you were hanging around with a known child molester?"

"What?"

"Damon Fletcher has been wanted in Colorado for sexually assaulting a ten year old. So," he got really close to me, "why were you associating with him?"

"I wasn't." *Well sort of.* This is where having a computer to check on backgrounds would have been considerably helpful.

"Don't lie, Carolina. You were seen with known criminals, one by the name of Snake, and the other was Luka Detorio. They were part of a known motorcycle gang who deals in drugs." I hopped off the ambulance and pushed past him. "Don't you dare walk away from me," and he grabbed my shoulder.

That one touch made me react violently and I swung around and hit him as hard as I could. "Get the hell away from me!" Unfortunately, he jumped away and I hit air and fell forward into his arms. All heads turned our way and we both froze in position.

He righted me back up, "Tell me where they are now, Carolina, and perhaps...." He paused and spit on the ground. "Perhaps, I'll make things considerably easier on you." That caught my attention and swallowed.

"How should I know?"

"This isn't going to go well for you, Carolina." He got closer to me in the middle of the street. "If you don't start talking."

I don't suppose another car would come around the corner and break through the police barricade. Nope, nothing happened in those few seconds. Yep, that's what I thought, I couldn't ask for two miracles in a day. "Either arrest me or leave me alone, which is it?" I looked past the captain's lightning stare as Riley scooped up her little girl in her arms. Angelica's eyes were crystal blue and she smiled at me angelically. Peace drifted my way and a sense of calm overwhelmed me. Then, Angelica's eyes changed to cloud blue and she suddenly looked bewildered. Riley followed Angelica's gaze and mouthed thank you. I smiled shyly. No one had ever thanked me before.

"I'm keeping an eye on you!" He snapped his legs together and turned away.

"Yeah, whatever, go fuck yourself."

My statement to the police was quite clear. I noticed from my house somebody suspicious walking over to where Angelica was playing. I went over to check him out and he pulled a knife on me where I received my vicious cut. Then, I scrambled for Angelica, and the bad man was run over by the car. There were no witnesses. Carson had come out of the house after the screech of the tires, and the other one who could refute my story was road kill. Hopefully, nobody really checked on the logistics of the whole incident. I looked like a hero and everything was wrapped up into a neat little package. The captain kept his mouth shut on my "illicit" activities, which made me very suspicious about his intentions.

Finally, after what seemed like tortured hours, I went into my house, hoping to find two dead criminals. I was wondering how in the hell was I going to dig a big enough hole for the two of them, but there was only a large bloodstain on the floor. The bedroom was a mess, my dresser was tossed over, and the hammer lay beside it with blood and hair on it. Red splotches left a trail that I followed out the back door and then poof, nothing. *Fuck, they weren't dead.* But I wasn't really afraid of Snake anymore or I was in complete shock at the moment, who knows.

Chapter 30

"I'm not going to testify against Seth in the trial," I said, standing tall in front of the Albuquerque prosecutor. My knees were ready to run like hell. My little foray with Snake and his gang made me realize I was tired of being everyone's puppet. Lionel Hawk was an impassioned prosecutor with a ninety percent conviction rate. Beleaguered families raved about Lionel giving them justice for their loved ones. On the news, he was a tall, handsome, distinguished gentleman in his late fifties. Currently, he was standing behind his desk, with a surprised look in his eyes, shoulders slacked in a question mark in a custom made suit, and his mouth gaping open.

"What do you mean you are not going to testify?"

"Exactly that, I'm not testifying."

"Do you realize if you don't, Carolina, that a serial killer could go free?" The gold in his wedding band stood out among the strands of his pepper and salt hair as he whisked his hand through his scalp. He left a Mohawk trail on the top of his head.

"I understand what it means," I mumbled as I headed towards the door. I wasn't going to be anyone's toy again, even if it meant letting that psychopath go. Well, at least that was what I was willing to tell myself.

"How many women will be tortured and killed because you're afraid?"

I turned around and faced him. "Afraid?"

"Yeah, afraid, afraid to see him again, to face him in court." He sat down behind his desk. I paced back and forth around his crappy little office and wondered how much the city actually paid him.

"I was set up and used for bait." I plopped down in the chair across from him, trying to understand why my body was not walking out the door. "I don't want to testify!" My voice echoed inside the room and bounced off the walls. My voice resounded in my ears, but what I heard was the word "coward". "I don't want to go through this nightmare for anyone's entertainment. Not to mention my background isn't exactly stellar."

"We will get past that at the beginning of the trial. "Miss Stronghill," his voice started out stern.

"Carolina."

He cleared his throat. "Carolina, I know you've been through a lot." He had a look of concern in his eyes, and I had a sudden need to engross myself with a painting on his wall. "I know I am asking for a lot more from you."

"Yes, you are!" I got up from the chair so quick it flew across the room. "You have no idea what I went through." He grabbed a tissue from the box on the top of his desk and handed it to me. While he waited for me to dry my tears, he thumbed through a file—my file.

I slammed my hand on top of it and stopped him from reading. "I'm more than these words on a file. I was a human on that altar." He sat back in his chair and twisted the gold band around his finger. Slowly, he turned around and grabbed a frame. Then he handed me the picture of a chubby faced baby wearing a pink knitted hat that had a bright daisy on top. "She's beautiful," and I offered the photo back to him.

"Thank you. I know what Captain Stafford did, Carolina, but I'm asking you to please help me."

I sighed. I could promise him nothing but this, "I'll think about it."

Walking out his office like a warrior, I willed my knees to stand strong, but they were determined to act like jelly and almost crumbled beneath me. *Just take the car and run.* Running was something I was good at. In the hallway, my jellied legs passed an older couple holding a gold leafed metal frame with the picture I recognized as one of Seth's victims. They huddled together as tears ran down their eyes and fell to the floor. The tears pooled and washed away the footsteps of the convicted. They were a mother and father holding on for a dear life. The father was a short Hispanic man whose face was aged by grief. Deep creases were around his eyes, and they were filled with searing pain from having his soul wretched out of him.

He stood up as I walked by. "Are you the one who is going to testify?" I turned around and looked at the prosecutor's door. *Damn him.* He had them waiting for me, bastard.

I swallowed hard and turned back to the sorrowed man. "I …I…I'm not sure. I don't think I can relive that nightmare again. I'm sorry." A lot of sorries were going around for the destruction left by just one man.

"This is my Alisha," and he showed me the picture of a lovely young woman in her thirties, with silky long blonde hair. Her eyes were the color of whiskey brown tinted by gold.

"She's was a lovely young woman." The ice around my heart began to break.

"He took her away from us," and he looked at his wife who was huddled in a chair, her face wet with tears. She held a rosary in her hand and her lips were moving. My throat began to tighten and it was harder for my brain to refuse the rawness of the pain that stood before me.

"I know, but I can't," and I gently pushed the picture back over his heart.

He bowed his head. "Please, help us, Lord," but I couldn't tell if it was a plea for me or for God. My stomach became instantly nauseous.

The woman slowly stood up, her burden crushing her, she put her hand upon my shoulder. Her face was withered and old from feeling so much excruciating pain. I didn't flinch at her touch, but it was hard to take the electricity that coursed through me. She had long beautiful fingers that I imagined cooked, sewed, and wiped the tears away from her daughter. My mother never did that for me. "You can stand for her in court." She choked out the words between her tears. "I will give you this for strength. It was hers," a small silver medal on a chain dropped from her hand. "It's a medal of St. Joseph. When she was a baby," her eyes became big and round, stars started to shine in them, "she had pneumonia, doctors said," and she laid her head on her husband's shoulder. "Doctors said she wouldn't make it. We prayed to St. Joseph on our knees all night." She smiled as her eyes relived a sacred moment in time, "But she made it through the night." She lifted her head straight and she became tall, her burden lifted. "He will come through for her again because you will stand for her." She spread the fingers of my fisted hand open and gently placed the medal on the soft padding of my palm. My hand fell at the weight of every heart Seth stole. She took my fingers and folded them around the medal. Her eyes were fierce and by her sheer determination, I was going to testify for them. She melted into her husband's arms and walked away. As I looked down the hallway, they were bent over from the weight of the invisible cross.

Me and St. Joseph ran out the building looking for air. I just got drafted to be a soldier for God. I was no longer a victim but a way for justice, *mother of God, how do I get myself into these situations?* This punishment thing for the crimes of the past was going to continue to haunt me till the day I died. My palm opened and my eyes began to burn from the reflection of the medal. Sunlight bounced off the silvery gray of my scars. "Fair enough," I put my sunglasses on and looked up into the sky, "You win, but it's going to come with a price."

I hightailed it to the police station and demanded to see Captain Stafford. As I waited, fingers drumming on the counter, I noticed looks from various officers and heard the whispers that hung in the air. Rumor had been passed around like a beer at a teenage party and people were drinking it in that I wouldn't testify.

Captain Stafford sauntered down the hall, his lips pursed when he saw me. "I want to go to your office, now!" He stared down at me for a moment, then he turned and I followed right behind him. On the outside, I was a soldier, me strong, me tough, and on the inside, I was chocolate pudding.

We walked into his oh so familiar office and he sat behind his large desk. "Miss Stronghill, I heard you won't testify." Sunlight poured through his office and crawled up the shoulder of his jacket. His face remained in shadow. The aroma of sweet cherry cigars hung heavy in the air and permeated his office.

"I'm not convinced that I should as of yet."

"So you would leave the Myers' without justice." He gave a warm smile and I returned a cold sneer.

This man and the prosecutor should rot in hell for trying to emotionally blackmail me. "I wanna know why you chose me?"

"Ahh," he opened his drawer, pulled out two glasses, and procured a bottle of something brown, liquidy, and I very much hoped something very alcoholy. He poured one for himself, eyed me, and poured one for me. He pushed the glass over to me with the tips of his fingers and then quickly pulled back.

I grabbed the glass, raised it to him, and said, "Mazel Tov" and swigged the drink down. It immediately burned the back of my throat and seared my esophagus. I began to choke, "That's a little strong." My head began to swim as my insides felt like a slow-burning fire was consuming them. *This was good shit.*

"I really can't tell you because of the trial and all, I'm sure you understand my hands are tied." He sat back in his chair with a smirk on his face. He thought he had an out, the jackass.

I lifted up my chin like I was acknowledging the poor man's position. "Would you agree without my testimony, the prosecutor doesn't have much of a case?" I swished the devil's juice around in the glass. I wasn't sure I would take another drink. "From my understanding, all the evidence is very circumstantial, any first year lawyer could probably poke a lot of holes in the case and out comes Seth," and I lifted one eyebrow, "back into your city." His face became vampiric white, cold comprehension hit him of what the rumors meant. He didn't think I had a choice. I slammed the glass down. "You want me to testify, you're going tell me what I want to know."

The smirk was gone, replaced by a cold hard stare and a grimace. "I imagine you've figured out how I know you." He sipped the drink of the damned.

Recalling the picture from the last time I was here, "I do."

His chair squeaked as he turned and faced the window. *Oh, god. Here we* go and I waited for the assault against my sanity. "We were getting nowhere, Carolina. We knew who the killer was, we followed him everywhere, until his lawyer filed a suit for harassment." He quickly turned back around, his hands turned snow white as he gripped the arms of his chair. "We still followed him, but he slipped through our fingers at every turn." We both eyed his hands and then consciously, he spread his fingers out. "We had to create some sort of trap for him, something that would attract him. Something that was so irresistible to him, or someone," and his eyes pierced mine. "Then Harvey called and mentioned you were in town." He grunted, "Said I should look after you." He lifted his lip and exposed his teeth before he drank some more, "You were perfect, exactly what I needed."

A ball of pain exploded in my heart and raced fire through my veins; it burned the alcohol away. "You bastard, why didn't you tell me?"

"Honestly, would you have set yourself up knowing what might happen?"

"I don't know, but the least you could have done was tell me."

"We watched you." He said it like it was something of inconvenience for him. "We had you under surveillance at all times. We had no idea if the killer was coming or not. We even had someone on the inside to keep track of you."

Oh, that just made my head spin more. "Someone on the inside?"

"Then Seth started to show up at your front door. We knew we had him but that night, he slipped past the one watching you." He took a drink and stared straight at me. "Somehow."

Images of the room on fire and the captain's heading exploding invaded my thoughts. "How close were you with my father?" I nodded my head at the photo of all them graduating from the academy. Another photograph depicted the three of them, Harvey, my father, and the captain holding a softball trophy after victory.

He stood up straight and tall. Beads of sweat broke out on his forehead. "He was my best friend."

My hands began to shake. The liquid within the glass was splashing over the sides. Quickly, I put the glass down with both hands. "For god's sakes, why would you do this to your best friend's daughter?" One question hammered away at me—*why, why?*

He bent half his body across the desk and threw his fists on the top, his face filled with malice. "Because you owed him." Whiskey and spittle crossed my cheek. "He was a good man and you shitted on his memory when you ran off with that …that….that Snake," he said, his finger shaking in my face. "Then you," his face turned the color of big red beet, "you know what you did." He wiped his mouth with his handkerchief.

I reared up in his face, which made it a little hard to do considering I'm five foot three and he was six foot five. "And what would you call what you were doing to his grave, exactly?!" I pointed towards the picture on the wall. My hand was shaking so badly I put my hand behind my back to hide my fury.

"You know what you are?"

"What?" My arms crossed in front of me and I was managing to stand on very shaking legs. I wasn't sure how much of this confrontation I could take.

"A worthless piece of shit!" His hand waved across my body. "You should be proud you had the opportunity to redeem yourself. It was a small price to pay."

"I almost died!"

"How many good women died?"

"So you're judging my soul!" The fire raced up my throat and I screeched. "I was tortured for his benefit, you bastard!"

He plopped back on his chair, his skin turned waxy gray as he regained his composure. "I'm sorry it got that far. It wasn't supposed to happen that way." He was quiet and sounded almost remorseful. But all I could hear was the word "sorry" echoing in my head.

"You're sorry! You're sorry! You sick son of a bitch!" I shrieked at the top of my lungs. A spark of insanity ignited my hatred and I forced myself across his desk. The amber-filled glass spilled whiskey all over his papers. Grabbing his tie, I pulled him forward and twisted till his face turned chalky white. His hands were on my own trying to release my death grip, but the adrenaline rush and anger were stronger. The monster I thought I had buried became alive and laughed at watching his last breath. That small laugh brought me back to my senses and I slowly released my fingers that were red and white from lack of blood circulation.

Red swam back into his face as he rearranged his tie, "I did what I had to do with the piece of trash that I had to work with."

The silence was deafening, except for the ring of his voice in my ear. I was nothing to this man, a means to an end. What was one criminal's life to him? I was struck by the hammer of his justification.

"I'm not testifying till I get something from you."

"And what is that?" he sneered.

His attitude told me he still believed this would cost him nothing and perhaps he was right, "A guarantee that you won't press any charges for "associating" with known criminals."

He licked his lips and sat back down, his chair squeaking under the weight of the pressure.

"I want it in writing with your signature, in triplicate." Where the triplicate came from, I have no idea, probably from too many shows from the seventies. That made him scowl even more. "And I want to see you e-mail it to the prosecutor." If his eyes were lasers, I would be a big pile of ash right now.

He sat back in his chair and crossed his fingers across his stomach. "And if I say no to your little request...?" The bastard thought he still had me cornered.

"Who do you want more in jail, me or the serial killer?" He was about to answer. "Choose wisely."

"Why is that?" he sneered.

"Because I'll go to the press with every detail of this conversation." His jaw tightened and he stared me down, but I wasn't going to be intimidated. He punched the keys on the keyboard almost to the breaking point. I zeroed in on every word he wrote, and then he hit the send button to the prosecutor. While I waited for the printer to print out three copies, I handed him a pen and went back to the one picture.

"I want something else."

"Oh, yeah, what do you want now, a presidential pardon?" he signed the last copy and pushed them across the puddle of alcohol. I picked them up by my fingertips and flicked wet droplets on him.

311

"Those pictures of my father," and I pointed to the ones on the wall.

He stammered. "Those are all I have of him."

"I may not deserve to live, but you don't deserve to have those." I marched over and grabbed them off the wall. Pictures in hand, I faced him. "He would have never done that to anyone."

I stormed out the door, echoes of his last words ringing down the hallway. "Don't be so sure of what your father would have and would not have done!"

Chapter 31

The sun blared down on the courthouse steps and baked us all like Christmas cookies. I pushed my way through the throngs of reporters with microphones and cameras within inches of my lips, waiting for that one sound bite that would bring them an audience. This trial was fast becoming a media circus, and I seemed to be the main attraction. Lionel Hawk waited at the top of the steps, not moving an inch to come to my rescue. *Bastard.* A few steps below him was a short, squat man talking to a circle of reporters. He was laughing and slapping the back of the reporter closest to him.

"Is it true this was just a lover's trap gone wrong?"

"What?" I lost my footing on the steps and accidentally knocked the closest reporter to me off balance. All the talking heads turned to the reporter behind me.

"Miss Stronghill," a reporter shoved his way to the front, smirking. "Isn't it true you were just caught in a game of S and M, you're just accusing an innocent man of torture, a reverend at that?"

"I wha…." All the blood drained from my head and made my head spin. He was writing something down, my fist smashed down on his paper, and the pen flew up in the air. "Fuck you!" All the reporters around me began to write furiously in their stenos, not to mention the cameras got even closer. Would "Fuck you!" be the latest headline in big bold letters? The pen landed beside that particular nasty reporter and he smirked at me as he picked it up.

"That'll be all, ladies and gentlemen, Miss Stronghill has nothing more to say." Lionel parted the sea of journalists, grabbed my arm, and pulled me up the steps.

"Hey!" I wrangled myself from his manhandling. "What are they saying, that I did this for fun?" Turning on my heels, I was going back to give them a piece of what was left of my mind.

He grabbed my shoulder and stopped me. "Ignore them, this is Seth's lawyer setting up a defense."

I pushed his hand away from me. "They think I participated in some sick sex game!" My fingers and toes were tingling and my breath was erratic. Any moment now, I would burst out into a hysterical fit. A lingering reporter, who hadn't taken the hint, leaned in closer and scribbled something on a white pad.

Lionel pulled me further up the steps, his eyes were cold steel. "Carolina, get a hold of yourself." He looked past my shoulder at the chaos behind me. His hand bound my wrist and I couldn't shake him off.

"Get a hold of myself?! The city of Albuquerque believes I'm a vindictive donamatrix out to ruin an innocent man."

"This is a game of misinformation and tactics, Carolina." Lionel was very agitated, and sweat ran down his face as he continued to hold my wrist in a vise grip. My skin was writhing from his touch—it wasn't him, it was the fact that someone was touching me.

I tried to pull away. My scars were burning and I thought the rest of me would ignite any minute now. "I'm tired of being everyone's game piece."

"Then play the game to win and you have your life back. Put Seth in jail and you will never have to play again. If you don't," he eyed the defense lawyer smiling and laughing with reporters, "you'll never have your freedom. Seth will stalk you till the day you die." He let go of my wrist and walked into the courthouse. Well, that kind of put a whole new spin on things.

I sat on a bench and waited for my turn, bobbing my knee up and down. They assigned a young attorney with a thick Texas accent, to make sure I was figuratively shackled to this trial. "Ma'am, would you stop doing that." He put a hand on my knee and I jerked away.

"Stop calling me ma'am," I said as I chewed on some gum and kept popping it out loud. The last pop, the Texan poked a hole in it and flattened it over my lips.

"Ma'am.." he looked at me and I gave him the stare of death, "Carolina would you please stop chewing your gum." Tossing the gum away, I waited nervously, and then I jumped up and went to the water fountain. The water cooled the small smoldering fire in my throat. My eyes became fixated with how the water flowed in a silver shimmer into an arc and then plopped like raindrops on the basin and circled down the drain. A cop in a blue uniform rounded the corner across the hall and his laugh bounced off the walls of the hall. My heart stopped at the familiar voice.

He was clean-shaven, his hair shorn, and all his tattoos were completely covered, nothing like the

Gabriel I had fallen in love with. He was in a deep conversation with the redhead that I had seen him with all those months. She was also in uniform, with her brilliant blaze of red hair in a ponytail underneath a policeman's hat. He came to a sudden halt when my eyes met his and we stared at each other across the hallway. Memories, voices, images came rushing forward and shattered my synapses. My eyes looked to the linoleum and found myself trying to pick up all the little pieces of brain matter. He had known who I was all along.

Little pieces of broken heart and shattered brain were on the floor as I walked away. My eyes started to see double and then I was pulled from the brink of disaster by a heavy hand and a thick accent of "Ma'am."

It was my turn to testify and I really needed to see the insides of a toilet, but I was guided inside the courtroom, where all of the sitting heads screwed their faces to peek at the latest witness. Knees knocking, I stood in the witness box and placed my hand on a beaten up Bible, the edges worn and frayed. A couple of pages were loose and peeked over the edge of the rest of the beleaguered pages; the words "Fear not, I am with you" stood out against the background of black and white. The courtroom was as quiet as St. Stephen's Church from my youth and my voice rang out, "So help me God."

The prosecutor stood up and surveyed each member of the jury, slowly and methodically. I don't know what Lionel was thinking, but they looked like a tough crowd to me. Each member of the jury was either so bored, they were about to fall asleep or some were volleying back and forth between the faces of a killer and my own. Some members of the jury were looking so intently at Seth that I could see only one thought across their minds: He doesn't look like a killer. Seth had a button up shirt completely ironed, with creases and a white collar around his neck. That son of a bitch was still pretending he was man of God.

I sat on the witness stand pensive, waiting for those final moments to end. "Why did you go under the name of Danielle Clearwater?"

"I had to hide under an assumed name because I thought I was under a death threat." *Hey, how perfect was that nice and neat little package.* Lionel went on to give my background and why I was a witness to this case.

Lionel stood by the jury box very relaxed in his freshly pressed suit. "Tell us, Carolina, about that night."

I breathed and looked at the jury who seemed lulled into a dead stupor. So, that was the strategy, bore them to sleep till they heard nothing. Even after all the coaching, I still had no idea what I was going to say. "I met Seth…" and my throat cracked, I picked up the glass of water, my hands shook so badly that the glass looked like it had a miniature tsunami in it.

"Your honor, there is no need for jury to hear this, it is public record." The defense lawyer, Thurmond Straw, had jumped up out of his chair and his jowls bounced as he spoke. He didn't want the jury to hear what Seth had done; all the evidence in the world with blood spatters, hair particles, DNA couldn't match my words ringing in the jury's ears.

Lionel spoke calmly, "Your honor, she is a witness to the crime."

That was an understatement of the year. The judge thought for a moment. The silence electrified the air as everyone waited for their chance at voyeurism. Right about then, Gabriel slowly slipped into the courtroom and sat like a stone. My shoulders sank. *Oh, fuck me, he just made this ten times worse.*

The judge reviewed the file and looked up at all our intense faces; he just became the center of attention and was playing for all it was worth. Both lawyers were on the edge of their proverbial seats, waiting in anticipation.

"I'll allow it." I heard all the whispers rise above the crowd in the courtroom and then dissipate into the either like wisps of smoke, "Miss Stronghill, you may continue."

So I laid my soul down like carpet and let the jury see the weaves and tufts of yarn that had been spun between Seth and me. I showed them in detail the rugged edges of pain and torture, patches of my soul that were threadbare that had been walked on. My fingers were wrapped so tight around the St. Joseph's medal that there was a red dent in my skin where it had been. I glanced at Seth and he had a dreamy look on his face. The bastard was reliving my moments in brilliant Technicolor haze. Some members of the jury's eyes glistened with tears and others stared coldly at Seth. I hoped they saw the dreamy look of a murderer living his fantasy.

Thurmond Straw glanced at the jury and then he looked at Seth staring off into space. He looked down at Seth's waist and his eyes shot up. He nudged Seth hard and Seth seemed to have come back to reality. He leaned over to the whisper something in his lawyer's ear and then grinned. That shook me a little but I made it through every detail.

Thank you, Miss Stronghill. Your witness." Lionel went back to his chair and left me alone and isolated, a wooden box for my only defense.

Seth's attorney got up with a file in his hand and grabbed the knife that Seth used off the prosecutor's desk. Thurmond Straw was short, squat, and he reminded me of a toad I once saw jump into a dirty pond. He wore a custom-made suit that was tight across his stomach and shoulders, and patent leather shoes. A sheen of light reflected off his balding head as he took out handkerchief from his pocket and wiped his face. He could pass for someone's creepy grandfather, but I didn't underestimate him. Lionel mentioned that Thurmond Straw ate witnesses for lunch. I could only hope I gave him a nasty case of indigestion.

He flipped through a file and stood in front of me, holding the knife. The courtroom lights reflected off the metal and I had to blink. He read the file up and down slowly as I waited for the train to come down the tracks. He was making the jury drool with anticipation.

"Tell me, Miss Stronghill, how long have you been involved in wanton behavior?"

I wasn't expecting that. "I'm not sure what you mean?"

"How long have you enticed upstanding men of the community into sex games and then blackmailing them?"

"Are you out of your mind?" I moved to the edge of my seat and got closer to the gate that jailed me in. "Seth came to me, pretending to be a reverend. He's the one who…who hurt me."

"Yes, it is true that he came to visit you when he was a reverend visiting his flock. A man of God merely trying to put wanton women such as yourself back on the right path." He peered underneath his eyelids at the jury. Uncertainty was crossing the jury eyes. *Oh god, they were buying this load of crap.* The white collar had blinded them.

"He's no man of God, he's a psychopath."

"Let it be known that Seth Whitehouse is a reverend." His lawyer turned to the courthouse recorder. "Did you not stalk him at his church?"

Lionel jumped up. "Your honor, we know the defendant is a reverend, but he has no known affiliation with any church in Albuquerque."

Mr. Straw jutted out his jaw. "I stand corrected."

"Why were you stalking my client?"

"I wasn't stalking him. He said he worked at that Church." My voice became three pitches higher than normal.

"Were you not seeing someone else and my client?"

"Seth kept coming over and talking to me, he was the one stalking me."

"I'm sure you misunderstood, that he was just trying to show you the error of your ways."

"Error of my ways, you fat bastard, he's the one who came over to my house," and I pointed a finger at Seth.

"Did you not have a ruse for him when he was at your house?"

"What are you talking about?" He still had the knife in his hand and walked over to the jury.

"You wanted him to help you with the yard. Were you not taking advantage of his kindness?"

I was getting irritated to no end. "He offered to help me, then he barreled into my kitchen."

"Then you 'accidentally,'" Straw made air quotation marks, "poured sauce on his pants. Wasn't that your attempt to begin sex games with him?"

"What the hell is wrong with you? Sex games?"

He came closer to the jury box, his fingers around the hilt of the knife and I couldn't take my eyes off of it. My blood was still on the knife, crusted to black. "Tell me, Carolina, your boyfriend shows up and sees you with my client in a, shall we say, a very compromising position," his voice was slick as a snake's underside, "and now you want the jury to believe he was trying to murder you."

"No, I told him to leave me alone."

"And yet you invited him over to your house a few days later to make up for that night." Thurmond Straw lifted an eyebrow at me. He walked over to Seth and Seth looked at him with big puppy eyes.

"I did no such thing. I refused his invitation but he made plans anyways."

"Carolina, stop lying and tell the truth you wanted this to happen to you, you're very sick, you like to be hurt. Didn't you and Officer Gabriel like to play bondage games?"

Panicked, I searched for Gabriel. He was standing against the wall, his face white as sheet. We were having fun one night, just playing cops and robbers with handcuffs. I knew Gabriel didn't say anything. Then a cold chill had hit me, my spine straightened to a piece of steel. Seth had been watching me the whole time. All those eerie feelings I had blown off were real. I struggled to take a breath.

The defense attorney faced me. "You need help, Carolina." Then he turned to the jury, "we will get you the help you need, Carolina," he placed the knife on the witness stand and patted my hand.

All the anger and fear that was damned up behind a wall burst and I jumped up. "You fucking bastard, you think I wanted this to happen? You! You cut me with that knife!" I was screaming at Seth, who kept his cool eyes hooded, but I could see them.

I kept my eyes on Seth as Thurmond's words buzzed in my ears. "It's what you asked for, Carolina, you asked Seth to tie you up, you told him if he didn't tie you up and cut you, you would destroy him in front of his congregation."

"No, I did not!"

"Why would he lie, Carolina, he is a man of God, you wanted this and now you have the gall to haul him before court and accuse of assaulting you of attempted murder."

"I didn't want this!" I grabbed the knife from the stand, "You bastard!" I looked straight at Seth, "You did this to me!" and the knife pointed to the scar on my arm, "You did this to me!" I slammed my fists into the rail and threw the knife on the ground. The knife slid across the floor and the point hit the leg of Seth's chair. The courtroom was dead silent and I stood there shivering, staring at Seth.

Lionel sprang from his chair. "Your honor! He's badgering the witness!" The courtroom erupted in noise but I couldn't take my eyes off that bastard. Seth's white mask was solid but the corner of his porcelain mouth cracked ever so slightly. He was going to win. Deflated, my fingers one by one slowly detached from the wooden bar; *dammit he was going to win.*

The judge talked down to me like I was his errant child. "Miss Stronghill, you need to calm down, now. Order in the court! Order in the court!" The gavel rang out and the courtroom returned to a church-like atmosphere. "I will allow it."

The judge pulled a tissue from the box and dangled it in front of me. "Mr. Straw, you may continue." Shaking, I grabbed the tissue and hoped the blood returned to my head soon. My body ached as I sat slowly, waiting for the edge of the chair.

Thurmond gathered himself and pulled down his jacket. "Miss Stronghill, will you give us more detail on how you killed that bank guard in cold blood."

Fuck, fuck! Oh, fucking hell!

The prosecutor bounced up, "Your honor, that information is totally irrelevant to these proceedings."

Mr. Straw said almost in a whiny placating tone, "Your honor, I am establishing what kind of character witness Miss Carolina Stronghill is," and he looked at me with a stare and then eyed the jury.

"The jury will strike that last statement."

"When you gunned down that bank guard, did you know he had three young children?"

A wave of surprised noise boiled and erupted in the courtroom. Seth smirked and cracked the mask of innocence even more. My nails were digging into the edge of the jury box. *I will not cry, I will not cry, I will not kill the man in front of me.*

The prosecutor jumped up again and said, "This is irrelevant, your honor, he is badgering the witness. I demand a retrial!"

After the judge banged his gavel and calmed everyone down, Mr. Straw bowed his head, "I think the jury needs to know what kind of witness we have, your honor. She was caught red handed and is now lying to the jury." Thurmond walked behind Seth and placed his hands on Seth's shoulders. "My client had no idea of her background. She is a liar." Thurmond patted Seth's shoulders. "His life is at stake."

Lionel jumped up. "Your honor!" But the conversation was lost in high pitched hysteria between the two lawyers yelling at each other. I sat back in my chair, the battle lost. Seth had the ultimate look of pleasure on his face. This had literally turned into a three-ring circus. *Oh, for god's sakes*, this was the justice system, innocents lost to lies and speculation. The heads of Alisha Myers' parents were bowed in deep sorrow. Mr. Myers' arms surrounded the picture of his daughter in a tight hug, hoping she could feel his love. They had put their faith and trust in the wrong person. Out in the courtroom, the ghosts of Seth's victims were shedding tears and I couldn't stop the tide of pain.

"Order in the court!" The judge banged his gavel till it splintered and piece of wood fell into my lap. Finally, the courtroom became as still as the night as my eyes landed on the face of pure evil dressed in a clergy's outfit. The piece of wood was smooth between my fingers.

"Your honor, may I speak?"

"Are you sure, Miss Stronghill?"

"Yes," I paused, and tried to swallow. I sipped some water to ease my parched throat.

Lionel's eyes were as big as saucers shaking his head. Thurmond Straw smiled like a Chesire Cat as he sat down behind the defense table. Fingers shaking, I put the sliver of wood on the judge's desk. Slowly, like a well-rehearsed prosecutor, I looked into the eyes of the jury. All twelve pairs of eyes stared right back at me. "I am a murderer." That made the jury's jaw open a bit but I had their full attention. "I was an angry kid. My mother had left when I was young and my father died of a heart attack at sixteen. I was alone and scared."

"Your honor, this irrelevant," Thurmond Straw's fat head was in his hand with a bored look. He was confident he had won; the rest of the trial was just preliminary.

The judge said, "You opened the door, Mr. Straw." Thurmond sat deflated in his chair. "Continue, Ms. Stronghill."

"Someone came into my life and offered solace to me. And from that moment, I would have done anything for him." I looked at Gabriel. His gaze was so intense. "I robbed, stole, and was a general menace." I smiled at my own memory of that stupid girl. "Snake was everything and his words were like gold. We got tired of robbing convenience stores of money and candy; we wanted more," I searched in my memory of what we actually wanted, "more power. So we got this bright idea to rob a bank. A guard foolishly thought he could stop me. I had a gun and pulled the trigger."

I looked at the jury. I couldn't read their faces anymore, I could only see the people in the bank. "I took the life of a family man, a husband, a father. I left his kids alone. In just a flash, I had become a monster." My words were as simple and as pure as I could make them. I turned back to Seth. "The same kind of monster who ties each hand so the string cuts into their wrists, the kind of monster who listens to the heartbeats as they slowly fade just so that he can feel alive." Seth's eyes were becoming dreamy as we recalled the memory of our night together. Never taking my eyes from him, I spoke serenely so as to not disturb the sleeping monster. "I know he is guilty."

The defense attorney just smirked, "Well, how do you know this exactly?"

I stared into the coldblooded killer's eyes, "He's reliving the hunt," I paused and carefully said the next words slowly, "the torture." The words crept into my thoughts, *now I lay me down to sleep, I pray to the Lord my soul to keep,* my lungs stretched to the point of pain as I breathed because I knew personally what the last words meant to me, "the kill." The jury moved their heads in the direction of Seth and caught him daydreaming. The jury suddenly started to squirm in their seats, the horror movie came to life in front of them. The Myers' faces were stark white.

Lionel sat back in his chair and slumped. The young Texan at his side threw his pencil down and closed his eyes. I was probably their worst witness ever. But I had one chess piece to play.

Thurmond Straw sauntered over to the bench. "Miss Stronghill, this is just another lie, another tale. You can't make the jury see past your guilt and put it on my client. You have no proof." The corner of his lip twitched as he walked away.

"I know of his guilt," Seth's face had a wry smile, "because he bragged about all the women he murdered." Loud whispers flooded across the room and I couldn't take my eyes off Seth. His face drained of all color.

"Well, that information is alleged." Thurmond Straw said it like a cat that caught the mouse in his jaws. He leered at me, smirked, "probably something he said during," he licked his lips, "during an interlude."

I ignored his vulgar reference and put my remaining piece out on the board. I kept my eyes hooded from everyone, "Not alleged." Then I looked straight into the eyes of the killer, "I have his confession on tape."

Chapter 32

The whole court erupted in noise and chaos. Lionel screamed above the din. "Your Honor!" Thurmond choked on his mouse, and Seth's stared at me with his cold blue killer eyes. Calmness seeped in and comforted me as I stared back without blinking. *I got you, you bastard.*

The judge struck his new gavel. "Order in the court! Order in the court!" The court quieted down and all parties took their seats. Seth and I continued our stare down to the point that I had to tear my head away to answer the judge's question, "Miss Stronghill, can you explain?"

Slowly turning my head back to Seth, "He told me everything, each girl that he tortured and murdered."

"How did you come by this tape?"

"I put a tape recorder underneath my bed every night." I was a moth captured by the electric light of Seth's eyes. He radiated pulsating light that was trying to zap me dead. "I was upset that night," and glanced at Gabriel. His face paled and he looked away. "And thought a shower would help me relax. I put a new tape in my recorder and pressed play." My lungs filled with air before I spoke, "Then, like I always do, I put it underneath my bed before I took a shower that night." I couldn't help it, I flew right back to the path of Seth's eyes and we continued our staring match.

"We will obviously need to review the tape." The sound of the gavel jumped me out of my flight path,

"The jury will be excused for twenty-four hours." Everyone began to leave the courtroom. My legs gelled beneath me as I stood, the room swerved, and I grabbed the chair behind me. The courtroom officer was cuffing Seth's hands, his eyes still laser pinpoints doing their level best to turn me to ash.

Lionel came up to the jury box. "Why didn't you tell me about the tape?"

"I don't know." I watched the backs of people leaving the courtroom, including the blue of Gabriel's uniform.

"Carolina, it never had to go this far. He could have been in jail a long time ago."

"I know."

"Then why be so insolent as to not tell me about this?"

"I don't know."

He hit the stand with his hands and I flinched back further into my seat. He stood frozen for a moment. "I want that tape, now!" and he walked away. The echoes of his voice rang through the courtroom, till the creaking and the popping of wooden benches was the only noise I heard. I did know why. How could I listen to my own screams?

I drove home and was lulled into a daydream by the blur of streets passing me by. In the middle of the night, I screamed. Dad came rushing in. "Carolina, it's all right." So young and so small, he picked me up and cuddled me against his warm body. His skin had the soft faint smell of cologne and cigars. Tears flooded his shoulder as I listened to the sounds of the snowstorm pelting against the window.

"Carolina, there are no monsters inside the closet." His voice was a bit on the harsh side as he wiped sleep out of his eyes. He could tell that I didn't believe him. He sighed and took me off his lap, and gently put me in the big comfy chair. He surveyed the closet. "See, there are no monsters." He opened the closet door wide apart and turned on the closet light. All the shadows scattered away like cockroaches in sunlight. My weepy eyes rose above the blanket to look, but I was so frightened I stayed inside the chair curled up in a little ball.

"Okay, Carolina, wipe your tears away. I'll go and get something special to take care of all the monsters." He walked out of the room and left me in my protective ball, surrounded by the arms of the chair. He was gone for so long I thought he had left me alone with the monster in the closet. I knew that monster had hidden behind my Barbie dollhouse, but dad just couldn't see it. Finally, he came back with a silver-looking box in his hands. "Carolina, this will take care of all those monsters."

My little hands balled in fists were by my face. I was so excited to see what could make the monsters vanish. Then, my little heart sank. "It's a tape recorder, Dad," I said with all the disappointment in my voice I could muster.

"No, no, Carolina, this is a special tape recorder." He put it underneath the lamp and its metallic face captured the light and sent shimmering sparks to my eyes.

"Carolina, see, just press this button," he pressed the magical button of play and the recorder started to turn. "See, when this turns, it captures all the monsters.

Now, we'll just put this underneath your bed." I eyed the closet suspiciously as he slipped the tape recorder into darkness. "There, no more monsters, eh. Time for you to go to bed." He picked me up out of the chair and brought me to bed. I slid underneath the covers and brought them to my chin. He kissed my forehead and whispered goodnight, the scent of his cologne lingering in the air. The tape recorder would capture the monsters who danced around my bed and I slipped into sleep.

After a while, I stopped believing in things that go bump in the night and the recorder gathered dust underneath my bed. After prison, when I silently went through the memories of my house, I went into my bedroom and kneeled underneath the bed, my fingers reaching till they found what they were looking for. Amongst the dust bunnies and spider webs was the tape recorder. Since then, it has captured all the creatures of the night.

Chapter 33

"He's confessed, Carolina." Lionel stood beside me as I stared at the back of Seth's head. The police were taking him out of the interrogation room in shackles. "You brought a killer to justice. A lot of families can sleep tonight." Lionel's voice was like a bee buzzing incessantly in my ear, "That tape doomed him. He confessed to the murder to all the murders."

"Where are they taking him?"

Lionel looked pensive. "He's being extradited to the other states to stand trial."

Seth's shackled feet scooted along the hallway. I heard the slush, slush sound of his feet as he moved followed by the sound of clanking metal. "I want to talk to him." Lionel's jaw tightened and the skin shrank around his cheekbones. His lips moved to speak. I cut him off before I changed my mind, "Alone."

Lionel's face became a kaleidoscope of different shades of red. "Carolina, that's not a really good idea."

"I wanna talk to him, now." I stared at Lionel. "I'm not asking for your permission."

Lionel stared at me and then he licked his lips. "Hey, Peter!"

A surprised guard turned around. "Take him back to the room." The guard's face screwed up in a questioning look. Lionel motioned with his hand to Peter. "Just take him back." He shrugged and walked Seth back to the confessional.

After a few moments, Lionel came to me. "Are you sure you want to do this?"

I stood there for a moment trying to stop the room from spinning. "No, not really. I just need to."

"He's chained to the chair. You have five minutes."

I stood outside the door and tried to put on a brave face, my old familiar mask. Heart pounding, I touched the cold metal of the doorknob, turned it, and walked in. His cold blue eyes scanned me from head to toe, stopping at each scar he found. They burned under the ice of his eyes and I resisted the temptation to cover them. The light in the interview room dulled everything into yellow ash.

"Hello, Carolina." His speech had that same perfect vernacular. My name rung in my ears and I almost backed out. My hand was on the doorknob behind me holding on for dear life. Shards of pain radiated from the doorknob poking into the small of my back. "Come here, Carolina, have a seat." He motioned with his eyes to the empty seat. He hands reached for the table, but only his fingertips touched the edge. Pensively, I sat down, placed my palms upon the table, and looked into the abyss of evil.

"You were my favorite one, so far." He licked his lips. My fingers dug into the table. He flashed his brilliant smile. He hummed, "I told you, you would not forget me." Sweaty hand prints were left behind as my hands rolled up into fists. I couldn't do this; I couldn't hear his voice without reliving every single cut, every feeling of the knife flaying my skin. "You are wondering why, aren't you?" He sat back in his chair, the chains clanking against the metal legs.

He smelled of soap and sweat, but somehow my senses recalled the scent of vanilla, my stomach became instantly nauseous. "Not really."

He lips twisted in a vicious half smile and then he cracked his neck. "Ah, so brave Carolina. I might as well tell you anyways." He came as close as he could to the table and whispered, "It's what they all want."

"What?" I choked.

"This is what women want," *his eyes dulled into a hypnotic state.* "They like it. You liked it. It is how you knew I loved you." A drop of drool fell off his lips and onto the table. I got up so fast I knocked over the chair and it skidded across the floor, "Did you figure it out?"

My hand was on the doorknob. I willed myself to open the door. *Open it, dammit!* as I screamed at myself, but I couldn't stop the question. "Figure out what?" A tear burned its way down my cheek.

"Why you are so drawn to me." All my muscles tensed and I couldn't get the damn door open. "You are just like me."

I forced the door open and ran across the threshold. Lionel was in my way as I tried to get around him. "You're pale," he said, as he blocked my every move. All I wanted to do was to flee, leave, ride on the wave of pain and misery, and wash out the door. "What did he say to you?"

"I need to get out of here!" I was going to be sick. My name rang across the halls and bounded off the ceramic tiles. My brain was dizzy as I looked for the

334

exit. My legs were turning to mush as I finally found the door and pushed it open. I hurled myself into the sunlight and stood in the heat of the rays. A moment in the sun burned away all the slime and the sickness that was coursing through me. Gabriel's truck was in front of me and I reached out to the hot metal underneath my fingertips. Guided by the strength of steel, my hand ran along the hood till I could open the door. I crawled into the front seat and sat there trying to get back any piece of me I had left behind. Anger rose in waves and my fists pounded on the dashboard, skin broke and blood smeared across the metal.

In my flash of fire, I hit the dashboard so hard that the old glove box popped open and a rosary dribbled out over the door. I picked up the rosary and ran it through my fingers, the beads cool against my fingertips. It was the same rosary that Seth had placed around my neck that night. Hazy flashbacks came roaring back, Seth placing the rosary around my neck, Gabriel's wings, and then Gabriel gently taking it from around my neck. Gabriel must of have thought it was something personal to me. The rosary started to burn in my hands and I knew what I needed to do.

Exhaust scented the air as I started the old truck and drove to where I needed to go. The engine puttered through the security gates and I parked the Ford right in front of it. I hugged the wheel, sat, and stared at the storage door. Finally, I was forced by the heat of the sun to make a decision.

As I rolled the shed door up, the light from the sun slowly chased the dark away and my father's car was there waiting for me. My body melted into the car and I ran my hand along the dashboard, feeling the smooth texture of leather. The seats cupped me like I was being held in a big hug. Now, for the real test: I took a really deep breath and put the key in the ignition, turned it, and click, click was all that happened. "Dad, you know me." I tried again and nothing but the clicking noise of dead vehicle. I rested my head on the steering wheel, "Please, you're the only one. I know I lost my way but I'm here." I twisted the key again and the GTO roared to life in a rumble, the sound of the exhaust making popping noises as it adjusted itself to its existence.

The miles skidded underneath the car till I stopped at the spot of my dark transformation. The door creaked an old familiar song as I stepped out into the sand. The scenery was a panoramic view of still deep cobalt blue mountains against a light azure sky. A child's giggle broke the silence as I looked to see a young girl with ash blonde hair running from her father. He caught her, scooped her up in his arms, and hugged her close. The wind whipped blonde strands around my face, and broke my fascination with the bond between father and daughter. I got the rosary, shoved it into my pocket, and opened the luggage compartment and found a small shovel.

The shovel hit the ground with a thud and bounced back. *Oh, this is going to be a whole lotta of fun*, and then I continued on digging, wishing for a sledgehammer. A small whirlwind gathered sand and blasted it in my face. *Thank you, thank you so much for that* as I wiped dirt filled sweat and tears from my eyes. I slammed the shovel harder into the dirt with all the force of my anger and dug deeper and deeper till there was a small deep pit. Finally, my anger was appeased and I said a silent prayer. Bead by bead, I took the rosary out of my pocket till all of the rosary beads lay in my hand. It no longer singed my skin. Gently, I laid the blood encrusted rosary in the ground, spreading the beads in a circle with Jesus on the cross resting on a pillow of dirt in the middle. "Now I lay me down to sleep…" and began filling in the hole. Pushing the last bit of dirt over my nightmare, I sat there. The girl's laughter broke the serenity and I looked over to the trees. The father scooped her up and they disappeared into the ether. For the first time in months, I felt peaceful, serene, almost clean. "I pray my soul to keep."

I stayed for a while and watched the sun set in brilliant colors. Finally, it was time to leave and as I opened the car door; I saw a black spot in the sage. A crow bounced out from under the bush. He looked so familiar but then again all crows looked alike. He slanted his head, gave me a hard stare, cawed, and took flight. The crow made lazy circles above my head as I got into the car and then he flew off into the sunset.

The air was scented with lilacs as I parked in my driveway. The trees budded with spring green leaves and the world seemed anew. My thoughts turned to doing a spring clean of the house, wiping the old cobwebs away, and maybe arranging some furniture. "I have lost my mind." As I sat on the porch, tea in hand, the stars unfolded in a diamond display. The old me that I had sealed away in the dungeon was released, except now there were deep scars across her.

The next day, I burst out of the house and began weeding, digging, and general yard chores with a real sense of vigor. I would probably lose that energy in about hour, but what the hell. I looked over at Gabriel's house and a sense of loneliness began to creep in. The sound of dogs barking broke the silence and there was Carson and Riley chatting over the fence. They waved and it was time to fess up and make friends with the real me. I'm sure they read all about me in the newspaper and wondered exactly what kind of neighbor they really had. My only redeeming grace was that I had saved Angelica from a child molester. The dogs ran up to the fence and yapped incessantly.

"Hey, Danni, or is it Carolina?" Carson really didn't mince words as she threw a ball for the dogs to catch. Both Carson and Riley looked at me.

"It's Carolina," and I let out that breath I didn't realized I had been holding. Suddenly, I felt very shy and crossed my arms and shuffled a bit. I couldn't look at their faces as I was waiting for the "Get the hell out of my neighborhood" speech.

Right about then, Angelica came running up to me with a dirt–stained, ratty old t-shirt. Her arms were wide open and she yelled, "Caro! Caro!" and she gave up on the rest of my name. Hmmm, my name must have been mentioned several times.

I picked her up and brought her in close to me. Her skin was warm and she felt like sunshine against my cold body. "Hi, Angelica," she had a stuffed giraffe in her hand, "What did you today?" Her smile was so big and it highlighted her chubby little cherub cheeks.

"I went to zoo!" My mouth dropped open with surprise.

"What did you see?"

"I saw an elwaphant and a raffe."

"Sounds like you had a lot of fun."

I looked at Riley's proud face. Angelica had broken her silence. All of us continued to chat like the events over the past several months never happened. I had no idea when the subject of my life would come up, but I wasn't afraid to tell them who I was anymore or what I had done. It was my experience, it was simply just me. The sun slipped behind the mountains as I said goodnight with the promise of chatting sometime in the near future. I opened my dilapidated gate and let the sound of the cowbell reverberate as I scanned the front yard. The destruction of snow had brought in new life. Plants I had never seen before were growing, old plants that were determined to stand the test of time, and of course, there would always be weeds.

The night was a bit chilly, so I escaped into the warmth of the house and straight into the kitchen. Cow cup caught my attention, and if I didn't know better, he looked terrified. "I promise not to throw you against the wall." I had my hand up with three fingers sticking up in a pledge, "When I get angry, I will count to five before I pick you up." He seemed to relax a little, then I threw in, "and I promise to get you a new friend." I thought saw him smile. Maybe psychiatric help is warranted in my case.

Cow cup in hand, I sat in the chair on the porch and watched the view. The sun set in golds, pinks, peaches, and then finally, purples. My thoughts were contemplative as the steam rose above my cup, and I thought of the possibility of guilty, not guilty, and living your life. I don't believe you can instantly just forgive yourself or someone else. I think it takes time. It takes practice. I didn't think there would be a day that goes by when I wouldn't think about Ronald, his family, and yes, I will always be haunted by Seth. But I thought that was the way it should be.

A cowbell broke the peaceful silence as Gabriel walked past the gate and stood there. The last rays of the sun bathed him in yellow ochre. His face was completely smooth, and his chiseled cut cheekbones were highlighted by the sunset. I didn't remember his chin being so square. My fingers ached to run through his long black hair that was no longer there. He wore new jeans and a plain white t-shirt with no hardware attached. He had metamorphosed into an unfamiliar butterfly.

"Can we talk?"

Frozen in my chair, I couldn't figure out what to do, talk, not talk. It was a huge divide between us and I was afraid I was going to fall in.

"How have you been?"

"Just dandy."

The birds were chirping, the wind rustled the trees, but what I heard most of all was the uncomfortable silence between us. I hadn't been with him since the

340

day he gave me his truck keys. I missed him, but it would feel like ash in my mouth to say it.

"I can't figure out what to do with you."

"I didn't know I was something to be done about."

"I've missed you Dan...Carolina." My name flowed across the wind, and the chimes rang in symphony. It was the first time I think I ever heard him say my name, except, I recalled a memory of Carolina whispered in my ear at the hospital. "You kept secrets from me."

Hmm, you think. "You kept them, too."

"I didn't have a choice."

"Neither did I. I thought...I thought I was running away from someone." I didn't realize that someone was me.

He sighed. "I'm an undercover cop." He shuffled his feet back and forth and put his hand in his pockets. "I was doing some surveillance for the gang unit." He looked so different. Did I really know him at all? "My partner...I was, God, I didn't think this would be so hard!" He slammed his fist into the post. "Fuck! Fuck!" He was visibly tense, his skin stretched over his bones. "My partner was shot. I crawled over to him." His fists were in balls. "I saw his eyes, I...." The sun had lost the battle against the night and cast him in inky dark shadows.

My eyes closed to waves of pain, "The nightmares."

"Yeah, the nightmares. I was stabbed before I could save him." He released his hands and moved his fingers. "I watched him die and I thought I would join him, but the cavalry came in and well, here I am. I was recovering when they asked me to watch over you." He put his head in his hands. "That redhead was assigned to be my new partner. What went down with my partner and I remained a secret." He leaned against the post and look out over the yard. "My cover remained and they wanted me to do some more surveillance at the bar. I didn't want anything to with what they were planning, Carolina." The new porch light suddenly came on and cut Gabriel's face, half illuminated and half in dark. "I did my best to stay away from you," his eyes brightened for a moment, "but I couldn't. Dammit, I couldn't!" Cautiously, he came closer to me, all of his being illuminated in light. "I need to know everything."

Twilight began with dark purple skies and the bursting of bright stars. The air was crisp with the scent of lilacs and the promise of rain. I whispered, "You heard it all."

"I heard what you wanted to tell. I saw the look in the jury's eyes. You made them believe you were a cold-blooded killer so they could see him as one. But, I don't believe you were that. The police report said…."

"What did the police report say?" What could it possibly say that would make me change who I was.

"Witnesses in the report said that Snake helped you hold that gun. That you started to shake and he helped you pull that trigger."

Tears began to well, shadows of ethereal images of me holding the gun to the man's head came with the wind and disappeared like smoke. "I'm so tired of reliving that nightmare so other people can understand." I shifted uncomfortably in my chair. "I think…I think you're looking for an angel, when there is only a demon to be found." He backed up and leaned his long body against a post, a shadow from the porch light behind him showed the round curve of a wing. "That I couldn't be that cold, so hopelessly lost." I kept my eyes on the horizon, hoping for a change of view, but it only got darker.

"I'm not. I just need to know."

"I wanted to shoot him. If I killed him, I thought the hurt would stop." My throat was incredibly dry, but I kept swallowing, "Until I saw the light of the bullet leave the gun and he fell to the ground." That shot still rang in my ears. "Then I watched him die." I turned my head to look in Gabriel's eyes. His eyes were illuminated by the candescent light, "I stole his life, and that was when I got my humanity back. But you see, it was a moment I can never get back."

"The police said you fainted."

Was he grasping for empty straws, excuses, desperately trying to change my past to meet his present memory of me? "Adrenaline was too much, I think. I don't know…I…." The vision of my father's face on that bank guard's face had overwhelmed my senses and shut down everything in that moment. I had no choice but to succumb to the blackness.

"You didn't even try to defend yourself. I read every line."

A loud rush of wind breezed through the trees; all the sounds of the courtroom proceeding became crystal clear. My mouth spoke the story, but it didn't seem to be attached to my tongue. I was lost in the shadows of the nightmare. I was in an orange suit standing, unwashed, hair covering my eyes, my wrists in shackles and my legs in chains. Blood was spattered across my fingers. My court-appointed lawyer stood at my side and did all the talking. I heard in the mist of the memory something about a plea of not guilty. "We will try and get it down to manslaughter."

Through the eyes of an eighteen-year-old, my lawyer was old with graying-blonde hair pinned in a ball against her head, wisps of gray poking out. She had a look of wanting to be anywhere but here, wrinkles surrounded her mouth like question marks, and her eyes were baggy and tired. She had seen too many like me. Behind my back, I could hear the screams of Ronald's wife and the cries from her children. Waves of "You killed my husband! You killed my husband, you're guilty, you're guilty!" crashed upon the back of my neck and I fell forward at the weight of those words. Guilty rained upon my head and battered my soul. I turned around and stared at my victim's wife's grieving face, the spit from her mouth and her eyes raging pain and everything became crystal clear to me in that moment. I turned back to face the judge, who asked me for my plea.

"Guilty."

"Tell me, Carolina, do you know what this means, your plea?" His face was stern and his eyes were bloodshot and bulging. I nodded my head and accepted my fate against my lawyer's protests.

The soft sounds of wind brought me back to the present and Gabriel's hand was on mine. I was so lost in my memory, I didn't know he had been close to me. He hadn't spoken a word the whole time. I think he was hoping for miracles, hoping something in that moment made me different. "Snake may have helped me pull the trigger but the intent to kill was there," and you couldn't run from the intent.

"Carolina," he whispered. "I'm not sure how this is going to work." He put his head down in my lap and I ran my fingers through his short hair. Something was missing between us.

"I have no expectations."

"I'm trying to say I love you." His eyes became before mine. The porch light cast a yellow ethereal light, but the intensity of his amber eyes was all I could see.

One tear ran spilled down my cheek. "I love you, too." He lifted me off the chair and cradled me. "We'll figure this out." He kissed my forehead. "We got all the time in the world." He sat in the chair and cuddled me into his lap. His skin felt like warm soft clay against the cool night air. I nuzzled my face into his neck and he smelled like rain. We listened to the soft night sounds of cicadas in the trees, cars slowly driving by, and the crickets sawing echoes through grass. There was a soft sound like wings unfolding and a small white feather gently fell on my knee. The future and the past collided in the stars above me and I remained in the present of the moment.

Chapter 34

I sauntered into the pizza joint after months of being absent and looked around. The place was exactly the same, sweltering heat mixed with Italian herbs. Marco raised his head from his receipts, then slammed his eyes shut and opened them again. He was chewing on a toothpick and an image of a cow chewing on wheat came into my head. My hand stifled the laugh that was about to come through. I managed to slap a coy look on my face; at least I hoped that was the look, I didn't have a mirror available. He was still staring at me as I scrunched up my face to the saddest puppy look I could manage. My brain sent out waves of psychic communication—*I'm really sorry and can I please have my job back*? He grumbled something that isn't repeatable even among sailor's company and threw me an apron. My hand caught the dirty apron just in the nick of time.

"Hurry up, Danni…Carolina," his voice questioned the Carolina part.

"Definitely Carolina." He gave me a sharp look and started muttering something in Italian. Yea, I was in trouble already. I walked back to my area and everything was in place exactly as I had left it. The routine began as it always had of flour mixed with water. I began rhythmic pounding and rolling of dough. Flour rose all around and instilled the air with white powder. For a few minutes, I looked around the room for familiar faces but they were all new juvenile delinquents. Mi familia was gone. They couldn't resist the call that had landed them in jail. It was their way of life and they couldn't imagine anything different. Sadness seeped into my heart as I rolled the dough flat. I had been given a second chance, and they blew their second chance into pieces.

"Danni…Carolina, or whatever the hell your name is, there's someone looking for you." Maybe it was Gabriel and butterflies began a battle in my stomach. I tried to rub off all the flour but it was hopeless, I kept leaving white trails of flour on my skin. "Screw it!" and I ran out of the kitchen with a big smile, expecting to see Gabriel, but there was just an old man about in his sixties with short cut gray hair, sitting in a booth. He wore a button up gray shirt with gray slacks sipping from a white Styrofoam cup, grimacing. He looked like a gray blob in a painting full of colors. I peered at the men's room, but the door was open. He was the only one in the place. *Damn, no Gabriel, just one old guy.* My face had been plastered in the papers and subject to the talking heads, so I got stares from strangers once they placed a face to the name, whispers as I walked by, even a few who wanted to know with sick fascination details of my torture. This asshole was probably one of them.

"Were you looking for me?"

His eyes were glazed over when he looked up. It took a few minutes but his pupils suddenly became pinpoints.

"That depends if you are Carolina Stronghill."

347

"That's me in the flesh." Silence ensued as he stared at me. I couldn't take the quiet anymore. "Look, Mister, I'm not telling my story…."

"Have a seat," he said it like a command that I needed to obey.

"Uhhh, sure." Like an idiot, I sat down promptly and stared at him, waiting for the next order. Not a word was spoken as he slurped his coffee. He had a long face with a salt and pepper stubble on his chin. The wrinkles around his eyes were deep crevices that made his Roman nose seem even longer. He was probably quite handsome at one time, but his face was beginning the process of withering. His cheeks were slightly sunburned, putting color into his white, pasty skin. His eyes bore melancholy, like a thought had turned him from stone into melting sand. "Well…Mr. …," I smiled, "Mr.…."

He put his coffee down and stared at me. He grunted and then said, "How does a murderer come from someone as beautiful as your mother?"

Ignoring his question, my heart leapt, "My mother—you know my mother?" Little wisps of memories came up and started a fire of the last time I saw her.

"I'm her husband, Kent Dumont." He did not put out a hand to shake mine, just merely looked at me, "Or rather, was her husband."

"What do you mean 'was'?" That can't be good, another husband left by the wayside, more children behind. A hard knot of anger and bitterness formed in my throat.

Tears brimmed on the edges of his eyes. He quickly picked up a napkin and blew his nose. He tried to speak, but his lips opened and closed like a fish out of water breathing for the last time. He grabbed a glass of water and sipped. Then he looked at me. "She passed away six months ago."

Taken back by that little bomb he just dropped, disappointment, and pain clouded my head. I had hoped to see her again, well, at least under better circumstances than jail. "Is this what you came to tell me?" I had sudden fascination with the old wooden table that was cracked, with little red ants crawling in and out the canyon they were in.

"No." His lips glistened from another sip of water. "She had only one request the day she died." He pulled out the gold necklace heart that she had worn around her neck. The necklace danced before my eyes and a memory flashed of me as a young girl sitting on her lap playing with that necklace. "She wanted you to have this." He handed the locket to me and quickly brought his hand back as though he touched fire.

"She said there is a picture of your father inside the heart."

So, she did love my father all these years, but why did she leave? There were so many questions to ask. I played with the locket inside my hands. Images of him as a young man danced across my imagination.

"She said it was important for you to know who your father was." He looked down at his coffee cup and his shoulders slumped.

If it weren't for the fact that he made an incredibly rude remark at the beginning of our little conversation, I might have felt sorry for him. Smiling awkwardly, I knew who my father was, and questioned my mother's sanity. My fingers deftly opened the locket...."Oh, my God!"

Epilogue

The steel rubbed his wrists; the guard seemed especially pleased to squeeze the cuffs tight around them. His hands were snapped to his body as the chain was wrapped around his waist and snaked down to his ankles. Seth remained quiet, almost dumb-like to his surroundings, but he was taking every detail in. The way a fly landed on the guard's ear and the guard's hand with a gold wedding band swatted it away. The look of defiance in the young guard's face as sweat ran down his neck. Seth stopped at the bus door and he sniffed the air of fear and perspiration. They shoved him up the steps and he shuffled down the aisle. Both guards locked him in place and slammed the cage. They rattled the lock, but Seth kept his eyes straight. He knew the less emotion he showed, the more it pissed them off.

The bus ride was long and boring. The scenery was unspectacular, until he saw the road signs announcing the penitentiary. However, with every passing mile, his skin writhed underneath his cuff and the sound of Carolina singing, "Small cell" echoed in his ears. His breathing increased and sweat pooled around his orange collar, but he kept his stony silence. His fingers twitched as they remembered the touch of Carolina's skin. The bus's brakes squealed and jumped him out of memory and into the sweltering bus, where he caught his breath as he looked out. The bars of the window outlined the large gray building. The building was one big square with concertina wire all around it. But Seth was not intimidated. All buildings, like people, had their weaknesses and it was just a matter of patience; just like with all his girls, time was all that was needed.

He was processed, deloused, and finally led to his small jail cell. He faced the steel bars and stood there motionless as they slammed the doors. His stomach rocked and panic crawled up through his veins, till it finally reached his head. He made neck circles and each bone in his spine popped in rhythm. Seth was able to forcibly stop the panic cold before it began to take over. He turned around to find a man sitting there staring at him. Seth tilted his head and took in every nuance of his new roommate.

The man's skin was dark. He had a tattoo on his neck, of a snake's head with green eyes, but the detail he concentrated most was the look that man had in his eye. A look he was very familiar with. A letter on the desk was made out to Diego. Seth smiled. This was going to be fun.

Seth sat down across from his roommate and they stared for a while, never speaking a word. Finally, Diego lay down and closed his eyes. Seth slowly moved his eyes over to the small writing desk in the corner. He got up quite succinctly and marked the steps to the desk—one, two, and he was there. His stomach rolled and Seth tried to occupy himself with some words that floated in his head. On the desk was a detailed pencil drawing of a beautiful girl with almond eyes that he knocked to the floor. He kept searching for something amongst the rolled up balls of paper, pencil shavings, till he finally found what he was looking for, a pure white sheet of paper. He grabbed the pencil, sat on the edge of the seat, and penciled in the first words.

Dear Carolina....

Outside the prison gates, a guard noticed something very peculiar. Five crows were lined on the gate cawing mercilessly.